Anne Brinsden is a former educator who grew up in rural Victoria. *Wearing Paper Dresses* is her debut novel.

Wearing Paper Dresses

ANNE BRINSDEN

MACMILLAN

Pan Macmillan Australia

First published 2019 in Macmillan by Pan Macmillan Australia Pty Ltd
1 Market Street, Sydney, New South Wales, Australia, 2000

A catalogue record for this
book is available from the
National Library of Australia

Typeset in 11.9/16 pt Adobe Garamond by Post Pre-press Group, Brisbane
Printed by McPherson's Printing Group

MIX
Paper from
responsible sources
FSC® C001695

The paper in this book is FSC® certified.
FSC® promotes environmentally responsible,
socially beneficial and economically viable
management of the world's forests.

*For Graham and Carolyn who listened for hours;
and for Daniel and Karli, Victoria and Emmeline
who have not yet read a word.*

A Woman's Point Of View

By Jennifer

CWA Cookery Book

The Country Women's Association of NSW has been responsible for giving housewives the best half-crown's worth of recipes on the market.

Their *Coronation Cookery Book* supplies 284 pages of interesting recipes, household hints, and all manner of kitchen lore. They have overlooked no possibilities, and if any woman does feel like giving an elaborate dinner party to titled guests, even that may now be accomplished (like the man on the flying trapeze) with the greatest of ease.

Valuable Information

Naturally, considering the compilers, the woman who lives in the country has been carefully catered for. No longer, if she decides to tan a sheepskin, will she have to go further than her own bookshelf to learn the method. She will also find how to: make a wool mattress; cure bacon; construct a bush ice chest and a fireless cooker; make soap and candles; and repair an iron tank.

The Land

Chapter 1

'It's NOT EVER going to be easy for you, Elise,' life had warned Marjorie's mother. 'I'm sorry, but you can't have everything. I have given you things which are so marvellous they could topple you over. My job, therefore, is to make sure you are well balanced with hard things,' it whispered as it went about gathering for Elise those particular terrors of hers.

Not that Marjorie really knew anything about that early on, because what could Elise tell of such things to those small, naive daughters of hers? So as far as Marjorie was concerned, there was nothing rickety back then. Those years were jammed full of steadiness. 'Sing us a going-to-sleep song, please, Mum,' her big sister Ruby would ask when Elise was tucking them into bed. And Elise would do just that. She hardly ever said no. She would sit herself down on the end of someone's small bed with its smoothed-down chenille bedspread. Those grey eyes would look at each of the two girls in turn. Elise would smile, and she would drift off as she sang: 'The Skye Boat Song', or 'Swing Low, Sweet Chariot', or 'Nessun Dorma', or 'I'll Take You Home Again, Kathleen', or 'Non, Je Ne Regrette Rien'. But those small girls were also drifting off, so they weren't in any position to notice their drifting mother.

These were the years when the city was soft and placid, and the three of them were at the kitchen table with the lace curtains moving gently and the door open to the backyard vegetable patch. When Elise had her wooden drawing box on the table. And the pencils and charcoals and pens and papers were spread in the sweet disorder of creation. 'Sit still, Marjorie,' Elise would say, her eyes studying Marjorie perched on the other side of the laminex table. 'I can't draw you if you keep wriggling. Why can't you sit still like Ruby?' There was never any drifting there with the pencils and paper.

Or when the distant salty haze swaddled their late Sunday mornings, and their house shimmered with the smell of a fresh brew. 'Elise, your coffee is ready,' Marjorie's father would be calling down the hallway to her parents' bedroom, where Ruby and Marjorie were tiny and contented in that big bed on either side of their mother. Where Marjorie could hear the distant trams, comfortable in their clattering and calling. And the air all around slow and secure from the smell of coffee; and warming asphalt; and clanking, stinking garbage tins holding their carefully rolled, damp newspaper offerings waiting patiently for the pre-dawn Monday morning garbo run. 'Thank you, Bill,' her mother would call back, as they smiled and lay there.

Marjorie loved it all. All that art. All those beautiful songs suspended on the melancholy breath of Elise's wonderful voice. 'Nessun Dorma' was Marjorie's favourite. Which, if she had been paying proper attention later on, Marjorie would have realised was a problem. Given that it was a tenor's aria, not a contralto's. And that those small girls were requesting a lullaby and the song was called 'None Shall Sleep'. And that Princess Turandot was crystal clear beautiful and very good at killing anyone who tried to love her. Just like a salt lake in the Mallee. But Marjorie didn't know anything about the Mallee then.

So she would not have understood at all if Elise had taken the time to confide her innermost fears of haphazard personal tarnishment. And Marjorie wouldn't have believed her mother then, anyway.

Others believed it, though. 'That Elise is a bit too highly strung, don't you think?' neighbours would whisper.

'She is tender. Those nerves of hers take advantage,' family and friends would say, nodding at each other, when Elise was not about.

But both neighbours and family knew more about Elise than the threat of nerves being strung too high. They all knew that Elise had talent, and the magnitude of Elise's talent was never in question. So they were blithe – all those friends, neighbours, family roundabout Elise. Every one of them truly believed those remarkable talents of hers could defeat anything. Even though Elise was never so sure. But what could she do?

And what of these talents of Elise? Those matters of small human glory that seemed so capable of blotting out to the world the truth of herself? 'You will study opera, and piano,' Elise's father had told her.

'But I prefer painting and drawing,' Elise said.

'No,' he replied. 'That is for bohemians. With opera you will go far. We can see it in you.'

'I don't know,' said Elise. *What can you see in me?* she wondered. *What if I go too far?* she thought.

Elise was not at all like Marjorie's father. She was not at all like Bill. For one thing, Elise made her debut and Bill didn't. For another thing, Elise had to be taught how to dance and Bill didn't. Marjorie knew all about that because she'd asked one day while sitting in the kitchen among the strewn finery of her mother's decorations for the inaugural debutante ball: 'Did you do your deb, Mum?'

'No, I did not, Marjorie,' Elise replied. 'I made my debut. A lady makes her debut at a debutante ball. She does not *do a deb.*'

Marjorie shrugged. 'Did ya have to learn how to do ballroom dancing to do your deb?'

'Yes. I was given dancing lessons.'

'Dad must have done his deb too then?'

'No. Your father never made his debut. Why do you ask?'

'Well, Dad dances a whole lot better than you do, so he must have had lessons.'

'Your father never had dance lessons. No one around here had dance lessons, before now.'

'Well, how come everybody can dance then?'

'They are self-taught, Marjorie.'

'Well, why have a deb then?'

'Because there is much more to making your debut than dancing lessons. There are deportment and speech lessons. There is etiquette to learn. Your grandfather was very strict about it all. A young lady making her debut is undertaking her introduction to society. She is presented to the world at her debutante ball,' Elise said to that. She paused for a bit. 'It's not quite the same thing here,' she then said.

But even though, in later years, when Marjorie was made to understand the fundamental difference between a *deb* and a *debut*, she didn't really know of the magnitude of first appearances that a person could undertake. Or of a life such as Elise's that was lived in the years before. A life that was not at all like Bill's life. A life lived within the orbits of various debuts. Like when Elise sang her first principal opera role. 'Your singing was wonderful, Elise. We will celebrate. We will have tea in the botanic gardens,' said her father of Elise's prima donna debut. So Elise did. With her mother and father, with their hats and gloves and pearls. There in the cool of the cafe. There in the gardens aflush with their rhododendrons and their gardenias. Sitting poised and still in her cashmere twin set, while her parents drank their tea, and she sipped her coffee. From china you could see through. How could Marjorie know any of that?

Bill didn't know of it either. His was a world that expected you to get on with it: to toddle, as soon as you were able, onto the dance floor and figure it out for yourself. He didn't have any experience with debuts back then. And he knew nothing at all of any prima donnas. Bill first laid eyes on Elise at his factory. Then he heard her. 'We have invited a young lady here today to sing to you all,' the boss had announced. 'In appreciation for all your unstinting efforts over the past couple of years. You can all be proud as we do our bit once more for the Commonwealth.' Because Bill had been working for ten years in the city now to save the farm back home and that was plenty long enough for the world to appreciate that the War to End All Wars hadn't sufficiently done its job. And that they were all obliged to think about going back to have another go.

Bill turned around and there she was. Standing with the boss in the middle of the factory floor. She carried a slight and hesitant beauty and reminded him of his horses left behind on the farm – beautiful and shy, nervy and flighty at once. Elise sang 'Danny Boy' and 'We'll Meet Again' and 'Lili Marlene', and other songs in a foreign language that he had never heard before. Bill was transfixed, and his essential war effort truck tyres and insulated electrical cables were left unfinished where he stood. 'I will marry her,' he declared.

Bill wasn't one for worrying about any niceties of life, like where a person's proper station in society should be, so he barged around to backstage one night and told Elise what he thought. 'You sang at my factory and I have been to several of your concerts since then. I have never seen or heard the likes. I don't know much about these operas and these foreign languages. But I know you,' he said.

And Elise noticed that Bill's eyes were blue and green at once, like the sea on one of its soft and wistful days. And like the sea on one of those days, his eyes were translucent. She could look right through to the bottom of him. So she knew that Bill had tallied up everything about her. And still he didn't seem to mind. He was not like all the other men.

But even so, and despite the small glories of her talents, Elise was ignorant about many things. She probably couldn't even boil an egg. She certainly couldn't kill a chook and pluck it. Bill knew how, though, so he cared for Elise and that settled it. And Bill was from the Mallee, which meant he didn't muck around either. He asked Elise to marry him – even though she was a non-Catholic. And out of his league.

Their parents didn't approve. 'She's a flamin' non-Catholic. And she's from the city. What does she know about anything?' Bill's father roared.

Bill said nothing.

'He is not educated. He does not understand the finer things of life. So how can he understand you?' her father asked.

Elise smiled.

Bill and Elise had as good a wedding as you can muster when you are bereft of a Catholic priest, education or standing. It is a fact that non-Catholic dignitaries, operatic scholars, artists and others attended. And that a wedding march was played on a quietly magnificent organ, as light streamed through the understated splendour of the stained-glass window behind the pulpit. Speeches were made and the couple was toasted. Bill promised Elise's father to look after Elise. And Elise's father nodded. Because despite the dexterity of talent to win out over high stringing, he needed Bill to do just that. Even if he was a Roman Catholic.

It was an absolute fact that Elise had a magical and marvellous wedding dress full of lace and crystal beads, because Ruby and Marjorie found it many years later, and Elise confirmed it. It was a fact, too, noted by the Catholics and the non-Catholics alike, that Bill and Elise were good for each other. And despite this feeble non-Catholic start to things, they were happy. But Marjorie didn't know any of that.

One day Elise came home from the doctor's and told Bill she was going to have a baby. Their first child was born one warm January morning. She was bonny and beautiful and knowing. She had auburn curls and confident eyes. Bill and Elise called her Ruby because she was a precious gem. And, like a precious gem, they got Ruby out and polished her up. They dressed her and showed her off. And their friends and family smiled because Ruby was indeed beautiful.

A second daughter was born a year later. This time in March fly season and in Lent and right before a second go at a world war. And it was not so much like the magical birth of Ruby because her parents knew what was in store – and because this baby resisted life from the outset and wouldn't be born. She eventually arrived, screaming in anger and protest at the forced entry to life outside the comfort and safety of a womb. The doctor was not impressed with Elise or the baby. 'This,' he said to Elise, 'has been a very difficult delivery and your insides are now ruined and you are not to have any more children.'

This child was not like Ruby. She was not pretty. She was vague and absent-minded – even before she needed to be. She had no hair. 'This looks like a stubborn one,' said Bill, staring into the hospital bassinette. Elise didn't say anything, probably on account of being exhausted from nearly dying in the giving-of-life process, and probably on account of worrying. They called this daughter Marjorie just because it was a name they liked.

Marjorie could see Ruby knew things, so she attached herself to Ruby, quietly and sneakily. She stuck close. Like mistletoe on a Mallee tree. And despite Marjorie's alignment with March flies and Lent and a world war that bettered its predecessor, life was good. It was soft and kind and had its own rhythm. Until one day Bill got a call from Aunty Agnes. 'Your mother is slipping away. She won't last,' Aunty Agnes told him. 'Your father called me on the telephone,' she said by way of explanation and with no explanation at all for why Bill's father had not thought to call Bill himself. So Bill, with his suitcase and a thermos of hot black tea, headed back to the Mallee.

*

The sun was low when Bill stopped to open the farm gate. Dust kicked up by the car insisted on hanging in the air around him. You could see it, too, stubborn and rusty in a line above the road for miles back, watching from a distance the closer dust jostling around the car. Bill ignored it. A bunch of galahs startled at the sound, erupting into the air from a paddock over the road. Bill tipped his face to the sky and watched the pink and grey flying overhead. He turned to drag the wire fence gate, with its line of barbed wire and bit of a Mallee stick prop, through its arc across the track. Then he got back in the car to head for the house.

But his mother slipped away faster than he could drive and died before he arrived. His father was on the front verandah and Bill could tell straight away that loneliness had already marched into the house with its own fat suitcase, and he was too late. 'Your mother's gone,' Pa said. Bill nodded. He did what he could in the face of that loneliness and grief. He leant forward and shook his father's hand.

So Bill found himself once again in that little wooden Catholic Church of his childhood in the Mallee. With his sisters and brothers-in-law, aunties and uncles, and all the other Catholics from roundabout. And with his father. Still tall and stern, but with his chin up. Now gaunt and afraid as well.

Low, sad Latin was said but Bill could not remember any of it. Instead Bill remembered the dust that came to pay its respects – drifting past the light of the amber church windows, moving softly through the gloom of the small church towards the heavy, seductive incense smoke. The candles putting in their bit with their melting and burning beeswax. The clink of the ecclesiastical chains as the priest swung the censer back and forth and across and back over the coffin. And afterwards, outside, the caress of the warm dry perfect autumn day. It was a good and honourable funeral when all was said and done. It paid due and Catholic respect. Before all the cars drove single file and slowly out to the cemetery, with its scrolled metal-and-wire gate and peppercorn trees, and stopped at the Catholic section.

It was time then, there at the bare and stony graveside, to pay due and proper respect to Pa and the family. The women hugged each other and patted hands and cried a bit and gathered in groups, clutching hankies, and talked about Bill's mum. The men, with hats on heads, faced each other and maintained a time-honoured four-foot distance. They shook hands and nodded. A slight twist of the right side of the head. A lowering of the chin towards the left shoulder. 'Pa' or 'Bill' would be said. Which was acknowledged with a returning nod and name.

The paying of respect moved on to the local hall, for the eating of sandwiches and scones and lamingtons and the drinking of very hot tea. In solicitous and practical custom, prepared by the non-Catholic women for their Catholic friends in need. And by the Catholic women for their non-Catholic friends. Before finally, the paying of respect concluded with a wake at the local pub.

Bill stayed for a couple of days, sleeping in his old bed with its striped ticking and kapok mattress. Then he stood on the front verandah, his tired brown suitcase packed and waiting in the boot of the car. His hat already on the back window ledge. The thermos filled again with strong black sugary tea and lying on the front seat. His father stood beside him – tall and straight and lonely. His pipe clamped in his mouth. His eyes staring ahead.

Bill reached for his own tobacco and a packet of papers.

'What's wrong with a pipe?' his father growled.

Bill didn't answer. He smoked his smoke and stared at the farm track leading back to Elise and Ruby and Marjorie and his good life in the city.

*

And that good life stayed good for a fair while after the funeral, until one day Pa called Bill on the telephone. 'I won't be saying much,' he said. 'It's long distance. Can't be extending every three minutes.' But Pa then straight away forgot about the expense of a long-distance call. He stopped and said nothing for a while – wasting precious time and money. Bill waited. He heard his father draw a breath before he went on to say: 'I'm not too old, mind. But a man can't manage a farm on his own these days. You're not needed there in the city now that blasted war is over. Your sisters can't do it. What does a woman know about farming? And anyway, they've got their own husbands with their own farms to worry about. But a farm is not for losing, don't forget, and a real man doesn't shirk his responsibilities. Not like a woman might.'

Pa was right. It was a short telephone call after all. Over before it hardly started. With Elise and the girls in their lounge room in the city, all warm and innocent and unsuspecting. Pa hung up. And Bill hung up. Pa asked no questions, but Bill knew that really he had. Pa had asked Bill to go back to the Mallee and take over working the farm. To save the farm one more time.

Marjorie didn't know any of this either. And what things she did know about were discoloured and bleached by now. She had soggy memories. Memories crusted and calcified so the truth of them was hard to locate. Memories that were swamped – like a salt lake had overtaken them. One of those salt lakes that had been rudely woken from primal seabed slumber by the uninvited. That then seeped up from under the clay and the sand to rage savagely and silently against the ignorance of the intruders.

But one of the things Marjorie could remember was running. There was no calcification on this memory. This memory wasn't soggy. It was Ruby who started it and Marjorie, as she did with most things handed to her by Ruby, took to it with a great and thoughtless joy. She never questioned if they were ever running *from* or running *to*. The reason was of no consequence then. Ruby would provide the answers if Marjorie ever wanted to know.

As for Ruby, she didn't take her decision lightly. Other negotiations were tried at first, around reasonable time and attention. 'Open the door, let us in,' she would call as they sat on the back step, hands on knees, staring at the backyard.

'When are you going to get out of bed?' she would cry from the kitchen, where their pendulum legs busied themselves ticking against the chair, their elbows plastered to the laminex.

And it would be uncalled-for to suggest Elise didn't try. She made an appearance. She fed them and dressed them and combed their hair and put in hair ribbons. For a while. But Ruby had a fair idea Elise was not going to be able to sustain that sort of effort for the long term. And she was right. Before too long, bits of Elise started to fade. And Ruby had Marjorie – all vague and thoughtless and clinging on like a strangle vine – to look after. So Ruby had a go at things. 'Come on, we're going up the street,' she would say. And they would be off. Away from Elise and her pitiful melancholy non-compliance. Looking for others that might do.

They ran, day after day. Sometimes they squeezed through the loose fence paling at the end of the backyard and ran through blocks crowded with scotch thistles, massing staunch and stubborn, looking down on Ruby and Marjorie and shaking their heads in the breeze each time they passed. They ran, with nothing above but the thin ribbon of sky carefully resting between the tops of the thistles, and no sound except the quiet thud of their shoes on the dirt. Nothing other than

Ruby with her auburn curls streaming down her back, bouncy and gleaming in the sun. And that was all Marjorie needed.

Sometimes they ran out their front gate and straight across the warm asphalt road with never a thought to look. Fearless in their small child ignorance. Running to the houses and yards on the other side of the street. Ruby taking charge. Marjorie following. Sometimes they got down on their stomachs and squeezed under closed gates – ruining their dresses and patent leather shoes; leaving hair ribbons forlorn and flapping on the wires. Ruby would stand on tiptoes then and ring doorbells. And Marjorie would put her head back and gaze up at people in doorways, so tall they didn't have any heads on. These grownups would say *hello* to Ruby and Marjorie and the girls would go inside, and then Elise would be there and the talk was soft and Elise would take her daughters home.

After a while, Ruby and Marjorie started to run in bare feet, and without ribbons in their hair.

'What about socks and shoes?' asked Marjorie.

'Who cares about socks and shoes?' Ruby replied.

'Shouldn't we have our hair combed? What about hair ribbons?'

'What's a hair ribbon going to do?' Ruby called into the warm wind.

And it was true, Marjorie had no idea what a hair ribbon was going to do. So there they were, feet bare along the warm footpaths, the asphalt soft and melting. The tarred road welcoming with its summer softness. And they were still fearless and ignorant. Hair free of ribbons. Feet free of shoes. Those neighbours talked oddly to Ruby then, asking questions: *Where are your socks and shoes?* and, *Where is your mother?*

The neighbours got together one night when everyone had eaten their tea. They invited Bill over and they talked to him about this running. They had all watched Bill and Elise and knew of their decision about the farm. And they were afraid for them – not sure they had made the right decision. But that was a hard conversation to be had and, anyway, they had no right to that conversation on account of them not being from on the land. What did any of them know about the workings of a wheat and sheep farm? But they all did know of some woman or other who was nervy – whose insufficient woman's disposition made them a sitting duck for bad nerves from time to time. And they all did know about children and running.

Bill sat in the kitchen. He was handed a glass of cold beer – inviting and hospitable in its amber and froth – and he drank it. Placing it carefully between sips on the table's clean laminex surface – thoughtfully avoiding the tablecloth so he wouldn't leave a wet beery mark. He took out his tobacco and papers and rolled a smoke. He looked at the faces gathered in the small kitchen.

'How is Elise?' the menfolk asked.

'We don't see her much anymore,' the womenfolk said apologetically. 'Just the girls.' Watching Bill. 'Those littlies running around the place on their own . . . Without their socks and shoes . . .'

And the men and women looked at Bill before looking away at their beers or their cups of tea or pausing to examine the thoughtfully pristine tablecloth.

The talk went on for a long time and Bill listened to it all. When, finally, the talk was done and there was nothing more to be said, Bill planted his hands on the laminex and pushed himself up from the table. He thanked everybody and shook the hands of the menfolk before going home. He thought a lot about what the neighbours had said. But he kept packing.

Bill took Elise and Ruby and Marjorie to live in the Mallee. He went back to help Pa run the farm. Just in time for the wheat harvest.

Chapter 2

THE HOUSE LAY in wait. It was like a huge spider – a golden orb – with a web of red, sandy tracks reaching for miles in every direction. All sorts of things were caught in that web. A small dairy was stuck down the back of the yard. A wash-house and bathroom, huddled and anxious about their segregation, were netted just outside the back door. Chooks and dogs were caught outside the house yard fence. A shearing shed and a windmill were at the edges of the web, hidden behind sandhills. Neighbours were wedged miles out of sight – caught in sand at every corner. The house squatted in the middle of the web. Severe in its ragged wooden verandah. Accusing in its unpainted asbestos-sheeted austerity.

They moved in with Pa. Elise's music was put on the old pianola in Pa's lounge room. Her art materials were shoved under the bed in her and Bill's bedroom. Bill and Elise hid things. Which was odd. Because how can you hide things from a house?

'It's just for a bit, love,' said Bill to the wide eyes staring out of Elise's head. 'Then we'll go back.'

Ruby and Marjorie roamed Pa's house looking for things, like reason and explanation. One day they discovered a magical crystal and lace dress. They took it to Elise.

'This,' said their mother, 'is the dress I wore on my wedding

18

day.' And she smiled and touched the crystal beads and ran her hands through the lovely lace.

They did it again. Two small girls arriving in the kitchen, walking in a cloud of crystals and lace. This time Elise's face burned with fury. And Marjorie was afraid because she didn't know why the burning fury was there or where it had come from so suddenly.

'Why have you got that dress out again? For Pete's sake! Put it back.'

Ruby looked at her mother with quiet dignity before walking from the room. Marjorie followed, red-faced and trying not to cry. Stumbling along with her portion of crystal and lace and her sudden fear. *What is the matter, Mummy?* is what Marjorie wanted to ask. But that was a very big question for a small girl burdened with crystal and lace.

Once, they found a beautiful crown high up and tucked away. So high and tucked away Ruby teetered on a chair to discover it. And Marjorie, watching her bring out this treasure, was speechless and gawking with the beauty and magic of it.

'What is it?' she asked.

'It's a crown,' said Ruby. 'It's for wearing.'

So that is what they did. Until, one time, Ruby's teetering and reaching brought out a smashed and broken crown. The pearly flowers broken and hanging. The stiff green leaves twisted and bent. Marjorie gazed at the ruined treasure. She touched the beautiful broken pieces. 'Why would someone smash the crown?' she asked.

Ruby looked at her sister.

'I didn't smash it, Ruby,' said Marjorie.

'I know you didn't, stupid!'

'Well, who did?'

'Who do you think, Marjorie?'

'I don't know. Maybe the possums ate it?'

Ruby flung the damaged crown onto the shelf before climbing off the chair and marching to the door. She paused and looked back over her shoulder at Marjorie, still standing beside the chair. 'You know who did it,' she said.

*

Elise had a fight on her hands with that house. She knew as soon as she saw it. But she gave it as good a go as she could anyway. Elise decorated. She put rugs on the threadbare lino, and hung lace curtains on the vacant, staring windows at the front of the house. She sticky-taped prints in the long, disdainful hallway.

'Waste of bloody time,' said Pa, watching the careful sticky-taping. 'That stuff won't last the summer.'

And he was right. He knew the sort of fight this house had put up before – and won. The sticky tape turned yellow and brittle, and fell off – but not before leaving its own sallow tattoo. The prints curled and died in the heat. The lace curtains didn't stand a chance, waving sloppily in the hot summer gusts with their tattered lace bottoms flapping.

Bill had tried the same once, back before he had to go to the city to save the farm. The side verandahs were Bill's doing, but the house was having none of that. It already had a front verandah and a back porch. Anything more than that was excessive. So it had always managed to keep those side verandahs at bay. If you arrived suddenly and took the house by surprise you could see them, the side verandahs struggling to hang on. Like their roofing tin was separate. Like their posts didn't belong. Given this previous experience of Bill's, you'd think he could have given Elise more of a hand in accepting a person's limits with this house.

He didn't though. So that first autumn Bill and Elise did give the house what for. Ruby had started school and Marjorie was waiting out the year before she could follow. Bill and Elise had moved out to the sleep-out off the front verandah for the summer. But when the Mallee finally turned from the relentless baking tyranny of summer to the serene warmth of autumn, they didn't move back.

That didn't bother the house. It replied with a momentary shudder of the roof trusses in the heat of the day. A louder than usual creaking of the floor joists in the cool of the night. A larger than ordinary warping of the front verandah posts and a warning splitting of the front verandah boards. An imperceptible flaking and dusting and scattering of the bare asbestos circling the house. Then all was quiet. The house didn't care if they stayed out forever. They were of no consequence. It would outlast them.

Bill thought a garden might help Elise to settle. Something green, something growing within the perimeter of the sagging and belligerent eight-foot-high wire netting fence surrounding the house. 'It's autumn,' said Bill. 'Let's plant a garden.'

They ordered seedlings from the city then stood, eager and hopeful, on the bright crushed-quartz platform waiting for the train. Waiting to collect their babies. Each tiny plant carefully wrapped in wet newspaper by a nurseryman hundreds of miles away, stacked upright and close together like small children on stage for the annual school choir, then shoved in a cardboard box for comfort and security during the journey.

'Gunna do tomatoes again, are ya?' asked the stationmaster as he handed Bill the damp newspaper babies from the guard's van. 'Just like the old days, eh?'

'Yeah,' said Bill as he took possession. 'Give it a go, I reckon.'

Bill knew what it took to grow vegetables in the Mallee. He built walled cities. Tomato plants with stakes, and cabbages on stalks, each surrounded by a moat and a red dirt wall. 'I'd better get out there and check those vegies,' Bill would say as he pushed his chair back from the kitchen table. And he'd head out the back flywire door into the warm evening stillness. Out to his walled vegetable city to check for any chinks in the fortifications. Then, reassured that all was well, and within the contentment of the heavy tomato and cabbage smells hanging on the night air, Bill would get the garden hose. He would fill the moats and breathe in the smell of dam water coming out of the hose and hitting the dry dirt.

Elise's garden was out the front. She wanted lavender and roses and bulbs. Irises. Belladonna lilies, pink and naked. Not vegetables. She wanted her garden to show the house who was in charge. A path from the gate to the front verandah. Gardens either side of the verandah steps. A path going around the side to the back of the house. Neat red bricks set on an angle to define the garden beds.

Bill dug lines of red sand. Working from the right to the left and back again – the shovel stocking-stitching row after row of that red dirt. He raked the rows of piled dirt and corralled them behind the angled red bricks. He got out the dust broom and went to work on the paths so no stray gum leaf dared remain, and the dirt was pristine and free of all stones. But he was worried. 'How about some geraniums? They might do better than irises.'

'No geraniums.'

'They don't take much water. Especially if I put them in

tins. And they come in all manner of colours. I can get some cuttings . . .'

'No geraniums in tins.'

'It's not going to be as easy as back home. There isn't enough water hereabouts, and what is here is too briny. They'll burn. I don't think the belladonnas will do much good at all. Too far out of their natural place.' But Bill had overstepped the mark with the talk about the lilies. He saw the warning change in the soft grey of Elise's eyes and the crumple starting in her face.

'But we'll give it our level best,' he said, rushing to iron out the crumple. 'We'll see how they manage.'

And the garden was planted. Further orders were made down the telephone to the city. Further deliveries were deposited onto the platform with its hot quartz surface. This time, wrapped in the cocoon of damp newspaper, delicate irises and assorted bulbs, buoyant roses and hard-wearing lavender. And Bill threw in an order of stocks as well.

'Irises, Bill?' asked the stationmaster handling these babies. 'Naked ladies?' His mouth screwed up in concern. 'Do ya think them bulbs are gunna go alright out there in this heat?'

'Won't know if we don't try,' said Bill.

'Keep the water up to them,' the stationmaster called as Bill walked off, by way of encouragement.

Bill took the babies home, bolstered by the kindness of the stationmaster. Kindness wouldn't guarantee success, though. Those plants looked at Elise out of their damp red dirt. They did their best. They tried to be buoyant and they tried hard to wear well. But it was just too difficult to stay afloat in the Mallee and even the best cast-iron of hardware eventually succumbs. Just ask those steadfast Furphy water tanks lying defeated in their rust across farms everywhere. Just give the

Mallee time. Bill battled hard for the flowers. He nursed the stocks through an entire season. But the hard-wearing lavender showed it didn't have enough wear and tear for the Mallee. The roses burnt to death in the heat and the salt. Nothing was ever seen of the bulbs. The Mallee smothered them in their infancy.

Pa looked on while Bill dug and planted and watered. He waited for the sure-thing failure of that garden.

'You were a bloody fool to think anything was going to grow there,' Pa snorted one night, gesturing to the dying plants. He spat in the dirt. 'You've gone soft, boy. This is the Mallee, not some namby-pamby city place.' Pa turned to Elise. 'Grow some geraniums in tins and show a bit of bloody common sense.'

Still, Elise didn't surrender easily. And when she did yield, it was with a peculiar dignity, telegraphing an inscrutable message to Pa and to the Mallee. She watched the garden wither until it was dead and dry then got down on her hands and knees and scrutinised the soil to make sure it was utterly devoid of moisture. She tipped water on it and watched to see the dirt surge up and reject the water until the water had no option but to bunch up into dirty little pearly balls and run away.

She refused to grow anything then. Instead, she kept a garden of hot dry red dirt. She raked the dirt. She swept the paths with the dust broom. But no living things and especially no geraniums were planted in those red brick flowerbeds ever again. Unless you think plastic is alive.

*

Elise's cooking was like the Mallee. It, too, was uncompromising. It, too, delicately balanced beauty and ugliness, lurching from nasty gelatinous porridge, clinging stubbornly to the wooden spoon, to fairytale pink and blue and green

French meringues that almost floated in the air and which Marjorie scoffed. From lamb flaps, boiled and drowned in their own congealed fat, to a succulent and tender roast lamb with crispy roast vegetables and gravy that made Marjorie's mouth water.

Pa was suspicious of Elise's cooking. 'What's this?' he would ask as he sniffed at the meringues. 'Call that a chop?' he would growl at the offering on his plate. Bill and Ruby and Marjorie didn't care. The bad cooking they endured. The magical cooking they admired.

But Bill had been away too long. Cooking in a Mallee kitchen was serious women's business. He should never have forgotten that. And cooking in the Mallee was sensible and predictable. It had boundaries and substance and the firm foundation of *The Country Women's Association Cookbook* to keep you on the right track. Unlike the Mallee, cooking could never be extreme or eccentric. If Bill had remembered, he might have had the sense to warn her.

Elise battled the wood stove. She had no choice; there was no chance of a city girl's newfangled gas cooker or electric cooktop coming over the sandhills to save her. There was just wood. Bill helped at first. He collected the kindling and chopped the Mallee roots into small, stove-sized nuggets. He showed Elise how to light the stove. And then, with autumn, came the shearing season, Elise's first test. She had to confront hardened shearers – navy-singleted and sweating men who could denude a sheep before you had time to take the lid off the billy. Shearers who had sweated and denuded right across Australia.

'What are you doing for their dinner?' asked Pa. 'And what's organised for smokos?'

Elise looked at Bill in alarm. She hadn't organised anything. Shearing was men's business. 'What do I know about smokes? I expect the men to get their own smokes. And they are sleeping in the shearers' quarters. They can get their own dinner,' she said.

'Don't worry,' said Bill, quieting the panic. 'You just need to make sandwiches and some cakes for smoko – morning and afternoon tea. And some cups of tea.' He grabbed the distressed hands rushing to cover her mouth.

Elise had to make tomato sandwiches on white high-tin bread with pepper and salt, and boiled fruitcake, and scones with butter and jam, and biscuits and slices. And a billy of scalding black tea with optional sugar, and optional milk for the sissies (of which there were none among the shearers' ranks).

The shearers sat outside the shearing shed, lined up in the shade of the corrugated-iron wall. It was the first day and it was time for smoko. The shearing plant was quiet. It had sighed and slowed at the yank of the shed hand on the leather pulley line above his head. The shearers had kicked the last of their naked sheep through the wooden trapdoor to join their already stripped comrades, then stretched and swayed to ease their tired backs. The last of the morning fleeces was thrown on the sorting bench. Relief and expectation danced in the air with the bits of flying fleece. Wafts of engine steam and engine oil wandered out into the welcome break and sat with the hazy lanolin smell. Smoko was a good time.

Elise did alright on the sandwiches and the tea, but the rest were a failure by anyone's standards.

'What are these things? Biscuits?' asked mystified shearers sniffing at Elise's scones.

'I think these are probably the scones, fruit scones,' said others as they poked the boiled fruitcake. 'Never seen those things before, though,' they added, shaking their heads and squinting their eyes at the pink and green and blue French meringues.

The biggest mistake, however, was placing the sandwiches and the other failures on her beautiful plates. The shearers were fretting now. They smoked their smokes and picked bits of tobacco from their bottom lips as they contemplated the inadequate morning tea. Talk was low and troubled. The idling shearing plant popped quietly in the background, made queasy by the unsatisfactory offerings. It was a hit-and-miss engine, and there certainly was a lot of hit-and-miss about this smoko. The ragged gum trees – overseers of countless sensible shearings and satisfactory smokos across the years – stirred. They dragged and scraped their dusty leaves across the tin roof of the shearing shed, splattering tiny gum nuts into the billy and onto the red dirt below as they surveyed the smoko. The sheep waiting in the yards outside bumped and sidled against each other, pushing their large woolly sides against the rough Mallee-pine rails, heads to the side, their horizontal pupils eyeing the foolish food in sheepish dismay.

Shearers mobilise quickly and effectively. They have a long and proud union tradition and they take this with them as they traverse the sheds across Australia. When smoking was finished and talking concluded, the appointed shed representative approached Bill. 'We can't have this, boss,' he said, jerking his thumb back over his shoulder in the general direction of the offending food. 'The missus will have to give us proper scones next time. We don't mind if we don't get the nice biscuits and things every time, but we have to have scones. And we have to have fruitcake – not that fruit biscuit thing.' The shed representative frowned. 'And what the hell are those plates doing here?' he asked. 'Ya know everything has to be wrapped in that lunch paper the womenfolk use. How's it all going to stay fresh on those?'

Both faces turned to gaze on the silliness of plates and the deficient morning tea.

'And, boss,' continued the shed representative as Pa came over, 'what the hell are those pink and green lolly things? We're shearers, not pansies. We can't be having them again.'

The other shearers nodded and spat in the dust while they cleaned their shearing combs, to show collective support for their representative.

'Serves yourself right,' said Pa to Bill. 'What the bloody hell do you think that city girl is giving them there? You can't be giving shearers that arty-farty muck to eat. And what are those silly bloody plates doing there?'

'It won't happen again,' Bill promised. 'I'll make sure you all get a proper feed from now on.'

The shearers were decent blokes. They had known ahead of time – from conversations and information hitching shearing sheds together across the nation – that Bill had come back to the farm and had brought a city girl back with him, and what did a city girl know about cooking up a decent feed? But she could learn. She deserved a go. So they shrugged and nodded and went back to the job of shearing, giving Elise another chance.

Magnificent scones and butter and jam appeared for afternoon tea. And a credible boiled fruitcake as well. It was a suitable feed and the shearing was uneventful from then on. Bill had taken on the job of making the scones and the boiled fruitcakes himself. Pa watched on, shaking his head in disgust.

*

Mallee life was like a hessian bag – sturdy and no-nonsense. It was hard-wearing. You could cement hessian bags if you wanted to. You could make a hut out of them. Plates did the same job as hessian bags in the Mallee. Life was cemented solid by sensible plates. Sometimes it was the grand finals – footy or tennis or cricket. Or the local dances, or the school break-up. Other times it was a wedding, or a funeral. Whatever it was, the ladies would *bring a plate*.

So Elise brought a plate to the annual dance at the end of the shearing. This was shortly after Marjorie started school, when they had been there for just over a year. Elise had brought a plate on various occasions over the previous year, though since the shearing she had stuck to sandwiches. This time was different, though. Elise turned up in her city clothes and styled her hair with Permanent Setting Lotion. She put on lipstick and high heels and pearls. *Dressed to the nines*, some of the women whispered. *Does she think the Queen's coming or something?* And on her plate were the wondrous, coloured, floating French meringues.

It was at this particular dance that Marjorie saw she wasn't the only one who loved her mother's meringues; Jimmy Waghorn did too. They always took Jimmy to the dances if he wanted to go. Jimmy was Bill's old childhood mate. He had lived in the area his whole life. If you asked him, he would tell you he was born under one of the gum trees down near the dried-up creek, but no one really believed him, because he also said the creek used to have water in it and nobody had ever seen that. Now, though, he lived in the old hut in the paddock next to the house paddock.

'These are alright, they are, whatever you call them,' he said to Marjorie as he crammed them in – his face now a French meringue testament with its bold, continental sprinkling of pink and green and blue. But he would say that. He would cram them in. Because he was kind. And he never seemed to care what anyone else thought. Marjorie had always liked Jimmy. She knew that Jimmy Waghorn was someone to stick close to – just like Ruby. But that night, long before she understood how right she would turn out to be about this, Marjorie knew that she loved Jimmy. She loved his brown face with its foreign pastel dustings. She loved him staring around at everyone, nodding and genial. She loved him cramming them in.

And Jesse Mitchell, that messy, skinny boy from one of the neighbouring farms who had started school with her. He was shoving them in too. Marjorie's mouth dropped open. What would that Jesse care about French meringues? He always seemed to be too busy hunching around the schoolyard and scowling at her and everyone else to know anything about anything. She watched him delicately placing seconds in his pockets. Marjorie wasn't surprised at that; Jesse always seemed to be hungry and looking to pinch food.

He turned to those two dusty little brothers of his who were never too far from creeping behind. 'Here,' she heard him say. 'Have one of these, you two. They're magic. They're from France. That's on the other side of the world.' And Marjorie watched those little boys as their mouths exploded with coloured meringue, and their eyes lit up and they crowded in against that big brother of theirs.

She watched him take some to his mother, whose shoulders seemed too snowed under ever to manage to hold her head up, her hands lying sad in her lap. 'Try this, Mum,' he said. 'I reckon you'll like this.'

But he didn't take any to his father. Everybody hereabouts

knew his father would have been too busy with his amber fluid to bother about food. And everybody hereabouts knew better than to interfere with Jesse's father when a barrel had been tapped. He would have been approaching full by now, standing outside at the barrel, staring over the top of his glass with its familiar, comforting mantle of froth. And anyway, he was all skin and sinew and bunched arms and jumpy legs, with shoulders that were always ready for action and eyes that never tired of watching. He seemed to have too much energy for one body already, so he probably didn't need any food.

Bill ate a couple. 'Now that's mighty fine tucker, Elise,' he said with a nod and a wink – even though those egg white French things did not really go with beer.

Pa headed for the lamingtons.

There were not too many others at that dance who touched Elise's French meringues, though, so they stood alone and fabulous among the scones, tomato sandwiches, jam slices and lamingtons, the fruitcakes, ginger fluffs and cream sponges. People were curious, but they skirted around them. These foreign concoctions were not to be found anywhere in *The Country Women's Association Cookbook*, not even in the most recent edition, so with the exception of Jimmy and Jesse they were not scoffed or crammed, not how the rest of the supper was scoffed.

'Here's your plate, Elise,' said Shirlene Doherty after the women had finished the cleaning up. 'My plate's empty but there are still quite a few left on yours.'

'You may take them home if you like,' said Elise.

'No thanks,' said Shirlene. 'My menfolk couldn't eat that. They need real food.' Shirlene studied the meringues, trying to pinpoint just where they failed. Perhaps because they were

French? And what would the French know about good food or proper farming . . .

'I'll have one,' said Aunty Kathleen, Bill's sister who had years before married a local farmer out the other side of the town. Aunty Kathleen had been keeping an eye on Elise from the backwaters of the supper eating – giving her city sister-in-law an honourable amount of time to do the right thing and stand up to Shirlene. But Aunty Kathleen had seen that Elise had been stumped as far as standing up for yourself goes. 'Thanks, Shirlene,' Aunty Kathleen said as she snatched a meringue from Shirlene – a courageous act of kindness.

'Me too,' said Aunty Thelma, Bill's other farmer-married sister snatching and grabbing and cramming – just like Jimmy Waghorn and Jesse Mitchell.

You might wonder why Elise didn't stick to sandwiches. Why did she, after all this time and all those sensible sandwiches, turn her aproned back on the sage judgement those shearers had declared about meringues?

'You're not doing sandwiches then?' asked an alarmed Bill when he saw the tiny fluffs of coloured egg white.

'I am sick and tired of sandwiches,' said Elise.

'Why don't you try a boiled fruitcake then?' asked Bill.

'No,' snapped Elise. 'I am making meringues.'

Bill saw the strange light in the eyes so he said no more.

Despite the alien subtlety of the meringues, though, Marjorie knew it was less the plates and more the drink that was at fault. 'Would you like a cup of tea?' Mrs Cameron asked after the rebuff of the meringues at the dance. She knew a cup of tea could solve a lot of problems.

'No, thank you. That is very kind of you, Mrs Cameron, but I prefer coffee,' said Elise.

'Oh,' said Mrs Cameron. And all the ladies in the supper room looked up from their cups of tea with milk and sugar and examined her once more, looking for a clue as to why any proper Mallee farmer's wife would refuse a cup of tea. For coffee.

Later on, the coffee drinking would be a relief to these women struggling to comprehend. It would provide a means of understanding why Elise was failing. 'Poor Elise,' they would say, shaking their heads as they washed up. 'It was never going to work out. Not when she could never have a cup of tea.'

'No,' they would agree. 'It isn't good, you know, drinking all that coffee. Not with those nerves of hers. And has anyone seen that concoction of a thing on her stove that she brews it in?'

The concoction they referred to was a wonderful aluminium stovetop coffee percolator with a glass lid brought by Elise from the city. At first Elise would offer her guests a choice: a cup of coffee or a cup of tea. But she didn't do that for long.

'Humph,' sniffed Shirlene Doherty in response. Afterwards, she said, 'She'll kill herself with that thing one day.'

'It's not poison,' Mrs Cameron pointed out.

'Humph,' said Shirlene. She was treating coffee warily. It was not normal. No one else in the Mallee drank coffee.

So the coffee percolator sat on the stove and bubbled and popped and percolated for Elise alone. It didn't mind, though; it was devoted to Elise. So, it bubbled steadfastly on the stove through the Mallee summers and winters. And it witnessed the dwindling visitors to Elise's kitchen.

'Keep that flamin' contraption away from my tea,' warned Pa, but Marjorie loved that coffee percolator. She dreamt of the day when Elise would give her a cup of coffee. 'Can I have a cup of coffee?'

'Of course you can, Marjorie. You are certainly able to have a cup of coffee. But the question you should ask is: *May I have a cup of coffee?* Mind your grammar. You are not a street urchin. And no, you may not have a cup of coffee. You are too young.'

'But I am older.'

'Not old enough.'

Until that time might arrive, Marjorie took comfort from the coffee percolator's otherworldly shape, its soft, wet burbling. She stared as the bubbles popped into the glass top – brown and curious – and down again out of sight. It was a thing of comfort and magic. It was a thing that made Elise happy.

But no amount of percolation could make Elise happy forever. Marjorie realised that over time. Because the coffeepot was not sensible like a teapot. It was kindly but foolish. It aided and abetted Elise and insisted on providing hot coffee percolations right through any blasting summer when only a cup of tea or a drink of water would really do the trick. If it wasn't for the coffee percolator, Elise might have worked out how to properly *bring a plate*, especially in the hot weather. As it turned out, though, Elise refused to compromise, regardless of the season. It might have been different if she had not been so stubborn. She might have been happy if the coffee percolator had stayed out of things. Because summer was the season when heat and dust and flies ran amok in the Mallee. Where sunburn and sunstroke flourished. It was the time for dust storms, empty rainwater tanks, sheep trapped and dying in the shrinking, stinking mud of the dams. But it was also the season for harvest.

'Crop looking good this year?' farmers would ask each other as they peered from under their hats at the sky.

'Reckon it might see us through the next couple of years, if this weather keeps up,' they would reply with a nod.

And that weather they would be referring to was a hot, dry, relentless summer. 'How many bags to the acre do you reckon?' they would ask as they rubbed warm, dry, golden wheat grains in the palms of their hands, and gazed enraptured as summer gusts lifted the husks and swirled them up into the incessant heat and desiccating dry of the heavens. This scorch of summer was necessary, because this was what the wheat needed. The Mallee knew that.

Mallee scrub lived lazily and effortlessly in its essential stinginess. It used little water and sprouted few leaves. But it had to work in summer. It would bend its niggardly leaves side on to the sun and refuse to part with any moisture, waiting out the turning of the sun.

Birds sat mute and motionless in summer. No complaining from the crows, no squabbling from the galahs. Vacant skies. Silent skies. Baking skies. Waiting for night-time.

Sheep retreated to the hard-baked clay of the dam bank, where they stood in silent dusty bunches and eyed the dwindling water and stared at the colleague stuck hard in the mucky clay. Or they stood together in the middle of a bare paddock, in a line, one behind the other, each patient sheep face tucked into the tiny patch of shade created by the sheep in front. Hundreds and hundreds of sheep in a line, forbearing and quiet, until nightfall.

Even the flies had trouble. In the boiling heat of summer the flies had no option but to gather together in whatever shade they could find. And the paltry shade of a back was as good a place as any. There they would congregate in as big a bunch as they could get away with – quiet and still.

But then there was Elise. She was unfit to live in the Mallee. Elise and her nerves were tight and reverberating and the Mallee wouldn't tolerate that. But Elise knew that piano strings work best when they are rigid – they are not magnificent if they are tractable – so she refused to modify. Even though everything in the Mallee had to modify in order to survive. And people who survived knew austerity and frugality were paramount in the Mallee – you could not be magnificent and thrumming and think you could survive with that; you needed to conserve. Mallee people were frugal with water. But Mallee people were also frugal with behaviour. They were thrifty with their speech and prudent with their dress and parsimonious with their movements. But not Elise. She was profligate. She was lavish.

When Elise was introduced to someone in the Mallee, she would step forward to shake their hand and would say, 'How do you do?' when she should have stayed where she stood and simply nodded her head and said, 'Hello.'

Elise, when asked how she was, would answer, 'I am very well, thank you – and how are you?' when she should have said, 'Good, thanks.'

Elise, when asked what she thought of the weather, would answer, 'I find this summer weather intolerable. It has been over one hundred degrees in the shade for ten days and nights now. When do you think it will pass?' when she should have said, 'It's hot enough.'

The Mallee could see Elise was unfit. It was always good at spotting an easy target and it assaulted her relentlessly throughout summer. And the arrogant, undressed asbestos house collaborated. All that baking heat, day and night after day and night, climbed right on top of everyone's nerves. But everyone in the

Mallee prepared for this. It happened every year. So, while it did climb right on top of everyone's nerves, it could be tolerated in the long run if your nerves were in good condition. But if you were a bit high-strung, then the chances were that any baking heat getting on those sorts of nerves would dry them right out and string them even higher. Make them twang.

Chapter 3

MARJORIE WAS OUTSIDE on one of those necessary, baking, hot summer days. It was school holidays and she had just finished grade two. She was playing absently in the dirt when Ruby rushed out the back door. 'Quick. Get up,' she said, pulling Marjorie out of her dusty play and onto her feet. 'They've left us behind.' She hauled Marjorie towards the path leading to the front gate.

'Who's left us behind?'

'They have – all of them,' said Ruby, dragging Marjorie through the gate and turning towards the farm track. 'Come on. We have to catch them.' Her legs flew down the track after the disappearing car.

Marjorie didn't argue. Ruby knew things.

The girls rounded the top of the sand ridge and saw the car. It was halfway to the gate. They kept running. *The car is tiny*, thought Marjorie. *I could pick it up and put it in my pocket.* The car was stopping. They saw Pa get out to open the gate.

'Wait for us! Wait for us!' Ruby yelled.

Pa pulled the wire loop off the top of the fence post and started dragging the wire gate across the track to let the car through.

'Wait for us! Wait for us!' Ruby yelled as the car moved through the opening and stopped on the other side. 'Wait for us!

Wait for us!' Ruby yelled as Pa dragged the wire gate back across the track. 'Wait . . . Wait . . . *Wait* . . .'

Pa climbed back into the car. The car started off again along the track through the paddock and into town.

The galahs near the gate saw what was happening and rose into the air, swirling around the car in a pink-and-grey chattering warning cloud, trying to get the car's attention. But no one noticed the galahs, or the two running girls. And now the car had all but disappeared through the standing stubble of last year's wheat crop.

'What will we do?' called Marjorie.

'We'll just have to run after them all the way into town.'

They ran for miles. Ruby in front and Marjorie behind, her small legs and arms pumping for all they were worth. The sun above and the dirt below. Brawny golden wheat stubble on either side, standing neatly in the red dirt, row after row in dependable, perfect lines.

They were halfway through the paddock when the farm ute appeared over the hill, driving along the track towards them. And in that ute, doing the driving, was Jimmy Waghorn. Jimmy who lived in the hut on their farm. Jimmy with his salt-and-pepper hair and his eyes like a stirred-up salt lake.

Jimmy's ute slowed and stopped. A classy slowing and stopping. Executed with effortless precision that left the wound-down driver's side window placed exactly opposite Ruby: the red dust cloud doggedly tailgating the ute hovered momentarily behind it, nonplussed at the unscheduled stop and displeased by the prospect of having to go on alone.

'You two having a bit of a run, are ya?' asked Jimmy, pushing his hat onto the back of his head before leaning his elbow on the wound-down window. 'Where're ya heading?'

'We have to catch them. They went off without us,' said Ruby to Jimmy Waghorn.

Marjorie watched from her careful position behind Ruby. She was busy. She had a lot to keep track of, simultaneously afraid at the tremor in Ruby's voice and transfixed by the appearance of Jimmy Waghorn in her father's ute.

'I reckon you've gone about far enough,' said Jimmy, studying the girls. 'Probably done a couple of miles. Want a lift?'

'No, thank you, Mr Waghorn,' said Ruby. 'We need to get into town and you're going the wrong way.'

'I could turn around.'

Ruby looked at the track and the ute and the stubble and thought about the turning around. Marjorie looked up at Jimmy Waghorn.

'Or I could take you back to the house. To make sure the gates are shut. Then I'll take you into town. What d'ya think?' Jimmy smiled and waited for Ruby.

'Alright, Mr Waghorn,' said Ruby; she knew the importance of making sure farm gates were shut.

'Good-oh then.' Jimmy alighted neatly from the driver's side. He picked both girls up at once and deposited them in the ute – Marjorie near the passenger window and Ruby in the middle. He glanced at the girls and unhooked the dusty water bag from the front fender before getting in the ute. 'Want a drink of water?' He unscrewed the cap and handed the water bag to Ruby. Ruby grabbed the damp ball of hessian and handed it to Marjorie, who suddenly realised that all she wanted to do was drink a lot of water from a water bag.

Jimmy Waghorn watched as the two girls drank then said, 'Let's go.' He smiled, his teeth perfect and white against the brown of his skin as he pulled the column shift in towards himself and down, and started off down the track.

Marjorie sat there on the hot, red leather seat with the lines of stitching – hoary and broken – rough against her bare legs and marvelled. She had run for all she was worth. And she felt sure that run could have lasted all the way into town. *This red seat is the seat of heaven*, she thought as it massaged her legs. *There is no way I would ever let Ruby down*, she whispered to the wound-down window. Marjorie gazed at her short legs sticking straight out over the end of the seat and listened to the burning and tingling coming from the soles of those bare feet. *I love you, Jimmy Waghorn*, thought Marjorie. She wanted to stay in that ute forever.

Jimmy drove the girls back along the track they had just run and stopped at the front of the house. Picking them both up again, he walked along the dirt path, then climbed the verandah steps separating the dirt gardens with their red-brick borders.

'Elise,' he called. 'Are you there?'

And there was Elise. At the front door. Staring. Looking from the face of Jimmy Waghorn to the face of Ruby to the face of Marjorie and back to Jimmy. The girls grabbed a harder hold of Jimmy and watched her.

'I found these two running into town. They'd run through the house paddick and were way down in my paddick – halfway to Smiths. Chasing the car,' said Jimmy, watching Elise.

'Why?' asked a bewildered Elise.

'They thought they'd been left behind.'

'But I was here. I was looking after them.'

'Were you?' asked Jimmy.

He scrutinised Elise. He noted the faded voice, the hair

41

and the hands. Elise tried to escape his gaze. But Jimmy Waghorn was good. He had seen enough. 'You going to make me one of those cups of coffee?' he asked, gently plonking the girls down on the verandah. 'And you got any of those pretty egg-white things?'

'Thank you, Jimmy,' said Elise so softly the girls could hardly hear. 'Come here, girls.'

The two girls walked to Elise and cautiously accepted her hug.

'Let's go and make Mr Waghorn a cup of coffee.'

Of course, Jimmy had more in mind than a cup of coffee and a meringue. He bided his time, sitting at the kitchen table and saying nothing. Elise put the coffee on and got out cups and saucers and plates while Jimmy watched the girls sitting at the table, eating their meringues. Ruby watching Elise. Marjorie watching Ruby. Jimmy was a patient man when patience was needed. He waited until Elise sat down. Then he launched a surprise attack. It was the best way. More humane.

'Why don't you play the piano anymore? What are you scared of?'

Elise spilt her coffee into her saucer.

'Don't hear you singing anymore either. Used to hear your singing when I was out and about. Could hear you clear as anything all over the place. Didn't matter which paddick I was in. Coulda been Guys, or Morrisons, or Smiths. Could still hear ya. What's the matter? Can't you walk over that hallway anymore?' Jimmy stopped talking and kept watching.

Elise carefully mopped the liquid from her saucer.

'You can't be letting the littlies run all over the place havin' to look out for themselves. It's not right,' said Jimmy. 'You and Bill been fighting?'

'No. Bill and I never have arguments,' said Elise.

'Good-oh,' said Jimmy as he got up from the table. He smiled at the girls. Four silent eyes above pink sugar cheeks latched onto his face.

'Well. Come on. Let's hear you play that piano. And you can sing too. In one of them foreign languages. Maybe Italian.' And Jimmy Waghorn rounded up that mob of women and drove them out of the kitchen, across the hallway and into the lounge room.

He shut the door and backed up against it. They would have to jump out the window to get away. And while Jimmy thought Ruby might try it (which meant Marjorie might follow), he knew for sure Elise was not a window jumper. Ladies did not jump out of windows. Not even to avoid playing a piano.

Jimmy smiled and folded his arms and leant against the door. He nodded in the direction of the piano. 'Off you go then.'

Jimmy Waghorn had them trapped in that lounge room, while he waited for the music to finish the job.

Elise sat at the piano, positioned the sheet music and lowered her fingers to the piano keys. The first sounds were hesitant, neither the piano nor Elise sure of the outcome. But then she surrendered to the magic of music, and the lounge room resonated with the sound underneath her fingers.

The house shuddered. But it had no weapon against this kind of extraordinariness once it got going. It creaked and groaned a bit. The corrugated iron on the roof popped and moved a bit. And then it was quiet. For the time being – defeated.

Ruby and Marjorie had been standing either side of Jimmy, stiff with the waiting, right up to the time Elise started playing. Now they leaned into Jimmy and drank in the fabulous familiar sound.

Jimmy waited until well after he saw Elise's shoulders and arms begin to mould into the rhythms of her playing. He watched until he saw a small oblivious smile. 'Now,' Jimmy said, 'what about a song to go with that?'

And without seeming to have heard and without missing a chord, Elise's hands changed the music sheets and Elise sang.

The house was outraged. This was an utter rout. The stove belched a gout of smoke into the kitchen. But that was all the house could muster. Jimmy and Ruby and Marjorie all leaned then. They leaned into the sound. Like the pragmatists they were, they drank it all in. Best to make use of it while it lasted. And it lasted for a very long time. Marjorie would have said it lasted for hours.

'Thank you, Jimmy,' Elise said to the sheet music. And shut the piano.

'Thank you, Elise,' said Jimmy.

'Would you care for another cup of coffee?' Elise asked the sheet music.

'Too right, I would,' said Jimmy.

When Jimmy had finished his coffee he said, 'I'm gunna go outside for a smoke now. I'm gunna wait there for Bill and Pa so I can have a bit of a yarn with them about the girls running all over the place.'

Elise shook her head, her eyes apprehensive over the rim of the coffee cup.

'And about you and that piano. And you singing.' He watched Elise's face struggle against a rising tide of panic. 'You can't just hide from a thing forever, Elise,' he said. 'It'll kill you in the end if you do. Sometimes you just have to run at it and grab it, both hands around its neck, and shake it until it's dead.'

*

Bill and Pa arrived home to see the farm ute parked out the front of the house and Jimmy Waghorn sitting on the front verandah.

'What's Jimmy doing here?' asked Pa.

'How the hell do I know?' replied Bill.

They had a long time to wonder. All the time it took to notice him on the verandah as they neared the house. All the time it took to drive into the car shed and all the time it took to get out of the car and walk from the car shed up to the verandah.

Jimmy was in charge, so when Pa and Bill reached the bottom of the verandah steps he started. All three men had their hats on: Pa and Bill on account of having just been into town and Jimmy on account of being outside. Their conversation went like this:

'Pa. Bill.' Slight left side to right side dip of the head from Jimmy in the direction of Pa and Bill.

'Jimmy.' Slight left side to right side dips of the heads from Pa and Bill to Jimmy.

'Hot enough for ya?' said Jimmy.

'Near enough,' said Pa. 'Reckon we'll get that cool change?'

'I dunno,' said Jimmy, scanning the sky from his perch on the verandah.

Talking stopped. Pa and Bill waited for Jimmy to get down to it. Which Jimmy did. Delicately. No point shaming anyone.

'Elise alright, Bill?'

'Why?'

'Just wondered,' said Jimmy. 'How are the two littlies?'

'They're alright,' said Bill, looking around as if he suddenly remembered their existence and expected them to materialise from out behind one of the side verandahs.

Pa folded his arms.

Jimmy took out his tobacco tin and rolled another smoke. 'Elise been playing that piano lately? Haven't heard it when I've been walkin' by,' he said, eyes on his smoke but ears pricked for the sound of the answer.

There was no answer.

Jimmy gave his smoke a quick check. 'She been singin' lately? I used to hear that voice everywhere. Could hear it from here to kingdom come. Didn't seem to matter where I was. Made me feel good. Can't say I've heard it for a long time now, though.'

There was no answer.

Jimmy Waghorn pounced, lithe and graceful. He looked up from his smoke and looked first Bill then Pa straight in the eye. 'You fellas need to look after your family. Elise and the girls are not in good shape.'

Bill and Pa were engulfed in their silence.

Jimmy started with Pa. 'You let her play that piano, you hear? Regular. Or look out. What sort of family business you doing round here? You're just chucking it out in the rubbish.' He studied Pa. 'And I'll be coming by now and again for a cup of coffee. I'll be asking Elise to play for me. And to sing.'

Jimmy nodded once at Pa and the matter was settled. 'You can go now if you want,' said Jimmy. And Pa, who hadn't uttered one word since the real conversation began, went inside. Because he knew Jimmy Waghorn hadn't really offered him a choice. Jimmy was just being polite.

Jimmy turned to Bill now. 'Come on. I've got a few traps set under the shearing shed.' He stepped off the verandah and they headed out the front gate and through the scrub towards the shearing shed.

Jimmy stopped when he got to the old split-post shearing shed fences and leant his elbows on the strangely comforting roughness of the top rail. Bill lined up beside him. The two old friends gazed in silence into the fallow paddock in the distance, watching the lowering sun painting the ridges of the fallow lines in gold, and the furrows in chocolate brown. A meticulous lino cut – line after line and curve after curve.

'The Mallee is gunna kill Elise if you're not on the lookout. You know what it does to you people,' said Jimmy, staring straight ahead. 'You know that for a fact. Why isn't she playing that piano and singing? And what about those drawings? She doing any art lately?'

'She's highly strung,' Bill said to the distant furrows. 'Folks around here are not the same as back home.'

'What do you mean?'

'She's having a bit of trouble settling in here.'

'Yeah? Settling in with which folks in particular?' asked Jimmy.

Bill just stared at the sheep yards for a while. 'And the settling in can make her a bit nervy,' he said.

'Who, Bill?'

'That Shirlene Doherty and her lot seem to be having a bit of difficulty with Elise.'

Jimmy nodded. 'Ruby and Marjorie ran clear through the home paddick and halfway through my paddick today,' he said. 'I dunno where they would have got to if I hadn't come along.'

Bill swung around at Jimmy. 'Eh? What did you say?'

'The girls were running into town, Bill.'

'Why?'

'They reckoned they'd been left behind. Didn't realise Elise was at the house.' Jimmy paused. 'Kids pick things up. You

47

know that. No different than when we were kids. Those girls know. At least Ruby does.'

'Elise's nerves get on top of her from time to time.'

'I know,' said Jimmy.

'And then she doesn't seem able to stop it.'

Jimmy nodded at the sheep yards.

'It's hard to know what to do when a woman gets a bit nervy,' said Bill.

Jimmy nodded.

Bill and Jimmy talked for a long time out there at the sheep yards. They talked until the distant paddock sprouted a ceiling of stars that popped out shy and pale. They talked long enough for those stars to end up fearless and brilliant in the velvet night. It took a lot of talking, because figuring how to ease off the tension on highly strung nerves is hard.

'Could you keep an eye on them for me, do you reckon, Jimmy? Elise and the girls? Drop in from time to time, like you did today?'

'I reckon I could do that,' he said.

'I'm tired to me marrow bones, Jimmy,' said Bill softly to the brilliant stars.

'I know,' said Jimmy.

*

'Jimmy Waghorn came over for a visit while you were gone,' said Elise.

'I know,' said Bill.

'I played the piano. And sang. Jimmy likes my singing. And my piano.'

'I know,' said Bill.

'He likes my coffee too.'

48

'I know,' said Bill.

'Do you mind?' she asked.

'About what?

'About Jimmy coming over and into the house?'

'Mind? Jimmy coming over and him drinking your coffee and listening to you play and sing? Mind? 'Course not! Why would I?'

Elise took to dressing Ruby and Marjorie in their dresses and shoes and socks once more, after that. She brushed and combed their hair and tied up Ruby's curls and Marjorie's sticking-out hair in ribbons and sent them outside to play. Where the sun sprayed their faces with speckles.

She marched into the abandoned bedroom and got out her pencils and paper, her paints and brushes. And the girls spent happy times at the kitchen table with Elise and her smile. Surrounded by paper and pencils, charcoal and peace.

She marched across the hallway to the lounge room. To the piano.

They were a long way from anywhere on that farm. There was no one around to hear. No one around to see. Except for Ruby and Marjorie. And that didn't count. Except for Jimmy and Bill and Pa, and that counted. Only Jimmy Waghorn, and the girls, and Bill, and Pa. And the crows, and the silent staring Mallee for an audience. It was good.

*

Jimmy's hut was over the sandhill from their house. He was close. Only about a mile away. Right in the middle of the next one-square-mile paddock that was once an entire farm for the Smith family. Jimmy lived outside his hut most of the time. It didn't matter what time Marjorie and Ruby turned up at that hut – if Jimmy was home he would be outside the back door. Sitting on an old blue wooden bench under the shade of an enormous peppercorn tree. Just in stick-poking reach of a campfire that never seemed to go out.

And he always let them sit on that bench there with him. He would never ask what were they doing there and shouldn't they clear off home? Jimmy would just pat the bench beside him, and Ruby and Marjorie would clamber on and they would all just sit. No need to talk. The only sounds were the four legs of the girls swinging against the bench, the shuffle of Jimmy's stick poking the fire and the soft swishing of the peppercorn leaves sweeping the dirt.

Pa caught Ruby and Marjorie halfway to the house paddock gate one day, running to Jimmy's place. 'Where the bloody hell do you two think you're going?' he said as he *whoa*'ed the horse to a stop, glaring down at them from the cart. 'Gorn, get back up to the house where you belong.'

'We're going to Mr Waghorn's place,' said Ruby.

Pa's eyes got skittish. 'Does Jimmy know you're coming? You can't just turn up, ya know.'

'We can turn up whenever we like. Jimmy said so. Didn't he, Marjorie?'

Marjorie nodded up at the face of Pa. The stubble on Pa's face jumped in alarm and his head tried to hide down between his shoulders. Ruby saw it. She was bold now. 'We've been lots of times. Since you went off in the car and left us behind. Haven't we, Marjorie?'

Marjorie nodded.

This time Pa's chin tried to burrow its way into his neck. But he had nothing more to say. He shifted his gaze from the girls and spoke to the air in front of him. 'Well, bloody go on then, and don't be late back, the pair of you.' He clicked his tongue to the horse, flicked the reins and headed on up the track.

Ruby and Marjorie laughed and turned to run to Jimmy Waghorn's place.

*

A number of the farms had swaggies camped on them: men whose exact ages could not be determined. Marjorie was near the end of grade five and the end of a year that added up to quite a few Jimmy Waghorn visits when the schoolyard decided to discuss their swaggies: Jack the Rabbiter, Johnny Bantam, Darkie, Bill the Smithy. And then it was Marjorie's turn.

'What's the name of your swaggie, Marjorie?'

'Jimmy Waghorn,' she said.

All conversation stopped. And everyone within hearing of Marjorie's reply swung around to consider the person on whose farm Jimmy Waghorn chose to live.

'How long has he been there?' ventured Jesse Mitchell.

Jesse was in grade five too, but he was one of the big kids. Even though he wasn't in grade six, he was a leader, because he was tall and tanned and good at both footy and cricket. He could also flatten anyone in a fight and often came to school on Monday morning with the bruises to prove it, though he wouldn't say where the bruises came from. But he always looked like he could do with some more food – him and his little brothers. Marjorie thought he should eat more of Elise's meringues.

'Dunno,' she said. 'He's always been there.' She stared at everyone staring at her. 'Why?'

'No reason,' said Jesse, now the spokesperson for the schoolyard. 'Ya talk to him, that Jimmy Waghorn?' he went on, looking at her out of the corners of his eyes. And Marjorie could see that all the schoolyard eyes really wanted to know the answer to that question.

Marjorie wished Ruby was there. Ruby would have done something or known why everyone was so interested in Marjorie's answer. But she wasn't there. Ruby was off somewhere with the other grade six kids so Marjorie had to manage on her own.

'Yeah, we talk to him,' she said. 'All the time.' Marjorie screwed up her eyes to better interpret the responses. But nobody was saying anything now and she had run out of things to say about Jimmy Waghorn. 'Probably nearly every day,' she finished lamely.

All of the kids, including Jesse Mitchell, stepped back from Marjorie. There was no sound from any of them, only the drumming of dozens of dusty school shoes scraping backwards in the dirt. No eyes left Marjorie's face. And at last she saw something she recognised – fear creeping up kids' faces and invading kids' eyes. Just like with Pa.

'Mum says you have to watch out for Jimmy Waghorn,' said Jesse.

'Why?'

'He reckons he owns the place.'

'Does he?' asked Marjorie.

'What?'

'Own the place?'

'I dunno,' said Jesse. 'How would I know?'

Marjorie surveyed the group and their collective fear churning and boiling. She took a gamble. 'Jimmy Waghorn comes and visits us a lot. He likes Mum's coffee. And her meringues. He has afternoon tea with Mum – coffee and meringues,' Marjorie repeated, just for the pleasure of it. Ruby would have been proud of her.

The fear cloud broke. It was rain now: raining all over the group. Including Jesse. 'And then Mum plays the piano and sings for Jimmy. Jimmy likes Brahms the best.'

It was a hot, dry Mallee day. Except for the raining fear. They had no idea who that Brahms character was but they were afraid. 'They do it all the time,' said Marjorie as she walked off to amuse herself on the monkey bars. She had those monkey bars all to herself for the rest of lunchtime.

*

Marjorie didn't learn much more about why everyone else roundabout was scared of Jimmy Waghorn. But they were. Neither did she know how music could talk to Elise and Jimmy. But it did. They were a duet. One fragile soul, fluttering and brittle in its disconnection, slowly twisting in the hot wind, like the failing sticky tape in the hallway. One fierce soul, solid and beautiful in its ageless connection. Watching, hidden and stubborn, like the Mallee.

No one hereabouts knew how to take that duet. Except for Ruby and Marjorie.

And Bill. Bill knew as much about Jimmy as anyone could. He knew Jimmy would be good for Elise. Even so, this duet stirred things up, made an eddying of those unreliable sands, a shuffling of wind through the scrub, a sideways watching from eyes busier watching other people's business than their own.

But no one and no thing roundabout was going to do anything about it. No one was game to talk to Bill about Jimmy. And no one was anywhere near game enough to ask Jimmy what he knew about duets.

Sometimes Jimmy would come during the day for no apparent reason. Sometimes he would just drink Elise's coffee, sitting there at the kitchen table. Sometimes he would come during the day, knowing Elise was drifting on shifting sands. Because Jimmy knew you could be drowned by a sandhill.

Often, he came by at night. Walking across the paddock from his place. Drawn by the sound of Elise playing and singing clear out into the carrying air. 'Come on in,' Bill would say out the back door to his old friend. Because, somehow, he seemed to know when Jimmy was out there. And now and again Jimmy would come in. And the two of them would sit in the kitchen with a cup of hot black tea and without any talk and they would listen to the music across the hallway. But most times he wouldn't. 'Nah, it's alright,' Jimmy would say. 'I prefer to do my listening out here in the scrub. There's no complications out here.'

And Bill knew what he meant. So Jimmy would stay outside the house. He would stand in the dark, under a Mallee tree, claiming his own space just outside that incomprehensible fence.

And Marjorie would watch for him from her bedroom window. Sometimes Marjorie would see him standing still near the tank stand. Other times she would see him leaning against one of the Mallee trees. Sometimes she would see him squatting comfortably, Mallee bloke style, in the dirt. Every so often she saw him early and easily – before the darkness coalesced into night-time shapes. Identified by the tiny glow of a cigarette being smoked in the dark. Marjorie was happy then. She would stand as still on her side of the window as the tank stand was standing on its side of the verandah. She would listen to Elise inside the house and watch Jimmy Waghorn outside the fence.

'Can you see him now?' Ruby would ask out of the dark lump of her pillow and blankets when Marjorie's shoulders stiffened.

'Yes. He's there.' She would smile into the dark of the night-time. And for just a little while, Marjorie was not scared. She had Ruby beside her inside the house and Jimmy alongside her outside the fence. She would give a tiny wave to Jimmy every time she spotted him. A wave of thanks. A wave of relief. Sometimes Jimmy would give Marjorie a nod, or a Mallee man's wave – the index finger up and down. Once.

'Do you reckon anyone else knows that Jimmy is out there listening to Mum?' Marjorie asked. 'Do you reckon Mum knows?'

'Does it matter?' asked Ruby, knowing quite well that it did matter. 'All that matters is that you and I know.'

And Marjorie knew Ruby was right and she was comforted by that, so she would climb back into her bed then.

Marjorie liked to think she saw Jimmy Waghorn nearly every time he visited. 'I can see him,' she would say to Ruby. She would turn from the window then. And Marjorie and Ruby would lie in their beds as the music soaked through the walls.

'I wish she would play forever, Ruby,' Marjorie would whisper across the lino.

'At least until we fall asleep,' Ruby would whisper back.

But Marjorie wouldn't let herself fall asleep because then she would miss out on some of the magic. And every time, when Marjorie reckoned her mother had reached that point of magic, Marjorie would get out of bed again, and stand at the bedroom window and watch once more. Out into the darkened scrub. Watching still for Jimmy Waghorn.

Mallee dustbowl now land of promise

By Mary Coles, staff reporter

Ern was a model farmer, hardworking and in love with the land he believed in. Year after year he collected prizes for his clean-fallowed paddocks. 'I used to go round after the weeds with a shovel,' he recalled, 'like a fussy housewife flicking a duster. Like my neighbours, I paid the penalty.'

As the years advanced he saw his land blow away, denuded of natural vegetation, anguished by dry seasons, by overstocking, and by relentless farming.

At four o'clock some afternoons Mrs Ruchel had to light a lamp in the house because raging red sand swirling outside completely blanketed the windows.

But the really tough break was finding themselves flat broke after the 1929 bumper harvest. That year the depression hit. The Ruchels watched other settlers quitting the Mallee in droves. Some just died there.

Australian Women's Weekly

Chapter 4

IF YOU THINK Mallee farmers are stubborn you need to think again. You need to think about the Mallee. Life in the Mallee is a deceptive, delicate balance and proper husbandry of that balance is necessarily brutal. Those farmers, though, are a hard-wearing lot. And they need to be, because the Mallee never gives up on sending hot winds and choking dust to blast sheds; salt and drought to ruin crops; blowflies and crows to torment sheep. Marjorie always knew that. She knew too about all those Mallee stumps: lurking below the dirt, waiting for their chance.

Mallee stumps can do anything. They can break a plough or damage a tractor or smash a man. And the farmers couldn't get rid of them. They put up a good fight in the early days, but it wasn't enough. The men, camping out there on their hot semi-arid selections with their swags and tents and their bright buoyant optimism, attacked all that scrub with axes. And the scrub laughed while its skinny little trees grabbed those axes and ground down all that dour iron into stubs of their former selves. So the men tossed aside their dismal axes and took to scorching the scrub with fire. But that scrub just stared back at their fires and stood and sacrificed its limbs to the flames. Then it turned its back on all those men and went underground. To wait them out. So the men, getting the wrong idea about the insurrectionary tactic, were cheered, made confident by their fires and the downed limbs, and they decided it was time to plough up.

Which was what the Mallee had been waiting for. That underground Mallee attacked. Because those lurking insurgent Mallee stumps had been setting traps. They broke ploughs, they smashed seeders, they upended carts. They were ruthless and relentless as they hit out at men and horses alike. So the men invented machines. Big Lizzie crawled in all her immense cast-iron might through the Mallee at about two miles an hour after that – day after grubbing day. Grinding everything in her path, grubbing out the stumps. She did her best. But she too failed. Even with all Big Lizzie's stolid might and belching oily effort, the farmers couldn't get rid of those stumps. If they had, they wouldn't have had to invent a stump-jump plough, which hurdled over stumps and dodged around them and left them obstinate and hidden below the dirt.

You can talk about *living* in the Mallee: Marjorie did. She talked about it and lived in it. So did Elise. And it is a funny thing because *Mallee* can mean more than one thing. You can talk about a Mallee tree and say how it is useless for climbing and useless for shade, and pretty much useless for furniture or fences. And God-awful to chop for firewood. But once chopped, it burns like the blazes. The Mallee tree is a dissident. It does not have a trunk like other trees; and the Mallee root – also known as a lignotuber – is not a root at all. It is the trunk. Stunted, twisted and underground. Growing below the sand. Sneaky and hidden. Those stunted spindles above the ground, which people mistook for the trunks, are stems, not trunks – not that anyone knew that back then. That is how it survives. It hides.

And you can talk about *the* Mallee: a land and a place full of red sand and short stubby trees. Trees short of leaves and short of shade and overall stunted from the effort of precarious survival. The Mallee is quiet on the surface of things in its own arid way, and seemingly insipid in its semi-desertness. With its emaciated trees, its restless shifting sand, its spear grass, its prickles and its prickle bushes. But it watches. Waiting for a chance to get rid of you. *Clear off, you lot*, it says. *Go back where you came from. There are too many of you here already!* There is no permanent fresh water in the Mallee. The Mallee won't allow it.

Elise didn't know anything about obstinate, insurgent land when she met Bill, though. Because she was not a Mallee girl. She had met Bill in the city.

*

'Do your best, son,' said his mother. 'Send money when you can.'

Bill was standing there at the dusty Mallee railway station with his old and scratched brown cardboard suitcase at his side and a wheat bag full of fear and responsibility on his shoulders. Watched over by one crumpled stationmaster, four resolute geraniums in tins and a couple of peppercorn trees. He stood there, waiting to be waved off by his two younger sisters with their anxious, damp eyes and their unsteady mouths; and his worn weary parents, dressed in the best they could manage and squinting into the glare from the dazzling crushed-quartz platform as they battled to save the farm. He bent and gave his mother and his sisters a quick peck on the cheek.

'You do your bit down there, you hear? We all have a job to do if we want to keep the farm,' his father had said. 'I'm buggered if I'm going to walk off. Not like the rest of them

61

are doing around here. I've been on the land for too long. I'm not about to give up on it now. Things will come good directly. And then you can come home.' Bill's father stopped. He was tired now and fidgety from all that talking. Because that was an excessive amount of words for a Mallee farmer to produce at any one time. He squared his shoulders and glared at his son. Bill nodded. He shook his father's hand, picked up the suitcase and climbed onto the waiting train.

Bill sat solitary then in a carriage, staring out a grimy train window at his fretting, receding parents until their tiny standing selves were swallowed by the silent, resentful Mallee scrub. He sat there, lonely and tired, wishing for all the world for a mother's cup of hot black tea while the carriage rattled and swayed and the miles of Mallee scrub lumbered past the window. Sitting there worrying about what living in the city would mean, or what would happen tomorrow or the next day, and whether the farm would be saved, or how a job would be got.

That train his parents had put him on puffed and clunked down the dusty lines for at least a day before disgorging him in the city to do his best at Aunty Agnes's place. A city strange and alien, with strange, outlandish gods. A place where people didn't bless rain.

'Beautiful day today,' his workmates would say as they smiled into one more of the endless days of blue above.

'It's too dry; the autumn rains are late,' Bill would reply. And he would shake his head as he scanned the flawless sky beyond the factory rooftops. That sky so skint of cloud.

'What in blue blazes do you think you are doing?' Bill's boss would ask when he saw Bill standing on the porch of the factory staring out at a perfect, belated rain.

'The rains are here,' Bill would call as he walked out to stand under it, letting it drip off the brim of his hat and into his face as he looked to the redeeming sky.

From the safety of the porch, his boss screwed up his face and blinked his eyes and shook his head at Bill.

'Where's the rainwater tank?' Bill would ask. Asking everybody, hunting all over the place, when he first arrived. Because there were no rainwater tanks to be found. Because people in the city had turned their backs on rain. Even his Aunty Agnes. Even she had abandoned it and left it alone to be snatched by the gutters and driven away down the drainpipes to waste. But Bill wasn't going to forget. He put out an empty forty-four-gallon drum and started collecting it himself.

'What's that?' his workmates asked.

'It's a water bag.'

'A what?'

'It's full of rainwater – to drink,' said Bill.

'Do you think that's a good idea? You should be careful of drinking rainwater,' they warned.

'Why?' Bill asked.

Bill did do his best in the city, like his mother had urged. His aunty helped. 'What are you doing lying about at this time of the day?' asked Aunty Agnes, leaning, arms crossed against the doorframe of Bill's bedroom, on his first day in the city. 'Why aren't you out there getting a job?' she said as the paper boy thudded the newspapers at the bedroom window. 'And wear your hat when you go for jobs.'

So he did. Bill – who knew nothing about life except life in the Mallee: the beauty of square miles of wheat ripened and proud and golden in the summer paddocks, and supple and green and optimistic in the spring paddocks.

Of tractors clouded in dust, pulling harvesters boiling with dust – patiently circling the paddocks. Of wheat bags plump, heavy, satisfied. Those bags piled up against each other in the middle of new stubble – a communal sharing of golden grainy glory. Of sheep running dusty and lumpy, peculiar and dismayed, ahead of the insistent silent energy of the farm dogs. Or the mood of shearing time – the hazy lanolin world of the shearing shed with brown woolly fleece flying through the golden air onto the grading table. Or the value of rain. And the beauty in sound and sight of a full rainwater tank.

Bill put Nugget on his shoes, and wore his hat. He clutched his Situations Vacant and his little cardboard tram and train tickets and headed out the door.

'Do your best,' said Aunty Agnes, holding hard on to the front door like she was sorting the sheep. 'And don't take off your hat, you hear?'

The trams and trains with their cardboard tickets and their conductors lugging their hole punchers and coin dispensers and peaked caps – they all did their job. They took Bill to join all those other men looking for work. And Bill stood in a long line with them. With all the men desperate for a job. A line of more men than Bill had ever seen even at the best of a footy grand final. Bill left his hat on and stood there hot in his suit in that long and silent line.

'Were you the only one in a hat?' Marjorie asked every time.

'Yes, I was.' And Bill was back there, like it was yesterday. He could smell the stifling city heat rising up from the dust and dirt of the factory yard, radiating out from the high red-brick walls of the factory building, falling down in snaking shimmers from the bright tin roof.

'I did my best, like Aunty Agnes said. I stood there in

the heat in that line with all the rest of them. Then I heard a window opening upstairs. A man leant out and yelled at us.

'*Hey! You there in the hat. Are you afraid to get your hands dirty?*

'I looked around to see if he was looking at me. *No!* I called up to him. *I'm not scared of dirt!*

'*Well, the job's yours then. The rest of you can go home.*

'And he slammed the window shut, and that was the end of it. I had a job. Aunty Agnes was right,' Bill would always say. 'Always wear your hat, Marjorie. Remember that.'

'What happened to the rest of them, Dad?' Marjorie would ask every time. 'Did they get a job? Did they get to keep their farms?'

But Bill didn't ever want to remember that long line of hot and hatless, desperate, silent men shuffling back out the gate.

'That's enough now,' he would say. 'Get and give your mother a hand to wash the dishes.'

*

Try as she did, though, Elise couldn't reconcile the ways of the Mallee. Her nerves wouldn't allow it. 'This is a dusty and stubborn place,' she whispered to Bill, her eyes wide, her strings a rabbit skin that has been left to curl in on itself and crack up in the heat – stretched and brittle and dry now from the sun. They were sitting at the kitchen table. Elise was fanning herself with a wet face washer but her hands were unsure of themselves. Their fanning was hesitant, lurching – like she had a fair idea already that there would be little hope of rescue for her strings in a warm wet face washer. Like Elise knew even now she was going to need a bit more than that. Ruby and Marjorie were hot, silent, watching. Even their legs were quiet and still under the kitchen table.

'The cool change will come through soon, love,' said Bill. His eyes were busy all over Elise's face.

'Mrs Doherty says I am not fit for here, Bill,' she said, her speech soft and slow as it struggled to cut through the damp flapping face washer. Her words labouring to cover the distance of the table top in all that heat.

'Eh? Who said that?'

'Mrs Doherty – Shirlene,' said Elise. She looked at Bill. She smiled apologetically and gave a ladylike shrug of her shoulders.

'She said, *You want to be careful. You're on the road to being a complete damn failure, the way you're going,*' said Marjorie.

Bill turned to Marjorie. Ruby tried to give Marjorie a warning kick under the table.

'She did,' Marjorie insisted. 'And she swore. She said *damn*. Which is a swearword.'

'Don't take any notice of Shirlene, Elise. I've told you that before. She's just a busybody with nothing better to do all day than try to upset people,' Bill said.

'But I must, Bill,' said Elise. She was distracted now, enthralled by Bill's eyes that were looking like the sea in a storm.

'What?'

'I have to be able to know when I am good enough,' she murmured, watching that rolling sea.

'You are bloody well good enough right now. Never you mind about that,' he said.

'Mrs Doherty said, *I don't think you are cut out for round here. Do you?*' said Marjorie. 'What does that mean, Mum? Cut out?'

Ruby tried for another warning kick.

'You girls go on outside and leave your mother be,' said Bill.

The two girls scrambled off their chairs and out the back door into the baking heat.

'Do you reckon we are *cut out for around here*, Ruby?' Marjorie asked.

'I think we are cut out for more things around here than Mum is,' said Ruby.

'Damn is a swearword, though,' said Marjorie. 'It's not a bad one. Not like Pa uses – more like what Mum uses.'

'Sometimes it is better not to say things, Marjorie,' said her sister.

'But damn *is* a swearword,' Marjorie said.

*

Swearing was like the Mallee. Swearing was elemental, no-nonsense, mulish. A necessary cover against the outside world. Ruby and Marjorie learnt the value and meaning of swearing from Pa. Because Pa was just like the Mallee. He was stubborn and he had precedence and he had expectations. And there is nothing more normal than swearing in the Mallee: it is good and normal. So Pa had no intention of listening to Elise with her soft city concerns and her anxious face and her timorous eyes.

'Please don't use that bad language in front of the girls,' she asked.

'What bloody bad language?' he said.

Pa swore all the time. And as far as Marjorie could remember, Pa's swearing was an indication of his underlying best intentions. Because it was mostly instructional.

Pa swore about the weather to instruct Bill on how to be a decent Mallee farmer instead of a useless one: 'It's going to be a scorcher tomorrow – I don't care what that flamin' thermometer is reading and that barometer ya keep tapping says. You're a damn fool, Bill. You can't go moving the sheep tomorrow. You'll bloody kill them all in that heat.'

He swore about the rounding-up process and its intended outcome – to instruct the dogs into better sheep yarding practices: 'Gorn, get in behind, I told you. Go way back. Go way back, you useless bloody mongrel.'

Ruby and Marjorie were the subject of Pa's swearing too. And it also was instructional. Pa swore at them to keep them safe when they climbed the sugar gums in the front yard: 'What are you kids doing up that bloody tree? Gorn, get down before you fall down and break your bloody necks.' He swore at them to explain science and geography: 'Shut that bloody wire door, you two. Do you want to let in every blowfly this side of the Black Stump?'

Pa proved to be a natural-born teacher. Even the cocky listened and learned. 'Shut the bloody gate,' the cocky said to anyone approaching the house. 'Turn that flamin' tap off,' the cocky said to anyone in the yard. 'Look out, you bloody fool,' it said to anyone passing its cage under the tank stand.

Elise swore and it was never instructional. Although, according to Elise, she did not swear. And she believed this as a tenet of faith even against the word of witnesses roundabout who knew otherwise. Because everyone in that house knew Elise swore. Except for Elise – she didn't know.

Marjorie took up swearing towards the end of grade five. She figured that if Elise could swear then so could she. She swore at the sandhills, the barbed-wire fences and the sagging gates. She swore at the dogs – when they were safely chained in their kennels, and couldn't sneak in behind and bite her on the back of the ankle. She swore at the beehives and their onion-weed honey and beeswax hoard. At Pa and his 1080 rabbit poison – swearing at him from the dubious safety of the inside of the house yard fence. And Marjorie took her swearing elsewhere. She swore at school – at Jesse Mitchell – and laughed. She never swore at Ruby, though, or at Jimmy Waghorn.

But swearing so copiously at school must have made Marjorie lazy, because Marjorie forgot herself and one day swore in front of her mother. Marjorie stood in the kitchen now, next to the stove, watched by an embarrassed and disappointed coffee percolator, popping brown coffee-infused water out its glass lid nonetheless. Standing before an enraged Elise.

'You are a bold, brazen little article.'

Marjorie's teeth were chattering. But not from fright. Or cold. They were chattering because Elise had Marjorie by the chin and was shaking her jaw up and down. Marjorie stared her mother in the eye as best she could.

'You should be ashamed of yourself. You are a filthy little guttersnipe,' Elise went on.

You're going to shake my head off in a minute, Mother.

'You are a disgrace. You are not a lady. You are a trollop,' she fumed.

Lucky I'm keeping my tongue out of the way. I could be in serious bloody trouble with all of this jaw shaking and teeth crashing going on.

'Your father will wash your mouth out with soap when he gets home.'

Do you think soap will eradicate the words from my brain? Or the will to continue? Go ahead and bloody well try. You and Father do your best.

'You're a disappointment,' said Bill, when he came home. He pulled Marjorie towards the washhouse. 'You'll think twice about swearing after this,' he warned as he grabbed the bar of Velvet soap and shoved it all around inside Marjorie's mouth.

I don't think the swearwords live in there, Father, thought Marjorie.

'Let that be a lesson to you,' said Bill as he threw the soap back into the wash trough and headed out the door.

'Why did you do it?' asked Ruby that night. 'I told you before if you were going to keep swearing then just make sure you didn't swear in front of Mum. You knew it would make her angry.'

Marjorie shrugged. 'I forgot. Anyway, I'm not going to stop just because Dad shoved soap in my mouth. I like swearing. It makes me feel better. You should try it yourself.'

Ruby sighed. 'What's the point of upsetting everyone all the time, Marjorie?'

'I was only swearing! I don't know what Mum is so upset about. And I already told you why – I like it!'

'Well, if you are not going to stop, then you need to learn not to swear out loud again when Mum and Dad are around,' said Ruby.

And while Marjorie might not have thought there was anything worth her while to learn from her father's lesson, she did think Ruby's lesson was worth something. So after that Marjorie only swore inside her head when in earshot of adults.

But when no adults were present, Marjorie swore often. She swore in the safety of the schoolyard, hemmed in by the drab schooling and listless learning of the budding crop of the next Mallee generation. Or in the middle of the paddock, encased by the stubble of last season's hopes; or bounded by the green and hopeful shoots of this season; or encircled by the lines of the resting and quiet fallow of the hopes and prayers to come. Marjorie swore long and loud. Because no one was going to stop her. Not even Ruby. Not even the bees could stop Marjorie swearing.

*

The house cultivated two beehives. One should have been enough for anybody. So how and why the house acted outside the boundaries of decent Mallee thriftiness and chose to acquire two beehives was anyone's guess.

The house harboured one medium-sized beehive under the side verandah, just beside Pa's bedroom window, where it hummed menacingly at anyone who came too close. The other hive was a monster. A huge ball of pulsating bee industry glued to the outside wall of the dairy. It hummed and swayed with its own life force and within its own thermosphere. It radiated collective purpose and dripped beeswax and onion-weed honey down the wall and onto the waiting red dirt. It was a law unto itself, and bees came and went in dizzying numbers, tiny machines dwarfed by the size of the sphere. These machines were fanatical in their devotion to the cause – armed to defend and itching to prove their worth. Minuscule transporters constantly landing and departing from that titanic sphere. It was a Buck Rogers, apriaristic space station.

The dairy was a sanctuary of sorts for Ruby and Marjorie. No cream or butter had been churned there since Bill's mother died, so the girls knew they had it all to themselves. It was cool and neat and clean and orderly – a relief from the encroaching chaos around them. But getting there was a trial of fear for Marjorie every time, on account of the bees.

'Let's go to the dairy,' Ruby would say.

'But what about the bees? I'm scared of the bees,' Marjorie would say.

'I've told you: the bees won't hurt you if you just leave them alone. And anyway, when did you last get a bee sting?'

That stopped Marjorie. Because Ruby was right. Marjorie had never had a bee sting. Not in all the times they had visited the dairy. But Marjorie knew a bee sting was bound to happen one of these days.

Ruby strode to the dairy. Marjorie crept, hunched and timid. Ruby would cast a calculating eye over the industrious beehive, before slipping quickly through the doorway. Marjorie sidled in behind, on the lee side of Ruby and the hive. Into the coolness and austerity of the clean bench and wash trough, and the gleaming stainless-steel strangeness of the milk separator standing in the middle of the room. Ready for action and still not willing to accept its separating days were over. The girls assembled the machine any way they liked. All those gleaming cones and discs and bowls and spouts. The separator would slowly wind itself into life as they cranked the handle, gradually increasing its effort until it whirred and spun under its own generated energy: a soothing, comprehensible energy. The girls would sit then, side by side, against the cool cement wall and watch the machine spin and spin until the separator got tired and slowed and stopped, and once more the only sound was the business of the beehive outside the door. Waiting for Marjorie to come out and face their music. But Marjorie always had Ruby with her. So she was safe.

*

Marjorie and Jesse Mitchell had just begun to join Ruby on the forty-mile round trip to high school when Elise decided to have another go at a flower garden. Not at the front, though. She ignored those gardens with their brick borders and clean-swept paths, waiting as they were for their plastic. This time she attacked the side of the house. Where the bees were.

Marjorie discovered Elise at the kitchen table one morning. She should have been getting their breakfast and seeing about school lunches. She should have been sighing and sipping a cup of coffee and slowly buttering bread. But Elise had more important things to do. She was drawing. 'This,' she said, slapping the drawing, 'will be a rose garden.' Elise was not hesitant or tired. She was aglow and aglitter. Marjorie's mouth fell open. A rose garden was too much to hope for. Some geraniums in tins would have done. Elise's glow enfolded Marjorie like superphosphate for wheat seeds.

'I will have paths here and here,' said Elise boldly. 'The roses will be everywhere. Here and here.' Elise was stabbing gaily at the drawing. 'I will have lavender too. And Queen Anne's lace.' The kitchen glittered with the brilliant light of Elise's enthusiasm.

Marjorie was foolhardy. She was swept away. She could see the garden in all its rose-coloured glory. She could smell its rich and comforting delights wafting and lingering in the warm evening air. All that heady purple aroma of lavender staunchly supporting the roses. Marjorie didn't know what Queen Anne's lace was but that didn't matter.

Marjorie could also see that Elise's planned bit of paradise was close to the biggest and scariest beehive – the one near the dairy. Her joy was not diminished by this either. They would surmount this obstacle, Marjorie and her mother. The bees would get used to it. They could make rose honey instead of onion-weed honey. It was a flawless plan. 'I will help,' said Marjorie. And Elise smiled a glittery-eyed and wild smile at her.

Chapter 5

MARJORIE STAYED HOME from school after that and helped Elise. They dug and raked and swept. And Elise was alive and burning with energy. Their waking hours were consumed with garden making. They piled red dirt into neat garden beds all over the yard, Marjorie imagining all the while the rose garden to come. Nothing else happened in that house for days and days.

'Why aren't you going to school?' asked Bill.

'I'm helping Mum,' said Marjorie.

Ruby gazed at her sister in her strange and penetrating way before walking out to the waiting car and the drive out onto the road to catch the school bus.

The house got messier and messier. The fire in the kitchen stove managed to stay alive by Elise and Marjorie feeding it thoughtlessly and arbitrarily. Meals appeared on the kitchen table in haphazard and ever-increasing absent-mindedness. Which was of no consequence to Marjorie. The weekly washing failed to make an appearance on the clothesline. The copper in the washhouse stood cold. The Simpson wringer washing machine stood idle. The clothesline, with its twin lines of crooked fencing wire propped up with forked sticks, looked on in naked puzzlement at all the garden-making activity over to its left. Elise gaily ignored it. There was too much work to be done in the garden for her to bother with any unclothed clotheslines.

Pa sat at the kitchen table on the first day of action, waiting for his boiled egg and toast and black tea for breakfast. But it didn't arrive. So he had to make it himself. Burnt toast clumsily constructed and angrily spread with treacle. Black tea slopped into his cup and splashed all over his saucer. Then he stomped out the back door in protest.

Pa stomped back into the deserted kitchen at midday and sat again at the empty kitchen table, tapping his fingers, waiting for his lunch. Elise missed this too, on account of being out in the promised rose garden and therefore too far away to hear. She was high and single-minded, concentrating on the job at hand. Pa was getting hungry. And desperate. 'Elise!' He flung open the kitchen window. 'Elise!' he yelled again at the bent back busy in the rose garden. 'It's dinnertime. Leave that damn fool digging be and get in here and make my bloody dinner!'

Elise looked up at Pa's angry face framed by the kitchen window. Then she bent again to the garden and called over her shoulder, 'There's cold meat in the refrigerator and bread in the bread tin. Get it yourself.' As dirt flew in clumps and clouds.

Pa gawped and Marjorie went quiet. She tried to blend in with the dirt – a pretty impossible task, but she needed to do something on account of expecting Pa to explode any minute. But he didn't. He slammed the window shut and disappeared back into the kitchen. Elise had already forgotten him. Marjorie was elated. *Bloody cop that, Pa!*

Bill must have made the meals. Marjorie couldn't remember her mother doing anything but the rose garden until that chapter had run out. Elise and Marjorie gardened from early in the morning, when Bill got up to milk the cow, until late in the evening, when Bill came in from the paddock. In the daytime, Elise was outside in the dirt. In the night-time, Elise was outside in the dark.

Marjorie lost count of when she had last gone to school. She could not remember when a roast lamb with vegetables and gravy was last provided. She didn't care that the same grimy, dusty clothes had not left her skin, day or night, for a now-forgotten number of days. Or that she had not sat in the tin bath in the washhouse for a long-forgotten length of time. Other things were more important. Elise was making a marvellous rose garden, and Marjorie was her right-hand man. Elise couldn't do without her. They were a team.

But the rose garden exacted things of Elise. It required her to wander outside and alone in the night. Marjorie didn't mind; she understood these demands, even if Ruby didn't. Because Elise needed Marjorie. And Elise was glittery, and excited, and full of beans.

Pa was the first to see it. He took a dislike to all that glitter and beans. 'The woman's mad,' he told Bill one night. 'What the hell are you doing letting her carry on with this rose garden rubbish? She hasn't cooked anything in a couple of weeks. I have to get my own breakfast, get my own dinner . . . And you're the one getting the tea – not her. You're doing woman's work.'

'I've told you before,' Marjorie heard her father reply, 'leave her be. Elise can make a rose garden if she wants.'

'You're weak. The woman is supposed to be in here in the kitchen. And you have her running around outside like a madwoman with that damn fool rose garden.'

'I said, leave her be, Pa.' Bill's fist thumped the table. 'And don't you ever call Elise a madwoman again.'

'When are you gunna tell her the truth?' snapped Pa. 'When are you gunna tell her this is a fool's undertaking?'

'In my own time. And it's none of your business when.'

'It is my bloody business!' shouted Pa. 'This is my farm and don't you forget it.'

Now Bill was shouting too. 'How *could* we ever forget it? And the least you could do is let Elise have a bloody rose garden!' Bill's other fist arrived to help with the table thumping.

'Bloody hell. You know there's no water on this farm to waste. Not on a damn fool bloody flower garden.'

The argument went on and on. It stuck to sensible things. Like what a proper Mallee farmer's wife should do. Like waste. Like water. Not about women and their defective nerves. And their words were like water pumping from a broken windmill.

'Get her back to doing that painting,' said Pa softly, at one stage. 'It's a good smile she's got on her face when she's painting. Not like what she's wearing now. That's a fool's smile. And painting doesn't waste water.'

Marjorie looked at Ruby, but her sister was fast asleep. 'Ruby!' she whispered as loudly as she could. 'Wake up!' But Ruby didn't. So Marjorie had to take matters into her own hands. She slid out of her bed and onto the tired lino floor. She crept over to Ruby's bed and crawled under it. Marjorie kept going until she was stopped by the tongue-in-groove boards of Ruby's side of the bedroom wall. And there she lay for hours. With the safety of Ruby's quiet breathing above her. With her hands over her head. Swearing in whispers to the dusty lino.

Pa stomped off to his bedroom. Bill sat in the kitchen, waiting for Elise to come back. Elise roved, euphoric and crazy, glittery and extreme, in the midnight dust, as the magic of

Marjorie's rose garden with its companion lavender and exotic lace from royalty curled up and died in utero. From the lack of a permanent water supply.

Marjorie tried to stay awake to hear Elise come back. Or to hear Bill go outside to find her. But she couldn't. She crawled out from under the bed in the early hours of the next day and looked at Ruby. But Ruby was still asleep. So Marjorie climbed back into her own bed. She pulled the sheet over her head and put her head under her pillow. And woke to the sounds of Ruby getting ready for school.

'Ruby . . .'

No answer.

'Ruby, I'm not going to school today either. I'm staying home again.'

No answer.

'Ruby, Dad and Pa had a fight.'

Ruby's back stopped and listened. 'They're always fighting,' it said.

'About Mum,' said Marjorie. 'And Mum keeps going off outside in the dark.'

Ruby turned to face her sister. 'I know that. She can go outside if she wants to.'

'I'm scared, Ruby.'

Ruby stared at Marjorie. 'What are you scared of now, Marjorie?'

'I dunno, Ruby. The bees? Maybe it's the bees? They're very close to where we're digging the garden.'

Ruby stared at her sister lying there in her bed for a long time. But there were no answers to be found on Marjorie's bed. She shook her head. 'I'm going to school,' she said. 'You can stay home. I'm not.' And Ruby walked out of their bedroom to see what she could do about making herself some breakfast, and some sort of school lunch.

Marjorie waited to see if Bill would make her go to school today. But her father didn't come. She stayed in bed and listened. To the complaining of the verandah boards; the starting of the car engine and car doors slamming; the noise of the car stopping at the house paddock gate, navigating sandhills and corners. She lay there until the sounds faded away.

On the other rose garden days, Marjorie would get up to find Elise already outside. But not today. Today was silent – the day was vacant and deserted. The only activity was the beehive. The only noise was the beehive. Marjorie had no clue what to do. So she sat on the path and watched the house and waited for Elise. Until Pa yelled at her, 'What the hell do you think you're doing, girl? Sitting out there in the blazing sun without a hat on. Do you want to get bloody heat stroke?'

Marjorie looked up through her dusty and sticking-out hair to find Pa at the kitchen window. She squinted up at him from her dirt path.

'Get in here and out of the sun. Damn fool girl.' And he slammed the window shut.

So Marjorie straggled off into the kitchen and stood, shoulders hunched and eyes squinting at Pa.

'Sit down and I'll get you some breakfast.'

Marjorie slid onto a kitchen chair, but her eyes remained locked on Pa. This situation needed watching. Even Marjorie knew that. Pa never cooked.

Pa got the bread from the bread cupboard, the butter and milk from the kerosene refrigerator, the treacle and jam from the pantry. Marjorie watched and said nothing. Pa hacked and sawed through the bread and speared the hapless crooked slice onto the toasting fork. Marjorie watched and said nothing. Pa flung open the stove door and thrust the speared bread at the Mallee roots burning inside. Marjorie watched and said nothing.

Pa made breakfast with the *flamin' useless toasting fork* and the *bloody useless bread* and the *useless flamin' kettle*. He threw the scorched and blackened bread onto a bread-and-butter plate and slammed it down in front of her. He shoved the butter in its paper wrapper and the treacle in its tin and the jam in its jar across the table towards her. Marjorie did not move. She waited until Pa concluded swearing and making breakfast. He sat down opposite her and poured black tea into his saucer and proceeded to slap his blackened and butterless toast with his treacle-coated knife. Pa had his saucer of black tea halfway to his mouth and was readying himself to slurp when his eyes met Marjorie's. 'Where is Mum?' she asked.

Pa put down his saucer of tea with uncommon delicacy. He took his time settling it just right on the bare kitchen table before answering. 'Well, you could at least flamin' thank me for gettin' your breakfast,' he said. 'Hurry up and eat it before it gets cold. And don't you have butter *and* jam. I've bloody told you before about that.'

'Thank you for my breakfast, Pa. Where is Mum?'

Pa sighed and looked kindly at Marjorie. And she stared back, wide-eyed and terrified. Because a kindly Pa was a most terrifying thing. 'She's still in bed. She hasn't got out of bed yet.' Pa watched Marjorie for a bit and was relieved to see she remained impassive and tearless. That, he interpreted as a good sign. 'Come on. Eat up.' He bent to his own burnt toast and black tea. Marjorie didn't know what else to do so she ate the burnt toast.

They finished their breakfast in silence. Marjorie cleared the table and stacked the dirty dishes in the dish pan. Pa poured hot water from the kettle. Marjorie stared as Pa took to the dishes with the long-handled wire dish washer with its Velvet soap compartment. 'What're you staring at? Don't you think I can wash a bloody dish?' said Pa.

No. I didn't think you could, thought Marjorie. She got the tea towel and dried and put away.

'I'm going to get the horse and cart and go round the traps now. I'll be back at dinnertime. Why don't you look in on your mother while I'm gone?' Pa's glance at Marjorie was too close to sympathy for Marjorie to understand. He walked quietly out the back door.

Marjorie waited in the kitchen for the longest of times for Elise to appear. She did all manner of filling things. Marjorie thought if she was full of filling things there wouldn't be room left for anything else. Like being scared. She filled up the firebox in the stove with Mallee roots. She filled up the coffee percolator with rainwater. She filled up the kettles before placing them on the stove; the tea tin with a fresh packet of tea; the milk jug with milk from the milk bucket; the jam dish with jam from the jam jar. She filled up the wood box on the back verandah. Then Marjorie sat at the kitchen table. She sat with her back to the stove and stared at the hallway door. She had run out of things to fill up. The kitchen helped her then by filling itself up with silence.

But Elise didn't appear. And the stove ate all the firewood. And the near extinction of the stove told Marjorie she would have to do what Pa said. She would have to go and check on Elise.

The hallway, meanwhile, had taken the opportunity to grow much bigger. Suddenly it was a long and lonely walk down that hallway. Out onto the front verandah. Over to the flywire door of Bill and Elise's sleep-out. The house watched Marjorie take her long and lonely walk. The hallway floorboards creaked in amusement at her wobbly, hesitant footsteps. And the front verandah boards squeaked in anticipation of the outcome. Marjorie paused just inside the bedroom door. There was no Elise. Just a lump in the bed facing the wall.

'Mum?' asked a tiny voice from the door. Quavery from the effort of the word.

There was no reply from that lump.

'Mum? Are you awake? It's time to get up.'

The bed and its contents were silent and still.

'Mum!' shouted a crying girl from the door. 'Everyone's gone. I'm the only one here. You're scaring me.'

The motionless lump in the bed sighed. Marjorie ran to the lump and hugged it. And words babbled and toppled out of her mouth and spilt all over that lump in the bed. They were words about Ruby having gone to school and Pa getting her breakfast and having done a bit of digging and stoking the fire and did Elise want a cup of coffee? And about getting out of bed so they could finish the rose garden. Marjorie's mouth ran out of babble and stopped. She wiped her wet face with her hands. Round and round.

'We won't be finishing the rose garden,' said the lump in the bed.

Marjorie stopped wiping. 'Why not?'

'I was foolish to think I could have a rose garden. I'm an utter fool.'

'But, Mum, you promised.'

The lump reared up from its bed. 'Promises are made to be broken, Marjorie. It's about time you learnt a thing or two about life. Hell and Tommy, what in damnation ever made you think we would have a rose garden? For Pete's sake. Don't be ridiculous, you stupid child. This house can't have roses. Now go away.' The girl stumbled backwards and the lump collapsed back onto its pillow. 'I'm tired,' it said and it curled into a lumpy ball and stared at the red dust carpeting the louvre windows.

Marjorie very much wanted to do just what the lump said. She wanted to go away. But how could she? How do you go away when you are on a Mallee farm? You could run for miles and miles and still be on the farm. Away was too far in the Mallee. The thought of running to Jimmy Waghorn's place had appeal. But Marjorie's legs had run out of fuel. They didn't have any running left in them after all this wobbling down the hallway. So she crept back to the kitchen and sat silent and still at the kitchen table. Waiting. Until it was dinnertime, which Marjorie knew because Pa came back. So they replicated their breakfast and had an uneasy dinner. 'How's your mother?' asked Pa over the top of his cold meat and chutney sandwich. 'Did you look in on her?'

'She's alright,' said Marjorie to her bread-and-butter plate.

'Where is she then?'

'She won't get out of bed.'

Marjorie glanced quickly at Pa, trying to gauge what she was supposed to do next. Pa's face was no help, though. It looked uncertain of the terrain ahead. His eyes stared at hers – peering over the parapets of the white stubble.

'She probably just needs a kip. Women are weak and she's been digging that damn fool garden day and bloody night. She's a city girl. Out there in all that heat. She'll come good in time.' Pa nodded at Marjorie.

'Mum said we are not going to finish the rose garden. She said, *What in damnation ever made you think we would have a rose garden? Don't be ridiculous. This house can't have roses,*' said Marjorie. But the relating of the conversation was too difficult. She looked at her bread-and-butter plate. So Pa couldn't see the water charging to invade her eyes.

Pa decided to stare at his plate after that. They finished the rest of their cold meat and chutney sandwiches in silence. Then Pa left, and Marjorie went again to sit by herself in the dust and the dirt and the blazing sun in the rose garden. The lump stayed in bed.

That afternoon, the Mallee got wind of the collapse of the rose garden and the discovery of the lump in the bed. As it always does get wind of such things. It sent a scout to reconnoitre. A willy-willy arrived. It skirled around and around the outside of the lumbering house yard fence, taking a look. Then it leapt the fence, jubilant at the evident truth of the story, and headed for the rose garden. It pivoted in the middle of the garden and tossed dust and dirt all over itself in triumph. It hopped from bed to bed, leaning and spinning and hurling. It noted Marjorie, scrunched in the dirt, and tried to lift her into its victory dance. But she was too much for it so it just shrugged and dumped dust and dirt on her. It expanded its dance into a series of connecting circles as it orbited the garden. It spiralled that garden to the sky before heading for the beehive to enlist support for its finale.

The willy-willy plucked at the bees and sucked at the bees until it had adorned the multiple layers of its spiralling dust and dirt with zealous bees. A beautiful, semitransparent vortex of sepia spangles and black-and-yellow jewels. Dancing and shimmering in the afternoon sunlight as it spun and swayed and buzzed and destroyed. As it wrecked and waltzed and droned. Around and around and around Marjorie.

*

It was after dark before anyone found her. Marjorie could never remember how long she cowered inside the dairy. The bees continued to drone and dance outside the dairy door long after the willy-willy had gone, while Marjorie hid. They only gave up and retreated to their space station when the light went out of the sky. And it was Ruby who found her. 'It's alright now, Marjorie,' she murmured. 'The bees are gone.'

'I knew you would come for me,' whispered Marjorie.

'I know,' said Ruby as she took her sister by the hand and led her out of the dairy, sheltering her from the possibility of any stray and still-excited bees.

And it was Ruby who held her sister's hand tight as she stopped in the moonlight so Marjorie could see the damage the willy-willy had done to the rose garden. And it was Ruby who ran a hot bath for Marjorie – even at that late hour – and made sure she had some soap to wash her hair. And found her some clean pyjamas to put on.

'Where is Mum?' asked Marjorie.

'She's still in bed,' said Ruby.

The lump in the bed did not emerge. Apparently it was too disappointed in Marjorie and her preposterous notions of a rose garden to tolerate her silly fears.

*

'Bees are no good,' said Marjorie the next day.

'The world needs bees,' said Jimmy.

'Bees wrecked our rose garden,' said Marjorie.

'What are you scared of?' asked Jimmy.

'Bees. Mum couldn't get out of bed because of bees.'

'Is that really why? Because of bees?'

'Yes.'

'Your mother couldn't get out of bed before the bees turned up,' said Jimmy.

Marjorie just looked at him.

'What are you frightened of, Marjorie?' asked Jimmy.

Marjorie stopped looking at Jimmy and looked at the fire instead.

*

Bill put Elise in the car and they drove the long miles to the nearest town with a doctor. It wasn't the next day that he drove Elise to the doctor, though; it was after any number of those days that it took Elise to finally manage to come back from being a lump in the bed staring at the louvre windows. The sad smile had come back from wherever it went and taken over her face by the time she finally managed to get out of bed. There was not one bit of the glittery smile left. And the beans she had been full of had gone as well. So the sad smile accompanied Bill to the doctor those many days after the collapse of the rose garden. Not the glitter. Or the beans.

Ruby and Marjorie didn't go with them. They stayed at the house with Pa. They had never stayed alone with Pa before.

'I don't want to stay here with Pa,' said Marjorie to Ruby.

'It'll be alright.'

'I would rather stay with Jimmy Waghorn.'

'Me too.'

'Why can't we just fend for ourselves if we can't stay with Jimmy Waghorn?'

'You don't have to worry, Marjorie. I am not going anywhere,' Ruby said.

As it was, the three of them – Pa, Ruby, Marjorie – all lined up on the front verandah and they all waved there in their line as the car drove off. Bill waved back. Elise didn't. She was too busy staring at the surrounding scrub.

Then they all went into Pa's lounge room and sat around, Ruby with her arm around Marjorie. Pa chopped his tobacco with the tobacco slicer and smoked his pipe and tapped his fingers on the table. And glanced at the two girls when he thought they weren't watching. But they were always watching. Especially Ruby.

Bill and Elise came back that afternoon. Ruby and Marjorie and Pa heard the car coming for miles. By the time the car was pulling up at the house the three of them were standing in line on the front verandah again. Like they had waited there all day. Bill waved as the car pulled up. Elise glanced at them standing there before shifting her gaze to stare again at the Mallee encircling her.

'Step aside,' said Bill. 'I can't help your mother up the steps with you lot gawking there.'

The three verandah occupiers stepped aside as Bill guided Elise down the hallway towards the kitchen. The three of them traipsed after them to find Elise sitting in her chair beside the kitchen stove. Near her coffee percolator. Studying a packet of cigarettes.

Marjorie was surrounded by smokers. Her father smoked smokes he made himself from bits of tobacco in a tin and tiny pieces of paper. So did Jimmy Waghorn. Marjorie was fascinated by their careful construction of the fragile fires. She would watch them: Havelock Flake Cut tobacco rubbed – heel of one hand into the palm of the other – while that tiny, delicate piece of paper sat poised on the edge of a mouth. The smokes were lit and puffed on once or twice, then left to cling precariously to the outer edge of the lower lip until they died from neglect.

Pa smoked a pipe jammed with tobacco hacked belligerently with a tiny cleaver. She liked to watch Pa. Scraping out the bowl of the pipe, banging it upside down, clamping the pipe stem between his teeth, holding the pipe bowl with one hand, the lighted match in the other.

Marjorie didn't know about ladies smoking, though. She wasn't too sure about that.

'The doctor said Elise should take up smoking. Help to steady her nerves. She'll be right as rain soon,' said Bill.

Pa opened his mouth but nothing came out so he shut it again. Marjorie opened her mouth and left it open. In case something might emerge later on.

'Smoking is not ladylike,' said Ruby.

'The doctor says cigarettes are alright. If a woman's nerves are gone,' said Bill.

Elise moved her eyes from the cigarette crouching between the first and second fingers of her right hand to Ruby's face. She looked pleased with Ruby. She smiled and nodded at her. Before moving her eyes to Marjorie.

Marjorie decided that now was the right time to shut her still-open mouth. Nothing had come out of it yet, so she concluded nothing was likely to come out in the immediate future. And because Marjorie was pre-empting Elise's reprimand to shut her mouth because *it's unladylike and young ladies don't go around with their mouths hanging open and what are they trying to do? Catch flies?*

This, astonishingly for Elise and her very impractical ways, was a very practical piece of advice in the Mallee. Because if you went around in the Mallee with your mouth open you would for sure swallow a fly. Everyone could testify to that. And it was only marginally (and subjectively and open to debate) less disgusting than accidentally snorting a fly up your nose. So Marjorie snapped her mouth shut.

Elise nodded and smiled. And proceeded to take her medicine. To smoke out any remaining, lurking glitter. Everyone stood around and watched. Even Pa was glued. Waiting to witness the health benefits of cigarette smoke on bad nerves.

Smoking did work for a bit – just like the doctor said. Elise's nerves relaxed in the drowsiness of the cigarette smoke and the tremor of the high strings slowed down to a soothing hum. The hum was a bit like the beehive – you could be lulled by it. And everyone was lulled. But somewhere along the line Elise stopped her treatment. She decided smoking would ruin her voice, and a magical voice was more important to her than cigarette smoke and good nerves.

Not too long after Elise did that, Marjorie also did a couple of things: she went back to high school, and she started – in private – smoking. Marjorie took up smoking for a number of reasons:

—Because Marjorie was conscientious and wanted to provide her own private and anonymous support to the local Mallee medical opinion.

—As a preventive measure, to get a jump start on any nerves that might manifest later in herself.

—Because both her father and her mother would not want her to.

—Because it would be a secret.

—And because – like swearing – she could. Let's face it. Bill would never miss the odd bits of tobacco from the tin or the few tiny slips of paper from the packet. And who was counting the matches?

Smoking was good. Marjorie liked it. Unlike Elise, she made a commitment to smoking. And smoking, combined with swearing, could certainly make you laugh.

The only thing she wasn't sure of, though, was whether smoking could have cured Elise's nerves if Elise had taken the prescribed medication for the long haul. Whether things might have been different in the end if Elise had decided good nerves might be worth more than a magical voice.

*

One of the other things that was never the same after the rose garden and the bees was the tea cosy. It wasn't too long after swearing and smoking arrived in her life that Marjorie realised tea cosies could have more than one purpose. Marjorie discovered a tea cosy didn't have to restrict itself to just protecting a good pot of tea because Elise had decided that if a tea cosy had tired of hot tea preservation it could become a hat.

'You've grown out of all your things,' said Elise one night as they ate their tea. 'That dress is far too short.'

Marjorie looked down in surprise and wondered where these extra-length legs had come from. Maybe high school was responsible?

Bill glanced up from the reverie of his potatoes and squinted at Marjorie. He wasn't worried about the legs. He was more concerned about the face. 'What're you doing with those pimples all over your face? You need to get rid of those.'

Marjorie switched from wondering where the legs had

come from to worrying about the spots on her face. Her face helped. It went red to try to hide the pimples. The legs weren't offering any help, though, so she just stuck them out of the way under the table.

But the longer legs and the pimply skin were not entirely useless. They gave Marjorie something. As recompense for the trouble they caused. They gave Marjorie a different optical perspective. And they also sharpened her hearing.

'It is important to dress properly,' Elise had always said to Ruby and Marjorie – usually as she was dragging a comb through a complaining Marjorie's resistant, sticking-out hair. 'A woman who is lazy with her dress will drift towards all sorts of slovenly behaviour.'

So Elise never went into town wearing her farmhouse dress. And never would she allow Ruby and Marjorie to go into town wearing their round-the-house clothes. They, too, must wear dresses and have ribbons in their hair. Regardless of whether the hair wanted ribbons.

'Here comes that Elise,' whispered Shirlene Doherty, peering through the tins of powdered milk and packets of salt lined up in the window of the town's general store. 'Hat and gloves, lipstick and high heels. Who does she think she is?'

Mrs Cameron scrubbed hard at the wooden counter top in her little shop and her face went red. Maybe she had pimples too. 'Hello, Elise,' she said. And her words rushed as kindly as they were able. Scurrying past Shirlene and her surly face.

'Good afternoon,' said Elise with a smile.

But Elise's diffident smile was no match for Shirlene. She turned to lean against the counter, arms folded, and watched Elise.

'Why do you bother?' Shirlene asked, her head moving up and down to take Elise in. 'It must be because you're from the city. Country folk don't get dressed up to the nines just to get the mail and papers.'

Elise faltered. 'Oh. I'm sorry,' she said.

But Shirlene was in too much of a hurry to wait for an apology. 'No. We don't have spare time just lying around so we can go into town in that sort of get-up,' she said. 'And how did you come by that dress, anyway? It's new, isn't it?'

'Yes,' said Elise. Her smile making a timid re-entry.

'Well, you're a bit hard up at the moment, aren't you? Why would you be wasting Bill's money on getting yourself a new dress?'

'I made it out of an old curtain,' Elise offered.

'A curtain?' Shirlene's teeth smiled.

There was something in that smile of Shirlene's that made Elise's own smile fall right off her face. She turned and her high heels ran out of the shop. The doorbell tinkled in alarm at the groceries left deserted on the counter and the girl left forgotten behind the flour sacks. Marjorie ran to follow Elise.

'Princess,' muttered Shirlene.

Marjorie used to love Elise's dresses made from fabrics strange and whimsical, and her hats and gloves and handbags. She was proud. But that was before the long legs and pimples. Now Marjorie was higher up and looking down. And from that superior height, she could see her mother for who she really was – which was that she was not fit for purpose among proper mothers. That she ignored the customs of women around her and made her own clothes. Out of curtains. Without any regard to local opinion. Or without any thought to what it meant for Marjorie and Ruby to have a mother who wore dresses made out of curtains. And the impact this might have on you once you had longs legs and pimples. And with flagrant disregard for any fashion catalogues. Not even the *Woman's Day*. Marjorie and her long legs and pimples burned at the humiliation. 'Can we *buy* clothes, like everyone else does?' she demanded one day.

'What makes you think we have the money to spend on buying clothes? What is wrong with the ones I make for you?'

'I would just like to have clothes that are like my friends' clothes for once.'

'Money doesn't grow on trees, Marjorie,' Elise said, drawing herself up to her full height and staring down at her daughter. 'Your father is working his fingers to the bone trying to keep the farm and provide you with a good education. And you have the hide to suggest we buy clothes. You are an ingrate.'

'She didn't mean it like that,' said Ruby. 'Did you, Marjorie?'

Marjorie wasn't listening to Ruby's warning, though. Ordinarily Marjorie would have been intimidated by Elise in full sail. She knew the consequences of antagonising Elise when she was in this frame of mind. But Marjorie was still suffering from the large dose of humiliation Elise and her outfit had caused.

'Why can't we be like everyone else? Just for once I would like to think we are like everyone else,' she said, hands on hips.

'Of course we are like everyone else,' said Elise in her beautiful voice and with her beautiful diction. 'Whatever would make you think we are not?' She smiled the smile of someone watching events from the high moral ground. 'And if you think I intend to lower my standards, you have another think coming, young lady. We cannot afford the luxuries. So for Pete's sake, Marjorie, get off your high horse.' Elise had a tremor of a glittery smile as she turned her back and flicked the tea towel to dismiss the subject.

Sometime after that, and perhaps to demonstrate both her innovation and thriftiness, Elise took to wearing the tea cosy for a hat.

'You've got the tea cosy on your head,' said Marjorie.

'Don't be ridiculous,' said Elise. 'Why would I wear a tea cosy on my head?'

Ruby glanced up from the mountains of homework she was always doing. 'Marjorie's right,' she said. Her talking was slow and attentive.

'I would certainly know the difference between wearing a tea cosy and wearing a hat,' said Elise, glaring in glittery indignation at Marjorie and Ruby in turn.

The glittery look was not lost on Ruby or Marjorie. 'It doesn't matter anyway, does it, Marjorie?' said Ruby quietly. And all talk about the tea cosy stopped.

The talk might have stopped but the hint of a glittery look and the wearing didn't. The tea in the teapot went cold from then on. But naked teapots and cold tea didn't bother Elise because she drank coffee – and coffee percolators didn't generally dress themselves in cosies.

Nobody mentioned the tea cosy on Elise's head. Ruby and Marjorie didn't mention it again. And Bill's powers of observation seemed to deteriorate with its arrival. 'Where is the tea cosy?' asked Bill, noticing the unclothed teapot.

'I have no idea,' said a cosy-headed Elise.

These days not even Pa was bold to say anything.

Ruby and Marjorie told Jimmy Waghorn about the tea cosy and Jimmy was quiet. He followed up his quietness with a cup of coffee and sat as the tea-cosy-capped Elise made coffee and talked about all manner of things. And glitter lurked at the back of her smiles. So Jimmy followed up with a yarn with Bill.

'You know about that tea cosy business then?' asked Bill.

'Yeah.'

'I don't care if she's wearing a tea cosy,' said Bill. 'If it makes her happy.'

'What people wear on their heads is their own business,' agreed Jimmy.

'But a man's got to worry a bit,' said Bill. 'About Elise. She's highly strung. A thoroughbred.'

'Things are fine, are they? With Elise?'

Bill shrugged.

Jimmy nodded. 'Who's it gunna hurt, anyway? That tea cosy?'

'Yeah,' said Bill.

They made no mention of the glitter, or who that might hurt.

Chapter 6

THE BUS CREAKED and groaned to a stop near the railway line. Ruby and Marjorie shoved forward and waited for the doors to slap open. It was the end of another hot summer school day. And nearly the end of Marjorie's third year of high school.

'Ruby, are you going to tell your mum?' called one of her friends as Ruby and Marjorie crossed the dirt road and headed for the ute waiting under the tree.

'Yes,' yelled Ruby.

'What will she do?'

'Dunno,' called Ruby.

Ruby and Marjorie rushed to get home. There was no dawdling tonight. No stopping at the railway crossing and checking for trains – even though they could have heard a train coming for twenty miles. No slowing at the neighbour's turn-off to check for cars even though they could have seen the dust cloud of a car coming for at least five miles.

Ruby drove over the sandhills, around the bends, through the clay pans. She slammed on the brakes at the front gate. They arrived at the house in record time. And barged hot, dusty, sweaty into the kitchen. 'Ruby is going to be in the school Christmas play,' shouted Marjorie.

Bill was there with Elise. He was often there these days. Sitting with her at the kitchen table at dinnertime, their faces

96

fixed on the wireless as they listened to 'Blue Hills' by Gwen Meredith. No good rains meant no decent crops which meant no real harvesting. So Bill tended to spend more time at the house. A spending Marjorie considered to be well worth the money. He could spend a bit more time tending the vegetables. And a lot more time tending Elise.

'What's all this then?' asked Bill. 'You can't be in the school play. You can't act.'

'Yes I can, Dad,' said Ruby. And she was glad of the hotness still in her face from the late-afternoon heat outside.

'Yeah. She can so. You should see her. She's going to be Juliet in *Romeo and Juliet.*'

'Is it true, Ruby?' asked Elise.

'Yes.'

'Well, congratulations. I am proud of you,' said Elise.

'You have to make Ruby some costumes. You have to make her a nightie and a dying scene dress, a wedding dress and a fabulous dress for the masquerade ball.' Marjorie nearly missed the look of alarm that passed between Bill and Elise. Ruby saw it straight away. 'What's the matter?' she asked.

'There is nothing the matter,' said Elise. 'Is there, Bill?'

Bill's face screwed up, a twisting that scared Marjorie. So she pushed her teeth together and concentrated on trying to keep an eye on both adult faces at the same time.

'We all need to cut back. The crop is bad. You know that. We have to tighten our belts,' he said.

'We must find a way,' said Elise. 'This is important.'

'How do you reckon we are going to do that, Elise?' Bill snapped. 'What would you know about *finding a way*? When have you ever had to *find a way* in your life? The bank won't extend the mortgage on the farm and you're talking about spending money we haven't got on a school concert. You think that's important?'

Bill's chair threw itself back from the table as Bill charged out the back door, grabbing his hat from the peg as he went. The flywire door clapped and clapped. Ruby and Marjorie sat rigid. There was no sound except for the flywire door and its clapping. The girls looked at each other across the table. They knew what the other was thinking. They had seen those thoughts in the eyes of farm kids everywhere these days.

'Don't worry. We will find a way,' said Elise brightly.

'How? There aren't any decent curtains left,' said Marjorie.

'That is uncalled for. An unkind comment,' said Elise.

'Stop it, Marjorie,' said Ruby.

But Marjorie didn't stop it. 'Maybe you could start cutting up the sheets and towels,' said Marjorie.

'Marjorie, I said stop it,' warned Ruby.

Elise sighed. 'Ruby, why don't you two go and tidy your bedroom while I have a think.'

Marjorie wasn't much for tidying. It reminded her too much of her solitary kitchen-tidying episode at the start of high school when Elise was a lump in her bed and the rose garden was aborted. But she went with Ruby and tidied. For Ruby's sake.

'I knew it wouldn't happen. Those sorts of things don't happen to us,' said Ruby in the bedroom. She began a frenzy of tidying.

'It must be the drought,' said Marjorie. 'Do you think Dad is worried we might have to walk off?'

'What?' asked Ruby as she stuffed clothes into the wardrobe.

'We'll have to leave a lot behind if we walk off.'

'What?' asked Ruby from the inside of the wardrobe.

'We won't be able to carry everything.'

'What are you talking about?'

'What about the clothesline? It will be just hanging there. With its forked sticks lying useless on the ground. What about the rabbit traps? Will we take those with us? And who will shut the house gate? It will just be hanging there, slapping and cranking in the wind.'

'Marjorie, it will be alright,' said Ruby.

'Do you know anyone who has lost a farm or walked off a farm?' Marjorie went on.

'No.'

'There's no crop, is there?'

Ruby stopped her tidying. 'No,' she said. 'There is no crop this year.'

'*If you lose your farm you've lost bloody everything.* That's what Pa always says.'

'Marjorie, everything will be alright.'

'How do you know? You can't know that. But anyway, the drought and having no money isn't as bad as Mum and that tea cosy hat!'

Elise appeared at their bedroom door soon after that. 'I know how I can make the costumes for very little cost,' she said. She made no mention of anybody walking off, or of the tea cosy.

'Well I would like to know how you think you can do that,' said Marjorie. 'Because we can't afford it, can we?'

'I said it won't cost much, Marjorie.' Elise's eyes settled hard on Marjorie and she folded her arms.

'How much? How much will it cost?'

'Stop it, Marjorie. Just listen for once,' warned Ruby, watching the hardening of Elise's eyes.

'They will all look lovely, I can assure you. Even to a selfish, self-centred little article such as yourself, Marjorie,' said Elise.

'Thank you, Mum,' said Ruby. *Shut up!* she mouthed at Marjorie.

'And the masquerade ball dress will be absolutely splendid. Come here, Ruby. I need to measure you up.'

Ruby was dragged across the hallway. Marjorie followed. Ruby stood beside the Singer sewing machine while Elise measured and noted. Elise copied measurements onto old newspaper, the newspaper transformed itself into dress patterns. And Elise and the Singer sewing machine treadled away.

The girls were now forbidden to enter the bedroom with the Singer sewing machine. They knew Elise was working on costumes while they were at school. And she was often working on them late at night after they had gone to bed. That was all they knew. They were fidgety and anxious. They were leery of the tea cosy.

'What do you think she is making them out of?' asked Marjorie as they lay in their beds listening to the rhythm of the sewing machine treadle.

'How would I know?' replied Ruby into the dark.

'I meant it about the curtains. There aren't any decent ones left.'

'I know.'

'And there are so many costumes. How could she make that many proper costumes?'

'I don't know.'

'It's going to be a public disgrace. We are going to be that family with the weird mother that everyone laughs at. Again!'

'Go to sleep, Marjorie.'

'And that tea cosy isn't helping. What if she takes to wearing it into town?'

'Shut up, Marjorie!' hissed Ruby.

The girls could have had a look any time at what was going on in the spare bedroom. But they did not.

'Why don't we sneak in and have a look?' suggested Ruby.

Marjorie shook her head. 'Why would we want to do that? If there is a costuming debacle in there and a public humiliation in the wings, it can wait, as far as I'm concerned. Why face it before we need to?'

So they settled on pretending. And why not? The adults in that house pretended. All the time. Ruby and Marjorie pretended the costumes were being made out of the beautiful crystal wedding dress hiding in its plastic bag in the cupboard while Ruby spent her time learning lines. It was better than nothing.

There were the kids at school to contend with, though.

'How's your mother going with those costumes?' asked Jesse Mitchell. 'She going to make them out of curtains?'

'No,' Marjorie said, scowling. 'She's making them out of old sheets.'

'Yeah, but what about the ball dress? Your dad's already too hard up and I reckon the bank isn't going to lend him any dough in this drought to spend on a ball dress.'

'I bet your mum's going mad trying to figure this one out,' said Kevin Doherty, one of the kids from Jesse's footy team. 'It's enough to send any decent sane person crazy, isn't it? So I reckon it must be having a field day with your crazy mother.'

'I don't know about any of that. But your mother seems to think she knows. Why don't you ask Shirlene?' suggested Marjorie.

Kevin's self-possession bleached. 'Yeah, well, you leave my mum out of it,' he said. Then he grabbed for the upper hand again. 'So what about that ball dress, then? Is she going crazy trying to figure out how to make it? Is the princess going crazy, Marjorie?' And dozens of schoolyard eyes swivelled to Marjorie and Ruby. Ruby shoved the grinning face out of the way and dragged Marjorie towards their friends. 'She's fine. She's making the ball dress out of old wheat bags, idiot,' Marjorie yelled over her shoulder as she stumbled after Ruby.

*

'I have finished the ball dress, Ruby – come into the bedroom and try it on,' said Elise one day after school.

The two girls looked at each other and Marjorie tried to make a run for it out the back door she had only just entered. But Elise was quick. Even for a lady. She rounded them both up and ushered them towards the bedroom.

Ruby and Marjorie stepped through the doorway into the bedroom with its Singer sewing machine and secret costumes and stopped dead as they banged up against magic. There were any number of other costumes there. But they were all beaten by the masquerade ball dress.

There, hanging glorious and solitary, was a ball dress fit for royalty. It took their breath away. And it took their voices away. A work of art was drifting in the late-afternoon light, surrounded by ministering spangles of Mallee dust. It was fabulous. It was gathered and tucked and layered. It was exquisitely stitched and sewn. No one could beat this. No matter how brand spanking new a Singer sewing machine might be. This dress was without doubt the best Juliet ball dress ever made. And it was made out of paper. Crepe paper. All the costumes were. Even the ones made out of old sheets and old curtains had been embellished with crepe paper. The two girls gawked at the delicate papery creation floating on its humble wire hanger.

'It's beautiful,' breathed Ruby.

'Where did you get all the paper?' asked Marjorie.

'It's crepe paper. It is very inexpensive,' said Elise.

'It's a dress made out of paper,' said Marjorie redundantly. Nodding at the wonder of it.

'Yes, it is.' Elise smiled. 'It's made out of paper. Try it on, Ruby,' she said.

And there, in front of Marjorie, her sister was transformed into a medieval crepe paper princess. Elise had put a mirror in the bedroom. Ruby twirled in front of it in her fragile, crinkly costume, and the paper crinkled and talked while she twirled.

'You will be the most beautiful Juliet ever to take the stage,' said Elise. The crepe paper dress whispered its agreement and so did the mirror.

In the weeks leading up to the concert Marjorie taunted her schoolmates. 'Hey, you reckon Elise is going crazy?' Marjorie had their instant attention. 'Well, you're right. She *is* going crazy trying to make those costumes. And you're right, Kev – trying to make that ball dress is driving her especially crazy.'

Marjorie smiled at the satisfied look on Kevin's face as she walked off. Then she stopped and glanced over her shoulder at Jesse standing beside Kevin. 'Remember when I said the dresses were made out of wheat bags? Well, they're not. They're made out of paper.'

'You're crazy like your mother,' said Kevin. 'How can you make a dress out of paper?'

'You're right. Costumes made out of paper? That would be

bloody stupid. That couldn't work. They're made out of wheat bags, boy,' Marjorie agreed.

Elise didn't stop at making a fabulous ball dress out of crepe paper. She made petite, crepe paper slippers as well, with tiny crepe paper roses to match the roses on the dress. And she rescued the crushed and broken crown lying forgotten on its shelf for so many years now. Elise cleaned it and straightened it and made it to fit Ruby's head of glorious red curls.

*

Bill drove his family to the town hall on the night of the concert. He was nervous for Elise. 'You've done your best and a person can't ever do better than that, so don't you worry about what anyone might think. Just keep your chin up,' he said, patting her hand.

Jimmy Waghorn knew how worried Bill was, so he came along to be there for both of them.

But for once, Elise was sure and confident. She didn't need any buttressing from Bill. Or from Jimmy. She didn't care what the Shirlene Dohertys of the world might think. And neither did the girls. They were quiet in the back seat, squashed there between Jimmy and Pa, buoyant in their fragile costuming secret: their approaching triumph.

Marjorie sat on a bench between Jimmy and Pa. Bill was on the other side of Jimmy. Elise was out the back helping Ruby with all that paper. Marjorie could see Jesse Mitchell's mother with her bowed head and Jesse's lanky, dusty brothers – all sidelong eyes and surly shoulders these days. She looked around but couldn't see Jesse. Aunty Thelma and Aunty Kathleen were there. She could see Shirlene Doherty and Kevin sitting with

Mrs Cameron. 'Are you ready, Kevin?' she muttered. '*For this is the winter of your discontent!*'

'What?' said Pa.

'Shh!' Jimmy whispered as the curtains began to rise.

Ruby and Marjorie were right to be confident. For that night, in the dusty town hall, Ruby was a princess. Ruby captivated as Juliet in her dresses of curtains and old sheets with their sprinkling of crepe paper, but the masquerade ball scene was a moment of sheer magic as Ruby and her crepe paper stepped onto the stage. Marjorie's steadfast, sheltering Ruby. Her glorious Ruby with the green eyes, the curling, tumbling red hair, the translucent skin, and that beautiful smile:

'*My only love sprung from my only hate!*

Too early seen unknown, and known too late!' cried Ruby in her fanciful creation.

Jimmy squeezed Marjorie's hand and Aunty Thelma and Mrs Cameron sighed at the ill-fated lovers.

'*You kiss by the book,*' she complained to Romeo, and all the girls laughed.

But Romeo was not put off:

'*O, she doth teach the torches to burn bright!*

Beauty too rich for use, for earth too dear!' he said.

And everyone in the hall, looking at Ruby in her fabulous dress, knew that those lines had been written hundreds of years ago in England for just this night in the Mallee. She ruled the stage in a glory of paper.

And it was a good thing it was a warm summer night, and the doors and windows were open. Because the gasp of awe from that compilation of Mallee folk was enough to suck all the oxygen from the hall. The hall could have become a mass grave site if the doors and windows were shut. As it was, though, the entire Mallee marvelled in open-windowed summer safety at the beautiful princess dancing, and loving, and dying in her magical crepe paper costume. It had truly never seen the likes. Pa was so captivated by Ruby he decided to help. He called out some of his own favourite lines during the fight scenes:

'"Put in the boot!" I sez. "Put in the boot!"

"Shame!" sez some silly coot!' yelled Pa.

Shirlene Doherty whirled around and glared at him and Pa grinned back.

'Good line, but let's leave C.J. Dennis out of it,' whispered Jimmy as he thumped Pa in the arm and grinned at Shirlene.

The supper after the concert was almost a disaster. People were so busy telling Elise and Ruby how wonderful it all was that the cream sponges were nearly forgotten. Even Shirlene Doherty tried hard to have a good word to say:

'Paper dresses,' she said. 'Made them yourself on your Singer. Well I suppose that couldn't have cost too much. And you can always burn them afterwards.'

'Look what Elise did,' said Jimmy, smiling quietly at Bill, watching the women crowding around his friend's wife.

'She's a marvel,' said Bill. 'A bloody marvel.'

'And what about that Ruby of yours?' said Jimmy.

'Yeah.' Bill smiled. 'I didn't know she had it in her.'

Marjorie hadn't been able to see Jesse Mitchell because he had been sitting right behind her. Not until the final scenes of the play had she realised this when she heard him whispering lines to himself:

'See what a scourge is laid upon your hate,

That heaven finds means to kill your joys with love,' he recited in time with the actor on the stage.

Marjorie turned and stared.

'It's alright, mate,' said Jimmy, who had also turned to Jesse.

*

There was a long, splendid autumn after the school concert and the stunning success of the crepe paper dress, as far as Elise and the Mallee were concerned. And Marjorie was like a wheat farmer after a good rain. She made the most of it. 'Hey, you, Kevin Doherty. I told ya Elise was making the costumes out of paper. What in tarnation made you think I would lie to you? I reckon you should believe everything I say from now on, if you know what's bloody well good for you.'

'Yeah, and what if I don't?'

Marjorie shrugged her bony shoulders. 'Up to you. But I go more than a bit crazy if I think people don't believe me,' she said. 'Crazy like Crazy Elise.'

Kevin hunched his shoulders and squinted at her. He looked around for backup, but he was a mean kid, even if he was good at footy, and as a result his backup was generally not reliable. The onlookers were already shifting off out of the perimeter of the conversation. Like farm dogs slinking away from each other after a fight.

Jesse Mitchell was still there, though. 'Leave him alone. He's not worth it.'

'Mind your own bloody business, Wheat Bag Boy,' said Marjorie.

'Just trying to help,' said Jesse, slowly shaking his head.

'Stop swearing, Marjorie,' said Kevin. 'She's swearing.'

'Go away, Kevin,' said Jesse.

'Yeah. I'll go. I'll go to the principal. To tell her Marjorie's swearing.' Kevin glanced over his shoulder, expecting the deserting spectators to halt their retreat. And they did. They liked the thought of Marjorie having to answer to the principal about swearing. They hesitated. But flagged their non-committance by looking side on and scuffing the dirt with their shoes. Those at the back of the group kept a handy eye on the safety of the shelter shed.

'Go ahead, Kev. It would be a very foolish bloody thing to do. But go ahead,' Marjorie said in an oddly soothing voice.

'Leave it, Marjorie,' said Jesse.

'Why should I, Wheat Bag Boy? You know Kev would be very bloody stupid to go to the principal.' Marjorie stepped towards Jesse. She poked him in the chest. 'Because,' continued Marjorie, poking him in the chest again to illustrate her point, 'young ladies' – poke – 'do not' – poke – 'bloody well swear.' Her hand shoved at Jesse's chest and landed him on his back in the dirt.

Marjorie stood over Jesse. 'Hell and damnation, Wheat Bag Boy. The whole world knows it's not seemly for young ladies to swear. Do you for one moment think Crazy Elise would allow me to bloody well swear?'

She watched as Jesse picked himself up and ran his hands through his dusty hair, before turning to walk after Kevin and the skulking retreaters. She watched until the bunch of them disappeared behind the comfort of the shelter shed.

Later, Marjorie was called upon to stand in front of the entire class and answer to the charge of swearing. Kevin Doherty smirked. Jesse stared straight ahead.

'I cannot believe this of you, Marjorie.' The teacher's face was squashed and pale – a rotten paddymelon. 'Were you swearing?'

'How could I?' asked Marjorie. 'You know my mother would never allow me to swear.'

'I know that. So were you swearing?'

'I could not have,' repeated Marjorie. 'My mother would be horrified.' She paused. 'And who do you think is the more likely to be swearing, Miss? Me? Or them?' Finger pointed towards Jesse Mitchell and Kevin Doherty. 'I could not have been swearing because my mother does not allow it.'

The teacher's face swung like a pendulum. It was caught between the aggrieved face of Marjorie, the righteous face of Kevin and the stony face of Jesse. Its bag of rotten paddymelon seeds swilled and clattered against its crinkled casing. She had been in the Mallee for a long time. She had seen a shearing shed or two. She knew about pulling the wool over someone's eyes. Her hands touched her face – to check on the condition of the saggy melon. The fingers climbed to her eyes – to see if there was any wool evident. The outraged claim of innocence from Marjorie was credible. The teacher knew that for sure: Marjorie's mother had schooled her daughters in ways of being more suited to a city life than life in the Mallee, and that included impeccable speech – not a vulgar word and definitely no swearing. She looked at the other end of the pendulum's arc: Kevin Doherty. And took in the apparent silent complicity of Jesse – a boy with a mother whose face never had the energy to raise itself out of the shadows. A mother whose interest in her children's education was lethargic at best and whose eyes spent their time studying her hands in her lap.

'Thank you, Marjorie. I believe I have to accept you are in the right. You can go back to your desk. And you two – you will stay in after school.'

'No,' said Jesse.

'I beg your pardon!'

'You can't keep me in. I have to take the littlies home.'

'You are skating on very thin ice, Jesse,' warned the teacher. 'Your brothers will stay here with you until you have finished your punishment. And then you can all go home.'

'That's not fair!' said Jesse. 'We'll miss the bus. How are we going to get home?'

The teacher stared at Jesse. 'I am disappointed in you, Jesse. I actually thought you might have been going to make an effort regarding your schooling this year. You will complete the essay neither you nor Kevin have yet submitted, and you, Jesse, will also write two hundred lines of *I will not engage in deceit, lies and impertinence*. I will phone your mother and let her know what has happened. It is up to you to complete your punishment before the school bus leaves. How you make arrangements to get home if you miss the bus is not my concern.'

'Stupid bloody fool,' crooned Marjorie as she glided past the desk of Wheat Bag Boy.

All in all, despite the legs and the pimples and the drought and the bank and the debt on the farm and the tea cosy hat, times were not too bad as far as Marjorie was concerned.

But while times might not be too bad for Marjorie, they were not that way for everyone. Because Marjorie didn't have to stay in after school that day. She was well and truly gone when at last Jesse and his scared and waiting little brothers raced from the long since empty schoolyard to start the lengthy run home, all by themselves, trotting as fast down those dusty roads as Jesse would let them. Their only companion the late afternoon sun that shone regretfully on them for as long as it could before it couldn't wait for them any longer and sank behind the distant sandhills.

And she certainly wasn't at home with their waiting mother.

With her beaten brow and her clouted ribs. Lying huddled and limp like a discarded rag there on the kitchen floor.

'Don't tell me you don't know where they are. Don't you give me that. You're a useless bloody excuse for a mother, you are,' his voice bawled at her as his shoulders and legs loomed over her.

And she certainly wasn't there with their father, waiting at their house gate with his jumpy legs and bunched arms, lurching and pacing with his flailing leather belt. Ready to finish the job.

Jesse slowed when he saw his father out the front of the house. Arms and legs of his brothers mashed themselves onto the back of his legs. 'Don't worry. Just keep walking,' he said to them. 'Go right past him and in the back gate. Find Mum and tell her I will be a bit busy with Dad for a while.'

'Will Mum be lying down again?' they whimpered.

Jesse's teeth gritted. 'If Mum is having a lie-down then get outside and do your chores. And stay out there. Don't come back inside until I come looking for you.'

'Where the bloody hell have you been?' his father yelled when he saw Jesse leading his brothers up the home paddock track. 'It's nigh on dark. How is this farm supposed to keep going with the likes of you never around to pull your weight?'

'At school,' said Jesse as twenty little-brother-fingers grabbed the back of his shirt.

'Don't lie to me. It's well past time for school.'

'I'm not lying.'

'And don't smart mouth me, either. By the crikies you're going to get a belting for this. The lot of you!'

'Leave the littlies out of this. They had nothing to do with it,' said Jesse.

Jesse's father stopped his pacing. His eyes glinted and narrowed. His hands knotted and they gathered his leather belt in a tight loop. 'I thought I told you not to smart mouth me, boy,' he whispered. 'Come here, you useless piece of shit.'

Jesse bunched his own hands into hard fists. He rolled onto the balls of his feet and faced his father. 'Go on to Mum and do what I said,' he told his brothers.

Jesse wasn't at school the next day. Or the day after that.

'What happened to you?' asked Marjorie a few days later when Jesse and a couple of fading black eyes and a chipped front tooth did finally decide to turn up at school.

'Went head first over the handlebars. My fault,' he said. 'I was riding in the dark.'

'So you stayed home from school because you fell off your bike? You're such a sook. And such a fool.'

Jesse shrugged and kept his mouth shut. He knew she could see the remnant colours of the black eyes but she didn't have to get too much of a good look at the broken front tooth if he could help it. Not just yet.

'Been a bad bloody week for you all round then, hasn't it?' said Marjorie. 'First, being kept in to write lines for lying about me swearing. And then stacking your bike and smashing your pretty face.' She shook her head at Jesse and laughed.

Chapter 7

IT WAS JUST an ordinary winter's night like so many before. The air was gloomy and heavy with the business of another pre-dawn frost. The kitchen windows were already cloudy, the kitchen doors were creaking, the tin on the roof above was popping in anticipation. Marjorie was setting the table. Ruby was putting out the plates. Elise, tea cosy on head, was checking the contents of saucepans and smiling vaguely at the girls. Pa was sitting at the end of the table smoking his pipe and tapping his fingers on the table. Irritated and impatient at the continued inability of any one of these women in his house to serve him some sort of decent tucker on time.

Bill came through the back door. 'Hello, dear,' said Elise.

'Where the bloody hell have you been all this time? It's way past teatime,' said Pa. 'I suppose you broke the bloody tractor again and had to walk back like a damn fool.'

Bill didn't answer. He looked at the girls. He looked at Elise. Vague Elise but contented Elise – no glitter lurking anywhere.

'I've been over at Jimmy's,' said Bill.

'What the hell were you doing over at Jimmy's at this time of night?' asked Pa.

'He's crook. I'll be taking him to the doctor's tomorrow.'

The kitchen went quiet. Pa took his pipe out of his mouth

and watched Bill. The walls, the windows and doors were quiet; the coffee percolator was quiet.

'Jimmy Waghorn doesn't like going to the doctor,' said Elise.

'I know. But he's ailing. He has to go.'

'I will come with you tomorrow,' said Elise.

'Thanks, love,' said Bill.

Tea was served. And eaten. A couple of cups of tea were made and gulped or slurped. A cup of coffee was made and sipped. Dishes were washed and put away. The girls got out their homework. It could have been any winter's night. Except Bill and Pa forgot to argue with each other. Even afterwards, when Marjorie woke in the early hours of the morning, it seemed ordinary. The same dark-time stillness. The same biting chill in the bedroom outside of her blankets. The same quiet pinging of the fuel drums out near the garage. The same alien brilliance of the stars speckled across the frosty sky framed by her bedroom window.

Tea that next night was not ordinary. Jimmy Waghorn loomed over the table. 'The doctor said Jimmy can't live by himself anymore. Says he's too old. He needs looking after.' Bill started the conversation by telling this to his plate. He raised his eyes and looked at the faces around the table to see if they were as shrewd as his plate.

Elise said nothing. She didn't need to. She already knew this.

Knives and forks were arrested in the middle of their duties. Forks hung stupidly in mid-air, laden with the hot food they were now unable to deliver. Knives were halted in their cutting. Some cutlery was dropped impolitely – clattering onto plates, or thumping on the table.

'How can Jimmy Waghorn be too old? He's only a bit older than you,' said Marjorie.

'It's different for Jimmy,' was all Bill said.

'He can live with us, Dad – in the spare bedroom,' said Ruby. 'We'll look after Jimmy.'

'We've already suggested that,' said Elise. 'Jimmy doesn't want to. He wants to travel up north. To be with his family.'

'But we are his family,' said Marjorie.

'No, we are not,' said Bill. 'Jimmy is sick and he has real family – kinfolk up on the river – and he wants to move up there to be with them.'

The tea table was silent. Everyone looked at their plates. But the plates said nothing. Because plates don't care.

'He never talked about having any family before,' said Marjorie into the silence.

'And why do you suppose that might be?' asked Bill.

'Leave her be, Bill,' said Pa. 'A young girl like that is not about to be knowing these things. How could she know? And it's Jimmy's business, anyway.'

'I'll be packing Jimmy up and taking him up to his relatives in the next couple of days,' said Bill. 'Now eat your tea. It's getting cold.'

'In the next couple of days?' Marjorie's face went red and her hands slammed the cutlery. 'What about Ruby and me? We've got to go to school. When do we get to say goodbye to Jimmy?'

'Don't raise your voice at your father, young lady,' said Elise.

'I've already said that's the end of it,' said Bill. 'Now eat your tea.'

So they all ate their tea. Because there is no sense in ruining even a half-good hot tea by letting it get cold.

'What are we going to do without Jimmy Waghorn?' whispered Ruby later that night.

'I don't know.'

'What do you think Dad will do?'

'I don't know.'

'What about Mum?' asked Ruby after a long dark silence. 'How do you think she'll go without Jimmy?'

'I don't know,' said Marjorie. Which was a lie. She had more than a fair idea and it all had to do with the dangers of strings getting far too tight.

'We're in big trouble,' whispered Ruby.

'I know,' said Marjorie.

Ruby flung herself back on her pillow.

'Let's wag tomorrow,' said Marjorie.

'What if we get caught?' whispered Ruby. 'It will just make things worse.'

'I don't care,' said Marjorie. 'I want to say goodbye to Jimmy. No one will know. We'll have to leave the ute home. We can ride our bikes so they can't hear us. We can leave early and ride off as if we were going to the bus stop then cut across the paddick to Jimmy's place.'

So that was what they did. Bill was gone before daylight so Ruby and Marjorie didn't have to be careful around him. 'We're riding our bikes today. Need some exercise,' said Marjorie as they headed out the back door. Elise didn't answer. She was busy with her coffee percolator. Pa was busy with his boiled eggs. The cocky was the only one who commented and he was more worried about personal appearance and farm safety than wagging. 'Girls, do your hair. Shut the bloody gate,' he said.

Just an ordinary school day. Wagging was so easy.

The two girls turned off at the first gate after the home paddock and headed to Jimmy Waghorn's place.

It looked like Jimmy was waiting for them. They left their bikes and walked over the sandhill behind the peppercorn tree – which was the opposite way to how they would usually arrive. But there was Jimmy Waghorn. Sitting on his old blue bench with a huge pile of wood stacked beside the campfire. His billy already nestled in its patch of coals at the edge.

'You girls supposed to be at school? You're not waggin', are ya?' Jimmy eyed them. 'I told ya already about waggin'. It's no good. Gets ya nowhere.'

'You and Dad used to wag all the time,' said Marjorie.

'Yeah, we did,' agreed Jimmy. 'And like I said: gets ya nowhere.' His face continued to radiate disapproval and for a moment the two girls were afraid he might pack them into his ute and take them all the way to high school. But his face softened and he patted the old bench. 'Come on.' He smiled that wonderful Jimmy Waghorn smile. 'I've been expectin' ya.' Jimmy Waghorn had business to do with Ruby and Marjorie. Things needed to be said.

It was a strange day for the girls. Jimmy Waghorn talked to them about a lot of things. 'People are scared of the wrong things generally,' said Jimmy. 'The only thing people should be scared about is if we haven't looked after each other. And drought. People should be scared of drought.'

The two girls looked at Jimmy and said nothing. They understood the bit about being scared of drought.

'All the time we are scared about ourselves. Worrying about whether we are good enough.' Jimmy gazed at the fire and shook his head. 'We shouldn't be worrying about what sort of hat anyone wears.'

'Are you talking about Mum?' asked Marjorie.

'Yep. I'm talking about your mother,' said Jimmy, nodding. 'Ya know people are scared of her.'

Marjorie stared at Jimmy in shock. 'No they aren't. They're not scared of Mum. They laugh at her behind her back. They think she's mental.'

'They don't know what to make of her, Marjorie.' Jimmy ignored the face glaring at him. 'They are scared of all those bits of her that are bigger than they are – like the piano, and the singing, and the drawing and painting. So they make fun of the way she talks and how she dresses.'

The girls said nothing.

'Like your Pa,' Jimmy went on. 'Why do you think he treats your mother that way?'

'Because he's just a mean old pig,' said Marjorie. 'He treats everyone bad. You should hear the way he talks to Dad.'

'I know the way he talks to Bill,' said Jimmy. 'And he talks to Bill that way for the same reason. He is scared of Bill. Bill can take it. But Elise can't.'

'What do you want us to do, Jimmy?' asked Ruby.

'Just make sure Elise is in good spirits, alright? Don't worry about the tea cosy hat.'

Marjorie folded her arms tightly across her chest and began kicking the dirt. 'You're asking us, the children, to look after our mother, the adult.'

'I am.'

Marjorie started kicking hard at the dirt. 'And who is going to look after us? Now that you're going?' Her voice was clipped and dirt was flying all over her shoes. 'She's the mother, Jimmy. She's supposed to look after us.'

'Elise isn't strong enough for this country.' Jimmy looked at them before moving to poke the fire. 'But you two are.'

'It's not fair!' shouted Marjorie.

'No, it isn't,' agreed Jimmy.

'It wouldn't be so bad if she didn't wear the tea cosy all the time,' said Ruby.

'Yeah,' agreed Jimmy. 'Just make sure she only wants to wear that tea cosy hat on the farm. You will know your mother is alright if she is only wearing that tea cosy on the farm.'

Ruby shook her head. She put her arm around Marjorie. 'I don't know how to do that. If I knew how to look after my mother, I would already be doing it.'

Jimmy nodded.

The three of them talked for most of the day. And the country roundabout kept watch. Jimmy and the girls took turns feeding the fire and making each other cups of tea. They watched the sun climb to sit above their heads. They had dinner and they talked. 'You doing that Leaving Certificate next year?' asked Jimmy.

'Yes,' said Ruby.

'You still want to be a teacher?'

'Yes.'

'You'll make a good teacher. You make sure you do that. Not enough good teachers,' said Jimmy.

Ruby smiled. But salt water was doing what salt water does and it was making her eyes sting.

'You could live with Aunty Agnes,' suggested Marjorie.

Ruby poked the fire and said nothing.

'What about you, Marjorie? Are you going to do your Leaving Certificate?'

'Yeah, probably.'

'What do you want to do when you finish school?'

'I want to make books,' Marjorie said.

'So our Marjorie is going to be a writer, eh?'

'No. I don't want to write books. I want to make books. You know: have a printing machine and make the books.'

'How are you going to do that?'

'I'm going to get an apprenticeship.'

'Oh! Marjorie is going to be an apprentice! Well, that's a funny sort of a job for a girl. But don't you let anyone stand in your way, Marjorie. If that's what you want to do,' said Jimmy.

They talked until the sun started heading towards its resting place. The girls knew it was time to go when the sun began painting the top of the gate in the distance. Jimmy had done all he could by then. 'It's time to go, girls,' he said softly as he stood up from their old bench. 'It's time to say goodbye to an old friend. And I don't want to be responsible if Bill finds out you've been wagging it at my place,' he added with a smile.

Jimmy hugged Marjorie. 'Don't worry about things so much, girl,' he whispered. 'Most things in this world don't amount to anything.'

Marjorie clung to Jimmy. Because she wasn't so sure. And she was worried about so many things. Like how was she going to manage now if Jimmy wasn't around anymore? Or Ruby?

'You are you. No one else, Marjorie. Remember that.' Jimmy lightly pushed Marjorie away from him so he could look into her eyes. 'You are going to turn out just fine, Marjorie. Too right, you will.' He nodded at her. 'And go easy on those kids at school. Don't be cruel.'

Marjorie smiled through the tears mustering at the back of her eyes. 'Wheat Bag Boy is an idiot. He got kept down a grade,' she said.

'He might not seem to be as good with the school books as you, girl, but he is not an idiot. He deserves better from you. Alright? And his name is Jesse.'

Jimmy hugged Ruby. 'Don't pay too much attention to what the people hereabouts are saying. They don't know much of anything.'

Ruby didn't say anything, but her arms tightened around Jimmy.

'Now the pair of you had best be getting home.'

'Goodbye, Jimmy,' said the two girls.

Ruby and Marjorie turned their backs on Jimmy Waghorn and walked over the sandhill to collect their bikes and ride home. They didn't look back once. So they didn't see him standing there watching them until they disappeared over the other side of the sandhill. They didn't see him walk after them to the top of the next hill and watch them ride their bikes down along the track through the stubble and out the gate. They didn't see Jimmy Waghorn standing and watching. Until he couldn't see them anymore.

The two girls never spoke to each other on the way home. They just pedalled and cried all the way into the spokes of their front tyres. Those spokes collected all the tears and converted them into delicate crystals, and danced them around and around before discarding them onto the red dirt.

No one at the house suspected a wagging. No one noticed the red crying eyes of the two girls. No one supposed the girls had spent the day with Jimmy Waghorn. Because it did not occur to anyone at the house that Ruby and Marjorie might need to say goodbye to him – or that Jimmy would want to say goodbye to them.

The two girls went to bed that night and cried quiet, desolate tears into their pillows and into the night. And into many other nights to come.

*

Nobody hereabouts ever talked about the business of Jimmy Waghorn, although everybody wanted to know. But Jimmy's business was Jimmy's business, and Jimmy had never invited his business to be discussed.

You never wanted to be found guilty of talking about someone's business without being invited. Because that would constitute a breach. And a breach resulted in a cold shoulder. And a Mallee cold shoulder was a hard and heavy thing to bear. It was high-priced. With payment imposed by everybody. And there is hardly a lonelier road than turning up at the local footy match, or the tennis or cricket match, or the local dance, and having no one to talk to, but lots of people to stare at you.

Still, everyone was uneasy. Because the legacy of Jimmy Waghorn was big in this part of the country. So they tried their best to find out.

'Jimmy's left the Mallee, has he? Gone up the river? He's got relatives up there?'

'Jimmy's got relatives up the river,' said Bill. 'Yeah.'

'Jimmy's been a bit crook lately, I heard?'

'Doctor said Jimmy needed looking after,' said Bill.

'Blimey. All this time. I never knew Jimmy Waghorn had any kin.' A farmer pushed his hat to the back of his head and scratched his hair at the front.

'Yeah,' said Bill. 'Jimmy has kinfolk.'

'Jimmy's coming back then?'

'The hut's still there,' said Bill.

Daft young farmers tried to squeeze information out of Pa. Choosing the public bar of the local pub.

'What about that rain? Wet enough for ya, Pa?'

A proper answer would be: *Could be wetter.* But: 'Call that a rain?' Pa said instead. 'I suppose you young whippersnappers are out there tearing round the paddick working up to plant?' Pa turned from the cold delight of his beer to scrutinise the pitiful insufficiencies of the younger farming generation. 'Young fools. Not near enough rain there to get a crop going.'

'Reckon we've got a chance at the grand final?'

'With that mob of pansies dancing around? They wouldn't know how to play real football if the football jumped up and bit them in the bloody neck,' said Pa. 'Not bloody likely.'

'Heard Jimmy Waghorn's not too good. He been a bit off colour lately?'

That was the question Pa knew they were all itching to ask. He paused from the beer to gaze once more at them. 'Why don't you take a trip out home and ask him your bloody self?' He gulped down the rest of his beer, watching over the frothy rim of his glass as their faces melted into dismay at the prospect of turning up at Jimmy Waghorn's place without an invite.

Pa slammed the empty glass down on the bar and walked out of the pub. Pulling his pipe out of the top pocket of his coat as he went. Grinning in delight.

Womenfolk huddled around Elise like chooks squabbling for the wheat.

'How are you, Elise? It must be such a strain for you.'

'What do you mean?' asked Elise. Because unlike Bill and Pa, she truly didn't know what they meant.

'We thought it looked like Jimmy Waghorn had slipped a bit lately.'

Elise gazed at the women as directly as good manners allowed, hoping she might find, very discreetly, a clue as to how she should answer. Trying to remember if Jimmy had tripped over lately. 'No, I don't think so,' she said cautiously. 'Jimmy has always been very graceful on his feet.'

Smirks and raised eyebrows buzzed between Shirlene Doherty and her friends. 'So he is doing well then?' she said.

'As far as I know,' said Elise. 'But you know Jimmy. He has never wanted to make a fuss.'

'No. He never has,' said the ladies, nodding wisely about something they knew nothing about.

So while they were all busy nodding and agreeing with Elise, Ruby and Marjorie slipped their arms through Elise's and steered their mother to safety.

'It's so nice of you to be concerned for Jimmy Waghorn,' said Marjorie over her shoulder as they walked off. 'Ruby and I will probably be going over to his place tomorrow. Do you want us to give him a message?'

'You're going over to his house?'

'Oh yes,' said Ruby, smiling at the women. 'Marjorie and I go over there all the time.' Completely without guile.

And so, for the moment, Jimmy's business, and therefore Elise's business, was safe. No one lied. The hut was still there. It always would be Jimmy Waghorn's place. And Ruby and Marjorie were still visiting.

In some ways, it was easier to manage the situation at school.

'Jimmy Waghorn's gone, hasn't he?' said Jesse Mitchell.

'None of your business,' said Marjorie.

'I know he doesn't live there anymore. Stop lying.'

'Shut up or I'll bloody shut you up.'

'You're swearing. I'm gunna tell the principal,' said Kevin, stepping in to support his footy captain.

'Shut up, Kev,' said Jesse.

'Go ahead, Kevin,' taunted Marjorie, ignoring Jesse. 'I crave to see you and your ridiculously flamin' stupid cronies being kept in again and having to write lines again! One hundred lines of *I must not bloody well be a stupid liar especially as it pertains to Jimmy Waghorn.*'

'Has he gone or not?' repeated Jesse.

'Like I said, Ruby and I go over to Jimmy's place all the time.' She paused for dramatic effect. 'You're welcome to come with us any time. I don't know how Jimmy will take people turning up without an invitation, but' – she shrugged – 'that's your problem.'

'Come on, Jesse. Forget it,' said Kevin, blanching at the thought. And the boys walked away before the situation became a bloodbath.

These were small victories, partnered by small comforts – because the girls were still visiting Jimmy Waghorn's place. They didn't mention their visits to Bill or Elise. They didn't have to.

'What have you been doing today?' Elise would ask when Marjorie surfaced in the kitchen after a long day of absence.

'Nothing . . .'

'What are you going to do today?' Elise would sometimes ask.

Marjorie would shrug her shoulders. 'Dunno . . .'

'The phrase is *I don't know* . . .'

The girls would do what they had always done when they visited Jimmy. They would collect the latest crop of hollow beer bottles and stack them neatly, triangularly, brownly beside the hut. Although there were no empty bottles huddling around the campfire anymore. They would tidy the hut. Even though it was now perfectly tidy. They would check the wood heap. They would light the fire and sit on the old blue bench. They would stare at the fire and poke it with a stick and talk:

'Not long now before you have to go to teachers' college.'

'Mum will be alright, Marjorie. Dad and Pa are there.

You'll be fine. Just try to think a bit first before you let anything come out of your mouth.'

'How do you reckon you catch a tram?'

'Aunty Agnes will show me. Are you listening to me? About Mum?'

'I wish Kevin Doherty would drop dead.'

'I wish I could show you how to manage with Mum. So you could make sure Mum is okay.'

'I'm not like you, Ruby. I wish I was like you.'

'I don't want you to be like me. You're fine the way you are. And Mum's always going to be Mum. Doesn't matter what we do, or don't do.'

'I wish I could come too,' Marjorie would say.

Ruby would take Marjorie's hand then. Or they would put their arms around each other's shoulders. 'It will be fine, Marjorie,' Ruby would say. 'Don't worry. We've got through more than me going away to teachers' college before. Me going away isn't going to change anything,' she would say.

*

What does it take for people to know how to properly tune someone's tight strings? What did Mallee folks know about tuning? They didn't know much. But there certainly were enough people who tried. Bill and his sisters, and even Pa. They all did their bit for the family.

Aunty Kathleen and Aunty Thelma knew that without Jimmy Waghorn to visit, Elise would now have no visitors at all. So, they would drive their various miles with the children bouncing and bobbing around in the back. Over to Bill and Elise's place for a cup of tea with Elise. 'Come on,' they would say in their kind and practical ways. 'Make us a cup of tea to go with that coffee of yours.' And they would bustle around in Elise's kitchen and ignore the tea cosy hat grafted to Elise's head.

Elise never knew just how to take all this kind and practical business, all this bustling and sensible generosity. But she knew it would be rude to refuse it.

'Would you play for us, Elise? Would you sing too?' the sisters-in-law would ask.

'What have you been drawing lately?' they would enquire.

They would stay for as long as they could. Because they were canny as well as kind. They knew if Elise agreed to play, the family business was in a fair-to-reasonable state. And if Elise agreed to sing as well, the family business was in a steady position – Elise might not be what she used to be, but, overall, she was holding her own.

'You know, you are very good, Elise,' they would say, when the singing and playing was exceptional. When the drawings and paintings were produced.

'I am not that good, really,' Elise would say. 'But thank you for saying so.'

Those sisters-in-law wouldn't listen to that, though. Because they were fair and honest as well as kind and canny. Even so, they knew they were no substitute for Jimmy Waghorn. And they knew, despite never having tuned a piano in their lives, that Elise's nerves were tightening. That over time, without Jimmy, Elise was becoming so highly strung that now she ran the risk of snapping more than one string at any moment. Snapping one was alright – you could still manage a bit of a tune. But snapping more than one meant Elise would become uselessly out of tune. And you don't have to be a piano tuner to know that if a piano isn't strung tightly enough it sounds terrible. But string it too tightly and the strings will snap. And sometimes it is only the tiniest of turns that make them snap. And you just never know when that tiny turn is going to be too much. Even the best of piano tuners has been caught out on that.

Ruby and Marjorie did their best. They had their own tuning methods.

'What's for tea?' Marjorie would ask when they got home from school.

On a good day Elise might pause from the potato peelings. She might adjust the tea cosy hat before smoothing her frock underneath the kitchen apron.

'It is not *tea*, Marjorie. It is dinner. Tea is a drink. Dinner is the evening meal.'

And the girls would be happy with that.

Other days Elise seemed to have forgotten an evening meal – even an ill-mannered *tea*. The girls, however, knew that any amount of rebalancing of high stringing could be achieved with a tuning fork. They had seen it done on the piano in the lounge room many times. But they didn't have a tuning fork. And they knew that neither the bone-handled main course fork nor the dessert fork would be of any tuning help when their mother had forgotten about an evening meal. So they tried to do the job with the music.

'Play the piano tonight,' the girls would then coax.

'Mendelssohn.'

'Brahms.'

And if all was not too bad, then Elise would agree. The piano would be played and the high strings would be lowered. Marjorie would lie in her bed with her hand on the tongue-in-groove lining boards. She would lie there – ears stretched to the air, her hand pressed to the wall. And that would do for Marjorie – there in the dark of the night. In the quietness of her bed with Ruby there in the room with her. 'Don't stop,' she would whisper to the wall when Elise's solitary recital would end. 'Another one, Mum. Just one more.'

Sometimes the plea would transmit from Marjorie's fingers, through the wall, fuse with the piano and meld with the keys. As Elise sailed between the worlds. And Elise might have the energy to do another lap.

Some nights, though, were not so. These times, the playing and singing might start well. But it would falter. The glorious singing would stop. The magnificent hands would crash down on the keys. Elise had the courage sometimes to give it another go. 'For Pete's sake!' the girls would hear as she attempted a correction. But, even so, the outcome for the night was sealed. 'Hell and damnation!' they would hear, and music scores would fly in panic across the room as Elise slapped them in anger. The piano would shudder and groan as it was clouted shut. Elise would rush from the room, slamming the door behind her. Fleeing outside.

And this was where Ruby and Marjorie were overrun. Because the family, in managing the tuning of Elise's high stringing, forgot about habit – and its outcome of complacency. It should not have crept up on them. They should have listened to the warnings. But they didn't. And it did.

So the family became accustomed to Elise and her involvement with the tea cosy hat, and her redistribution of family responsibilities, and her immoderate self-assessments of her talents. And neglected to see Elise had elicited reinforcements; and these reinforcements were creeping over the horizon.

The family could have tuned all they liked. But it wouldn't

have made any difference. Sometimes strings are just too far gone. And there are always those roundabout who are more than willing to assist someone with the final snapping of a too-tight string.

The months crept through winter and headed for spring. And Elise was able to extend on all fronts before anyone noticed. And before Marjorie had time to weigh up the obvious dangers of plastic.

PLASTIC FLOWERS *(with real)* *for* CHIC ARRANGEMENTS

By Margaret Berkeley

Plastic flowers, once despised as phonies, make artistic arrangements when used with garden green by an expert.

'I must admit I was reluctant to use them at first,' Mr Pickett said. 'But they have a great many advantages, particularly in very hot or very cold weather. On hot summer days, when cut flowers can die so quickly and disappointingly, plastic ones are wonderful substitutes. In winter, of course, they're a real standby.

'To clean plastic flowers, vacuum them. If they get really grimy, hold them under the shower for a minute or two.'

Australian Women's Weekly

Chapter 8

'How COME YOU two always drive yourself to the bus stop now?' asked Jesse as they shoved and clambered onto the school bus for the lumber to high school.

'Because we can. How come you do?'

Jesse ignored the question. Everyone knew Wheat Bag Boy had always got himself to school for as long as anyone could remember. 'How's your mum?'

'None of your business. Why?'

'Just asking.' Jesse looked at Marjorie very carefully and for a long while – like he would look when he was under the bonnet and checking the health of an engine. 'You still going over to Jimmy Waghorn's place?' the engine examiner asked.

Marjorie stopped in her tracks – halfway down the school bus and halfway to the prized back seat. She looked over her shoulder at Wheat Bag Boy. 'Also none of your damn business,' she said.

'I heard your mother wears a tea cosy on her head now,' called Kevin Doherty from the front of the bus. 'Still having trouble with that crazy business in her head, is she?' He grinned and looked to Jesse, who glared at him and moved down to slouch in the back seat.

'How is it there, without Jimmy Waghorn?' Jesse whispered to Marjorie as he shoved in beside her. He watched her from top to bottom now for her reaction – like when you check the oil and then put the dipstick back in and out, and in and out again – to see if it has changed. And he recognised that look from Marjorie – the wariness, the worry, the fatigue. It was there for an instant. Before her eyes pulled down the blinds and she turned her head to look out the bus window.

'There's going to be a variety concert in town soon. It's a drought fundraiser. You should get your mother to sing,' said Jesse.

Marjorie looked at him in surprise. 'Why?'

Jesse shrugged. 'Because your mother is the best we've got around here. It might do her good.'

Marjorie stared hard at Jesse. Trying to make him out. 'Who says so, Wheat Bag Boy?'

'I do. And don't call me Wheat Bag Boy.'

Marjorie paid no attention to that. 'And how would you know about such things?' she asked.

'You don't have an exclusive patent on knowing things, Marjorie.'

Marjorie turned in her seat. She looked fully at Jesse. She narrowed her eyes and studied him for some time. A part of her noticed the sun in his wavy brown hair and his long, tanned fingers resting lightly on the top of the seat in front. *That hair could do with a comb*, she thought. She shook her head and shifted to look out the window again, to stop the thought. 'No one likes Mum's singing. Or her piano,' said Marjorie to the bus window to stop her brain combing. *Only the family – and they don't count. Only Jimmy Waghorn – and he has gone away.*

'Get her to sing a song out of a musical,' suggested Jesse. 'Meet them halfway.'

Marjorie didn't answer. She reached for her schoolbag and pulled out the latest book she was reading. She gave Jesse one last quizzical look before sticking her head in her book and leaving it there – firmly stuck in the safety of paper. All the way until they arrived at school.

Marjorie said something that night, though. At teatime. 'The kids at school are saying there's a fundraising concert coming up,' Marjorie said between the peas and the mashed potatoes. 'Maybe you could go in it, Mum?'

'Eh? What's this?' asked Bill.

Elise put down her knife and fork and wiped her mouth with her serviette before looking across at Marjorie. Her expression was indecipherable.

'It's a drought fundraiser,' Marjorie ploughed on through her mashed potatoes. 'It's gunna be a competition – that's how they'll raise the money.' Her voice now decided Bill's question was scary, so it began to squeak. 'Mum could be a contestant. She could play the piano and sing something.' Marjorie bent to shove the mashed potatoes into her mouth to stop the squeaking.

But it was too late. The words had got out. Elise folded her serviette and placed it beside her plate and smoothed the tea cosy on her head. She got up from the table and left the room. Shutting the kitchen door behind her.

'Now look what you've done,' said Bill. 'You've gone and upset her. Why can't you leave well enough alone?'

Marjorie glanced over at Ruby and saw the look on Ruby's face. She supposed it was the same look that was now on her face.

'I thought it might help,' Marjorie apologised to her potatoes. 'I thought Mum might like the idea and it would get

135

her out of the house and she would win.' She faltered, red in the face.

The kitchen door opened again. Four heads swivelled to watch. Elise walked back in with a smile on her face and an arm full of sheet music. 'I would like to contribute to the fundraising concert. Thank you for bringing it to my attention.' Elise beamed at Marjorie before sitting down. 'What do you think I should sing, Bill?' she asked.

Bill looked at Pa and Pa looked at Bill. Ruby and Marjorie looked at Pa and at Bill and then looked at each other. Everyone trying to gauge the lay of the land. 'Go on then,' said Pa to Bill. 'Don't just sit there like a bloody useless nincompoop. Give Elise a hand.'

Bill nodded at Pa. 'Go on, you two,' he said to Ruby and Marjorie. 'Get and clear the table and do the dishes. I need to help your mother with the music.'

So Jesse Mitchell's suggestion was put into action. Bill nominated Elise for a singing item and Elise got to work to prepare for the concert. And the family got to work to support Elise as she got to work. Pa ascended the heights of patriarchal contribution and declared he would make his own breakfast – 'Just for the bloody time being, mind!'

Elise had chosen 'Wouldn't It Be Loverly' from *My Fair Lady*. This was not a funny song. So why laugh? Marjorie started it. One night when things seemed to be fine and the practice was going fine. 'You just swore, Mum,' Marjorie interrupted.

'I did not. You know I do not swear. It's unladylike.'

'You said *abso-bloomin'-lutely*. You told me *bloomin'* is a swearword.'

'As I am singing the words of a respectable song, it is appropriate for me to use that kind of language.' Elise laughed, and looked at Bill. And everyone laughed. 'Of course I would never use that word otherwise. It is vulgar. Therefore, you two are never to use such a word. Understood?'

Pa snorted into his saucer of cooling black tea, and Bill glared at him.

It was a good time – all this practising. Elise, in the hurly burly of practice, did not have time to tighten the strings on her nerves. Or administer her prescribed doses of self-condemnation. All she had time for was practising. Even Elise thought she was happy. But peace is never for the long haul. Everyone should remember that. And tranquillity can dry out so quickly in the Mallee:

'I can't believe you're entering in the concert,' said an eyebrow-arched Shirlene Doherty.

'Yes,' said Elise, smiling.

'Are you sure you're up to it? I hope it won't be too much for you.'

'Why would it be?'

'All that worry. It's going to be hard on those tricky nerves of yours, isn't it?'

'On the contrary. I am actually enjoying rehearsing for it,' said Elise.

'Well, I hope you'll be good enough on the night,' Shirlene Doherty warned. 'But it doesn't matter if you don't make it, does it? Everyone would understand. What with the sort of nerves you've got there and all.' And a solicitous Shirlene shook her head. She smiled as Elise and her nerves rushed from the store.

Elise never said anything but Marjorie felt it starting to leak after that. Out through the gaps in the floorboards and the ripples in the tin as the night of the concert loomed. Because, unbeknown to Marjorie, the high stringing of nerves is very sensitive to the concerns of solicitous folks. Therefore, the closer the concert came to the farmhouse the quicker the tranquillity ran out in that house. It was running out of Elise the fastest of all. But it was gathering tranquillity from the rest of them stuck in that house as it ran – like iron filings running after a magnet.

Bill stopped laughing and tried to help. He made Elise coffee. He made Elise date scones. He tried to soothe her with the tea cosy hat. 'Gorn, you two,' he said to Ruby and Marjorie. 'Get and give your mother a hand around the house.' To Elise he said: 'Old ma Doherty is a sour old cow. Don't listen to her.'

Bill did not tell Elise everything, though. He never said *you have the best voice ever heard in the Mallee and that is for sure.* That, for sure, was the truth. But he didn't say that because he knew it wouldn't have helped. He did mention some things to his sisters, though. In private. They talked about it when the children were in bed and Elise was busy practising.

So Aunty Kathleen and Aunty Thelma said something when they were both in the store next:

'Jealousy is one of the seven deadly sins,' said Aunty Thelma as she plonked her packet of Uncle Toby's rolled oats on the counter. She glanced over at Shirlene, who was leaning against the counter reading the magazines.

Mrs Cameron blinked in alarm.

'No it isn't,' said Shirlene.

'Yes it is. It's a mortal sin,' said Aunty Kathleen, nodding piously. 'I wouldn't be mucking around with mortal sins on my soul. Not with Father O'Brien only doing confession once a month now.'

They couldn't stop it, though. Elise's leak got bad. They did their best but it wasn't a leak you could easily fix – not like a hole in a rainwater tank. You could fix that with a bit of an old rag shoved through the hole and with the pressure on the inside holding it all steady. But Elise did not have enough insides to aid in stopping any leak. No matter how many mortal sins might be cut short.

It was Pa who brought the leak to a stop. Perhaps because he had lived in the Mallee the longest, and therefore knew what it took to really stop a rainwater tank leaking. 'Stay the course, girl!' Pa ordered one night when Elise's leaking was flooding the kitchen. 'It's not long now. Stay the course. Never you mind about that Shirlene Doherty. You show her. You show them all what a thoroughbred lassie like you is bloody well made of!'

The night of the concert was the longest and shortest of Marjorie's life. Some things that night went so fast Marjorie was never able to properly see them or hear them again – like what she wore. Other things that night pushed themselves outside time. They drowned themselves in resin and gave themselves back to Marjorie as garish resin paperweights. Staying with Marjorie forever – peering out at her from their resin prison. Things like Elise's performance, and the money, and the prize list.

The house sighed and creaked as Elise packed her sheet music and practised a few last notes and dressed for the concert. The verandah boards complained as she walked from the sleep-out back down the hallway towards the kitchen. And the tin on the roof rattled in agreement with the wind that suddenly rushed at the house in spite. But Elise withstood. She came into the kitchen dressed in a new dress she had made herself. Ironed – for hours – by Marjorie and the cast-iron flat irons, aided by the water-filled sauce bottle with the holes punched in the lid to dampen the garments. And wearing stockings and high heels. And a hat. With a handbag hung over her right arm. Elise was wearing gloves and a lipstick-enhanced smile. The coffee percolator popped a final bubble of encouragement. The stove puffed non-committal smoke.

Pa came into the kitchen dressed in his Sunday best – a three-piece pinstriped suit complete with grandpa shirt and watch chain and black hat. The white stubble had vacated his chin. He stood and surveyed the family. 'Bill, get that hat off her head!' he hissed, being discreet as he jerked his thumb at Elise while examining the ceiling above the kitchen cupboard.

Bill gently removed the tea cosy hat from Elise. He put it at Elise's place at the table. Patted it to let her know it was alright. And it was time to get going. Wood was put on the fire and the dampers were shut down and Bill went to get the car.

Bill had filled the car from the petrol drum near the shed earlier in the day. All the other farm drums crowded around while he did that and had all tinked enigmatically at Bill – not choosing to disclose whether they were barracking for Elise or not. Neither did the scrub. It just watched, silent as always, as Bill pumped away on the pump arm sticking out of the top of the forty-four-gallon drum. And it watched now, just as silently, as everyone got in the car. Ruby and Marjorie climbed into the back and sank onto the red leather seat. Pa climbed in – now as taciturn as all that night-time Mallee staring at him through the car window as he sat himself in the back next to Ruby and Marjorie.

There was nothing to be heard but the sound of the car engine toiling up and down the sandy track into town. No one said anything. Bill glanced at Elise when he could – without attracting attention. Every time he had to turn left, he looked at Elise. Elise looked out the side window the whole length of the trip and held tight to the sheet music. The myriad inscrutable stars looked down on her face gazing out the car window. And that face and those eyes of Elise's gazed back. Inscrutable in return.

Everyone from roundabouts was at the concert. All the kids from school were there. Except Wheat Bag Boy. Marjorie couldn't see him anywhere. 'Where's Jesse?' she asked his friends. They just hung their mouths open and stared at her and shrugged their shoulders.

There were plenty of people on the benches. Waiting for the entertainment and their opportunity to thumb their noses at the drought and let it know that no drought was going to force them to walk off their land. And plenty of people out the back behind the heavy red curtains. Waiting for their opportunity to perform and to thumb their noses at the drought and let it know that no drought was going to knock their town about. There was a barrel for the men – placed outside the hall so as not to offend the womenfolk. And a shandy for the ladies (but really they should stick to a cup of tea and looking after the supper).

There were murmurings and shufflings of feet and quiet coughings. Then the curtains were drawn and there was the concert. There were fiddle players and honky tonk piano players. There were reciters of poetry, reciters of prose, someone telling jokes and a couple of church choirs. There was a man playing the spoons, and a man playing the saw. There were children, singing and dancing.

And there was Elise.

Bill had to come in from the barrel and help Elise onto the stage. On account of the stage fright. Stage fright is enterprising.

It had managed to find its long and dusty way from the city right to that steadfast town hall. And stage fright was never to be laughed at. It would sneak up on you and ruin you in a moment whenever it pleased, wherever it struck. Elise was well familiar with stage fright. 'You better get in here quick, Bill,' the concert organisers rushed out to warn him. Because they could see what that stage fright was up to. It had rushed out of the curtains and nearly toppled Elise off the platform. Bill dumped his creamy glass of beer and raced to help her to the piano. He helped arrange her sheet music. He patted her hand. 'Keep your chin up, girl,' he whispered and left her there.

Elise looked in terror at the seething waiting mass of audience in that little town hall. No one there knew it except Elise, but that stage fright had beaten Bill. It had already bound Elise and gagged her. An aeon passed while she stared out in her mute terror at the expectant upturned faces. Until she heard someone yell at her from the audience . . .

'Open your flamin' lungs, girl!' the voice yelled. 'Out of the starting gates at full gallop. That's how you win a bloody horse race!' It was Pa. And it was enough. The stage fright couldn't hold the gag in against that sort of fair dinkum Mallee truth. It ran off. And Elise started to sing.

Elise wasn't aware of her hands moving over the piano keys. She just sang. *Wouldn't it be loverly?* But it was so much more than lovely. That voice coming out of her pounded at the ears of all and sundry; and pulled at the hearts of all and sundry. That voice was magic. Elise sang until the town hall groaned with the loveliness and thought it might have to cave in under the weight of the beauty. Elise sang. And the Mallee sand and the Mallee sky listened and acknowledged this talent – strange and alien to it, but it bent its knee at talent nonetheless. Those stars, enduring in their eternal desert landscape scrutiny, spangled – just for Elise. Elise sang. And she left those people believing in magic. She left them all in no doubt about it.

The town hall was silent and still when Elise finished. The only sounds were the sounds of Elise. Elise shuffling her sheet music together. Elise scraping her chair back from the piano. Elise's high heels clicking across the floorboards to centre stage to bow to the silence and stillness.

Marjorie was terror struck at the still and the silence. Too terror struck even to contemplate the terror on Ruby's or Bill's faces. Her eyes were stuck to the fragile face of her mother as Elise stood – all alone – surrounded by terrible, silent stillness.

Then sweet relief like the first drops of rain on a tin roof as the town hall exploded in a firework of untoward Mallee approval. Elise stood – timid and mute and incredulous – as every man, woman and child clapped and shouted and called and whistled (if they were a man). Boots and shoes rumbled on the floor. If that Mallee town had known there was such a thing, they would have called for an encore. It went on and on.

It was better even than the crepe paper dress night.

The applause finally wore itself out and Elise bowed again, in disbelief, and left the stage. Because the concert organisers had to allocate the prize winners. Which, being a fundraising concert, went like this: you took as much spare change as you could afford to the concert and you put all your money on the person you wanted to win. The person with the most money won.

Marjorie looked around at the audience and willed them to give money to Elise. She saw Jesse. He was late and was now standing all alone at the back of the hall and looking more dishevelled than usual. Marjorie didn't dare hope he would put his money on Elise. She saw Bill handing Ruby coins and saw Pa getting out his coin wallet.

But the truth was Marjorie's family was not one of the richest families – it was one of the poorest. They didn't have much to spare but even so – because of the secret family business of Elise, and more so because Elise was just plain good – they had all scraped together what they could. But it wasn't enough. The first prize went to a honky tonk player, the second prize to a fiddle player, the third prize to a poetry recital and somewhere down the long line of coins counted, Elise was given an honourable mention.

Elise's prize, in accordance with the latest home decorating fashion for the discerning Mallee farmer's wife, was a bunch of plastic flowers. It was a huge bunch. Large and lusty plastic flowers boldly decorated in numerous colours and bobbing pertly on their plastic wire stems with their sensible plastic leaves in tow. Elise nodded graciously as the organiser reminded the audience of Elise's talents. The organiser handed Elise the bunch. And spoke of the many virtues of the modern plastic flower in a semi-desert environment – they don't need to be watered, they won't ever wilt, they only need to be dusted.

There was a bit of talk on the trip home.

'You were a star, Elise,' said Bill.

'I didn't win.'

'You won as far as I am concerned. We just didn't have enough money.'

'Shirlene Doherty was right,' said Elise.

'What?' said Bill.

Elise said nothing.

'It's not like the Princess Theatre, I know, but you were marvellous.' He glanced across at Elise.

Elise said nothing. Marjorie thought that maybe the job of holding both the sheet music and the huge bunch of plastic flowers was taking up all her mother's energy.

But it wasn't that.

'There is only one reason I didn't win. I didn't win because I am not good enough. Shirlene Doherty told me that,' said Elise.

Ruby and Marjorie looked at each other and said nothing.

Pa didn't say anything. And neither did Bill.

Bill went into town early the next morning to get the mail and papers. But mostly to check out the conditions. It is what you do after a good rain. You drive around slower than you could walk, one hand on the wheel, head hanging out of the ute door, and look at the ground to see how it has turned out after all that rain. So Bill was in town to see how it had all sunk in the morning after the concert.

The men were gathered at the post office. They were relaxed. Old felt work hats pushed off the forehead onto the back of the head. Cigarettes hanging languidly off the corner of the bottom lip. A group of men in the red dirt near the cement water trough. Squatting in a circle, elbows on one knee.

'Bill,' they said as he joined the circle. Slight nod from each one.

'Gidday,' said Bill. Nodding back.

'Reckon it'll get to a hundred?' The farmers all turned their faces upwards. They squinted and examined the peerless blue sky. Maybe they could see a thermometer up there.

Someone shrugged. 'Might. Might not.'

'Yeah,' they agreed.

'How're those Merinos going?'

'Yeah. Not bad.'

Everyone nodded in encouragement.

'How's that arm of yours?'

'This one?' asked a farmer, flexing a sore shoulder.

'Yeah. That one.'

'Could be better. The wife says I should go to the doctor, but what's he gunna do?'

'Yeah.' They nodded again to support the immutable right of a Mallee farmer to resist.

And then down to business:

'Elise alright after last night?'

'Right as rain,' said Bill, tensing just a bit.

'Elise is something special. The wife says she has yet to see anything better on a stage. Or even the wireless.'

'Yeah,' they agreed, and confirmed their agreement by looking at Bill and nodding.

'We're lucky to have her. And that's that.'

'Yeah. That's for sure,' they said.

'If there's anything we can do, Bill . . . Anytime . . . Sometimes a bloke needs a few mates to help around the farm. Every now and again. When you might need to be closer to the home paddick.'

'Yeah,' they all agreed, and Bill stared around the circle.

'Nuthin' much. A bit of fencing. Help with the sheep. That sort of thing . . .'

Shrugs and nods rippled around the circle. 'Yeah,' they said. And looked at the sky, or the dirt. Or retrieved the smoke from their bottom lip and looked at it in surprise. Like they had just noticed it had gone out.

And so Elise got a foothold on the Mallee. And the Mallee finally had to admit that Elise was more than a bit like it. Because a Mallee tree is hidden. The trunk lives below the dirt – twisted and gnarled and living a precarious life. It is unpredictable and obscured by the sand above. It does not include anything about nerves: because tree trunks do not have nerves, do they? But the menfolk had made up their minds: nerves were never to be spoken about to anyone who was not a local. And nerves were never to be spoken about to Bill or Pa.

But nerves *were* talked about. That is for sure. By those locals who were brazen and careless with decisions of the menfolk, and were without manners. 'She's far too nervy for my liking, that one,' said Shirlene Doherty. 'She's not suitable. She can't even play the piano by ear.' And she would sniff. Because maybe there is a particular smell that hangs around bad nerves.

But the menfolk were not backing down. 'All women are nervy,' they said. And that was that. Those farmers applied the stump-jump plough principle and decided to ignore Elise's bad nerves. No sense aggravating them when they were safely under the sand.

Talk got back to Marjorie and Ruby. Which was that everything about Elise's performance was better than what you see in a variety performance on the stage in the city. Marjorie and Ruby had to take their word on that, on account of not ever having seen a city variety concert.

Pa celebrated the concert success immediately. He was not one to wait for any *bloody ignorant comment* from any *bloody stupid nincompoops* to make up his mind. He made his own mind up during the night. And rose the next morning with a grin across his stubbled face and a shout in his lungs.

'Where's my flamin' breakfast?' he roared as he stomped in triumph down the hallway. 'Where's my flamin' eggs and where's a man's bloody cup of tea?' he roared as he charged through the kitchen door. And pulled up short. Because there it all was – eggs, toast (with dripping), and a cup of strong black tea. Pa looked suspiciously at the breakfast as he lowered himself into his chair. By the time he had finished lowering, though, he had made a decision.

'Sit down, girl,' Pa said, waving his dripping-clad knife at Elise's chair. 'I've got a few things to say. And I am gunna bloody well say 'em. And you keep your mouth shut, you hear?' he added, jabbing the knife in Marjorie's direction.

Elise sat down and looked at Pa.

'You are a remarkably queer girl, Elise,' said Pa, getting straight to the point. 'You're not fit for the Mallee. You with your queer ways and hoity-toity habits. This Mallee's gunna bloody kill ya. You mark my words.' Pa proceeded to jam egg and dripping-laden toast into his bristly mouth. 'But you did alright last night. You tore out of the starting gates, raced down that straight and won by a couple of bloody lengths. I couldn't have done it better meself.' Pa banged his hand on the table for emphasis.

Marjorie's eyes squeezed into their corners to get a look at Elise while still trying to keep a good look at Pa. Elise said nothing.

'You showed 'em what we're made of, don't you worry about that,' said Pa as he tipped hot black tea into his saucer. 'You're still a bloody useless non-Catholic. But you're family.' Pa drank the tea. He nodded at Elise and shoved his chair back from the table. 'Well, can't be like you womenfolk – lying around the house all day with nothing to do.' And Pa, pleased with himself and the family, stomped out the back door.

*

Things were lovely for a while. Everyone was happy. Elise, despite not being good enough, got out her pencils and paper.

And Elise and Ruby and Marjorie talked about all manner of things while Elise did wonderful things with charcoal and paint.

But Elise didn't know what to do with the plastic flowers. She didn't understand them. She put them in a vase. She stared at them and questioned their place in the world and moved them all around the house. A constant movement of gleeful colourful plastic, bobbing. Elise put them in the kitchen. In the hallway. In the lounge room. She dusted them and didn't water them and put her ear close to their plasticky petals and tried to hear what they were saying. She put them on the front verandah and they stayed there for weeks, jauntily greeting all those entering the house, before Elise brought them back into the kitchen and put her ear again to their flashy plastic. She listened. She went so far as to take off the tea cosy hat so she could press her ear closer to the plastic messages. It was a simple enough message when she finally heard it.

You were not the winner, the petals whispered from the midst of their plasticky plume.

'I know that,' said Elise. 'We didn't have enough money.'

Is that really why you didn't win? sighed the mournful bunch of gaudiness, their natural synthetic ebullience worn weary after all these weeks by Elise's stubborn refusal. They stared at her dolefully.

So Elise marched the plastic flowers out to the back porch, where they sat in the dust and flies. And Elise went back to playing piano and practising arias.

She moved them out to the washhouse, where they had to suffer the indignity of being overcome with steam whenever Elise stoked up the copper to boil the sheets.

149

But Elise couldn't ignore them forever. One morning, forever came to an end. The girls had driven off to catch the bus. Pa had left to check the fences. Bill was ploughing way over in Morrisons.

That morning Elise's strings started to twang. She walked out to the washhouse. She retrieved the bunch of reproachful plastic flowers and brought them back inside. Elise cleaned them off – deliberately and carefully – with the tea cosy hat and placed them on the washing-up bench. Where she could ignore them no longer. Elise sighed. She put her head in her hands and cried. Long, sad crying. Crying that cried and cried until it washed out the last stubborn remnants of refusal. Into her kind tea cosy hat. As Elise accepted the pert plastic flowers' truth. Elise did not win because she was not good enough.

*

Pa was back home first. He found Elise in the kitchen peeling potatoes and chopping cabbage. A fine and sensible task for a woman. He thumped the empty thermos on the table and tramped off to the lounge room to listen to the wireless.

Ruby and Marjorie were home next. The house heard the ute coming from way back near the Smiths paddock sandhill. It knew something was up, so it got ready.

The girls had a routine. Talk was cheap. They knew that. They also knew talk was very cheap where high stringing was concerned. So all talk these days between Ruby and Marjorie was short.

'What are we having for tea tonight?' asked Marjorie as she threw her schoolbag in the back of the ute and climbed into the driver's side.

'It's Tuesday. It's chops.'

'Oh yeah. I forgot.'

'It amazes me how you can so conveniently forget things.'

'You have to do the vegies tonight,' said Marjorie. She backed this up with a start of the engine, a jerk into first gear and a screech of the tyres as she forced the ute to turn around and go home.

'It's your job.'

'Yeah, but I've got too much homework.'

'Too bad. That's your problem,' said Ruby, staring out her side window.

Marjorie shrugged. It was an ambit claim. 'Suit yourself,' she said.

Ruby glanced across at her sister forcing the ute up the resistant sandhill.

Marjorie wrenched the column shift into third gear, and the ute roared down the other side. 'Who's feeding the chooks and collecting the eggs?' she asked.

'Me,' said Ruby.

'I'm not feeding those damn mongrel dogs.'

Ruby looked straight ahead. She knew Marjorie was scared of the dogs. 'I'll feed the dogs when I do the chooks,' she said.

Marjorie nodded her thanks at the windscreen and threw the ute into a corner slide to line it up for the run to the farm gate. Ruby watched the squall of dust and dirt and stones escaping the tyres. 'You're going to cop it when Dad sees those skid marks.'

'Dad can bugger off,' said Marjorie as she reined in the ute just short of the gate.

'And I'm setting the table,' she called from the driver's-side window as Ruby dragged the wire gate with its tree branch post through its arc.

Ruby shrugged and smiled. She didn't care. Marjorie always liked to set the table.

Ordinary talk always ended at the gate. By the time the gate opener and closer got back into the ute for the run to the house, the talk turned to tuning. 'Anybody say anything at school?'

'Nope,' said Marjorie. 'No, wait. There was something. One of the kids asked how the plastic flowers were going.'

'What did you say?'

'I said they are as unalive as when we first got them, so clear off.'

'What did they do?'

'They cleared off,' said Marjorie, grinning. 'Anybody say anything to you?'

'No,' said Ruby, chewing her lip. 'But you can't help thinking they were saying something just before you got there.' She looked across at Marjorie and Marjorie nodded. There was no need to say anything to that. They were at the house now and the house was waiting for them. Marjorie had parked the ute in the niggardly shade of a Mallee tree, ready for tomorrow's journey.

'Do you reckon the tea cosy will ever get its proper job back?'

Ruby sighed the sigh of a person who has shouldered fully loaded wheat bags for too long and without any thanks from anyone. 'I don't know.'

'I'm scared,' said Marjorie.

'I know,' said Ruby, not looking at her sister. She wanted to say, *So am I*. But she couldn't say that. She had Marjorie to look after. 'We just have to take it one day at a time,' she said instead. 'Lamb chops day then cold meat day then shepherd's pie day then lamb stew day then roast lamb day – one day at a time.' Ruby pushed open the car door and clambered out.

'Come on,' she said, shouldering her schoolbag. 'Let's see what lamb chops day has for us.'

The two girls walked down the path and up the steps to the front verandah, down the hallway and into the kitchen. Where they found Elise peeling the vegetables. Unlike Pa, the sight of it scared the wits out of them. Probably because they were weak women and scared more easily than men. They stood crowded together just inside the kitchen doorway – Marjorie with her arms dangling by her sides, and Ruby with her arm around Marjorie. 'You're peeling the vegies. That's my job,' blurted Marjorie.

Elise looked up from her peelings. She blinked at the girls. 'For Pete's sake, Marjorie. How many times do I have to tell you? It is *vegetables*.'

'For Pete's sake yourself, Mother. You're peeling my vegies,' repeated Marjorie, raising her voice. Her legs had frozen. She couldn't move her arms. She didn't know what to do.

Ruby moved forward. 'It's chops tonight, isn't it?' she said, putting her schoolbag down on the kitchen floor as slowly and quietly as possible. All the while not taking her eyes off Elise. 'Is there anything we can do to help?'

'That would be lovely,' said Elise brightly. 'Why don't you go and feed the chickens and collect the eggs? Marjorie can set the table.'

Marjorie's eyes tried to jump out of their sockets in an effort to grab Ruby and keep her in the kitchen. Ruby's eyes told Marjorie how very quick the chook feeding and egg collecting would be.

Ruby tore out the back door so fast it clacked a multitude of clacks in disapproval. She raced down the dirt path, out the back gate and headed for the chook shed. No time today to check for snakes in the feed bin. Ruby slashed the bucket into the seconds wheat and headed out the shed door in the same movement. She slammed through the saggy wire gate of the chook yard and sprayed the startled chooks with wheat before charging into the chook house to ratchet the eggs as quickly as possible into the bottom of her skirt. A quick spew of water into the forty-four-gallon-drum water trough, lock the gate and stumble home – fully egg-laden – as fast as she could stumble.

Marjorie loved setting the table. A properly set table was a sign of steadfastness. Of dependability. It was a measure of the health of a household. A person who could set a table properly day after day was a person of self-discipline. A person who could set a table properly day after day was a person in control of their own life – despite who might have been peeling the vegies.

Marjorie snapped the tablecloth high above the bare wooden table and let it drift downwards to clothe the undressed. She walked around the table and smoothed the corners before moving to the cutlery drawer.

Five square-shaped bone-handled knives, yellowed and weary from use. Five forks. Marjorie placed these precisely, as she always did. Knife and fork for Bill at one end. Knife and fork for Pa at the other. Knife and fork for Elise on the left side of Bill. Knife and fork each for Ruby and Marjorie. With the knife edges facing into the middle and the fork tines facing upwards. Back to the cutlery drawer. Five dessert spoons and dessert forks. And the walk around the table was repeated. With the bowl of the spoons and the tines of the forks facing upwards. Marjorie scrutinised the placement to make sure the edges of the cutlery were in exact alignment.

Over to the pantry cupboard for the cut-glass salt and pepper shakers – to be placed in front of Bill. In line.

Touching. Then over to the fridge – quietly burping its kerosene into the hallway – for the butter. She collected the butter knife and the butter dish. Marjorie sliced a slab of butter from the square and placed it in the butter dish. And placed the butter dish, with the butter knife, in front of Pa.

She collected five serviette rings with their serviettes rolled up inside. And walked around the table carefully placing serviette rings and serviettes squarely across the top of the table settings for each person.

Marjorie was adrift from the Mallee. Floating tranquil in a place where order and pattern and place mattered. She had just stepped back to survey the completed table when Ruby and the eggs burst back through the kitchen door.

Marjorie looked up at Ruby. Startled by her sudden reappearance. She looked down at the perfect table and smiled. And remembered her mother.

Ruby glided across the kitchen and began moving eggs from her skirt to the washing bowl. 'How is she?' Ruby whispered while watching Elise's shoulders checking saucepans on the stove.

Marjorie stared at Ruby. 'I dunno. Same?'

'Marjorie!' hissed Ruby. 'Haven't you been watching Mum?'

Marjorie stared. 'No,' she said.

By the time Bill came in from the back paddock, Pa was seated at his end of the table and tea was ready to be served. It was a tea like they had not had for a very long time. Elise had fried the chops black and hard, and boiled the cabbage until it sagged limp and exhausted on the bottom of the saucepan. But it was a nice bright green because she had not forgotten to add the soda. Ruby had salvaged the burnt potatoes by mashing them with a chopped raw onion. Elise was putting food on

155

plates and handing them to Ruby and Marjorie to place on the table. 'Hello, Bill,' said Elise.

Marjorie and Ruby watched Bill as he studied Elise for the positioning of the tea cosy hat. He looked at Ruby and Marjorie. But they were not going to give him any of their carefully collected information. They were just kids. They went back to placing the plates of brutalised chops, exhausted cabbage and salvaged potato on the table. Bill looked at Pa and Pa was looking happy with the world. A man's life was back on an even keel if a woman was cooking his tea again. Everyone sat down at the table.

'Who cooked the buggery out of these chops?' asked Pa, stabbing them with his fork. 'You don't need to flamin' butcher them. They're already dead before they hit the frying pan.'

No one answered. Everyone was looking at their plates. Everyone except Elise. Who was smiling brightly.

*

'Maybe it's a good thing,' said Marjorie later that night.

'Who knows?' said Ruby.

'I'm sick of having to do all the work. It's about time our mother started acting like a normal mother.'

'If cooking and cleaning and washing makes you a normal mother, then you and I are already normal mothers,' said Ruby.

'Why didn't Dad say something?'

Ruby was tired. She had been carrying that wheat bag on her shoulders for a long time now, and she had too many people in it. 'I don't know. You should have done more than just set the table.'

But that comment from Ruby was silly and it scared Marjorie. So she rolled over to face the wall.

Chapter 9

THE HOUSE SETTLED and shifted on its foundations as the seasons changed and the air moved from hot to cold. And Elise settled and shifted on her foundations as she allowed the truth to seep in and get to work on cutting away the vanity from her mind.

Ruby and Marjorie shifted too, after that night. They shifted back into tuning. They listened and listened. But were not able to detect anything. They crept into the house each day after school, wary, jumpy for signs, tuning forks at the ready. But all they saw was Elise doing the things a normal mother should do. So after a while they relaxed.

But Elise was busier than they realised. She wasn't only peeling the vegies and getting the tea and doing the washing and ironing. Each day, in the peace and quiet of her kitchen, Elise was listening to the plastic flowers – for instruction. It was some weeks before anyone noticed. And it was Marjorie who noticed first. 'Have you noticed Mum smiling a lot more?' she asked one night.

'Isn't that a good thing?' asked Ruby's pillow.

'Do you think the smile is a little bit glittery?'

Ruby raised herself on an elbow and stared across the darkness at Marjorie's bed. 'What do you mean?'

'I dunno. Glittery. Like that time Mum made the rose garden,' whispered Marjorie, so the walls wouldn't hear.

Ruby said nothing for a long time. But Marjorie knew Ruby was still propped up on her elbow. Checking. Because that was what she would be doing if Ruby had asked her that question. 'You're right. It is a bit glittery,' Ruby said.

Ruby and Marjorie watched Elise and Bill and Pa over the next few days. Elise cooked and cleaned. She burnt the potatoes and stewed the cabbage. She scorched the roast and clagged the porridge. She played the piano and sang. She didn't draw.

And Elise got more and more glittery. At least, to Ruby and Marjorie. They watched Bill and Pa, but they seemed serene. Only Ruby and Marjorie seemed to notice any glitter.

The girls started watching out for bad nerves again. The back of the ute seemed full these days. Other things besides schoolbags were catching a lift home and interrupting their conversations. 'The railway kids are saying Mum looks happy lately,' said Ruby.

'How would they know?'

'Exactly.'

Or: 'Wheat Bag Boy cornered me today. He said, *Jimmy Waghorn can't help your mother anymore, can he?*'

'What did you say?'

'I just looked at him.' (*I looked at his chipped front tooth, his mouth, those hazel eyes. I looked at him leaning against the lockers with his hands in his pockets – waiting to help. I wanted to tell him I was scared. I wanted to tell him I don't know what to do; and I wish I could run away with Ruby until everything is alright. That I could turn up at the hut and find Jimmy Waghorn on the old blue bench. I wanted to tell him everything is hunky dory*). Marjorie's eyes screwed themselves up at the memory. 'He asked if there was anything he could do.'

Ruby and Marjorie kept watch for the bad nerves. But it was too late. Elise had already moved on. The lessons with the powerful plastic preachers had finished. They had gaily passed on all necessary instructions. And Elise set about putting the instructions into practice.

With the practice consisting of cleaning. Because cleanliness is next to godliness. And God, unlike Elise, was decent and not proud and did not presume to have talent. Elise was released at last from the burden of presumptive talent, and was content. She spent her solitary days in that house – cleaning. She was a cleaning industry. Single-minded in her quest for cleanliness.

Everyone was happy. Pa was happy because the dams were full and Elise was smiling when he got back. Bill was happy because the cropping was good and Elise was smiling when he got back. Elise was happy because the beautiful plastic flowers had waved and bounced and told her to clean. Because cleaning would result in absolution: from pride and presumption. Only Ruby and Marjorie were not happy. But they were just kids as far as Bill and Pa were concerned. And what did kids really know about happiness – even if they were old enough to be in their last years of high school?

Ruby and Marjorie crept off to school each day – trying to leave no footprint on the pristine lino they crossed. And they crept about school each day – trying to leave no imprint on the pristine lives they encountered everywhere. And they crept home again – trying to contain their gathering dread at the growing glittery smile, and the expanding industry of cleanliness. While they waited for their father to do something.

But Elise didn't have time to wait for Bill to do something. Elise discovered she had been imperfect in her cleaning industry. And contentment started to run out of her like the sullied water she was now constantly sloshing out the back door into the dirt. She knew she had to step up and do more. Late into the night, Elise sat alone in the lounge room, playing all manner of music from masters much greater than her, and singing all manner of opera from composers far superior to her.

Bill was relieved because Elise was singing and playing. The singing and playing made no difference to Pa. Ruby and Marjorie watched and waited. The piano and the singing were as wonderful and beautiful as always. But it was also clamorous and gleeful. Those girls could pick out a crescendo. They could hear it building.

And Elise was further away than ever from Marjorie on the other side of the tongue-in-groove wall. Elise was a hive of industry and Marjorie tried not to remember the other beehive and the other industry and what came after.

'How come we don't see your mother around town any- more?' asked Jesse. But Marjorie was too exhausted to answer. Worn out from too much glitter and cleanliness and energy.

But Elise wasn't worn out. And one night Marjorie's mother entered an all-night vigil of cleaning. And cleansed pride from her soul.

*

Marjorie knew it was three o'clock in the morning. Because spotting three o'clock in the morning is the same right around the world. The Mallee outside her bedroom window was still and knowing and quiet, waiting out the remaining hours for the dawn of a new day. There were sounds but they were all of the night, familiar and carrying on the pre-dawn air. The shrill of a fox hunting through the paddocks. The answering call of the barn owl hunting through the night. The pinging of the forty-four-gallon drums, sucking themselves in and complaining in staccato about the chilly semi-desert air. And across the night – the second train. The wail of the train whistle arcing through the miles as the train headed out along the lonely Mallee distances. The rhythmic beat of the wheels on the train tracks carrying clear and perfect for miles and miles and miles in the dark of the still, Mallee, three-o'clock-in-the-morning time.

She was woken by Elise in the kitchen. Bill was always first in the kitchen. Way before sunrise, summer or winter, Bill would be up. He would light the fire, fix the percolator for Elise and put on the kettle to make a cup of tea for himself and Pa. But it was Elise who Marjorie could hear in the kitchen. Moving and singing. Marjorie's ears tried to burrow into the pillow. But it was too late. They had already heard it. And ears know you can't take back a hearing once it has been heard.

'Ruby,' Marjorie whispered across the post-midnight darkness in the bedroom. 'Ruby. Wake up. I think I heard Mum singing. To those plastic bloody flowers.'

But Ruby didn't wake up. So Marjorie had to go and have a look all by herself. She crept up to the kitchen door and listened to that marvellous voice singing softly to the receiving plastic. She pushed on the door to find Elise ecstatic and full of glitter in her transcendence.

'Hello, dear,' said smiling, glittery Elise, glancing up from her cleansing washing and her redemptive singing. 'Be careful of the clean floor. You will have to sit on the table. Don't touch anything.'

Marjorie stood and stared at her mother. And Elise smiled happily back. 'Well, don't just stand there, young lady. You'll leave marks on the floor. Get up on the table.' So Marjorie climbed up on the table and sat there with all the kitchen chairs – which had already been ordered onto the table – and watched as Elise briskly cleaned and softly sang.

Marjorie tucked her feet into the bottom of her nightie and hugged her knees. She was cold and scared. Elise had cleaned everything. Saucepans were scrubbed and shiny. Cutlery had been washed – again – and was laid out in perfect rows under one of the chairs on the table. Cooking pots and pudding bowls and mixing bowls and baking pans were washed and sparkling and stacked everywhere. Crockery was clean and stacked on the bench. Glassware was sparkling and glinting. The walls were dripping soapy tears down their tongue-in-groove surfaces. Even the old stove had been given a baptism, and it gleamed obsidian and malice at its treatment.

But Elise hadn't finished. She was administering to a huge preserving pan on the stove and a bucket on the hearth. 'Wait there,' she ordered. 'I have the copper going in the washhouse so I can have more boiling water – the kettle isn't up to it all.' Elise shook her head at the kettle. She knew what it was to be deemed not up to something. 'I won't be long,' she said as she disappeared out the back door and into the distant gathering dawn.

Marjorie sat, perched on the table in among the chairs. She didn't know if she was imprisoned by them or shielded by them. And she waited and watched for Elise to come back in, tottering under the weightiness of a full bucket of restorative boiling water.

'Don't you think you've done enough for one night?' ventured Marjorie as she watched Elise pour the boiling water into the pan. 'Don't you think it's time to go to bed?'

Elise was outraged in an instant. 'Don't you tell me I have done enough, young lady!' Her lovely grey eyes glared furiously at Marjorie. 'What would you know about enough? You are nothing but an ingrate.' The startled bucket sprang from her hand and clattered and splattered onto the kitchen lino.

Marjorie cowered into the meagre protection of the kitchen chairs and hugged her knees. She felt scared and she felt cold, so she shivered for the both of them. Elise went back to her cleaning. Leaving Marjorie there to watch for an eternity. And beg for an eternity. Elise scrubbed and boiled and disdained Marjorie's fleshly beggings, and reminded Marjorie of her shortcomings: 'You are a bold, brazen little article, Marjorie,' Elise said as she threw more items of sacrifice into the pot.

'I'm sorry,' Marjorie whispered, looking out at Elise from the bottom of a lake of tears.

Marjorie must have dozed, sagged against the legs of the chairs, because suddenly Bill and Ruby were in the kitchen, and the kitchen was full of early-morning sunlight. And even more clean things. Elise was sitting quietly by the fire, drinking a cup of coffee. No singing to be heard. No righteous anger to be seen.

'How long have you been here?' Bill was asking as he put a blanket around Marjorie.

How long have you not been here, Dad? Marjorie wanted to ask Bill.

'Mum needs to go to bed – and so does Marjorie,' said Ruby.

'No! I need to go to school,' shouted Marjorie. Starting up in terror of the idea.

'I need someone to look after Elise,' said Bill.

'Why don't you give it a try?' said Marjorie. 'Isn't that your job?' Her panicked arms dislodged the chairs and tumbled them onto the immaculate floor.

Elise moved her head at the clatter. Ruby and Marjorie saw the look of wrathful indignation strut into her face. 'Still here, are you, Marjorie? Still destroying all that is clean and pure – after all I have done for you?' She went back to her coffee. 'Get out of here. You are a filthy little guttersnipe. I'm sick of the sight of you. Go on to school!'

But it was going to be a bit hard getting to school today. Marjorie had just noticed the cleaning that had occurred while she dozed. Elise had excelled herself. She had finished with a cleaning crescendo of all things plastic. Including the plastic flowers. It was an adoration of the plastic. And the adoration was painstakingly arranged all around the room. Pristine glasses held bunches of colourful toothbrush flowers – bobbing and curtseying in a wild dance of love. Sturdy tin mugs sensibly held hair combs sprayed and fanned in a polite salute. Anxious jam jars caught now bent and boiled hairbrushes. Stolid hairbrushes with their scalding injuries, serious in their endeavours to bow from the waist.

And the plastic flowers were caught in eternal giddy obeisance to each other. Leaves flung in all directions in an outpouring of pleasure at the work of Elise. Stems caught weaving and flowing in sublime delight. Petals twirled and coiled and curled. 'What have you done with the brushes and combs?' yelled Marjorie. 'How can I go to school if I can't do my hair? And what did you do to the toothbrushes?'

'Don't speak to your mother like that,' Bill warned.

'Why not?' Marjorie screamed into Bill's face. 'She's boiled the guts out of all the brushes and combs and toothbrushes. They're all bent out of shape. They're useless. How can we go to school now?'

Ruby grabbed Marjorie. She put both arms around her. 'Come on,' she whispered. 'Let's just get ready for school.'

'She is the cat's mother,' said Elise.

'See that? Hear that?' Marjorie pushed Ruby away and pointed at Elise. 'Do something. She's turning into a lunatic.'

Ruby tried to grab Marjorie again.

'Don't you speak about your mother like that,' warned Bill. 'By the crikies, I'll give it to you.'

'Leave the girl alone,' ordered Pa as he stepped into the kitchen and in between Marjorie and Elise. 'The girl is right. Bloody do something.'

Marjorie stared. Shocked at her unexpected ally. 'Do you have a brush and comb, Pa?' she said.

''Course I bloody do. Got bloody hair on my head, haven't I? Go on, you two,' said Pa. 'Go have a look on my dressing table. Then get yourselves off to school.'

So Ruby seized Marjorie again and shoved her out of the room before Bill or Elise had a chance to do anything.

They didn't waste time. They were not going to be around for another aftermath of a glittery smile. Ruby threw books and whatever into their schoolbags while Marjorie threw clothes on herself. Then Ruby shunted Marjorie down the hallway, grabbing Pa's hairbrush and ramming it into her schoolbag as she went.

Ruby stopped the ute halfway to the bus stop. She reached across and grabbed her sister's hand.

'Cigarettes from the doctor aren't going to stop it this time, Ruby,' Marjorie whispered.

Ruby stared straight ahead. She nodded.

Ruby and Marjorie spent the school day traversing all the necessary people and mundane activities. They did their utmost. Like pretending the worst thing that could happen to you was not doing your French homework. It was a practised art. A necessary skill. 'Aren't you two eating any lunch?'

asked someone more intent on other people's business than their own.

'We're fasting. It's a holy day, isn't it? You're such a non-Catholic pagan,' said Marjorie. It was enough to deflect, but Marjorie was exhausted. She slumped.

Ruby jumped to her feet and pulled Marjorie up. 'Come on,' she said piously. 'It doesn't mean we can't drink water.' And she steered them away towards the bubble taps.

The two girls bent and drank. They paused for a bit to catch their breath then drank some more. It was all they had to fill their stomachs and they still had the whole rest of the afternoon to get through. They were not even going to think yet about how they would manage life after school. They stopped when they couldn't force any more water down their throats. Now they had to find a safe place for the rest of lunchtime. A place where curiosity and conversations could be minimised. 'We could go to the library?' Ruby suggested.

'Yeah,' said Marjorie.

The two girls walked into the school library, avoiding the gaze of the librarian at the front desk. They grabbed a handful of books and headed for a table in the corner, behind the bookshelves.

Where they almost collided with Wheat Bag Boy, who was lurking there clutching his own pile of books. A collision would have been a disaster. Books would have clattered. The librarian would have materialised. Kids and teachers would have noticed. 'What are you doing here?' hissed Marjorie in alarm. Imprisoning her books tightly between her arms and her chest.

Jesse looked at Marjorie, then at Ruby, then back at Marjorie. He might have been sizing them up. Choosing which one was going to be butchered for this fortnight's supply of mutton. 'You two alright?' he asked softly.

'Yes, thanks,' answered Ruby. 'Just doing a bit of research. Come on, Marjorie.' Ruby pulled Marjorie away towards a waiting table.

'So am I,' said Jesse, watching Marjorie. 'Doing a bit of research. A library is a fine place for research.'

'Bugger off,' whispered Marjorie, as forcefully as she could in a library. But Jesse did not. He followed Ruby and Marjorie to their table at the back of the library stacks. And seated himself and his own heap of books at the table next to theirs. He sat with his back to them and stretched out his long legs, and began to casually leaf through his own assortment.

Jesse seemed to take no more notice of Ruby and Marjorie. He seemed to also pay scant attention to the several curious wanderers. He would just glance up at them, and the raised eyebrow and the look in his eye and the casual stance of the legs and the shoulders all said one thing: *Come any closer and I will skin you and gut you and leave your skin to dry out and crack up, crucified and choking in the dust on a lonely barbed-wire fence somewhere.*

That lunchtime in the library saved Ruby and Marjorie. No one came near them. Jesse spoke to them once more during that library lunchtime. 'Want a sanga?' he asked, waving one half of a half-dead tomato sandwich at them.

'You can't eat in the library,' Marjorie whispered, looking around for any librarians with a good nose for a warm tomato sandwich.

Jesse shrugged. 'Suit yourself,' he said and started to eat.

'We'll have it. Thanks, Jesse,' said Ruby as she grabbed it out of his hand.

Marjorie even went to sleep for a time. Guarded carefully by Ruby. Guarded just as carefully by Jesse. But before she wanted it to, the bell rang and it was time to begin the long slog of the afternoon. Marjorie sighed. She was not sure she had enough energy left to attend to the irrelevancy of school today. And then, before she ever wanted it to be, it was home time.

Marjorie avoided everyone on the school bus by doing what she always did – flinging herself into a seat and burying her head in the latest book she was reading. She tuned out the world of the school bus. She tuned out the world. Ruby sat beside her but Marjorie had no idea what Ruby did. And then, before she ever wanted it to be, it was time to get off the bus.

Marjorie and Ruby stood there in the middle of the road as the school bus lumbered off with its crowd of dust. The old ute was parked under the usual tree. On the other side of the road an immense goods train was rumbling over the railway crossing in a deliberate, persistent procession of wheat trucks. Marjorie turned and watched. 'We could jump that train,' she said.

Ruby said nothing.

'It wouldn't be hard.'

Ruby threw her schoolbag into the back of the ute.

'We could jump on and not go home.'

'Get in the ute,' said Ruby.

'We could go somewhere else. We could go and live with Aunty Agnes. Or just live forever on the train. Just travel all over the country . . .'

'Get in the ute, Marjorie,' said Ruby.

'We could stay away.'

'No. We can't stay away.'

'Not go back.'

'Marjorie! Get in the ute!'

So Marjorie got in the ute.

Ruby drove home. Slowly. And Marjorie opened the gates. As slowly as possible. They didn't talk. There was nothing to talk about. They had no plan.

The house gate was swinging in a warm northerly wind when they got home. Swinging and slapping and waiting for them. Marjorie grabbed it and slammed it hard shut behind her as she went through. And followed Ruby up the front steps of the house. The house was quiet. There was no creaking, no rattling from the wind. It watched, accepting as it did the tinking of the questioning sticks and stones on its roof, cast there by the wind.

Ruby and Marjorie walked side by side down the long hallway to the kitchen.

They found Pa sitting in his chair at the table. 'You're home,' he said.

They nodded.

'Get yourselves some tucker then.' He nodded at the pantry cupboard.

Marjorie stared. Suddenly understanding that Pa knew they had fled to school without any food.

Pa looked away. Embarrassed that his weak concern had been so easily discovered. 'Gorn,' he said. 'Get some tucker into ya. Stupid buggers. Tearing off without any breakfast. Not taking your bloody lunch.'

The two girls ate quickly and in ravenous silence. Food shoved in mouths. Milk gulped. Mouths wiped with backs of hands. With no regard whatsoever for a polite thin slice of bread or a proper allocation of butter or the correct use of a bread-and-butter plate. Or a butter knife. Or a serviette. When they had finished, they looked at Pa. 'Your father has taken your mother to the doctor's. Your mother is ailing,' said Pa.

The girls stared. 'Thank you for your hairbrush,' said Ruby. Marjorie nodded.

'Humph,' said Pa. His fingers tapped themselves on the table.

Marjorie started to rise, her chair scraping along the lino. 'I suppose I better do the vegies.'

'No,' said Pa. 'There will be no tea here tonight.'

Marjorie stood. The two girls watched their grandfather.

'Your father called on the telephone. The doctor said your mother has to go away – to a bloody city hospital. She needs treatment. We don't have it here in the Mallee,' said Pa. And his tapping fingers could have said, *That is because us Mallee folk don't generally need that sort of treatment.*

'What do you mean? What sort of treatment?' Marjorie glared at Pa.

'You know what I mean,' growled Pa. 'Your mother's not right for this place. I said the Mallee would kill her in the end. And it's having a pretty damn good go at it right now.'

'No, we don't know.' And Marjorie was shouting again. 'We don't know anything! We're never told anything!'

'Yes you do. You bloody do know!' shouted Pa. 'You know as well as I do. We all bloody do.'

'Where is she going, Pa?' Ruby asked quietly, and her look stopped the pair of them short in their shouting.

'A damn fool mental hospital in the city,' said Pa. 'Your mother's gone stark raving mad.' His hands slapped down on the table. 'Now gorn and pack a case. When your father gets back, we have to drive to the city.'

But what about school? What about the chooks? What about the dogs? Who's going to milk the cow? Who's going to check the windmill? Who's going to go round the sheep? What am I going to say to everyone at school? These were all things Marjorie wanted to ask but she didn't have time because she only had time to pack a suitcase.

*

Marjorie and Ruby had made the car trip to the city before. Holiday trips. Long trips but happy ones. This trip, though, was interminable. The Mallee did its best to hinder them. Slowing them with splatters of dust and dirt. Or bursts of kangaroos out of the darkness on the sides of the road. The girls and Pa sat motionless in the back seat, Marjorie once more clinging to Ruby like a strangle vine. Bill drove silent in the front. Elise sat at Bill's side and sang quietly to the darkness – or to Bill. And conversed throughout the night-time miles with the plastic flowers left to guard the kitchen in her absence. She ignored Ruby and Marjorie. Except for the various times she was bidden to scold Marjorie once more for being *a bold, brazen little article who jolly well needed to be taken down a peg or two!*

It was a night strangely similar to the previous night. There was Marjorie, sitting trapped while Elise used her wondrous voice to sing and to scold. Marjorie was grateful for this night, though. There was no kitchen light swinging and illuminating on its brown cord. The car was dark. Marjorie couldn't see the glittery smile.

Like the night before, Marjorie eventually dozed. And woke to a pre-dawn city sky silently passing the windows of the car. To the comfort of tram wires overhead and electricity wires overhead and those strange Marshalite traffic signals with their red, orange and green dials on a giant clock. The comfort of things telling Marjorie she was not in the Mallee, and that there were others besides Ruby who might help.

Bill deposited Ruby and Marjorie at Aunty Agnes's place as the city sun poked over the rooftops to see what was going on. They scrambled out of the car. Pa got out and grabbed their suitcases from the boot. He threw them on the footpath while Bill struggled to keep Elise in the car. Pa climbed back in to help Bill with Elise for the rest of the journey. They had a commitment to keep.

Aunty Agnes fussed over Ruby and Marjorie. 'Bill used to live here,' she said. 'When he had to come and work in the city to save the farm.' (As if perhaps the girls did not know Bill had been used as ransom to save the farm.) She made them open their suitcases and have a bath and wash their hair, which she then insisted on brushing. She forced them to eat poached eggs on toast and drink milk poured from a milk bottle with a beautiful tin foil hat. Then gave them a shopping basket and her purse and made them go to the corner shop and buy things for her – like bread that had been baked just that very day. And boiled lollies. Aunty Agnes told them to go into her lounge room and watch the television set and eat the boiled lollies.

It was well after dark when Bill and Pa came back. That would have been normal for Bill in the Mallee. But it was odd and scary in the city.

'How is she?' asked Aunty Agnes.

'Bloody hell, Agnes,' said Pa. 'Give us a chance. We've only just got home.'

'How is she, Bill?' Aunty Agnes asked.

'She's committed,' replied Bill wearily. Placing his hat on his old peg behind the door.

Dad is sad. And scared, thought Marjorie. And she was very frightened, so she charged into the conversation. 'What does that mean? Committed?'

Bill stared at Marjorie for a very long time. 'It means,' he said, 'that your mother is in a mental hospital. She will be there until she is released.'

'How long will that take?'

'I don't know,' said Bill, rubbing his hands over his face.

'When will you know?' Marjorie glared hard at Bill.

'Come on, Marjorie,' said Ruby. And snatched Marjorie away to the safety of their Aunty Agnes bedroom.

*

It soon became apparent to staff at the mental hospital that the commitment was for the long term. It was estimated to take weeks and weeks. Evidently Elise had suffered a major nervous breakdown. And that takes a long time to repair.

A major wheat harvester breakdown only takes days to fix. The same for a major tractor breakdown, and for a major car breakdown. A major shearing plant breakdown only takes hours. You break down a gun to clean it. It is a good thing. Marjorie was at a loss to know why it should take so long for the major nervous breakdown of Elise to be fixed.

After the first couple of weeks, Bill and Pa and Ruby and Marjorie had to go back to the Mallee. Pa went back to checking the water in the dams – because he could still manage a farm, couldn't he! Bill went back to the back paddock – because that was a long way away and a man had the time to cry like a man should back there. Cry for his wife, cry for his daughters.

And Marjorie went back to school. She would have liked to never go back. But Ruby needed to finish her Leaving Certificate.

'What will I say tomorrow?' Marjorie asked.

'Don't say anything.'

'But what about when they all ask?'

'No one's going to ask anything.'

'Of course they are. Why wouldn't they?'

'Because, Marjorie, they don't have to ask. They would have figured out weeks ago what's happened,' said Ruby.

'How would they?' asked Marjorie, her voice rising in panic at the thought. 'How could they? We haven't told anyone.'

'Who do you think's been looking after the farm?'

And, of course, it was the locals. Those stalwart, loyal locals who had pledged to lend Bill a hand in the event the family was under the weather – in the event Elise might not be one hundred percent. They had all pulled together. Nothing had been said to anyone who was not local. But all the locals hereabouts knew about Elise and her nerves that had managed to break down. So they had been doing what they could for Bill and Pa and the girls.

The school bus trip was hard, Elise and her commitments now being everyone's business. So Marjorie made sure she had a book with plenty of pages in it. The classrooms were the same, so Marjorie made sure she sat up the front where nobody else wanted to sit. And at lunchtimes, Marjorie developed a passion for study and the benefits of solitary library research.

All the school watched. But Jesse Mitchell was the only person game enough to interrupt. He waited for Marjorie against a corner of a classroom block one lunchtime. 'Sorry to hear about your mother,' he said, stepping out in front of her.

'Thanks,' Marjorie said to the ground as she attempted to sidestep Jesse.

'How is she going?'

'Fine,' muttered Marjorie to the ground as she attempted another sidestep.

'She'll be alright,' offered Jesse. 'She'll get better.'

'What?' snapped Marjorie, and she couldn't stop her eyes from leaving their contemplation of the ground to glare at Jesse.

'That mental hospital will fix her up,' he said.

Marjorie jerked her head up high. 'What would you bloody know? She is not mental. So bugger off, Wheat Bag Boy.'

And Marjorie ran for the girls' toilets, where she locked herself in a cubicle for the remainder of the lunchtime – biting on the bunch of school dress she had shoved in her mouth to stop water bursting from her eyeballs and sobs bursting from her mouth. She was safe after that. And left alone.

*

Bill went back to the city after the weeks and weeks of necessary repairs to the nerves had been completed. He collected Elise from the mental hospital. Elise gathered together as much of herself as she could manage from the bits and pieces she had scattered around the place, and packed them into her suit-case. She brought back as much as she could find. Bill drove Elise back all those hundreds of miles. And so much of Elise came back most people hardly noticed it was not all of Elise.

Even so, everyone tiptoed around her. Because of all the breakdowns that occur regularly in the Mallee, a nervous breakdown was not one of them. And a major nervous break-down was not what the Mallee knew about.

Marjorie and Ruby held their breath for days and days. But nothing out of the ordinary seemed to happen. Elise seemed tired – but she was tired before. She seemed also to have left the glittery smile in the mental hospital – and that made

Marjorie and Ruby think maybe things had a chance to settle back down. Perhaps their mother's tight stringing nerves had taken the opportunity to ease off a bit while she was in that mental hospital.

Old routines re-emerged. Ruby and Marjorie got themselves ready for school. Bill took the tractor out to the back paddock. Pa dealt with the rabbits. Elise sat in the kitchen – next to the stove – next to the coffee percolator – and wore the tea cosy hat. Things were pretty normal.

Except for those plastic flowers. One day Ruby and Marjorie came home from school to find Elise had collected the whole twisted and contorted and boiled bunch of them, and planted them in those bare red-dirt front gardens.

Marjorie saw them first, out of the driver's-side window. 'Ruby, look.'

The girls got out of the ute cautiously. Trying not to disturb those gaudy plastic petals bent to the sun and bowed to the dirt.

'I'm scared,' whispered Marjorie.

'Of what?' asked Ruby. 'A bunch of plastic flowers?'

'Yes,' whispered Marjorie, trying to climb behind Ruby.

They walked up that dirt path, never taking their eyes off the flowers. Every one of those bent and twisted flowers had been stuck in the flowerbeds, with their edges of perfect pointed bricks. The flowers were in rows. Perfectly distanced from each other in every direction. Sensible plastic flowers in the barren red dirt. It was a work of art.

The two girls walked into the kitchen. But Elise seemed alright. 'There you are, dears,' she said with a smile. And went back to sipping her coffee.

'Those plastic flowers are in the dirt out the front,' said Marjorie.

Ruby watched Elise.

'Yes, dear,' said Elise, smiling still. 'I planted them. I've always wanted some flowers at the front of the house.'

'They're not real,' said Marjorie.

'Of course they are real,' chided Elise.

'They're plastic.'

'They are, Marjorie. They are plastic. They are modern and will not wilt and will not need water. We will not need to prune them or spray them for insects.' Elise lost interest in the subject and went back to drinking her coffee.

'Are you peeling the vegetables tonight?' asked Ruby, very carefully.

Elise looked at her and smoothed her tea cosy hat. 'Vegetable preparation is Marjorie's job,' she said. 'I am too tired for such matters.'

Ruby and Marjorie looked at each other.

The girls waited for Bill or Pa to say something that night at the tea table. But no mention was made of the plastic flower garden. The girls waited another day and then a few more. But nothing was said by Bill or Pa. So the girls decided to say nothing to them.

Elise took to caring for that gaudy, garish garden of curved and crooked plastic in the same way she had cared for its predecessor garden of dirt. Meticulously.

And Marjorie would creep between the garden beds, hugging the middle of the dirt path and trying not to look. But, try as she might not to look, her eyes always made her – she had to note the gardening. She wanted to ask Elise why she changed the flowers perpetually. Because Elise did. Elise would move them from row to row. From side to side. From front to back. And back again.

But Marjorie was too scared to talk about those plastic flowers. She was too scared because no one else in the house seemed to be scared about the plastic flowers. No one else seemed to notice them at all. Only Marjorie and Ruby.

Chapter 10

BUT IN THE end, it was Elise's art that snuck up and tripped Marjorie over. It wasn't the plastic flowers at all. Marjorie had never been scared of art because art made Elise happy. So Marjorie was caught off guard. She was ambushed because she was not on the lookout.

It happened some time after Elise had fulfilled her commitment at the damn fool mental hospital. It seemed her commitment included a reassessment of the value of some, but not all, paper. Like Elise's charcoal-and-ink drawing of Marjorie with her elbows on the kitchen table and her chin propped up in her hands. One day that paper disappeared and it took its drawing with it. 'Where is the drawing of me?' asked Marjorie. They were in the kitchen. And the kitchen was calm and unperturbed. Elise was painting. Ruby was doing her homework and Marjorie was sitting there, leafing through Elise's folio while she painted. It was a lazy, contented leafing.

'That dreadful thing? It is over there.' Elise's paintbrush waved in a vague way towards the back of the kitchen.

'Where?'

'Under the cocky's perch. The cocky needed some paper.' And Elise went back to concentrating on her painting.

Marjorie looked over at the cocky, sitting in its pink-and-grey perfection on the back of a kitchen chair. The cocky caught her gaze and began walking with quick and imperious cocky steps – back and forth, back and forth along the back of the chair. He held her gaze and started nodding with intent – up and down, up and down – and raised his beautiful crimson cocky crest at her. Marjorie looked down at what the cocky was trying to show her. And there indeed was the drawing of Marjorie. Sitting on the chair. Put to a much more important use than being a more than half-decent study of Marjorie, drawn by her mother. She stared at the drawing, now embellished by the efforts of the cocky. The cocky looked Marjorie in the eye and bobbed up and down once more before pausing to deposit a further glistening pearly blob onto the paper. The drawing had become a collaborative piece.

The cocky put its head on one side and gazed at Marjorie out of one pink-circled eye. *What do you think?* it asked Marjorie. *Collaborations can often be tricky. More opalescence to the left, perhaps?*

Marjorie had learnt things about struggle by now. About when it was wise to be scared. About when it was prudent to be careful. But she still grappled with rushing things. She wished she was like Ruby, who was so careful, so delicate. Ruby never rushed. Ruby was a shimmering circus juggler in the middle of the circus ring, performing while the stars and the moon and the midnight sky moved outside. Beautiful and poised. Serene and calm in the concentration of her craft. Never dropping the juggle, no matter how complicated it was. Elise and the tea cosy hat, and the garish plastic flowers bobbing in the blazing sun, and the hot red dirt could be kept aloft – spinning and spinning and spinning – by Ruby. It seemed effortless.

Marjorie was already feeling the prickle warnings as she watched the cocky. She should have trod cautiously at that point. But she rushed. Like a bull in a china shop. 'Why did you do that? I liked that drawing.'

'The cocky needed some paper,' said Elise, concentrating on her painting.

'What was wrong with using newspaper?'

'For Pete's sake, what is the problem?' Elise put down her paintbrush and looked at Marjorie. 'It was a frightful drawing.'

'But it was a drawing of me,' said Marjorie. 'You did it.'

'I know that, Marjorie. I also know it was a very bad drawing. And being my drawing, I have the right to do with it what I jolly well want!' Elise picked up her paintbrush and resumed her painting.

'You only did it because it was a drawing of me. You could have used newspaper,' said Marjorie.

Ruby had put down her schoolbooks and was watching her mother now. 'I am sure Mum will do another drawing of you, Marjorie.' She spoke slowly and quietly.

'You couldn't be bothered with any newspaper, could you?' said Marjorie, ignoring Ruby's efforts to rebalance the spinning.

'The drawing had no redeeming artistic merit. It was an embarrassment for any true artist,' sniffed Elise, shaking her head and dislodging fragments of glitter.

'You could do that, though, couldn't you, Mum?' coaxed Ruby. 'You could do an even better drawing of Marjorie.'

'You're just raving on, Mother. You couldn't be bothered and gave it to the cocky to shit on because it was just a drawing of me. You wouldn't have done it with any of the drawings of Ruby!'

So the bull trampled and crashed all over the place and the delicate, paper-thin porcelain of Elise's mind wobbled and swayed. And Ruby's juggle was toppled.

'You are nothing but a selfish and self-centred little article, Marjorie,' said Elise, throwing her paintbrushes down. 'For Pete's sake! It was a piece of paper. The world does not revolve around you, young lady, and it's about time you realised that!'

Marjorie scrambled off the kitchen chair. She abandoned that marvellous folio and that sea of art paper and ran for the back door.

'Why don't you have a rest, Mum? Let me make you a cup of coffee,' Ruby was saying as Marjorie slammed through the flywire door as hard as she could. The door slapped against the asbestos sheeting of the porch as she ran. Slapping again and again as it watched her stumble off the back step and onto the baked-hard red dirt of the backyard. Slapping and clapping while Marjorie's tears splotched onto the limestones and splattered and bounced on the red sand.

It was getting dark when Marjorie walked back into the kitchen. Her tears were out of sight. They were dammed and drowned. Elise and Ruby were still there. All Elise's art materials were put away. There was no sign of the collaborative effort under the cocky either. Marjorie wasn't surprised. The collaboration would have ended a long time ago – in the kitchen stove.

Ruby looked at Marjorie. Elise looked at her coffee. Marjorie went to the pantry cupboard and started doing her jobs. No one said anything.

'Why did you upset Mum like that?' Ruby asked later, when they were in bed.

'She was using that drawing of me for the cocky to shit on.'

'There's a time and a place to talk to her about those things,' said Ruby. 'And that wasn't it.'

'I didn't start out to upset her. I just wish it wasn't always all about her. That sometimes she could see how other people feel.'

'That's what Mum said about you.'

Marjorie stared into the dark. She blinked her eyes hard and for a long time, before rolling onto her side and facing the bedroom wall. She could hear the house smirking.

*

Marjorie did a queer thing that night. She lay stiff as a board in her bed. She stared at her bedroom wall and contemplated the blessings of darkness while she listened for Ruby to fall into a deep sleep. And for the house to settle into its midnight quiet. She waited a very good length of time – a sensible scared-of-getting-caught length of time. Then Marjorie squeezed quietly out of bed and did something she had never done before. She collected her clothes and shoes and crept out of the bedroom, crept carefully down the hallway – avoiding the squeaky floorboards just itching to turn her in – and crept out the back door.

Marjorie stood in the middle of the backyard. She got dressed. Supported by the light of the blazing, inscrutable stars. She shoved her nightie under the tank stand and set off. Heading out the back gate, down the hill, across the paddock and towards Jimmy Waghorn's place. It was the first time she had ever gone there in the night.

Marjorie walked quietly and carefully for longer than she needed so she could be sure she would not be heard by the house. Then she started running. Sure-footed in the dark. With only a thin moon to help the stars in any guidance. A loping, easy stride. She could have run into town and back.

The night air was cool and it brushed Marjorie as she passed. *You are not like your mother,* said the soles of her feet and they beat a softly padded drum to supplement their message.

The night air daubed its soothing ointment and whispered its agreement with the feet.

Marjorie squeezed through the wire triangle at the gate, and kept running. *You are not like your mother, you are not like your mother*, her feet kept chanting. She was running to Jimmy's place. But she had to make a stop before she got there. She had never had to do that before. But this time Marjorie had to pull her run up short when she saw, in the night distance, the glow of a fire right next to Jimmy's place.

She swallowed an enormous mouthful of panic: hands scrabbling at her face as the dread tried to force its way past her teeth. There was a paddock fire ahead! A grass fire in front! A racing, roaring out-of-control monstrosity galloping amok in the middle of the night through the tinder-dry stubble in Jimmy Waghorn's paddock! Blazing negligently away. Cavorting across the wheat stalks while all decent CFA volunteers were blissfully ignorant and asleep in bed. When any half-decent wet wheat bag that she might have used to bash the fire out was bone dry and stashed miles back in the grain shed.

Why didn't she always carry a wet wheat bag with her? She raged at herself. How stupid could she be? She mustn't have put the fire out properly earlier on. And now here she was without a wet wheat bag. Only a selfish, self-centred and thoughtless person would run off into the night with never a thought to bring a wet wheat bag in the very likely case of a raging grass fire in a stubble paddock. She was going to be responsible for letting the whole bloody farm burn down, didn't she know?

But an instant later Marjorie realised that she, and the whole bloody farm, were safe, despite her abject stupidity. The fire was burning constant and contained; it was not spreading. Marjorie blew out an enormous mouthful of relief – equal to the enormous mouthful of panic she had just swallowed. And started off running again.

She ran right up to that fire. It was an ordinary Jimmy Waghorn fire, burning in his old campfire space: just like she and Ruby might have lit. She walked around it, double-checking to be sure none of the fire had escaped into the surrounding paddocks, before she sank down on the old blue bench.

And sucked in her second enormous mouthful of panic for the night when a voice spoke to her from the base of the peppercorn tree.

'Night-time is the best time to come here,' said Jesse, unfurling his long legs and pushing himself up from the sculptured bole of the tree. He pushed aside the drooping fronds – aromatic and delicate on the slight, middle-of-the-night breeze. 'Don't know why you haven't tried it before.' He glided – casual and taut – towards open-mouthed Marjorie. 'Shut your mouth, Marjorie,' he added. 'If the sun hadn't gone down already you would have a gob full of flies by now with your mouth hanging open like that.'

Marjorie slammed her mouth shut and watched Jesse move over to the old blue bench – *her* old blue bench! She watched Jesse fold himself up again, settle to the red dirt and lean against the bench. Right next to her. One elbow casually resting on the seat. Both eyes casually resting on Marjorie.

'What are you doing here?' demanded Marjorie.

'Visiting Jimmy Waghorn's place,' said Jesse, watching Marjorie.

'You can't.'

'Can't what?'

'Can't come here to Jimmy's place.'

'Yes I can,' said Jesse – suddenly fierce.

'No you can't,' said Marjorie – missing Jesse's fierceness.

'You don't own this place,' said Jesse. And Jesse lurched to his feet. 'This is not your place. This is Jimmy's place.' Jesse was standing over her. His eyes – hot and angry – stared at her as he threw himself back down to sit beside her, this time on the bench.

Marjorie knew enough from her own life about probable consequences of sudden anger. She did not press the point. She chose instead to stare at the fire. 'How long have you been coming here?' she asked.

Jesse glanced at her before looking away at the fire. 'Years,' he said softly. 'I've been coming for years.'

'What?' Marjorie's arm shot out sideways and whacked Jesse in the chest. 'Don't be bloody ridiculous.'

'Years,' Jesse repeated to the fire, ignoring the whack in the chest. 'Way back when Jimmy was still here.'

'Bullshit,' Marjorie exploded. 'You're a bloody liar and full of bloody bullshit. Jimmy never told me you were here.'

'And why should Jimmy have to tell you, Marjorie?' Jesse balled his hands into fists and folded his arms tightly across his chest. 'You don't own this place and you never owned Jimmy Waghorn either. Jimmy didn't have to ask your permission.' Jesse's voice was tight. Like his fists.

The stump in the middle of the fire burnt out its heart and slumped, sending a shower of sparks into the night sky. Marjorie followed its lead and slumped, but without the accompanying beauty of the shower of sparks. She watched as the stump turned to bleak ash. *Now I have nowhere left to go. Not even Jimmy's place is safe.* In fact, she realised, it never had been. Wheat Bag Boy had been sneaking around and stealing Jimmy all these years. She was such a fool. Now all she had left to run away to were books. But there was no point letting Wheat Bag Boy know how she felt. She too folded her arms across her chest. And the two of them sat there on the bench, staring at the fire.

Marjorie broke the silence. 'When exactly did you first start coming? I remember you practically wetting your pants at the name of Jimmy Waghorn.'

Jesse scuffed the dirt with his boot. It was true enough. 'Right after that paper dress concert. I came the night after you had me kept in at school for falsely accusing the lovely, ladylike, teacher's pet Marjorie of swearing.' Jesse looked at Marjorie.

Marjorie grinned. But Jesse wasn't grinning. 'Hang on – we were only kids then,' said Marjorie. 'I must have been about thirteen. You couldn't have been older than fourteen. What were you doing running about in the dark?'

Jesse didn't answer for a long time. 'Secret family business, Marjorie,' he said finally. He looked up at the stars. And back down sideways at Marjorie. Who was sitting there once again – with her mouth open – staring at him. He leant across, put his index finger under her chin and pushed upwards until her mouth shut. 'Did you think you were the only one around here with secret family business?' Jesse smiled a crooked smile at her.

Yes! thought Marjorie, still feeling Jesse's touch on her skin.

'I used to watch you all the time. I knew your family had secrets.'

'How did you know?' Marjorie blurted.

Jesse sighed and shook his head and didn't bother to answer. 'I used to try and figure out how you did it,' he said. 'You were so skinny and tired-looking. So scared of everything all the time.' Jesse was talking softly to the night-time.

187

'What do you mean?' said Marjorie. 'I wasn't scared.'

Jesse shook his head and didn't reply.

'How I did what?' asked Marjorie into the silence.

'Survived it.'

'Survived what?'

Jesse shook his head again. 'Marjorie,' he said, 'I am stunned at how very stupid you are for such an intelligent person.'

'What?'

Jesse ignored her. 'Anyway,' he continued, going around the blatant stupidity beside him, 'as a kid would back then, I decided it might have been due to having Jimmy Waghorn living on your place. So I decided to risk it and find out.'

Jesse bent and picked up a handful of stones and started throwing them one by one into the fire as he talked. 'I decided the consequences of turning up at Jimmy Waghorn's place without an invite couldn't be any worse than staying at my place.' Jesse shrugged, rolling inwards on his memories. 'I got here about midnight, I reckon. And there was Jimmy, sitting on this old blue bench like he was waiting for me. Like he had been waiting for me for years.' Jesse pushed himself off the bench to go and throw some more stumps on the fire. 'That's when I started coming.'

Marjorie watched Jesse hurling stumps onto the fire like he wanted to make a Guy Fawkes bonfire.

'Did you ever notice when I didn't turn up for school?' he asked as he sat down again.

'No. Maybe. Sometimes.'

'I didn't think so. So you didn't notice I wasn't at school the day after you got me kept in for lying?'

Marjorie shrugged. 'You fell off your bike, didn't you?'

Jesse fell silent and examined the horizon and the sky.

'Your dad get up before dawn?'

Marjorie startled at the question and the obvious reason for it. 'Yes. Always.' It was her turn to look at the horizon.

'You'd better get on back home then. Get back in through that bedroom window or whatever it is you do. While you still have time.'

Marjorie jumped up and looked at the fire and at Jesse and over towards the home paddock. She was calculating before she realised what she was doing: how much time she had to get home, how much time to undress and put her nightie back on, how much time to carefully sneak back into that house and get back into bed. Before Bill got up. Without waking the house. Without waking a soul.

'I'll put the fire out,' said Jesse. 'You get going.'

'Thanks,' said Marjorie absent-mindedly. She was concentrating on her calculations. She had already forgotten about Jesse. She was off. Heading into the dark and back towards the house paddock.

Jesse stood at the fire and watched her – watched her move from the light of the fire into the dark of the night. He watched until he couldn't see her anymore and couldn't hear her anymore before he bent to put out the fire.

Marjorie stopped at the backyard fence. She stayed there until she was no longer breathing hard. Then she carefully squeezed between the gap in the gate and the fence post, and went to retrieve her nightie. She paused on the back porch to gauge the interest of the house. But it didn't seem fussed. So with her clothes and shoes bunched tightly to her chest, Marjorie crept down the hallway towards her bedroom. She was almost betrayed by a sneak floorboard trumpeting a squeak. But no one stirred. She paused at the bedroom door

189

to listen to Ruby's breathing before creeping over to her bed and climbing in. She lay there, flat on her back, clutching her clothes and her shoes and staring at the tongue-in-groove ceiling boards parading out of the pre-dawn gloom.

Marjorie heard Bill get up. She heard Ruby start to wake up, so she rolled over to face the wall and pretended she was asleep – clutching her clothes and shoes – and waited until Ruby left the bedroom before charging out of bed and into a furious dust storm of getting ready for school.

'What's the matter with you?' asked Ruby, glancing up from her school sandwich making as Marjorie sidled into the kitchen.

'Nothing. Why?'

'No reason,' said Ruby. 'I could ask Mum to do another drawing of you.'

'No! You already did that yesterday and she didn't seem too keen on the idea. So forget it!' Marjorie grabbed the bread and started to lay into it with the bread knife – hacking and sawing. 'I don't want another stupid bloody drawing.'

'Suit yourself. But it would make things easier with Mum if you asked.'

'No!' shouted Marjorie.

*

Marjorie managed to get on the bus without looking at Jesse. She pushed and shoved and elbowed to the back seat and threw herself into the safety of a book. And straight away went to sleep. But Jesse had managed to sit beside her and he elbowed her in the back so she jerked awake as Jesse murmured to the bus window behind her ear: 'Just act normal.' Which for Jesse meant climbing into a seat on the bus and falling asleep.

Both ways. Going to school and coming home again. Instantly asleep as soon as the bus took off. Instantly awake as soon as it stopped. But Marjorie never slept on the bus.

She sprang up in her seat. She knew what he meant. She had spent the morning at home scanning to see if anyone could detect anything that wasn't normal. And now here she was – giving it all away. *Attention, everyone on the bus! I was out at Jimmy Waghorn's place most of last night. And that is not normal for me. I have not slept so am very tired now. So I am just going to go to sleep on the school bus – which is also not normal for me.*

'Back of the library. Lunchtime,' Jesse muttered to her before he fell asleep. But he kept his elbow placed at her back to jab, solicitously, apparently in his sleep – any time he thought Marjorie was falling asleep.

Marjorie somehow managed to stay awake until lunchtime. She jammed her lukewarm Vegemite sandwich down her throat and drank more than lukewarm water at the bubble taps, before heading to the uncertain sanctuary of the back of the library. Jesse was already there. And once again, he had managed to clear the perimeters. They had the place to themselves. Jesse had also made preparations. He had a couple of large piles of books – big and solid – scattered in studious disarray. It was like he had made a queer little blockade on the table.

He grinned at her questioning stare. 'Done this often enough. You can have a good sleep here. Libraries are always good for the mind.'

By then, Marjorie was just about asleep on her feet. She slumped into the chair next to him, folded her arms on the table, put her head in her arms and was asleep.

Jesse let Marjorie sleep for half an hour before he woke her and made her help him put all the books back. Marjorie still wanted to sleep but Jesse had enough prior experience to know a good half-hour would get her through the rest of the day. They went their separate ways for the afternoon and didn't speak again that day. Or for the next number of days. It was almost as if the night at Jimmy Waghorn's place hadn't happened.

About a month after that, Jesse was suddenly at Marjorie's side as she headed for the last class of the day. 'Half-moon tonight,' he said, looking for it in the sky. 'Be cold, though. Frost most likely.' He must have thought Marjorie needed an update on the weather forecast because that was all he said before he ambled off.

Marjorie stared straight ahead. She didn't even give him the time of day. Because now – on account of Jesse's unsolicited weather report – she didn't have any time of the day to spare. She had to reserve all available time to spend on thinking about what she was going to do. She thought about it all the way home on the bus. She tried to think about it all the way home in the ute. But Ruby kept interrupting.

'Things alright at school?'

'What?' replied Marjorie, concentrating on the driving.

'The kids giving you any trouble about Mum?'

'No. It's alright.'

'She's started making a nativity set. Out of plasticine. Has she shown it to you?'

'No.' Marjorie glanced at Ruby in fright. 'How long has she been doing that?'

'A couple of weeks.' Ruby glanced at Marjorie. 'She probably hasn't had time to show it to you,' she said, trying to soothe Marjorie. But kindness couldn't hide the truth. They both knew the rules.

'I suppose she'll talk to me again one day.'

'You know how it is,' said Ruby. 'She'll get over it.'

'When do you suppose that might happen?' said Marjorie. 'Based on our previous experiences with the immaculate bloody Elise, it might be Christmas. What do you estimate? How about a wager on a Christmas truce?'

Ruby sighed. 'Try to be patient with her, Marjorie.'

'Why should I?' Marjorie jerked the gearstick. 'I don't want to do this anymore. Normal mothers don't do this, Ruby.'

After Jesse's weather forecast conversation in the school-yard, and now the revelation of a plasticine nativity set that Marjorie was not part of, it was very easy for Marjorie to make her decision.

She did her jobs in complete silence. But the inside of her head was rowdy. She had to plan what to wear, where to stash, where to change, what time to leave, how to leave, how to get back in time. She also thought about food supplies. And decided against food. There was never enough in the house; any shortage would be missed. She considered tobacco and papers supplies.

But she didn't allocate any thinking time to what they might talk about at Jimmy's place – her and Jesse.

Her final decision was to go to bed earlier than usual. And pretend to be asleep.

'I'm going to bed now,' Marjorie muttered when the washing-up was done after dinner. Bill looked fleetingly surprised. So did Ruby – lifting her beautiful head momentarily from her endless homework. Tea-cosy-hatted Elise didn't move from her seat in front of the stove.

In no time at all, the house was silent, Ruby was sleeping, nearly half of a moon was climbing above the sand ridge in the distance, and Marjorie was sneaking out the back door with a stash of tobacco and papers.

It was an easy run. The night was half-lit by the half-moon, and Marjorie loved it. She ran fluently and lightly, her long legs relishing the crisp air and the concentration of effort. For a brief moment of bliss, Marjorie forgot about Ruby, forgot about Bill – she almost forgot about Elise. She didn't even notice herself slow to dart between the gap in the paddock gate or pick up the pace for the small hill – didn't even notice the waiting glow of the fire. She forgot about Jesse.

And suddenly she was there. At Jimmy Waghorn's place. And the fire was burning and waiting for her. And Jesse was cooking and waiting for her. Damper and billy tea and rabbit on a stick. 'I could hear you coming a mile off,' said Jesse, glancing up from his cooking. 'You need to run quiet in the night.'

'I can run quiet if I need to,' said Marjorie.

'You should always run quiet,' he said to the rabbit. 'Then you won't need to.'

'Stop talking rubbish.' Marjorie claimed a spot on the old blue bench, untied the coat from around her waist and put it on.

'You been here since I was here the other night?' she asked.

Jesse shrugged. ''Course I have. That was weeks ago.'

'How many times?'

'As many as I needed.'

'Why?'

'I told you why. You don't have exclusive rights on secret family business hereabouts, Marjorie.' Jesse waited for the question. But Marjorie never asked it. So he went on. 'I come when I need to. That's what Jimmy said to do. And that is

194

what I do.' Jesse grabbed the rabbit from the fire and threw it on a tin plate sitting on the bench. He hastily pulled it apart. Darting at it with his long fingers so the rabbit couldn't attack him with its heat – its last, defiant fight. Jesse sat down, the rabbit-loaded tin plate between him and Marjorie. 'Here,' he said. 'Have some.' And started to help himself.

They ate the rabbit in comfortable silence. It was delicious as only campfire roast rabbit can be. They ate the damper with butter and jam. It also was delicious. Marjorie sighed a deep sigh of contentment. A very rare sigh. She was used to sighs – sighs were normal in her life. But not sighs of contentment.

Jesse started making a cup of billy tea so Marjorie pulled out the tobacco and papers and started rolling smokes. She rolled a slender smoke. She examined it and nodded to herself – gave it a couple of swift jabs of a matchstick in either end – before laying it on the bench for Jesse and making another one for herself. By the time she had finished both smokes, Jesse was back on the bench and watching her with more than a glint of amusement in his hazel eyes. Marjorie didn't notice this. She was still busy. She hadn't finished. She handed Jesse his smoke and held the match to his mouth while he drew breath. She lit her own, drawing air through the smoke until it was alive and awake.

'Such a refined lady,' said Jesse through the smoke of his cigarette. 'Not only do you not swear, but you also do not smoke.'

'Bugger off.'

Jesse laughed. A rich, melodious laugh that lit up his face. And showed his lovely teeth. With his chipped front tooth from that time a few years ago when he'd gone head first over the handlebars of his bike and turned up at school with black eyes and a broken mouth. Marjorie stared at Jesse. Shocked. She had never noticed Wheat Bag Boy laugh before.

The two of them stayed there at Jimmy's place that second night and looked back out at the Mallee as it pondered them. They talked and talked about nothing, and gazed up at the frosty stars glistening overhead, and watched the Southern Cross turn slowly over. They watched the fire and listened to the thoughtful exchange of the plovers discussing matters of vast avian import out in the dark of the paddocks.

And they paused, and listened as one to the first goods train of the night as it made its slow, lonely way through the miles and miles of railway lines etched into the fabric of Mallee farm life. They heard it from one side of the night horizon to the other. Faintly, then clear and crisp on the frosty air, and then fading. A pendulum swinging slow and methodical across the night. The whistle and the wheels. Eternally hauling the wheat and wool of the Mallee. The goods train: as paradoxical as everything that survived in the Mallee. It clickety-clacked, clickety-clacked, clickety-clacked soft, then loud, then soft – determined and business-like as it carried the heart of Mallee farm survival on its back. And it moaned and wailed and shrilled soft, then loud, then soft – solitary and desolate as it carried the source of Mallee landscape devastation on its back.

'Time to pack up,' said Jesse. 'If you're back in bed before the second train, you'll get enough sleep.'

Marjorie didn't answer. She got up, took her jacket off and tied it around her waist again, and helped put out the fire.

'See ya,' she said, staring in the direction of the house. Then Marjorie was off and running.

'Yeah,' said Jesse. He stood and watched her leave, as he had done the first night, before turning on his heels and walking the other way.

Chapter 11

WHY DID MARJORIE turn up at Jimmy Waghorn's place in the dark? Why not? She had always gone there. Since she was so tiny the ripened golden heads of a good crop of wheat could lean in to her ears to whisper a warm and golden message as she ran.

Why go in the middle of the night – covertly? Again: why not? Secrets were the mainstay of her life in that house. And if you were already, day by secretive day, weary and spent from the toil of keeping secrets, then some of those secrets should be of your own making. These midnight campfire meetings were compensation for the struggle, payment in kind. And Marjorie discovered it was recompense enough. Besides, Marjorie was sixteen. Jesse was seventeen. Both well old enough to be running around in the dark on their own.

So, Jesse and Marjorie met at Jimmy's place secretly and commonly and in the dark from then on. They sculpted a tiny, secret life for themselves in the middle of the night, hidden inside the reality of their wintry daytime lives. Marjorie's upbringing helped. She was brought up on the obligations of masquerade – of living a secret – and was used to having to adapt quickly to arbitrary changes to this facade. So she was speedy. She tuned herself in right away to finding Wheat Bag Boy at Jimmy's place that first time even though there was no time for a proper sit-down tune-up. It was like when you have to fix a tractor breakdown right out in the middle of the paddock. And just like a middle of the paddock tuning can sometimes be, this one turned out to be perfect. Jesse and Marjorie never missed a beat at all these night-time meetings, over all those passing seasons, the two of them together there in that Mallee.

There was a comforting and unusual sameness about their visits. They ate food provided by Jesse. They drank tea made by Jesse. They smoked smokes provided and made by Marjorie. They watched the night-time Mallee and heeded the night-time Mallee. They packed up and left before the second train warning.

Their conversations held the comfort of sameness: Marjorie made statements and Jesse answered. Jesse asked questions and Marjorie answered. Or didn't. Either way, over time the two of them were knitted together by their conversations and their collusion there at Jimmy's place. With conversations that lived only at Jimmy's place – conversations that waited around at his place from one night-time to the next one, so they could be finished off then. Or at the next night-time after that.

*

'My mother Elise is making a nativity scene out of plasticine.'

'Why do you call your mother by her name so much? Why don't you call your mother *Mum*, like normal kids do?'

'Dunno. I only do it sometimes. And maybe I'm not normal.'

'Why is she making a nativity set?'

Marjorie shrugged.

'It's not anywhere near Christmas,' Jesse pointed out.

'She's good at art.'

'It's not even shearing time. Christmas has only just happened,' Jesse pointed out.

'She's really good.'

'What does it look like?'

'Dunno.' Marjorie stiffened.

Jesse waited. Marjorie said nothing more. Jesse had to wait right until the next visit.

*

And then at the next visit:

'Mum isn't talking to me.'

'Why not?'

'Dunno,' said Marjorie, poking the fire and clamping her teeth shut – and the conversation shut.

*

And at the following visit:

'Your mother talking to you yet?'

'No.'

'How long will it take?'

Marjorie shrugged. And her shoulders put a halt to the conversation.

*

And at the next visit after that:

'Sometimes it's only a few days. Sometimes it's a couple of weeks,' she explained as the campfire light reached out and grabbed her emerging from the night-time and dumped her on the old blue bench. 'But it's already been weeks and weeks this time. Mum not talking. Elise being angry. Her carrying all her disappointment about me on her shoulders for us all to see.'

'Why does she do that?' asked Jesse.

Marjorie looked at Jesse like she used to look at Wheat Bag Boy. 'Because I've done something wrong. Elise will talk to me when I've been sufficiently punished.' Marjorie turned away, and Jesse knew she had said as much as she was going to say about this topic at this visit.

*

All in all, it took about half-a-dozen night-time visits to Jimmy's place to complete the conversation. Night-time visits that ran up to crutching time. And ran out the other side of crutching time.

And it took Elise about the same time – a season of punishment, much more than a few months, if you are counting time as a linear concept – to deem Marjorie suitably punished. One night after school, Ruby and Marjorie walked into the kitchen. 'Oh. There you are, Marjorie,' said Elise. 'I have been making a nativity set out of plasticine.' And, as arbitrarily as she had been confined to solitary, Marjorie was arbitrarily allowed out.

Over the years, Marjorie had tried to find a weapon to ward against arbitrary assaults. But any lasting defence seemed elusive. Which was ironic. Because for all her inability to understand and accept the Mallee, Elise was a lethal expert of the most common form of attack wielded by the land – the arbitrary assault. The random deadly willy-willy that crushed the promise of a good harvest. The indiscriminate dust storm that choked and shredded and buried as it raged across the Mallee.

Marjorie should have known better than to think she could escape the effects of the assault. She saw what arbitrariness did to the Mallee. But each one of these random attacks managed to catch her unawares. Each one left her reeling and determined, that this time, it would be the last. And the ending of each punishment was soaked in relief and the belief that it was the last that would ever be.

But it never was. Just like the lurking Mallee stumps, it was waiting. Just like the inevitable drought, it was biding its time.

Marjorie smiled a rich smile of relief and dumped the wheat bags of guilt and disgrace off her shoulders. She glanced at Ruby, who gave her a rueful, apologetic smile. Only one of them could be in solitary confinement. This time it was Marjorie's turn. Although there were no turns really. Even that was arbitrary.

'Hello, Mum,' replied Marjorie. Two words full of pardon. 'I bet it's wonderful. I would love to see it.'

'Of course you may see it, dear girl.'

*

'Mum showed me the nativity set,' said Marjorie as she stepped out of the darkness and into the first visit to Jimmy's place after Elise's pardon. She paused to untie the jumper from around her waist, and to shake her head at the thought of all that delicate plasticine beauty.

'So your mother is talking to you again?'

'Yeah.'

'Why? What's different that made her want to talk to you again?'

'I don't know,' said Marjorie. 'Maybe I have done my penance . . . Maybe she couldn't be bothered anymore . . . Maybe she forgot . . .'

Silence arrived. Jesse moved to throw a couple of stumps on the fire. They sat on the bench and smoked a smoke.

'What does it look like? That nativity set?'

'Beautiful,' breathed Marjorie, remembering the art and loveliness of those tiny plasticine statues. She started talking. She hadn't intended to say any more about it but, all of a sudden, there she was. Talking her head off. A summer rain storm of talking as she described the tiny beauties made incongruously out of a child's play stuff. Jesse listened transfixed. And before they knew it, the train was coming across the horizon.

*

A thought came to Marjorie after a number of times and a couple of seasons of campfires and night trains. Marjorie and Jesse hadn't ever stopped meeting at Jimmy's. They met there right through autumn and the ploughing, and right through winter and the planting. Right past the beginning of spring and into the lambing.

And Marjorie's thought was just like the Mallee spring – cautious about emerging in case the rains didn't follow. But one peerless, starry night on that old blue bench with Jesse at her side, a tiny part of her weighed up the idea of taking a risk. Of opting to take a gamble on looking out for someone else – not just herself – if she wanted to. And she decided she did want to.

'You lied,' she said. 'You didn't go over the handlebars, did you?' Pointing at Jesse's chipped front tooth.

Jesse shook his head.

'What happened?'

Jesse watched the fire.

'Who was fighting?' she asked.

But Jesse was too busy staring at the fire to hear.

'Who did it?'

But Jesse was too busy jabbing at the fire to answer.

So Marjorie watched the fire too because she was suddenly scared and couldn't think of anything else to say or to ask. But the firelight was bright. It showed Marjorie something she hadn't seen before. She saw something about Jesse. And about herself. 'Did you cop it at home after I got you kept in after school?'

Jesse nodded and hunched down into his shoulders so he could get a better look at the fire.

'Why?'

'There doesn't have to be a reason why.'

'Who hit you? Does your dad hit you?'

Jesse just shrugged and stared at the fire. 'I used to hide them – my mum, my brothers – when my brothers were really little. I'm pretty good at it now – I've had years of practice. I know which nights are going to be the bad nights. But I was too late that night. And I knew I would be. I knew as soon as I was kept in and given all that stuff to do. My brothers and I didn't get home until nearly dark. He had already belted Mum. He started on me and I lost it. I laid into him. He might have split my lip but I flattened him.'

'Why don't you tell someone? Why don't you get some help?'

'Why don't you, Marjorie?'

Silence was making a habit of attending their campfires. It turned up now at this one too. So Jesse and Marjorie sat side by side and stared at the flames for the rest of the night. They only moved to put wood on the fire, or to roll another smoke. And that was all they did until the train told them to go home.

Marjorie lay in her bed back at the house and thought for a long time about the night that had just happened. She was not sure whether it was the roast rabbits, or the billy tea, or the stolen and rolled smokes. Or maybe it was just the magic of Jimmy Waghorn living on in the peppercorn tree and the campfire.

'Does anyone else know about this?' Marjorie had asked before the silence turned up.

Jesse had shaken his head. 'Not anymore,' he said. 'I tried to tell the teachers once. But they didn't want to know. Then one day I saw Jimmy Waghorn looking right at me. One of those days when I had a black eye. Looking at me like he knew what was going on. I got up in the middle of the night after that – just like you've done now – and came over here.'

'Does your mother know you come here?'

'My mum doesn't want to know much about anything. So, no. She doesn't know.'

'What will you do if your dad finds out and tries to stop you?'

'I'll flatten him!' said Jesse.

*

'My mother isn't normal,' Marjorie said the next time they met in the dark. Right after the cup of tea. Even before the first smoke of the night.

Marjorie wasn't about to mention Jesse's story about why his tooth was broken or how he could turn up any time with bruised eyes. That was Jesse's business. But she could let him know her stuff. Marjorie had never talked about her stuff to anyone before except Ruby. So she stared straight ahead at the fire so the flames could help her in the telling and the smoke could help her in the remembering.

Jesse looked at Marjorie and nodded. And looked away

again. 'And how would a fine young lady like you define *normal?*' he asked, trying to make it easier for her.

Marjorie switched from being scared to being haughty. 'I define *normal* in terms of balance – how a thing balances out in relation to something else.' She used her hands to demonstrate a set of balancing scales. 'Bloody hell, Jesse. It's pure science.' And they both burst out laughing.

The laughter was what she needed. Her words from then on did speak about balance: the wondrous balancing of Ruby, who seemed to so effortlessly keep Elise on an even keel. And the fragile balancing act of an artist carefully walking between creativity and chaos. Marjorie showed it all to Jesse. Bit by bit. Starting with the easy bits.

'My mother makes her own clothes out of patterns she thinks up in her head, and out of old curtains. No one else does that.'

Jesse shrugged.

'My mother makes fancy-coloured meringues and can't make a scone to save her life – or ours. Other mothers make useful tomato sandwiches and sensible fruitcake.'

'I like them. Them *fancy-coloured meringues.*' He grinned at Marjorie and she smiled ruefully back. She was running out of the easier items.

'She drinks coffee. Every other person in the entire Mallee drinks tea. There is no other coffee to be had in any other Mallee kitchen.'

'Jimmy Waghorn drank coffee,' said Jesse. 'At your place. He told me.'

Marjorie drew in a long breath and let it slowly out. 'Mum wears a tea cosy on her head – all the time. It makes her feel better.'

Jesse remained silent and still beside her.

'Mum planted those bloody plastic flowers she won,' Marjorie went on. 'She talks to them. And she thinks they talk to her.'

Jesse, carefully like a fox, moved to face Marjorie, so he could look her in the eye. 'Yes. But what does all that do to you?' he asked.

Marjorie spent a long time bunching all her thoughts and trying to decide which one to pull out of the pile. 'For as long as I can remember,' she whispered, 'Mum has gone away. My mother goes away inside herself and stays there. Sometimes it's not long. Sometimes it's for days. Sometimes it's for weeks. Sometimes I know it's my fault. Sometimes I have no bloody idea why she does it.' She shook her head. 'She gets so angry.'

'How is it your fault?'

'I've said the wrong thing. Or I've not said anything. Who knows?' Marjorie shrugged. 'All I know is it wouldn't have happened if it wasn't for me and I need to try harder. Like Ruby does. Like Ruby can. But I've never been able to try hard enough.'

'What do you do?' asked Jesse. But Marjorie didn't seem to hear him.

'It's not Mum's fault,' Marjorie went on. 'I'm too loud. I'm too boisterous and clumsy. I make her angry without even trying.'

'What did you do when you were little? What do you do now?' asked Jesse, and Marjorie heard him this time.

'I used to latch on to Ruby. I was so bloody scared all the time. Remember when I told you I wasn't scared?'

Jesse nodded.

'Well, I am scared,' said Marjorie. 'Mum and I tried to make a rose garden – just after I started high school. I was so happy.

Mum was so happy. Then she went to bed and wouldn't get up and we never got that garden. I got caught in a willy-willy with bees in it. We got bees instead.'

There was a long silence after that. They smoked in silence and smoked in silence again.

'My mother has nervous breakdowns, Jesse.'

The peppercorn tree had been holding its breath all this while, listening to Marjorie, wondering if she had the courage. Now it breathed out. It soothed and sighed around them. Its leaves whispering and swaying softly in the night breeze.

'Sometimes my mother is a complete lunatic. Sometimes she is totally mental. My mother went completely mental over those plastic bloody flowers and had to go away to a damn fool bloody mental hospital for mad person treatment.'

And, having broken the rules and betrayed the family and exposed the secret business of Elise, Marjorie sighed a gulping, gut-wrenching sigh of relief. 'That is not normal,' she said, using her arms and hands again to demonstrate the scientific balance of normal.

Marjorie looked at Jesse and they both burst out laughing. They laughed and laughed. They kicked the dirt with their laughter. They rocked the old bench with their laughter. They scared the plovers and the rabbits and the foxes.

The laughing finally wore out, so Marjorie rolled two more smokes.

'I don't think I can do all this without Ruby,' whispered Marjorie. 'She has always been there for me. She even made sure she was born before me so she could look after me.'

Jesse put his arm around Marjorie at that. Because he knew two things: he knew what it meant to be the one who always had to look out for everyone. And he knew what it meant to see frightened eyes staring at you all the time. Marjorie sat there, leaning into his shoulder. They smoked their contraband and waited for the train to tell them to go home.

'It's your turn next time,' said Marjorie as she tied her jumper around her waist.

*

So on the next Jimmy Waghorn night, Jesse did the talking. Staring straight ahead, just like Marjorie had done. And it was Jesse's turn to be supported by the flames and smoke of the fire.

Marjorie sat there beside him on that old blue bench. She stared at the fire too. It was lucky for the pair of them that the fire was there and could carry the night by itself. Because Marjorie had nothing at all to say. Because Jesse might not have let too many words come out of his mouth, but the words he did let out had way too much to say. About his own particular, peculiar way of managing life on his farm:

'My father is a drunken useless father who has been drunk and useless since the day I was born,' said Jesse. 'My little brothers have not known anything except being scared to death when their father comes home. I am the big brother who has spent so much time jamming and hiding them in cupboards since they were small.'

'No wonder you never do your homework,' said Marjorie.

'The concept of homework at my house is misplaced,' said Jesse.

'You need to tell someone,' said Marjorie.

'Why?' asked Jesse. 'You don't. Do you?' He looked at Marjorie until she turned away.

'I am the cause of it all, anyway,' said Jesse.

'How could you be?'

'My father had to marry my mother. And I am their firstborn. So, I am both my mother's and my father's ruin. I really loved Mum when I was little. But that's what little kids do. But now sometimes I think I hate her. She is a worn-out mother, an ingratiating, placating, fawning woman, who totters around and around the drinking, then the arguing, and then the hitting and the fighting, only to get up the next day – or the day after that – and sign up for it all over again. My brothers and me are trapped. We're like those sheep who have got stuck in the mud in the middle of a nearly empty dam. Killing ourselves just trying to survive.'

'You could call the police.'

'Why? What would they do?' Jesse grabbed a lump of wood and threw it hard into the middle of the fire.

'My mother is a hoarder,' he went on. 'She collects things for all of us. Like broken teeth and split lips. She used to hide things. Like my little brothers in cupboards, and our bruises under the jumpers. But that's my job now. And my mother is a wordsmith. She transcribes things – like being bilious instead of being beaten. And I do too,' he said, looking at Marjorie. 'Like the time I told you about a bike accident instead of a bashing.' And he smiled a lopsided, chipped-tooth smile at her.

Marjorie felt sick at the relentless dread that boarded at Jesse's place. She felt the helpless fury of Jesse when he hid his little brothers all over the place; she felt the abject futility of any effort his mother made. And Marjorie had a measure of sympathy – just a bit – for her own mother and her desire to go inside herself and shut the door on the world. Because that was exactly what Marjorie wanted to do with Jesse's story.

She was gentle when Jesse finished talking. 'Having a deranged and mentally unstable mother isn't that bad, I've decided,' she said. 'At least we have some good times.' She rolled a smoke and handed it to him.

Jesse smiled, his face crooked and sad. 'I'd like to see those plasticine nativity things your mother is making. One day.'

And it was Marjorie's turn to comfort Jesse. She slid her arm around his back. But she knew one arm wouldn't be enough for this kind of story. So she slid her other arm around his front. She put her head on his shoulder. Her hands joined – they let Jesse know. And Jesse and Marjorie sat there, waiting for the train.

Because Marjorie saw that some people are chipped and damaged, cracked and frayed, exquisite and talented. But they care. They love whenever and wherever they can. In spite of their madness and their sadness, they still try.

But some people are just mean bastards.

*

No one at the house ever found out about Marjorie's night-time schedule. Because no one there could have contemplated her getting up in the middle of the night and running off. And Marjorie couldn't blame them for that. Even she found it all a bit hard to fathom. Someone who was scared of bees and a life without Ruby, just getting up in the middle of the night and running off across the paddocks by herself, alone and in the dark.

So it was no surprise, really, that nobody ever knew. But there were certainly enough indications there if they cared to pay attention. Because the house kept trying to warn them with its creaks and its squeaks. Every time Marjorie ran off. Every time she snuck back in. And maybe they should have known. Maybe they should have been trying a bit harder to look out for Marjorie. Perhaps things might have turned out differently if they had known.

Marjorie and Jesse met at Jimmy Waghorn's all the rest of that year. They had already gone past the early winter frosts and the emergence of the plasticine nativity scene and into the shearing season. Through the sleepy, silent woolly sheep and the quiet, blinking naked sheep. They had sat and listened to the night train lug away the carefully sorted and graded and baled wool. They had sat around that campfire through the ploughing and the sewing. They had eaten campfire rabbit as pale green wheat poked through the damp red dirt. And met all through the winter and into spring, watching as those hopeful baby shoots changed from pale green to deep green; and from deep green to the promise of harvest. The two of them had thrown Mallee stump after Mallee stump on that fire all through Ruby's last year at school. All through the apprehension of her exams, the elation at her results and the relief at Ruby's acceptance into teachers' college. And Marjorie's terror of a life lived without her.

All the while Jimmy Waghorn never failed to provide a midnight haven. And in the middle of all those months, Marjorie ran smack into love.

Love was sneaky. Like a lot of things in the Mallee – sneaking about, waiting to knock you down. So Marjorie wasn't prepared for love to turn up on the school bus. That's the last place it should have been but there it was, lying in wait. Rolling around under the seats like a discarded, half-sucked gobstopper. Sneaking about until it could get in behind and bite her on the ankle.

Marjorie was tardy that day in shoving to get to the back seat, so she missed out. And the only seat left was next to Jesse.

'There's a seat there next to Jesse Mitchell,' said Ruby as she grabbed the other vacant seat.

But Marjorie and Jesse never sat together on the bus anymore. Marjorie wouldn't. She was scared of anyone, especially Ruby, finding out about her and Jesse and their night-time runs. So that was her rule: no sitting together on the bus. Except for this morning, when she had no choice.

'Go on,' said Ruby. 'I don't think he bites.'

Marjorie had no choice. Refusing a seat and standing up for the whole trip would have drawn attention to herself. She always fought for a seat. So she pushed past Jesse's knees and sat next to the window. Maybe it was pushing past his knees that did it? She wasn't sure. It certainly wasn't looking into his eyes that did it, because she carefully avoided looking at him as she elbowed past. But what she did know was that as she bent to get her book out of her bag she noticed his long brown fingers. All those fingers staring at her underneath their covering of crossed arms. Marjorie liked those fingers. She wanted to touch them. Right there on the school bus.

Her mouth dropped open. She straightened up and twisted around to stare at Jesse. At the same time that he turned to look at her. He smiled. Marjorie loved that soft mouth, and that lovely smile, with its chipped front tooth. Why had she just realised this? And there was that smell of him that she knew so well now. She breathed it in. No one else but her should be allowed to smell that smell of Jesse.

'Shut your mouth,' whispered Jesse. 'And stop staring.'

Marjorie all of a sudden wanted to grab his hand and hold it and lean into him and smell him. But she couldn't. She wanted Jesse to put his arm around her and pull her into his chest. But that couldn't happen. She was on the school bus. So she shut her mouth and did her best to read her book.

That night Marjorie ran to Jimmy's place. Her run was purposeful – like it always was. But she had never had a purpose such as this before.

She ran into the firelight. Jesse was putting down an armful of firewood and he turned towards her as she ran in. Marjorie didn't bother to say hello. She didn't stop either. She untied her jumper from around her waist, threw it on the old blue bench and walked straight up to Jesse. Marjorie walked slowly and carefully. But even so, she didn't stop until she had walked straight into him and his body stopped her. She didn't say anything. Just looked at him – slow and close up. First at his wavy brown hair, the ends glinting copper and gold now from the fire; then at the skin on his face – brown and smooth; and then into those complicated coloured eyes fenced in by all those long, thick eyelashes. She leant in towards his neck and smelt him. Before pulling back to look at that lovely mouth of his with its chipped front tooth.

And before she knew what was happening she was kissing that mouth. And it was soft, and warm, and Jesse had his arms around her and was kissing her back like he thought this was something they should have done a long, long time ago. And Marjorie didn't want to stop. Because love had been standing there, waiting for Marjorie, for a very long time, there at Jimmy's place.

But Marjorie had no idea how strong that love was. It took her by surprise. It grabbed her and bowled her right over. Threw her down and left her there, gasping in the dirt.

Chapter 12

IT WAS GETTING so close to Christmas people were out everywhere scouring their favourite sandhill to bags a fine native
pine for a Christmas tree. It was a proper time for a nativity
set. 'Do you remember that plasticine nativity set I said Mum
was making?' asked Marjorie.

Jesse was sitting in the dirt, leaning back against their bench,
his knees comfortably bent. Marjorie was sitting in front, the
back of her head against his chest, her arms wrapped around
his knees. Jesse had one hand resting lightly on her head and
a smoke in the other one. They were sharing the same smoke
these days. The fire-poking stick was lying in the dirt in easy
reach as they sat there, staring at the fire.

'Yep,' he said. Blowing smoke at the peppercorn tree.

'Do you still want to see it?'

'Yeah!'

'Come over and take a look. Ruby's playing in the tennis
grand final next Saturday, and everyone's going to watch her.
I'll say I have too much study to do. I'll get away with that. It
isn't a lie. I just don't intend on doing it. I'll meet you here.'

'All that scheming – I'm impressed,' said Jesse. 'I won't have
to say anything at my place. And no one will ask anything either.
Your life is so much more complicated than mine – living in
a house with people who actually bother to think about you.'

'I'm sorry, Jesse.'

'Don't be. I wouldn't be here with you if it wasn't for them,' Jesse said, his breath as he spoke making soft, warm currents in the hair on top of Marjorie's head. 'I'll be here on Saturday – waiting for you.'

So that Saturday was different. This time they met in the middle of the day at Jimmy's place. And this time, for the first time, they walked off from Jimmy's place in the same direction.

Marjorie fell silent as they approached the house. Jesse was the first person she had ever been brave enough to invite there. It was a perilous thing to do. Even with love to support her. They could have gone through the back door. That would have been quicker. But Marjorie took Jesse around the boundary of the house yard fence so they would go in through the front door. If she was going to let him see her house, then she was going to let him *see* the house.

Jesse was silent too now. He could see the bare house yard with its inappropriate eight-foot-high wire-netting fence. He, too, felt the wind pushing the fence backwards and forwards at them. *Shove off!* it was saying as it strained to jostle them. But Marjorie kept walking until they were at the front gate and staring at the front verandah.

The gate squeaked and clattered and moved in the wind. A sudden gust came to its aid and it slammed shut in front of them. But Marjorie was used to this. She grabbed it and slammed it back open, throwing it hard against its hinges. And they walked the bare dirt paths to the beautiful gardens with the immaculate red-brick borders and the jaunty, perpetual plastic flowers. Marjorie flung out her arms. 'Elise's plastic garden. The one I told you about. It is, apparently, without end.'

Jesse said nothing. He crouched down and studied the

plastic flowers. 'Next?' he said, looking at the verandah boards and the sullen, shabby curtains.

It was a staccato of explanation from Marjorie as she marched into the house and down the hallway:

'Dad and Mum – sleep-out . . . Pa – bedroom . . . Spare bedroom – never used except to conceal clandestine artwork and to make paper dresses . . . Ruby and Marjorie – bedroom.' Thumbs jerking to the right and to the left.

Jesse stopped Marjorie at the girls' bedroom. 'Which is your bed?'

'That one,' said Marjorie, pointing to the messy one.

'So that's where you dream your dreams.'

'I try not to dream dreams here. They're usually bad if I do. Come on,' Marjorie said. 'We haven't finished the tour.' She headed for the lounge room. 'This is where Pa spends most of his time when he is not outside distributing poison and setting traps.'

'I like your Pa. He's not really the cantankerous old bastard he likes to think he is.'

Marjorie shrugged. 'I couldn't really see anything else when I was younger because of all that meanness hanging around him all the time. But he managed to get Ruby and me out of the house once when Mum was stark raving. And gave us his hairbrush. I will always like him for that. Anyway,' Marjorie said, entering the lounge room, 'this is where my mother plays the piano and sings.'

Jesse noticed the smells of things first. The smell of Bakelite tobacco pipes, and the smell of new tobacco. The smell of old dead ash on chimney hearths. And the scent of a piano.

The piano was an instrument of power in that room. It had Jesse transfixed, even though it had not uttered one sound.

He ran his fingers over the wood and sniffed at it. He sat on the piano stool, lifted the lid and touched the keys before turning to stare at the careful castle of pianola rolls guarding one end of the piano. And at the mountain of sheet music gathered way down the other end, propping each other up on the top of the piano – arias, sonatas, concertos. Jesse picked up a sheet and studied the pencil scribbles and notes and comments. 'Your mother has the most beautiful voice I have ever heard.'

Marjorie nodded.

'And she plays the piano like I have never heard,' Jesse said.

Marjorie nodded.

'And now I'll show you the nativity set,' she said, leading him to the kitchen. And the piano knew that even though it had the power to spellbind many, it had nothing to compare with the power of the plasticine.

Jesse walked through the kitchen door behind her and the first thing he saw – delicately balanced on one leg with three legs moving through the air in a frozen moment of running, its mane and tail blowing in a non-existent breeze – was a perfect tiny horse. It was dancing in the middle of a piece of old newspaper, in the middle of the kitchen table. Jesse walked around the table studying the tiny horse from all sides. He crouched down to table level and looked at the horse from that angle. He pulled up a chair and just sat in front of it and stared at it, his chin resting on his hands.

'There's more of them,' said Marjorie after a while.

'Where?'

'Everywhere.' said Marjorie.

And they were everywhere. As Elise completed a piece, she would position it according to some complex design known only to her. Some pieces were on the windowsill. Others were on the washing-up bench. A few were in the crockery cupboard. A collection of them were precariously balanced on the dado board at the top of the tongue-in-groove boards lining the kitchen. They were animals of Elise's deciding regarding the make-up of a nativity set. There were sheep, cattle, dogs, more horses, a pig, chooks, a cocky and a cat. There were men and a mother and a baby. There were kings and presents and camels.

Jesse studied them. Some he touched with just the tips of his fingers. 'How can she do that?' he asked. 'They're like tiny pieces of magic.'

Marjorie stared. First at Jesse, then around the room at the nativity pieces. She didn't see it that way. She saw delicate beauty and unmatched talent. But it was hard not to examine everything for the lurking, suspect gleam of madness. To peer furtively at her mother in case a tinge of glitter be found in the intense concentration. To stop herself from seeing an artful sprinkling of it in the allocation of space and position. She knew the nativity pieces were good. But she was scared of what Elise could do when glitter was around. So she answered Jesse as best she could. 'Dunno,' she said shrugging. 'Do you want a cup of coffee?'

He looked up. He had been so absorbed in the pieces. 'Yeah,' he said. 'I've always wanted to have a cup of Elise's coffee.'

So Marjorie poured coffee and they went to sit on the back porch.

They were sitting, lazy and comfortable, talking and drinking coffee and smoking, when the dogs started barking. Somehow, they had not noticed time leaking sneakily out behind them. And now they heard the car coming back. They should have heard it miles back but they were not paying attention. It was nearly at the house paddock gate. Marjorie rose up in a panic. 'They're home,' she said. 'Quick. What will we do?'

Jesse raced back into the kitchen. He called over his shoulder as he ran. 'First rule, Marjorie. Just act normal.' He scanned the room to see what was out of place. 'I'll fill the coffee pot and wash the cups. You get your schoolbag and stick your study stuff everywhere. Make a mess. You've been studying hard.'

Marjorie raced to get her schoolbag. 'Quick. Out the back. They'll come in the front,' she said as she threw books and pens on the table and scattered notepaper around. 'Get going.' She slid into a chair and buried her head in a textbook.

Jesse glided out the back door, melted through the back gate and merged with the waiting scrub. He was gone.

He took one of the plasticine horses with him. He couldn't resist all that beauty stuck with such thoughtless ease in an old chipped cup in the crockery cupboard. No one would notice one less perfect, tiny horse, he reasoned.

And he was right. No one noticed. Only Jesse. He noticed it every day.

*

Marjorie might have started looking at other people besides herself, but she was not very strong. She couldn't afford to just keep adding wheat bags of people to the pile on her shoulders. She was likely to collapse under all that weight. So when she put Jesse on, she dropped others off. She neglected to watch her mother and she forgot to look out for her sister. And then there was Christmas to think about as well. Everyone was bustling with Christmas. Womenfolk were cleaning the town hall for the Christmas concert. Menfolk were downing a giant Mallee pine for the hall Christmas tree. Some dad somewhere was practising in the Santa suit. Bill was servicing the kerosene refrigerator, and checking the Coolgardie safe to make sure they could cope with the extra Christmas load. Pa was out in the horse and cart, scanning the sandhills for their own Christmas tree.

Marjorie loved Christmas. Because Elise loved it. It was a good time. Elise and Marjorie and Ruby sat at the kitchen table on warm summer nights and made things. They were wishful and gentle as they talked of life for Ruby after the Leaving Certificate. As they swathed the kitchen and the lounge room with crepe paper chains. As they watched their mother finish off beautiful hand-drawn Christmas cards, as they wrote in them and readied them for posting. Last year's Christmas cards were transformed into Christmas tree decorations. The house smelt lovely – of pungent Mallee pine. And the only glitter to be seen anywhere was the properly placed glitter on the Christmas decorations.

But even with these happy times, Elise was eroding. Drifting away. Not even Christmas could stop it. She was like a sandhill battered ever so insistently and ever so slowly by a hot north wind, the hill diminishing as the stuff of the sandhill was dragged away by the wind. But the pull of the wind and the diminution of the sand was subtle and unremarkable. The sand drifted over the crest of the hill, gradually leaking away until the sandhill was not what it used to be. Until a whole lot of what it used to be was on the other side, blocking the road.

No two motives with Elise were ever the same. But there was a pattern. A gradual dissolution – triggered by something only known to Elise (but dust storms are like that); an unhurried, distracted walk to madness; a time of terror as madness pulled Elise through its door; and then the return.

This time Elise chose religion – which was convenient, because she could hide in her gradual, devout deterioration for a long time before anyone noticed. And she could contemplate at her leisure all those thoughts about her failure of sanctification.

Marjorie and Jesse continued in their pattern as well. They were a habit. They ran at night and in the dark and in a secret known only to the two of them. And in the dark at Jimmy Waghorn's place they shared their secrets. They loved each other.

Ruby went to live with Aunty Agnes after Christmas. And Jesse and Marjorie started their Leaving Certificates and took to sitting beside each other on the school bus. They didn't talk. They just sat. Marjorie with her head stuck in a book and Jesse sleeping. They didn't need to talk during the day and they didn't want to talk during the day. Talking was for the night and for Jimmy's place.

*

It was spring of that Leaving Certificate year. Everyone else was off at the local field day. And Marjorie organised another tour of the house. This time to see Elise's art folio. They drank Elise's coffee and smoked Bill's smokes. And Marjorie showed Jesse the treasure. A haphazard pile of forbidden bohemian talent shoved under the bed in the spare bedroom.

Jesse was awestruck at the richness of Elise's art. He sifted through them all – charcoal and pencil drawings, unfinished sketches, finished and unfinished oil paintings. Paintings of the Mallee. Drawings of Ruby and Marjorie. A sketch of Bill. One of Pa. 'Why doesn't she hang any of them up?'

Marjorie shrugged. 'We don't know. We've asked. But it's not worth it.'

Elise was not the same, though, when Jesse visited the second time. She was meditating on how to absolve herself of her terrible sins. There were signs, if anyone wanted to pay attention. But Marjorie was too busy with her study and her Jimmy Waghorn runs. And Ruby was too busy with her teachers' college and living at Aunty Agnes's. And Bill was too busy down the back paddock. And Pa was too busy with the rabbits.

Elise sang and played the piano. And it was particularly beautiful. It was all about religion. But much of the masters' works were based on religious themes. And, anyway, with a voice like that, who was going to tell Elise not to sing Rossini's 'Born but to Labour in Sorrow'; or 'Ave Maria'?

With all that busyness from everybody roundabout, Elise was left alone. She had the blessing of solitude to meditate uninterrupted – like a cloistered nun. This time she didn't need the medium of plastic flowers. She had undergone a transfiguration. Now she only needed to listen to the messages in her head. So Elise sat there, in her kitchen, and watched the fire in the kitchen stove. The coffee percolator popped and burbled. And the message murmured so kindly to Elise was comforting, because it was familiar.

What are you doing this time, Elise, so your sins can be absolved? What are you doing about your perilous lack of grace? What is your fitting and enduring penance so that you can be made good enough? For you are not hallowed.

The fire burnt bright. Until it was nearing Christmas again. School holidays were just a few weeks away, and Marjorie was looking forward to Ruby coming home; and to her and Jessie and long, lazy, summer nights at Jimmy's place. Then Marjorie came back one night from Jimmy's to find the kitchen light on. She stood in the dark and saw Elise moving about. It was a warm night but Marjorie shivered. She changed into her nightie and walked – slow and careful – into the kitchen.

'Hello, Marjorie dear,' said Elise, unperturbed by the sight of her daughter walking through the back door in the middle of the night. Elise was at the stove, shoving paper into the fire. She had piles of paper screwed up at her feet waiting their turn. The heat from the stove blasted Marjorie and she felt chilled to the bone.

'What are you doing?' she asked. 'It's way past midnight.'

'I'm just cleaning out the rubbish.'

Marjorie moved towards Elise to try to see what she was burning. 'What rubbish?'

'My old rubbish. Useless things.'

Marjorie couldn't think of anything to do but watch. So she sat and watched until the whole pile waiting at Elise's feet had disappeared into the stove. When the last piece of paper had gone Marjorie spoke. 'Come on, Mum. It's time we both went to bed.'

'Yes, dear,' Elise agreed cheerily. 'That's enough for one night.'

It took Marjorie a long time to get to sleep. She was scared again.

Marjorie didn't tell Bill. He was too busy with the harvest down in the back paddocks. She didn't tell Pa. He would have thought it was a good thing Elise was cleaning up. She didn't tell Ruby. She was not here anymore. Marjorie kept an eye on Elise. And told the only person she could tell.

'Mum was up when I got back last time. She was burning stuff.'

Jesse stopped poking the fire and watched Marjorie. 'Does that matter?' he asked.

'I don't know.'

'Have you noticed anything else?'

'No.'

'Maybe she was just cleaning up?'

'Maybe.'

They were right, of course. Elise was cleaning up. She was cleaning up her life. It was hard to get rid of such an accumulation of wickedness, but the fire offered constant encouragement. And Elise's smile changed. She didn't need the trappings of earthly glitter in her smile this time. Now she smiled the serene smile of the acolyte as she drifted down her chosen path.

'How is your mother?' asked Jesse the next time.

'Still burning stuff.'

'Anything else?'

'No. Apart from all the burning, everything else seems normal,' said Marjorie. 'For our house, anyway.'

'Why don't you tell your father?' suggested Jesse. 'Maybe he's noticed something too?'

Marjorie just looked at Jesse. And Jesse shrugged. They knew each of them had their jobs to do in their families. And they just had to get on and do them.

'Apparently God has no longer forsaken the Mallee,' announced Marjorie at the next meeting.

'What do you mean by that?'

'Mum always used to complain about the *godforsaken Mallee*,' said Marjorie. 'But God forsakes no longer. Mum's changing religions. She's going to become a Catholic.'

'Is that a problem?'

'I don't know. The Catholics are all over the moon. Pa is smug.' Marjorie stared at the fire. But the fire wasn't giving any help. That, apparently, was a special dispensation afforded only to Elise.

'She's spending all her time on religious stuff. But I suppose she has to.' Marjorie stared again at the non-responsive fire. 'It's probably nothing.'

Jesse didn't say anything, but he was not so sure.

*

A few nights later Marjorie started awake in the dark of the night. Woken by the train traversing the horizon and calling out to her – clickety-clack, better wake up, clickety-clack, better wake up. She stared into the dark and registered it was the second train. The one before dawn. And realised why the train had warned her. Elise was up and in the kitchen. Marjorie could hear her singing and moving about. There was a burning smell.

But Marjorie was wrong. Elise wasn't in the kitchen. And neither was the fire.

Marjorie wanted to call out to Ruby across the dark, like she always used to. But Ruby couldn't possibly have heard her from all those hundreds of miles away, tucked up nice and safe at Aunty Agnes's place.

Marjorie crept out of bed and followed the smell and the sound. A fire full of embers and sparks, crackling, and charred paper, and scorched Mallee trees. Panic lurched and swayed and leapt out of the shadows at her. She ran – all crooked-armed and wobbly-legged in her panic – down the hallway and out the back door.

The bonfire down by the tank stand was busy. The tank stand and the back gate and the Mallee crowding around in the dark were glowing from the reflected heat and the anticipation of participation. Elise was pulling pages from a notebook and throwing them onto the inferno. Each page was caught by the fire and consumed before the jubilant fire released it to the night. Glowing and flaming pages danced overhead, fluttering off into the Mallee in all directions. Elise was singing. She was bright with energy. Bright with burning.

'What are you doing with that fire?' Marjorie tried to run at her mother, but her legs couldn't do it. It was like a huge salt lake had shoved itself between her and her mother and she was spluttering – drowning in salt water. She flailed her arms.

Elise paused. She stared at Marjorie. 'Shut the door. You were not born in a tent.' She resumed her beautiful singing.

'What are you doing, Mum?' shouted Marjorie. 'This is not the kitchen. You're outside.'

Elise stopped – notebook in one hand and a torn and crumpled page poised for sacrifice in the other. 'Don't be ridiculous. Of course this is the kitchen. Ladies don't go out in the dark and light fires willy-nilly.'

'What is that? Give me that.' Marjorie, recognising the book, grabbed at Elise. It was Elise's sketchbook.

Marjorie was yelling now. 'They're your sketches. Stop it.' She lunged again and grabbed the book.

Elise rose up. 'How dare you? Give that book back.'

'Get away from me,' Marjorie shrieked as she ran for the other side of the fire.

But that wasn't going to stop Elise. She had eternal absolution to consider. Elise chased after Marjorie. 'You are not worthy. Give me the book,' she said, stumbling and swiping.

The fire took this opportunity to invite the tank stand to participate. So the tank stand quickly bent one knee at the devotion displayed by Elise. And just as quickly offered its remaining limbs to the holy conflagration. The scrub nearby was ecstatic with the blessing of the floating, flaming pages. It, too, joined the worship as its leaves crackled and burnt. And the sun decided to peer over the sandhill to see what the disturbance was all about.

Elise emerged through the smoke, purified and determined. She was calm. Smoke was drifting from her dress. 'You are not worthy, Marjorie,' she said. 'You are a bold, brazen little article. Give me the book.' She held out her hands.

'Wake up!' Marjorie screamed into the air and tears burst from her eyeballs. But the water was as useless as ever. She couldn't see where she was going because of the tears. She couldn't see where Elise was going because of the tears. And even though the tears were bursting from Marjorie's eyeballs like water spurting out from the top of a windmill tank when someone had carelessly forgotten to turn the windmill off, there was not near enough of them to put out the fire. 'Dad, Pa, where are you?' She was sobbing now – another useless activity. 'The tank stand's on fire. The trees are on fire. Mum's on fire. Please!' She ran from Elise and her holy inferno.

Time decided to leave Marjorie. She seemed to be running forever with smoke and burning trees and crippled tank stands running with her. With Elise somewhere in the fire-coated darkness demanding her book. But suddenly there was Bill with a bucket and he was throwing water over the holy fire and on the tank stand and sloshing it at the trees. Pa was there – still in his pyjamas. Not Ruby. She was safe with Aunty Agnes. 'Mum is burnt. Mum is burnt,' said Marjorie over and over. She clutched the remains of the sketchbook to her chest, sank down in the dirt and howled. Despite their inability to do anything useful, the tears would not stop breaking out of her eyeballs and spilling down her ashen cheeks.

Before proper time came back to Marjorie, Pa had put out the fires. And Elise was coaxed gently into the kitchen by Bill. Where the family then dealt with the burning disaster and the management of secret family business:

—The burnt tank stand was useless but the rainwater tank was alright: Bill's assessment.

—The fires were smouldering but no longer a threat; Pa would be on fire watch just in case: Pa's evaluation.

—Elise was burnt; someone would have to take Elise to the doctor: Bill's evaluation.

—Elise was raving mad; someone would have to take Elise to the doctor: Marjorie's evaluation.

—Who had let Elise get like this? Everyone's question.

—Why didn't someone stop her? Everyone's question.

—*Why didn't I stop her?* Marjorie's question.

Marjorie went with Bill. He was going to need help with Elise in the car. Sometimes Elise was quiet and contemplative – she sang and prayed out loud to saints across the centuries. Other times she tried to climb over the seat to flail and rail at Marjorie. 'You stole my Act of Contrition,' Elise wailed over and over, as the car trudged through the early-morning sandhills to the local doctor.

Marjorie sat, teeth clenched and face stony. She had nowhere to go. She was trapped in the car and she didn't even have a book she could run into.

'The burns are superficial. Nothing to worry about,' said the doctor. 'But I'm worried about her state of mind. I wouldn't say she is floridly psychotic. But she's close to it.'

'What does that mean?' demanded Marjorie, watching her mother's incessant pacing.

'Don't be rude, Marjorie,' said Bill.

'It means your mother's sanity is compromised.'

Elise took a print from the surgery wall and smashed it over Bill's head. 'Horrible thing,' she said. 'I can't abide bad art.'

'Can we give her some drugs?' asked Bill, holding Elise tight.

'I will give her an injection now to calm her down,' the doctor said. 'And a prescription for tablets to try to keep her calm. But you need to be prepared. We might be heading for another serious nervous breakdown.'

Bill blinked rapidly and his eyes got moist. Bill and the doctor talked and planned. Elise muttered and whispered. Marjorie sat and stared.

Everyone did what they could.

The doctor sent Elise home with veins full of drugs and hands full of tablets. To tide them over.

Bill tended Elise with the greatest of gentleness. While to Marjorie he cried: 'How did she get like this?'

I don't know! thought Marjorie.

'I asked you to look after your mother. Can you just do that one thing? Can you just tend to your mother?'

No, thought Marjorie. *I can't. I can't do it.*

Pa took to coming in the back door any old time of the day. 'Won't hurt if those flamin' rabbits are left for a bit,' he said. 'Might just sit here in the kitchen and read the *Sporting Globe*.'

'Flamin' hell,' said the cocky.

The doctor made enquiries – in case the compromised sanity wasn't reparable and a major nervous breakdown turned up.

Bill and Pa made preparations in the event of another drive to a mental hospital. Just in case.

The telephone exchange operator spent hours in a frenzy of porcelain plugs and snaking brown cords. Family roundabout were called. Locals were called. Family far away were called. Ruby had to come home to help with the watching.

Ruby and Marjorie watched their mother. And watched her. Elise humoured them. She put the tablets in her mouth with some rainwater to wash them down.

But Elise had her own ideas about what to do with tablets. It was hard work and had to be done carefully – so as not to scare and scatter. Much like yarding a couple of thousand head of sheep and separating the ewes from the wethers. Elise pursued the tablets relentlessly like a well-trained sheepdog. She rounded them up and separated them from the water and yarded them on their own under her tongue. Because Elise was not prepared to forgo her own spiritual commitments – not even for self-deposited, pre-paid, damn fool mental institution commitments. So when Ruby and Marjorie were not looking, Elise opened the yarding gate and popped the tablets into the waiting stove.

*

'One of our tank stands caught on fire a couple of weeks ago,' said Marjorie, jogging out of the Mallee night into the waiting campfire light.

'*Hello* would be an appropriate conversation starter – given the length of time since you were here last,' said Jesse. 'Where have you been anyway?'

Marjorie untied her jumper from around her waist and pulled it on. 'Home,' she said, glaring at Jesse.

Jesse studied her for a long moment. 'Tank stands generally don't volunteer to catch on fire.'

'Well, this one did.'

'Who set the tank stand on fire, Marjorie?'

'I bloody didn't.'

Then Marjorie was mortified to find words wouldn't come out of her mouth properly and she was shaking for no apparent reason. And Jesse was beside her, and was putting his arms around her, and was making her sit on Jimmy's bench. Jesse made tea. He rolled a couple of smokes. And the Mallee night listened once more while Jesse heard about burning sketches and burning scrub. And the invention of tablets to repair a possible major nervous breakdown which was apparently, at this stage, only a minor nervous breakdown.

'I can't stop her,' said Marjorie. 'I'm trying as hard as I can. Ruby's had to come home early to help. I can't fix it, Jesse. I can fix the ute. I can fix the tractor. I can even almost fix the sewing machine. But I can't fix this.'

Marjorie was speaking in a whisper now. The peppercorn tree swayed and rippled in the summer night-time air, its fronds straining and fluttering to hear. Jesse hardly spoke. Because there was nothing to speak about. Because he knew he couldn't fix it either. 'Come here,' was all he said. He pulled her tight against his chest. Marjorie buried herself there, safe inside the circle of his arms. Surrounded by the smell of him. Listening to the steady beat of his heart – solid and dependable like the train. And they just sat. There on the old blue bench – sitting until the train, ever faithful, reminded them it was time to go home.

*

'I won't be committing myself to a mental institution,' Elise said some days and many burnt tablets later. 'I don't have time for that. I am committing myself to the convent. I am going to become a nun.'

'Don't be ridiculous. You can't be a nun. Nuns are virgins.'

'Don't be impertinent, Marjorie. You are speaking sacrilege,' snapped Elise.

'Shut up, Marjorie. You'll only make it worse,' said Ruby. But it was too late. As if to demonstrate the sublime difference between impertinence and piety, Elise moved around the room collecting all the exquisite nativity statues. And started to kill them. All the while adorning the deaths with pronouncements. 'There is no place for guile in the sanctuary of a convent, Marjorie.' As sheep were crushed into lumpy humility. 'Fleshly self does not cohabit with piety, Ruby.' As royalty and their gifts were smashed into plasticine oblivion.

'Stop it! Stop it!' screamed Marjorie, while Ruby tried to salvage the tiny statues. But between the three of them, they succeeded in destroying every one. Most, Elise grabbed and pulverised, others Marjorie and Ruby killed – collateral damage – during the saving of them. And Elise was satisfied.

Bill and Pa came home to a lumpy indiscriminate plasticine graveyard tended by two frightened young women and a serene novitiate of the convent. Pa's mouth opened. It hung there before shutting again because nothing came out. His eyes opened wide before screwing themselves tight.

Bill's lips turned on the dead smoke clinging to his bottom lip. And chomped on it. Up and down. Up and down. Like his lips couldn't stop. 'I thought I told the two of you to look after your mother?'

'We couldn't stop her,' said Marjorie. And Ruby's stricken look agreed.

'How about a lie-down, love?' said Bill as he gently led Elise from the killings and the kitchen.

*

'I'll have to build bookshelves everywhere,' said Jesse.

'What?'

'Our house,' said Jesse, poking the fire.

'You're getting a new house?'

'No,' said Jesse, shaking his head at Marjorie. 'A house for you and me. Next year. When we leave here. It's going to need a lot of bookshelves to hold all our stuff. Especially all those books you are going to be making. They will be everywhere.'

Marjorie shook her head then.

'What? I can build bookshelves!'

But Marjorie was shaking her head to try to shake some things out. She was trying to make room because the bookshelf house was having difficulty fitting into her mind along with everything else that was in there now. But it just wouldn't fit, no matter how much her head shook. So she had to toss it out and leave her mind to be filled to the brim with Elise. And talk of nuns and convents. And scenes of tank stand fires and lumps of plasticine. 'We smashed the plasticine nativity set,' she said.

*

'Where will we live, do you reckon?' asked Jesse at the next visit.

But Elise was crammed tight into Marjorie's head now. She was crouching in every corner, taking up every available space. Before, there was no room for a house. Now there was hardly any room to fit Jesse in either – her head couldn't hear him. 'My mother told me my endless selfishness and pride might be redeemed if I look after other people and not just myself for once,' said Marjorie instead.

'Why aren't you taking your mother to the city?' said Jesse. 'She needs help.'

'How can I bloody take her?' Marjorie swung from the fire to shout into Jesse's face. 'What do you suggest I do, Jesse? Shove her into an empty wheat bag and throw her into the back of the ute?'

Jesse put his arms around Marjorie. He held her tight and stroked her hair. Once again, he listened for hours and hours. Marjorie talked, with the comfort of someone to listen to what she was saying. She had so much talking to do she didn't have time to do any listening herself. Because they both knew, despite all the consolation of words and campfires and old blue benches, there was nothing either of them could do about Elise.

Chapter 13

IT TAKES A deal of time and energy to round up a couple of thousand head of sheep and properly yard them all. And the hardest part is not getting that mob into the yards; it is drafting them – separating them once they are in the yard. Everyone knows that. But what people generally don't know is that it also takes quite a deal of time and energy to round up a few hundred tablets and properly yard them too. Elise was tried and Elise was tested. To see if her claims of piety and service were up to the mark. She had her cross to bear: daughters constantly at her side – watching and proffering and preventing; Pa turning up and sitting, fingers drumming on the kitchen table, eyes glaring at her; Bill tending and doting. But Elise was resolute. Because despite the cloying, ignorant love of her family she had a vocation. Elise smiled serenely. And Elise steadfastly, privately, fervently rounded up and burnt.

'Look after Elise,' Bill pleaded. Anxious to stay but that wheat needed harvesting and that dry paddock needed a man's desperate, lonely tears. 'Look after your mother, you two.'

But Marjorie didn't have the energy to look after her mother. She didn't have the talent. Marjorie and Ruby would take turns to sit at the table and watch their mother, day after day. Elise sat quietly near her fire and lulled them both into inattention.

After weeks of tablet fasting, a glittering, joyous evening arrived. It was Marjorie's turn to watch her mother and Elise chose a moment of inattention and darted for the kitchen door. Before Marjorie could understand that the moment of spiritual action had arrived, Elise was running down the hallway and into the spare bedroom. She snatched her art folio from under the bed and dashed back for the sanctification of the fire.

'Out of my way,' said Elise, shoving Marjorie aside as she raced to kneel before the blessed, expectant stove.

'Don't do it, Mum. Give it to me,' said Marjorie. She moved towards the fire and made a grab for the folio. But Elise was too quick. She pushed Marjorie with the strength of the zealot. Marjorie stumbled and fell. By the time she'd scrambled back to her feet, Elise had embarked on her holy mission.

The first into the fire was a lovely autumn landscape. Elise shoved the scenery through the firebox into the flames and the fire loved it. It roared through the chimney on the splendour of the canvas and the oil. Elise opened the top of the stove. She crushed a charcoal portrait of Bill and threw it in the top, and the stove ate it. Elise saw Marjorie start towards her again. 'You are a wicked girl,' she said. 'You are doing the work of the devil.'

'Please, Mum,' Marjorie begged.

But Elise was alive with glittery conviction. She rolled canvases and stuck them upright in the top of the stove – miniature chimneys atop the stove. And the chimney glowed in appreciation. Marjorie lumbered forward – a bull in a china shop. Marjorie reached again to wrench the folio from Elise. As she shouted to Ruby for help. As Ruby heard Marjorie's cries. As Ruby ran for the kitchen. As Ruby called for Pa while she ran. As Marjorie turned again to her mother.

239

By the time Ruby got to the kitchen, the fire was stretching out the top of the chimney, carrying Elise's offerings to the heavens. Marjorie was lumbering and charging. 'Stop!' she was shrieking at her mother. 'Ruby!' she was screaming at the door. But Elise had no care at all for Marjorie's screams and less care for Marjorie's clumsy lurching. Elise was batting her away with graceful, fervent ease.

'Mum!' Ruby cried in horror when she burst through the door. She ran towards the fire and the folio. Marjorie and Ruby both grabbed at Elise but she swayed away – serene and stalwart, folio held aloft like a liturgical candle. Marjorie and Ruby charged again, this time to grab the folio and haul it from Elise, as a delicate pen-and-ink sketch floated and burnt.

'*Et tu, Brute?*' Elise said to Ruby with infinite sadness. 'Are you also the work of the devil?' Elise knew that Marjorie was too late for salvation. She was proud and haughty and rebellious and refused to contemplate humility and righteous acts of contrition. She was hard and stony. But Ruby was different, virtuous. There was hope of redemption for Ruby. As Elise contemplated her, she was rewarded for her holy contemplation, and granted an epiphany. Ruby, in her virtue, deserved to participate in the revelation of Elise's glory.

So Elise, in an act of religious generosity, decided to share her chosen path with Ruby. She stepped aside and invited Ruby to participate. She made way so Ruby could run and fall. So Ruby could join her – sacrificial and redemptive, on the cleansing, burning stove.

Marjorie screamed a soundless, useless scream as her sister stumbled forwards on Elise's path of deliverance. Marjorie's hands scrabbled and clutched at Ruby as she went past, but her frantic grabbing had no chance against this invited salvation.

Marjorie was a sinner so what could she fathom of sublime purpose? Marjorie was not a penitent so how did she think she could thwart divine intercession? Her feet were glued to the lino and her legs had turned to jelly as Ruby staggered towards her sanctification. Marjorie was no match for such piety.

Ruby's eyes were wild, hands outstretched and waving towards the deliverance of the waiting stove. And Marjorie stared, aghast and incapable, as her beautiful sister fell and fell onto the red-hot surface – a cast-iron altar, burning in its desire. Her screams pierced the air. They were accompanied by a quiet contralto humming from Elise and Marjorie's whimpers. And the house shuddered.

There was no serenity this time when Bill and Pa rushed into the kitchen. There was sacred chaos. Ruby was screaming a soundless scream now – her mouth open but nothing coming out, as she waved and jerked her hands and arms in front of her. One side of her face was busy trying to shed all its ruined skin. And her hair was on fire. Marjorie was throwing water over Ruby. Elise, however, had made a commitment, and she was determined to honour it even amid the unholy chaos. She had returned to her task, and was savage now in her crushing and rolling and feeding. 'What have you done, Marjorie? What have you done?' shouted Bill. 'Why can't you ever do as you're told? You're bloody useless, you are, Marjorie. Bloody useless!'

'We've got to get Ruby to a doctor,' said Pa to the kitchen, helping Marjorie wrap damp tea towels over the butter they had slathered on Ruby. 'She's going into shock.'

Marjorie felt the kitchen pause and take stock so she did likewise. An ethereal quiet suffused Marjorie. A bubble of disconnected time enfolded her. So Marjorie sat inside that quiet and that time and listened to the muffled sounds of

241

the shouting and the screaming and the singing all around, noticing and assessing.

—Ruby was on fire. She was very badly burnt. The skin on her face, hands and arms was trying to escape her body. It was dangling and flapping like bark from a tree caught in the gust of a hot summer wind. Ruby stank. Because her hair was burning and her skin was flapping. That was what Marjorie concluded about Ruby.

—Dad was wet and watery. Dad had salt water diving out of his eyes. Marjorie had never seen Dad's eyes with salt water coming out of them. And yet here it was. That was what Marjorie noted about Bill.

—Pa was soothing. Pa was quietly organising everyone and was making soft decisions and was not substantiating his case with any invective at all. That was what Marjorie logged regarding Pa.

—And Elise. Marjorie felt her shoulders shrugging themselves. What was there to assess about her mother? Elise was being Elise.

But what about herself? Marjorie didn't need to note anything about herself because her mother had done that for her already. Elise smiled at Marjorie. And Marjorie could see as plain as day in that smile that Bill had been right all along. Marjorie was to blame.

And with the acceptance of her responsibility came a welcome and quiet peace. Not about the water coming from Bill's eyes – that was not normal and was very scary. Not about the absence of swearing coming from Pa's mouth – that also was not normal. Not about Elise – that was too typical for this family. So this only left Ruby. Marjorie raised her right arm and twirled, arm outstretched, until she faced the wreckage of her beautiful and brave sister. Marjorie studied her before turning her head to Bill. 'If Ruby was an animal we would get the gun and shoot her,' Marjorie said. Calmly – as a matter of fact and of human decency. 'Get the gun, Dad.'

Elise, transcendent, seemed not to hear. But Bill and Pa were staring at her and their mouths were open and nothing was coming out. Marjorie could see they had failed to grasp her meaning. 'Look at her,' Marjorie said. 'We should put her out of her misery.'

The ethereal quiet ricocheted around the kitchen. Spiralling into the eye of the storm. Elise smiled at Bill and dropped the remnants of the folio on the floor. Bill roared a wordless outrage and lunged at Marjorie. Pa roared an expletive-devoid warning at Bill and charged forward to slam the gate shut on Bill's advance on Marjorie.

'Leave the girl alone,' he said sharply to Bill. 'That's shock talking.

'You'll have to stay here, girl. That'd be best for all,' said Pa to Marjorie kindly.

Marjorie stood and watched and listened – remote and detached – as Pa ever so gently took Ruby and her spread butter and damp tea towels and herded Bill, Elise and Ruby down the hallway and out to the car.

Marjorie was still. She stood and listened for the slamming of the car doors and for the passage of the car down the home track. She stood. Until the sound of the car engine faded into nothing, and the house went back to its job of popping corrugated iron on the roof. She stood still and listened as a gust of wind came by to find out what was going on, and banged the flywire door at the back a couple of times in its passing.

Marjorie stayed at the house while Bill and Pa did what needed to be done for Ruby and for Elise. Because even with her being so bloody useless and so bloody liable, the rest of them couldn't do everything. Besides which, Marjorie now accepted she was truly responsible. And she had jobs to do. The first of which was having to get on the telephone and let the doctor know they were coming. 'If you could manage that without making a mess of it,' yelled Bill as he rushed out of the house.

Marjorie dialled for the exchange operator and asked to be connected to the doctor. She told the doctor to:

(a) expect Ruby who had somehow accidentally burnt off all the skin on her hands and face and arms and set her hair on fire on the kitchen stove; and

(b) expect Elise who might need to be reassessed regarding the efficacy of the magic tablets to ward off a further commitment to a mental hospital.

The conversation was later repeated of course, many times, by the exchange operator, who was listening in. As was her duty.

The Mallee was listening too. And it was thinking it was probably the last time it was going to hear Marjorie's voice.

Marjorie followed up that job with the job of cleaning up the kitchen. This job took a long time. She swept up all the remnant ash and scraps of burnt paper: innocent victims of Marjorie's blasphemous intervention. Without mercy, Marjorie threw the pile out the back door.

Marjorie restored the stove to its right and proper order and function. She put the fire plates back on the stove, emptied the ashtray and restocked the fire with proper fuel – appropriate, crumpled, pre-read newspapers, and clods of Mallee roots. She watched the fire until she was sure it was alive before closing down the dampers. It was a good fire. Maybe because of all her experience with fires lately.

It was the rest of the room's turn then. Marjorie collected and tidied the remains of Elise's folio and put it back under the bed. She collected Ruby's red hair – curled beautifully on one end and burnt beautifully on the other. She sniffed it. She smoothed it, and placed it on the kitchen table. There is nothing in the world like the smell of burnt hair.

Marjorie bent close and examined Ruby's skin – sloughed off like a snake discarding last year's out-of-fashion collection. She touched it gently, delicately – this fragile, lacy, stinking assemblage. Marjorie didn't know what to do with a person's burnt skin. Especially not her beautiful sister Ruby's skin. It didn't seem right to sweep it out the back door. So she picked it all up and placed it beside the hair on the table. Marjorie swept and washed the floor to remove any signs of burning.

It was the outside's turn now. Marjorie fed the chooks and collected the eggs; she fed the dogs and watered the vegies. She checked the sheds and sorted and tidied. Then she went back inside to her room. Marjorie packed clothes for Ruby. She packed clothes for Elise. Because the family was going to have to go to the city again. That was for sure. And then she packed things for herself.

After all the jobs were completed, Marjorie went back to the kitchen and sat quietly at the kitchen table. Alone with the house. Waiting. She sat for some time without moving – listening to the house creaking and popping as it acknowledged the night-time overtaking the day.

She stirred when the night-time shift started. She roused and looked around before lovingly collecting Ruby's hair from the table. She revisited the bedroom and Elise's folio – where she

245

took out an exquisite, tiny, pen-and-ink drawing. She placed the drawing and the hair inside the remains of the sketchbook. Then she went back to her bedroom and put the book, with all its precious contents, in with the clothes and other things she had already packed.

Marjorie walked into the kitchen one last time. She took tobacco and papers and matches, and odds and ends from the pantry cupboard. She reached up to the mantelpiece and took down the old tea caddy, and she stole Bill and Elise's money. *And now I am a thief as well*, Marjorie thought. *I really am responsible.*

The telephone rang sometime after that. It was the telephone exchange operator passing on a message: 'Ruby has been very badly burnt. She has to be driven in the ambulance to a hospital in the city. Bill is going in the ambulance with Ruby directly to the city. Pa will drive the car home. You are to wait there and look after the animals until the neighbours come over to give you a hand.' This was what the operator wanted to say.

'That would be because of stinking Ruby and her skin falling off. And because Elise – my mother – did, in fact, need to honour a commitment to that institution for the mentally insane. And if you want my tip, it is that my mother is most likely going to have to honour that commitment for the long haul,' is what Marjorie might have said to the operator if she had picked up the receiver.

The exchange operator rang and rang. Dreaming birds, perched on the wire of the party line, opened their eyes as their feet read the wire's urgent message. The house, smug in its accounting of the recent event, was quite happy to admit its urgent call.

The telephone tried its best – ringing and ringing into that quiet night. But the operator didn't get her opportunity to pass on the message to Marjorie. Marjorie had already packed her possessions into her schoolbag and shouldered it. She'd walked one last time through the kitchen and threw for one last time a collection of Mallee stumps in the fire. She'd slammed the kitchen door behind her. Marjorie didn't hear the telephone ringing. She was outside the house – running.

It was dark outside. There was no moon, just the blazing of millions of stars, as Marjorie ran down the home track, watched all the way by the scrub, which knew for certain now that Marjorie was good for nothing and responsible for everything. She ran with her usual lightness but with a greater decisiveness.

She did not run to Jimmy Waghorn's place. Although she should have. She did not bother to wonder if Jesse was already there, waiting for her. Although she should have. She did not bother to offer Jesse Mitchell the gift of an explanation of her decisions and her intentions, or the gift of a goodbye. Although any decent person would have.

Marjorie ran instead the length of the house paddock track. She paused to push through the gap between the wire gate and the fence post. She set off running again. She and the load on her shoulders ran the length of the farm track until she got to the bus stop and the train track. And there she rested and waited, opposite the railway crossing and in the gloom of a Mallee tree.

Marjorie and the scrub listened for the sounds of the first night train coming down the track. It took its time, as it always did, and gave plenty of warning, as it always did. Marjorie had been as quiet and still as the Mallee tree she was leaning against as she listened for the train whistle wailing across the Mallee distance, and the growing sounds of the train wheels. She waited until she heard it slowing for its approach to the crossing before turning to watch it arrive. The night wind, quiet until now, had been watching Marjorie all this time – furious at her. And the night wind was determined to let her know of its condemnation. So it gusted hard and slammed the guard's van door open.

But Marjorie wasn't intimidated by that. Not at all. The train slowed as it always did. Just in case. And whistled as it always did. Just in case. The wheat trucks lumbered past Marjorie as they always did and Marjorie acknowledged each one of them as they passed. Nodding and acknowledging until the guard's van arrived.

Marjorie threw her bag then, nonchalantly, into the passing guard's van. She took one quick look behind her at the darkened track to the farmhouse, then followed her bag into the van with an easy, graceful leap. Marjorie might have been incompetent with her mother but this running and leaping onto trains was something Marjorie executed with absolute competence. And the train, after all these night-time years, was at last rewarded for its endless nocturnal patience. And so was the Mallee.

Marjorie huddled in a dark corner of the guard's van. She didn't shut the door. She sat there staring out for hours, watching the glooming night-time Mallee staring right back at her. Countless bunches of silent cement wheat silos were passed. Countless lonely night-time roads were crossed. Marjorie felt the slowing of the wheels and listened to the warning whistle each time and waited for others to join her in the safety of the night train. But no one did.

Once or twice, Marjorie saw a car stopped at a crossing, paying homage to the train, waiting for it to pass. And she wondered if it might be Bill and Pa and Elise and Ruby. But Marjorie dismissed the thought. *Ruby won't be in the car*, she thought. *She's probably dead by now*. Mostly Marjorie just sat and stared and wondered about nothing at all. Because that was the only sensible thing to do.

And the train let her sit there and think about nothing at all because that train, as always, was kind and dependable. And it did the only thing it could do for her that night. It took her carefully through the rest of the night. Down the miles and hundreds of miles to the city.

Marjorie listened to the clickety-clack, clickety-clack and clickety-clack of the train. And she was soothed by the familiarity of the rhythm as it harmonised with her other comforting rhythm. Because inside her head Marjorie was running. Running away, running away and running away. Because isn't that what any sensible person would do? Isn't that what any normal person would do after what she had just done?

And all the while, throughout those night-time miles and hundreds of miles, that glooming Mallee watched, and judged, and was satisfied.

Marjorie's decision was a triumph, the Mallee decided. Someone was leaving. The Mallee delighted in its victory throughout each and every one of those hundreds of miles. And that watching and triumphant Mallee was as sure as any semi-desert environment can ever be that the leaver was never going to come back.

Chapter 14 .

BUT THE MALLEE was only half right on a number of fronts. Probably on account of being only a semi-desert.

So that Mallee might have given a knowing nod at the passing train with its crushed and crumpled cargo lurching and swaying, the eyes staring out into the dark from the guard's van. It might have stood back and folded its arms in the middle of that night-time gloom, in its relentless, eternal, implacable semi-desertness, and said, *Yep. Knew that was gunna happen. We could all see that coming a mile off.*

But all through those decades, in its unrelenting unthinking determination to overtake, that Mallee had made a mistake. It was blinded by the shimmer of its own fervour. It failed to see just how much of itself it had managed to insinuate into Marjorie. So it was wrong about Marjorie never going back. Because Marjorie never entirely left. A portion of that Mallee was going to be there with her wherever she went. Even if she didn't know it. Even if that Mallee couldn't see it for the glare. That Mallee had spread out under her skin in all directions just like one of those salt lakes creeping slow and sly and silent across the terrain. It had burrowed right in and now lurked below her surface just like those Mallee stumps resting quiet and watchful below the red sand in the paddocks. Just like the water, waiting brackish and stubborn beneath the clay pans.

And the Mallee forgot about salvage. It might have thought about the dirt and the scrub and the water and their collective drive to repossess. Their drive to get back what was taken. To fix what was discarded. But it forgot that a person – a person such as Elise, and even a person such as Marjorie – will also be dogged by what is so recklessly discarded. They too will be haunted by the need to collect all those broken, abandoned things lying around and stick them back together again. Somehow. As best they can. One day they will return to these things, and they will do whatever it takes to convert them into something handy, something useful. Because they will have remembered that you don't waste anything in the Mallee.

And it forgot, too, about the peculiar way of people from the Mallee to congregate in their groups: in the red dust and dirt out the front of the post office; at the supper table after the tennis grand final; leaning against the bonnets of cars; clumping at the bar of the pub; or collecting and huddling in the ladies' lounge. To crowd together, stubborn and steadfast, to barrack for that person who was doing their best to mend something. Because nobody should ever underestimate the abilities of fencing wire or baling twine. Or the capacity of a person to fix any amount of broken things with enough of either of them. Even if that person took a long time to do it. Even if they were not very good at it.

And it was also only half right on account of where was Marjorie going to go to anyway?

Marjorie went to Aunty Agnes. But it took her more than a week to get there. She had thoughts of having to fend for herself in the city. Down by the river. Trapping rabbits in the vacant lots and under abandoned warehouses. But Marjorie, just like the Mallee, didn't account for a person's need to salvage.

It didn't take too many days before she was overtaken – there by her campfire, staring at the river and smelling the sea, all by herself with her cooked rabbit and her billy tea. So, all she could do was pack her things back in her schoolbag and head for Aunty Agnes's place.

Agnes had been keeping a lookout ever since the telephone call. Pa had telephoned her about the accident. His voice snaking down through the miles. 'There's been a bastard of a turn up here, Agnes,' he bellowed down the line. 'Elise's had one of her nervy turns. A bad one. Bill's had to take her back to that lunatic asylum. She'll come good eventually. The doctors reckon it's going to take a hell of a long while this time, but what do they bloody know about anything? She'll come good. But Ruby got burnt on the stove.'

'What? How?'

'Elise was stark raving mad. The girls were there with her. They were trying to look after her. Crikey, we all were. But it was Elise and her mad bloody fit that did it.'

'How badly is she burnt?'

'She might die, Agnes. Skin hanging off everywhere. Half her hair burnt off her head. Her arms and legs, stomach – all a mess. The ambulance met us at the doctor's. We put butter on her – Marjorie and me – it's the best we could do. The poor kid trying to scream but nothing coming out. Marjorie all of a shake and starey-eyed.' Agnes's brother ran out of words. He took a deep, raggedy breath. That breath managed to suck in some more words but the new words weren't as stout as the earlier ones. They were thin, crusty words. 'I don't know if our best will be good enough, Agnes,' the new words croaked. 'I don't know. I reckon there's a good chance Ruby could be bloody dead by the time they get her to the city.'

Agnes listened to her brother. She stared at the Sacred Heart of Jesus standing in his alcove at the end of the hallway while her hand stuck to the receiver as if refusing to let go of it might save Ruby.

'Are you still there, Agnes?' Pa said.

'Yes,' she said.

'And Marjorie has taken off.'

'What?' said Agnes as the Sacred Heart gazed serenely at her.

'She's bloody gone. Shot through. I came back home here after the ambulance left the doctor's and she wasn't here. She was supposed to stay here and look after things until somebody got back, but the place was empty. And nobody has any flamin' idea where she's got to.' Her brother's voice was wobbling to a standstill now. It was tired from all those wire miles it was riding down. So very tired from having to say these things.

'Has she taken anything? Books? Clothes?' Agnes asked.

Agnes listened as her brother heaved a sigh large enough to shake all the waiting crows off the miles of listening telephone lines. 'How the bloody hell would I know, Agnes?' he said.

'Poor Bill. Poor Elise. Those poor girls,' she said.

'Yeah,' said Pa. Then: 'You haven't seen her, have ya?'

'No,' she said.

'It's a bloody mess I tell ya, Agnes. It's really bloody shook me up, all of this,' he said. His voice scraped and stopped. He tried again but his voice splintered. It had had enough and it gave up and left.

*

Marjorie and her backpack crept up to Aunty Agnes's kitchen window. The sun had dipped itself down behind the rooftops on the other side of the house – tucked itself in and pulled the covering of those tin roofs and tiled roofs over its head. So Marjorie knew she would be safe in the shadows on this side of the house. She could see Aunty Agnes there – sitting at her kitchen table – washed over gently with the glow from her kitchen light. Marjorie reached out and pressed her hands flat against the window and touched her forehead, then as much of her face as she could, to the glass. She blinked as the water crept around her eyeballs. Marjorie knew this glass, and she could tell that it knew her. It was as hard and as cold, as thin and brittle and transparent as herself. 'Aunty Agnes,' she whispered, as one hand curled and tapped on the window. As the other hand stayed splayed and pressed against the cold hard rigid surface. 'It's me.'

*

It was Marjorie's turn now to stare at the Sacred Heart of Jesus. She could see it through the door, reproving – staring at her as she soaked up those precious, undeserved Aunty Agnes hugs. Watching aggrieved as she wrapped both hands around a cup of hot, milky Aunty Agnes tea. Marjorie was sitting at the kitchen table with her back to the stove. She stared at his hand cupped under his Sacred Heart – there to catch the drops of blood perpetually falling. Falling now, no doubt forever, because of Marjorie and what she had done.

Aunty Agnes was in the hallway next to the Sacred Heart. She was on the telephone. Making a call that couldn't wait any longer than giving Marjorie a hug and getting her a hot cup of tea. She was standing with her back to Marjorie and talking as quietly as she could given the distance the words had to travel to be heard. It was Bill on the other end of the line this time. 'How is she?' he was asking.

Aunty Agnes shrugged. 'She's not on an even keel at all. But what would anybody expect, after all that's happened? And her thinking she had to run off and fend for herself like a swaggie down by the river all these past days?'

Marjorie could hear the soft murmurings. But she was tatty and shabby now so she had no strength left to try to understand what the words were saying.

'Could you see if you can get her to come to the phone, please, Aunty Agnes?' Bill asked. His voice snaking down through the hundreds of miles of brown cords with their efficient porcelain plugs. Travelling the lanes and multitude miles of telephony.

'It's your sister,' he said when Marjorie took the receiver. 'It's Ruby. She's gone.'

Marjorie moved from staring at the wall. She turned her head to stare down the hallway at the stained-glass window in the front door. She waited patiently while the words bashed themselves at her ear, trampling their way in.

'Are you there, Marjorie?' she heard her father ask.

'Gone where?' she said.

'Passed away,' said Bill. 'She's died.'

'Why?'

'Crikey, Marjorie,' Bill's voice splattered down the line. 'What sort of a question is that?'

Marjorie shrugged.

'Are you there, Marjorie?' her father asked.

Marjorie shrugged.

'The burns were too bad. We tried our best: you and Pa putting butter on – you remember? – and the damp tea towels. But it wasn't enough.'

Marjorie nodded at the wall.

'Are you still there?'

'Yes. I'm here. Where would I go?'

She heard her father sigh. And thought about how a sigh can sound when it is coming on brown cord from hundreds of miles away.

'You've missed the funeral. It was last Saturday week. Everybody was there. It was a really big turnout.'

'Did my mother go?'

Bill stopped short at the other end of the line. 'She's been admitted to the mental hospital again. Your mother is in a very bad way. Of course she didn't go!'

Marjorie nodded again.

'Marjorie?' Bill said.

'What?'

'Put Aunty Agnes on, will ya?' His voice was soft and slow like a gentle autumn rain. But Marjorie couldn't hear that. Perhaps it was too hard to hear that sort of thing after so many miles of telephone wire.

So Marjorie handed the receiver to Aunty Agnes and Aunty Agnes talked quiet, murmuring talk into the telephone again before hanging up the receiver and coming back to Marjorie in the kitchen.

Go on – I dare you. Marjorie glared at the Sacred Heart of Jesus. *Try and drop just one holy red drop on Aunty Agnes's carefully scrubbed lino. If you bleed even one tiny drop I swear I will blast your entire bloody colourful plaster body from here to kingdom come with every bit of water in my eyes.*

'Thought you would want to know all this, love,' Aunty Agnes was saying. 'It is best you hear it from us. We can go up on the train on the weekend. Bill can pick us up from the station. Take us out to the cemetery.' Aunty Agnes stopped until Marjorie looked up at her. 'None of this is your fault, dear. It's not anyone's fault,' she finished.

Which bit did you think I would want to know? Do you really think I want to know any of this? What good is knowing? she thought. 'She's better off dead,' Marjorie said, nodding at the Sacred Heart of Jesus. Nodding at its accusations.

'You can stay here as long as you like, dear,' was Aunty Agnes's reply to that. And her voice was like her nephew's. A kindly, soft breath coming out of her throat.

*

Aunty Agnes looked after Marjorie back there in the Mallee. She had Marjorie hidden behind the veil of a short-brimmed, black straw hat with spotted netting. She barricaded her behind a black long-sleeved dress, and black gloves Marjorie never took off. While Marjorie stood there in the naked sun of that cemetery. As Marjorie thought about the funeral this Mallee had, a short while back, produced for her sister. With its dust and its candles in that timid little wooden church, with Ruby lying stranded out near the altar – trapped in her coffin, in front of everyone. With Bill and Pa and Aunty Agnes sitting in the first pew, staring at Ruby's new home. *Although*, thought Marjorie, *Ruby would not have been stuck in front of everyone. Because not everyone was there. Mother and I were noticeably absent.*

'We put on one of our best for Ruby. No doubt about that. It was one of our best. A one-hundred-to-one perfect Mallee summer's day,' said a kindly Pa, nodding. And Marjorie was grateful. She knew what that day would be: with its strings of lacy thin clouds trailing high in the immaculate sky, its bleaching sun, its satisfied stubble with its collection of fat bags of wheat. So the sun and the sky and the stubble soothed her a bit. Because she also knew there would have been all the crying women with their bunched hankies; the staunch men with their lifted chins. All of their glancing-away eyes with their discomfited uncertainties. There would have been the cups of tea. The plates.

'It's good to see you, Marjorie,' the platform standers had said when she got off the train that morning. 'How are you doing, love?' they asked.

Why is that? Marjorie wondered. *Why is it good to see me?* And she thrust her gloved hand at them to parry away the hugs before any of them could get near her.

Jesse wasn't waiting on the platform. He waited at the cemetery. He didn't come over while the depleted, bereft little family walked to the hump of red sand and limestone pebbles piled fresh in the Catholic section. Their covering offerings of roses and daisies and geraniums as burnt and dripping and dead as Ruby by now.

What do you say to a sister you have killed? thought Marjorie as she stared at the hump of dirt that had now come to be her sister. *I didn't mean to. I didn't ever mean to do any of it, Ruby,* she cried inside herself. That was the most she could say.

They were all lined up neatly there at the grave and, like anybody does, they stood and stared silently down at the dirt lump. Pa was standing on one side of Marjorie. Aunty Agnes and Bill on the other side.

Pa cleared his throat. 'I'd best be heading back to the car for a sit-down,' he said. But Pa had something else to say before he left the line of graveside starers. 'I'll be helping you with the dishes tonight, Agnes,' he announced as he lifted his gaze to stare into the middle distance in front of him.

Agnes yanked her head around to look at her brother.

'I can dry a dish if I want to, Agnes,' Pa said to the air directly ahead. 'Marjorie's had too much on her plate lately. It won't hurt for all of us to step in and give the girl a bit of a rest.'

Aunty Agnes nodded and the corners of her mouth moved a tiny bit as she watched her brother walk back to the waiting car.

'Looking back on it, I don't recollect giving you much of a hand about the place. But I didn't see all this coming,' said Bill. He was staring straight ahead, like a soldier on parade. Marjorie stood still and silent like she was one too. Then she raised her head to the bright, clear blue sky. To tip the lurking tears back into her eyes. *What am I ever to do in the rest of this world now?* she thought. *Here without Ruby? Here in this world without Ruby?* As her eyes drifted over the installation of the dead – dead body, dead flowers, dead pile of dead dirt.

'Pa's right. It was too much for your shoulders, Marjorie,' said Bill. 'Nobody is holding you responsible. You did the best you could, girl.'

Marjorie didn't say anything. Aunty Agnes was busy with her hanky.

So Bill went on: 'But there are some things in life that are more than anybody's best. No matter how hard a person might try, some things in life are going to find a way to get the better of us.' And it was his turn to stare at the sky. His hand went out – sideways – as he stared, as his chin wobbled. That sideways hand, all through the staring and the wobbling, gave his daughter a pat on the shoulder. Not too much, mind. Just enough. Then Bill and Agnes walked together back to Pa, waiting in the car.

Jesse stayed under a peppercorn tree. He circled them from there. Circling around that small mob of them, never taking his eyes off Marjorie – like a kelpie watching the leader of the mob. He only stepped out from his patch of shade when he could see that Marjorie was about to go.

'I'm sorry about Ruby, Marjorie,' he said.

Marjorie's eyes blinked at him.

'Everybody is,' he added, watching her blinking eyes.

Marjorie's eyes switched to blinking at the peppercorn tree. She watched as it sighed and whispered its support for Jesse. Her eyes moved then as Marjorie stood there out in the open in the middle of this fenced-in, boxed-in, cemented-in patch of ground with its collection of bones and other people's memories. Those eyes looked up at this boy – a seeming stranger to her now; a boy that Marjorie had not so long ago believed she had known oh so very well, and loved oh so very well.

'When are you coming home, Marjorie?' this stranger asked.

Home? Marjorie wondered. *Home?* She shook her head. 'I am thinking about staying with Aunty Agnes for a while,' she said. 'I don't think I will be able to live here any longer.'

'What about us, though?' Jesse asked. 'What about me?'

'I am not so sure there is any *us* these days, Jesse. I don't see how there can be any *us* anymore,' she said, shaking her head. 'There is no time left in my life now for *us*. Not after what happened here.' Marjorie looked around like perhaps she might find some loose time she could use – maybe lying discarded among the stones and dirt here in the cemetery. But there was none that she could see. 'There was never going to be any room for *us* after that night,' Marjorie said, swinging back to face Jesse.

Jesse stepped towards her. 'You can't just decide that on your own, you know,' he said.

Marjorie put up her hands – palms pressed to the warm dry

air in front of her – ready to stop Jesse. Ready to push Jesse, if she had to, into the red dry dirt beneath them. 'Don't, Jesse,' she said.

*

'It is for the best. You know that. You need to get away from here for a while. Agnes will look after you. I've already talked to her about it. You can get a job in a factory like Bill did. Work in the city until all this has blown over,' said a kindly Pa.

'Yes. A fresh start away from all of this is the best thing. Give yourself a chance to get back on your feet. To get on with things,' agreed Bill.

'You're no use to anyone moping about here, girl. Least of all yourself,' said Pa. 'You take my advice and get yourself back to that city with Agnes. It'll only need to be for a while. You'll be home directly, when you've got back on an even keel,' said Pa and his voice was tender again. But these sorts of words had overexerted Pa. He tried to keep the rest of his words in but he was too tired now and they managed to escape. They were still words kindly meant and softly said: 'What the blue blazes do you think you could have done anyway to stop any of that flamin' bloody bastard of a mess from happening?' those words said.

'Watch that bad language,' Aunty Agnes said.

But Pa ignored his sister. He had some important facts to point out. 'Your mother was a raving bloody lunatic,' he said. 'No point denying it,' he said.

'That's enough of that talk. What good is that sort of talk now?' said Bill.

'Yes. So stop it right now, the both of you,' said Aunty Agnes.

Pa ignored them. 'What's done is done and there is no

flamin' point going over and over what happened. So best to just get on with things. And don't you listen to what anybody hereabouts is flamin' well saying, girl,' he said.

But I want to listen. I need to know what they are all saying, thought Marjorie. *I need to know what is my right and proper punishment for all of this bloody bastard of a mess.*

*

Marjorie stayed there for days with her father and Pa and Aunty Agnes – in that house – eating and roaming and sleeping once more in that house she had thought, not all that long ago, she would never see again. Tossing around, restless and staring-eyed in that house. Sleeping once more in that bedroom with its cold, accusing, vacant other bed. Until Marjorie finally answered them. 'I think I will go back to the city with Aunty Agnes like you said. For a while. Like you said. I can't stay here.' She nodded at each of them.

Marjorie was nodding because she had now come to accept things as they were here. She knew now that even though it had only been a few small weeks – which isn't much time in the life of a house – that this house would always be just the same as it ever was. And it had no damn right to be just the same as it ever was. It should have been so different. It should at least have had the decency to express in some way what had been happening there. What had happened there. It should at least have had the decency to admit to Marjorie, in the still small hours as the three o'clock train wailed across the horizon, at least some culpability. Instead of leaving all the blame to Marjorie. Instead of just standing there supercilious and silent.

So Marjorie found herself once more on that bright crushed-quartz railway platform. Standing there with Aunty

Agnes. Standing there with her father and his shivering chin in the warm air, his eyes blinking and blinking under the shaded brim of his hat, the sideways arm around her shoulders. Standing there with Pa and his jammed-on stiff upper lip. She gave them both a kiss on the cheek: one cheek full of furrows and white stubble; one smooth and full of tremors. She turned then and climbed into the carriage to sit beside Aunty Agnes and look at the two of them out of the train window. The men waved. Two farmers lifting their chins and squaring their shoulders in the face of yet one more catastrophe as the train started pulling Marjorie out of the station and into the trip back to the city to live with Aunty Agnes. For a while.

Take Care With Nervous Breakdown Cases

DEAR MIRANDA.-. There is one section of the community to which I would like to draw attention. They are the nervous type of people, people who have had a nervous breakdown . . . Other people never realise what a tremendous strain it is for them to make the effort to do the slightest thing.

Many times the fight back to health seemed hopeless but time has been on my side. But I do wish I could appeal to people not to be unkind to nervous children. Children who are afraid of various things will not be cured by a spanking. Parents are only sowing the seed of future trouble both for themselves and the child.

In my own case I was thought queer because I excelled at history, geography and art at school and could make no headway in handicrafts, knitting or sewing. Since I left school I have been regarded askance because I enjoy opera and not jazz, because I would rather read than play tennis.

Of course, everyone is not like this. Most of the people in the Mallee are good neighbours and always ready to lend a helping hand at time of trouble.

'MALLEE TREES'

The Weekly Times

Chapter 15

MARJORIE TOOK GREAT pains with Aunty Agnes's city. She didn't at the beginning. Not when she first turned up there – all by herself and saddled with everything. Marjorie already had too much of her own pain then, lumped on her shoulders like a whole mountain of wheat bags. She couldn't take on any more of anyone else's – even a city's. Marjorie's wheat bags were so heavy then that she had no chance of lifting her head high enough to get a good look at anything else that might be going on around her. She certainly didn't have any chance of really looking this city in the eye, to see it for what it really was.

And even if she had, she might have back then only seen it as so many others chose to see it. To see it as a taut place, a frantic selfish place crammed full of to-and-fro and noise. But that was only on the outside of itself. And if those who were so pitiless as far as the city was concerned would just bother to stop for a while and think, then they would realise things. Like: the Mallee wasn't on its own with a three-o'clock-in-the-morning soul. Like: this city wasn't without a heart. It had its own particular soft, three-o'clock-in-the-morning echoes when it quieted itself to a lyric drone and turned then to looking at things – things like Marjorie. When it nodded and hummed to itself because it could see what would be good for her. She was naked, it could see. And that was no way to live.

Marjorie was just like so many others who had already done what she had done – run away from their certain somewhere to here. Arriving in fright, without any decent covering to protect themselves. It was time that Marjorie needed more than anything, as far as this city could establish. Time to fix things after all that naked running. That, and the same thing that all those others were after. All those runners just like her who had arrived here to hide within the camouflage of its bustle. It knew that all they ever wanted was a decent chance to be somewhere else – somewhere other than where they had come from. And a good city always had plenty of both of those things: time, and somewhere else.

And it had Aunty Agnes to help – her there doing the sagacious watching:

'How is Bill going?' That was the first question she would ask her brother down the telephone line.

'What's a bloke to do? He's keeping a stiff upper lip. He'll get through in time,' said Pa.

'He might need more than a stiff upper lip to get through this one, I think,' she said.

'Eh? What's that you say?' said Pa.

Aunty Agnes shook her head at the Bakelite telephone on the wall. 'You know there are better ways of dealing with things than just ploughing paddicks and going out and killing more rabbits,' she said.

But Pa was so tired. And there were no women anywhere in the house no matter how hard he tried not to look for them. And he and his son were rattling and bumping around that lonely, empty house like the last grains of broken wheat in the chook bin. And he actually didn't know of any better methods for dealing with the sorrows of life than a good rabbit poisoning could provide, so he said nothing at all down the telephone line to that.

'I'm worried about Marjorie,' Aunty Agnes said into the silence.

'Why? She's doing alright there with you, isn't she? She's not the one stark raving mad and locked up in a bloody lunatic asylum,' her brother pointed out. 'She's not lying dead and buried. She's young. She'll be right.'

'She won't talk about it.'

''Course she won't. She's got a good head on her shoulders, that one. What's the good of yapping about a thing all day long? You think me and Bill sit around here all day long talking about it? What's the bloody good to be got from that?'

'A lot more good than two grown men pretending all day and all night.'

'What?' said Pa.

'Marjorie just stays in bed all day. Won't come out of her room,' Agnes said.

Notions of gardens and bees stirred in Pa. 'Eh?' he asked, and he was crumpling and slumping even as he did. Because try as he might to consider 1080 the best answer to life's unanswerable troubles, he did know what his sister was getting at. And he did know too that his son – out there every day from dawn to dark, furrowing up every paddock from here to kingdom come – he knew Bill already had far too much on his plate for one man to manage and the shotgun always ready and willing and capable there in the shed. 'Well, what are you letting her do that for? Go in and get her out of there, Agnes. By the cripes, do you want her to end up like her mother lying about in bed all day? And Bill having two raving bloody lunatics on his hands along with an already dead daughter?'

'She's suffering. She's like those soldiers you hear about that come back from the war all staring and not making any sound.'

'Suffering? Of course she's bloody suffering after what she's been through! But what about her father? Does she think he's not suffering? Put her on the telephone. Let me have a talk to her. I'll flamin' fix things.'

'And just how do you plan on fixing her? With dead rabbits? Or by ploughing a paddick?'

Pa was quiet down the line again. He was punctured and squashed by his sister's infernal questions; bewildered by lives that couldn't be fixed by farming. 'Does she ask after me, Agnes?' he whispered into his silence.

'She doesn't ask after anyone.'

'Go and get her please, Agnes. The girl can't stay lying about in the bedroom all day and not talking to anyone. Tell her I want to talk to her, please.'

So Aunty Agnes did as she was told and went to tell Marjorie that Pa was on the telephone and wanted to talk to her. And Aunty Agnes was shocked, because Marjorie did come to the phone.

'It's Pa here,' said Pa.

'Mmm,' Marjorie replied.

'How's the city treating ya, then?' Pa asked.

Marjorie shrugged.

'Starting to get on top of things then, are ya? Starting to settle in?'

Marjorie shrugged down the phone.

'You can come back up here, girl. I could do with a bit of a hand with the rabbits. Your father and I are rattling around in the place now. It needs a bit of a woman's touch.' Pa tried to fight it, but it was pleading that escaped from his mouth and raced down the telephone line, because what he really wanted to tell Marjorie was *I miss you. I miss both you girls. I am afraid for you and your father.* But that is not what a man says.

How can I go back there? Why would I go back there? she wondered. The girl sighed.

'Put yer Aunty Agnes on, will ya?' said Pa as his nerves undid themselves.

'The girl's in a bad way, Agnes,' he told her.

'Really!' said Agnes.

Vexation doesn't travel well over telephone lines though, it seems. And neither, it appears, does irony. So both must have leaked out by the time her voice got to her brother. 'Get her a job. Get her out doing a decent day's work,' he said. 'That'll usually fix things. The girl needs to start looking at what's in front of her. There isn't anybody that can do anything about what's in the past,' said Pa.

Pa was blundering. But he was right, so Aunty Agnes did. She did for Marjorie what she had done for Bill all those years ago. 'You can't be lying about the house all day, you know. You will never be able to pull yourself together that way,' was her softly delivered advice to Marjorie the next morning as she placed the newspaper gently, firmly, on Marjorie's pillow. 'We need to take your mind off brooding about things that can't be changed. Decent, hard work is the best medicine for most things in life. That, and a good couple of decades of the rosary,' she added as a seeming afterthought.

Marjorie's eyes followed Aunty Agnes. *What about in death, Aunty Agnes? Is decent hard work the best medicine for most things in death, too?* Marjorie said silently to her bedroom walls.

But Aunty Agnes had made up her mind now, and she had Pa on her side, so no amount of silence and dry dull eyes was going to change her mind. 'Come on, Marjorie. You need a respectable outfit to wear to job interviews,' she said. 'We will go to the department stores in the city. We need a decent pair of shoes and stockings. And we are going to the haberdasher's. And you are going to start looking in the Situations Vacant and start applying for jobs.' Aunty Agnes stopped and turned to examine Marjorie's hair messing itself all over her pillow. 'Did Elise ever attempt millinery?'

Marjorie spoke then. She said the first decent words to Aunty Agnes that she had said to anyone in a very long time. 'Millinery?' she whispered.

'Hats. Doesn't matter. I know how,' said Aunty Agnes, blinking and blinking at the whispered word.

*

'You look very smart,' he said from behind the carved oak desk. His head tilted at her. The gold-plated Schaeffer fountain pen reclining in its silver-plated desk set glinted at them. He reached for it and his right thumb rubbed it as he stared at Marjorie.

'You do indeed,' said the woman at his side. She smiled. 'Marjorie, isn't it?' she asked, glancing at the pile of job applications in front of her.

Marjorie nodded. She sat up straight. Hooked one ankle discreetly behind the other. Clasped her hands over the lines of the box pleats in the skirt. She imagined her father standing in that long line of hatless men out under the sun in that factory yard.

'It looks like a Chanel,' the woman had said when she directed Marjorie into the office. Her raised right eyebrow questioning the decency of a young girl wasting money on a store-bought Chanel suit. And if she could afford a store-bought Chanel suit, then why did she need this job?

Marjorie thought of Aunty Agnes's Singer sewing machine. It would be luminous by now, she knew. And redolent of metal and wood and Singer sewing machine oil. She could see the gentle afternoon sun creeping through the lemon tree in the front yard before it melted through the lace curtains in Aunty Agnes's front room. Before it laid itself softly all over the surface of that Singer sewing machine. It was not her mother's sewing machine. It was Aunty Agnes's. Marjorie smiled a bland smile – it was the only smile she had these days, but it seemed to suit everyone – and tried to tell herself that the palms of her hands were not sweating away underneath their protective finger clasp.

He had stopped playing with his pen now. 'So why should we give you this job, Marjorie?' he asked.

I really have no idea why. Because Ruby isn't here anymore? Or perhaps because my mother is here still. She is apparently busy fulfilling a long-term commitment at a mental hospital here somewhere. Is that a good reason for wanting this job? 'Because I have always loved books,' Marjorie said. She smiled. Her hand went to her throat and she clasped, as a comfort, the pearls that Aunty Agnes had given her. ('You have them, love,' Aunty Agnes had said. 'I want you to have them.')

'Ah!' he said. 'That is very commendable in a young lady. A love of good literature will carry you safely through life. But,' he said, 'there is much more to working here than liking books. We need someone with an enthusiasm for the enormous importance of all that this institution – its processes and procedures – stands for.' He leant forward, peering at Marjorie to see if she was fully appreciating the responsibility of the position. 'That is what I need,' he finished.

The woman nodded.

I need a sister. I need a mother. I need a job, apparently. That is what Aunty Agnes thinks will do the trick. That is what I need. 'I think books are important for a progressive society,' Marjorie said. *But books, it turns out, are not always as safe as you might think. So I will watch them very carefully for you in here from now on*, she could have added.

He looked at her legs. And at her high heels. 'There will be quite a lot of running around,' he said.

Marjorie smiled again. *I am good at running*, she thought. She nodded.

'Can you start immediately?'

'Yes,' she said and nodded again.

'How old are you, Marjorie? Do you have a driver's licence?'

'I can drive,' Marjorie said.

'Wait outside, thank you,' he said.

So Marjorie bent to pick up her handbag and gloves, then stood and walked from the room. Her high heels clicked across the tessellated tiles.

The chief librarian resumed rubbing his fountain pen as his eyes watched her legs – no doubt checking, as any boss had the right to do, that the seams of her stockings were straight.

Marjorie got that job. Aunty Agnes's job-getting magic had worked once more. And both Marjorie and Aunty Agnes always thought it was on account of the neat little hat perched on the top of her shiny dark hair. Because Marjorie didn't wear a tie, like her father had done so many years before when he got his job. But she did wear a hat. Just like her father had done.

*

The woman's name was Patricia (not Patsy!). 'Follow me,' she had said as she clipped off down the corridor. 'You are to start at the bottom. You will be trained on ephemera. Do you know what that means?'

'No.'

'Ah!' said Patricia. And she stopped momentarily to look at Marjorie with a slight, superior shake of the head. 'It is to do with all that does not last: newspapers, magazines, journals and the like. But I imagine you are too young to fully consider the enormity of all in this world that does not last.' Patricia glanced at Marjorie.

Marjorie smiled back. *You are so very wrong about that*, Marjorie thought, smiling pleasantly.

'You will begin with newspaper clippings. You will assist our patrons with their ephemera requests. You will then progress to magazines and journals, if you prove yourself. After that . . .' Patricia shrugged. 'We'll see,' she said.

She handed Marjorie a pile of newspaper clippings. It was a collection of articles about last year's Melbourne Olympic games. *Ruby loved the Melbourne Olympics*, she thought. On the top of the pile was a photograph of a young woman, her legs and her heart pounding their way to the fulfilment of glory. It was Elizabeth Alyse 'Betty' Cuthbert. Australia's golden girl running into Olympic and Australian history. It was a big year for running that year, thought Marjorie. 'Do you think she is running to or running from?' she asked as they both gazed at the photo.

'She's running to the finish line. For a gold medal,' Patricia said. 'She's just running.'

'No one just runs,' said Marjorie.

*

Marjorie surprised herself. She really liked her job. She wasn't making books on a printing press like she always imagined but she *was* surrounded by them. And that was something. She found too that she could hide away from everybody for hours within all that paper. For days and days and weeks and weeks. And she didn't have to talk hardly at all. And when she did it had to be hushed, slow, weighty talk. Which suited her just fine. Because paper is heavy. Even newspaper and magazine paper, if it is piled high enough, can be very heavy. And ephemera is so much more substantial than anybody ever realised. Except Marjorie. She soon realised. She fitted right in with this job because she appreciated the dead weight of impermanent things. So, Marjorie worked away – caring for fleeting, fragile, dead weight ephemera. There in the city.

And the city whispered into the air all around Marjorie as she watched it out of her tram window; out of her library window; out of Aunty Agnes's lounge room window. It brushed against this girl as she walked all alone through the midday lunchtime crowded pavements, or through the after dinner, early night, silent suburban streets. It sighed as Marjorie sighed. It spoke so kindly to her about such things as burnt, dead sisters, or mothers who preferred the sweet treasures of madness to her daughters, or a boy who would now be stranded and bereaved, slowly dying of thirst as he wrote yet another letter that would be crushed unread into a handbag before being taken out and smoothed down and laid against a cheek and breathed slowly in – then jammed neatly, unread, with all the rest of them in the bottom of an old brown suitcase at the bottom of Aunty Agnes's old brown wardrobe, as the boy clung by himself in the star-littered dark to a relic of an old blue bench. But even though it talked so softly, this city could see how hard it was for

Marjorie to listen, this city could see that such things as it had to whisper were hard to hear. And even though that was not what this city had in mind, this is what Marjorie did. She grafted bits of this place on. She mortared and stacked. Carefully plastering layers of it all over the place. Until she was encrusted. Until she was a slight, delicate, pretty, distraught thing – a piece of battered reef – a coral skeleton that had caked and iced its ethereal beauty all over those wheat bags. Until Marjorie's burden of wheat bags was practically invisible, non-existent to anybody who didn't know what was going on. Until the average Joe Blow could have been mistaken for thinking Marjorie had forgotten all about the Mallee and what could go on there.

A proper graft needs careful attention, though. It needs to be done precisely. It needs to be watched for a long time. There is no place for sloppy, slapdash grafters on a farm. Grafts will turn on those sorts of grafters. They will protest and wither and die and drop off – just to prove a point. And encrusting and encasing someone is no different. So it took Marjorie more than a year to do all that grafting.

But time taken doesn't bother a city. What are years to a city? And what Marjorie didn't realise was this city knew more about grafting than she did. It knew that grafting is a charity. It knew that a grafted thing is a healing thing – a graft lets things grow again. So the city helped Marjorie. For months and months. Streets and laneways, patient and gentle, whispered to her.

'I found another art gallery hidden down a back street in the city today,' Marjorie might say as she flung patent leather shoes and handbags at her bedroom door.

'Did you, dear? You mother always loved the art,' Aunty Agnes might reply – dauntless in the face of Marjorie's anticipated hostility.

'More books?' Aunty Agnes might ask, indicating the ever-increasing pile wobbling away in Marjorie's bedroom.

'Don't say anything about anybody!' Marjorie might warn.

'Look at all that rain – look at all that grass,' Marjorie might comment as she watched the men in Aunty Agnes's street cossetting their particular bit of nature strip with its perfect push-mower surface.

And Aunty Agnes watched as Marjorie's patent leather high-heeled shoes transported her anywhere she wanted to go in this city. As the city paraded its footy grand finals and its spring racing carnivals and headed for the magic of Myer Christmas window displays. As all those soft summer days courteously gave way to cool summer nights. Not like the Mallee, where the summer night leered and jeered at you from outside your totally ineffective bedroom window and blasted you with its dark, eighty-degree midnight heat. Yes, this city knew what Marjorie needed. And Aunty Agnes did her best to see that this job and this city were as mild and as kind to Marjorie over the next few years as they could be, given what she had done.

But it wasn't all like that. There was that particular bit of the city that dragged at Marjorie at the mental hospital. Try as she might, Aunty Agnes couldn't do anything about that. That bit of the city was like the Mallee. It showed no mercy. It was gristly and soggy, that bit of the city. It was sullen all around that mental hospital and it sucked at Marjorie and tried its level best to pull her into it. Because it knew that there were many times when Marjorie would have been quite happy to be pulled in. To be pulled under. To stay there. It was the still, silent sea of her waiting salt lake – shallow and stinking and biding its time until you stepped onto it. When its devious crystalline beauty would break under your feet and turn into a sucking black stinking morass. Grasping at you with its dank air, its lack of dust, its beautiful cast-iron bars, its beautiful lush gardens, its beautiful wrought-iron fence.

Marjorie went every month to the mental hospital. (So she said.) Month after month. Like going to confession. She should have gone with Bill when he came down to visit Elise – like Aunty Agnes did. She should have gone to the hospital once a week – when Bill wasn't there – like Aunty Agnes did. Like she had gone once a week, sandwiched between Ruby and Pa in the back seat of the car, to mass at the dusty little Catholic church in the Mallee. But once a month was better than nothing. And before once a month it had been nothing.

Aunty Agnes, though, went every week without fail. 'Perhaps it would help if you came along, dear,' Aunty Agnes had suggested early on. 'You might be able to settle a bit if you saw her.'

Settle a bit? I'm not a bloody bucket of milk that you want to get the cream off, Aunty Agnes, she thought. But Marjorie was not sharp in her reply to her aunty. She was mild and contemplative. And why wouldn't Marjorie be? Sheltered as she was now within her encrustations. She felt she could view the world with the serene detachment of an under-the-saltwater organism from where she was now – without having to actually touch any of it. 'No, thank you very much, Aunty Agnes. It is not convenient for me right now,' she said. 'Dad can go with you when he comes down again.'

'Your father keeps asking if you have been to see your mother yet. What should I tell him?' asked Aunty Agnes after a number of her lonesome faithful weeks of visits.

And Aunty Agnes must have caught Marjorie at low tide. Those encrustations must have been exposed to the air and dangerous. 'Tell him to bloody come down here and see her for himself! Tell him to do it! Tell him it's his job! Bloody hell, Aunty Agnes! Bloody hell!' Marjorie roared.

The face of her thoughtful and gentle Aunty Agnes turned red at that and crumpled in on itself. It was a sagging pavlova with leaking, syrupy sugar as tears sprang from her gentle old eyes to wind their way down the furrows in her cheeks.

That is a bloody awful job of ploughing they have done there on your face, Aunty Agnes, thought Marjorie as she watched the slow syrupy travel of an old lady's pain. *Those furrows are all over the place like a dog's breakfast.* Marjorie turned away from the wet, crumpled face. She stared out the kitchen door instead, at the Sacred Heart of Jesus with its perpetual bleeding heart. It was giving nothing away – as usual. But Marjorie could see it was sorely tempted today. She could see its index finger itching to break away from catching those drops of blood. Itching to point itself at her and break the seal of confession. *You are responsible, Marjorie*, those sorrowful eyes were saying. *Why do you bother me with your 'Bless me, Father, for I have sinned'? The fact is your mother has fallen into temptation and succumbed to the evil of insanity; and your sister threw herself on the pyre. And you failed to stop either of these things happening. What can I do? It is a sin. A mortal sin of omission. And now sins of torment as well, Marjorie?*

'Do you know anyone who has committed a mortal sin, Aunty Agnes?' asked Marjorie.

'Of course not, dear,' said Aunty Agnes.

Oh yes you do! thought Marjorie. And the Sacred Heart of Jesus won again. Because it showed Marjorie that pain and suffering needed to be looked at square in the face when you were a mortal. And Marjorie had to admit that her best opportunity to look pain and suffering squarely in the face was at that mental hospital with her mother.

Or maybe it was because she had already stared someone else's pain and suffering squarely in the face with those tears she caused to spill themselves from the kindly eyes of her Aunty Agnes. Maybe that was what made her do it? Anyway, Marjorie and her encrustations explained things thus: *What's the point of dwelling on your personal blameworthiness and letting it wear you out so that you end up dying early if you are only going to end up in hell for eternity, you and your pile of mortal sins?* So, Marjorie started going – once a month only, mind – to the mental institution. On Fridays – the day set aside by any Catholic worth their salt for eating fish, and for the perpetual remembrance of death. She went after work.

'Are you coming out for drinks after work, Marjorie?' workmates would ask.

'No thank you. I am sorry but I have charity commitments I must attend to now,' Marjorie would say. Except that many times she was lying. Sometimes she just stayed in the city and wandered the comfort of the streets. And she never felt the need to explain to anybody why she lied about this. Neither the boys at work who wanted her to go for drinks nor poor old Aunty Agnes who refused to let up on the belief in a mother's love to overcome everything bad in the world.

But every now and again, imprecisely, Marjorie would actually visit. Where, at this gristly and soggy place, Marjorie would watch. Marjorie's dry hard eyes would watch all its crying women with their feeble bunched hankies, their twisted and forlorn hospital dresses, their frightened eyes and their whisperings. Her face would screw up at its stark men with their lifted dribbling chins and their clenched jaws. Their jangling legs and arms.

Their useless mutterings. Marjorie wasn't a shirker, though. She took it upon herself to be responsible for things at these visits. At each of these fitful, sporadic visits Marjorie counted the half-filled, saucerless, teaspoonless cups of lukewarm tea scattered randomly, crouching anxiously on bare wooden tables everywhere in that room where the residents were marshalled to receive their guests. She counted the sensible tin plates with their scrubby supply of stale Arnott's Milk Arrowroot biscuits. She counted the tables and the sensible chairs. And Marjorie would sort these things out.

'Hey! Don't touch those. They're my tin plates,' one of the crazy men would protest. And he would lunge at her and stretch his insane eyes to their limits at her. But he was mistaken if he thought his insane eyes were a match for Elise's. He didn't frighten Marjorie. And Marjorie was quick. She would just step aside and let him sprawl on the floor, or stagger into chairs or other inmates. She really didn't care which. 'That girl is stealing all the biscuits again! Stop her! Someone get the help!' one woman with painted nails and impeccable diction would screech. But Marjorie was not deterred by her either.

There was never a thought to look around for her mother when she arrived. Marjorie didn't need or care to do that. She knew where she would be. Elise would be jammed as she was every time in that timid expanse of a visitors' room. With its silent, watchful orderlies in their white coats. Elise and all her companions sitting on those metal chairs. Or slumping, or squatting. Or not sitting at all. Elise always was sitting, though. Upright. Her head naked of any decent tea cosy.

And Marjorie didn't know either if Elise cared to watch out for her in those early days. Because Marjorie never bothered to look. She just went straight to work. She straightened the tables and chairs – even the occupied chairs, if she felt like it. She would push the chairs equidistantly into the tables and arrange the chairs equally among the tables. Then she would place the lukewarm cups of tea – equally, comfortingly, squarely in front of each chair. Then she would arrange the tin plates with the biscuits – grabbing them out of hands if needs be. She was methodical. She was at peace and with purpose as she carved out sensibility and order. As she set the tables.

She did speak to her mother, though. 'So this is your lunatic asylum, is it?' she said the first time she went. On subsequent visits Marjorie would say the following when she had finished her table-setting chore: 'There,' Marjorie would proclaim. 'The tables are set, Mother. There are no tablecloths. Or serviettes. It is a bit of a handicap to set a proper table under these conditions. I have done it appropriately other-wise.' And she would turn as she spoke to the empty fireplace near the window. Because that was where Elise would always be. Sitting in a chair beside the empty fireplace – staring at its emptiness. Marjorie would go over to her mother and would reach down. It looked like she was putting her arms around her mother to give her a hug. But she wasn't doing that at all. Marjorie had no hugs left these days. 'Why don't you spit some more tablets into the fire before I go, Mother?' she sometimes said.

Or: 'So, are you happy now?' she often asked.

Sometimes Marjorie left her mother a different message. It was a simple one. 'We did it, you and I,' she would murmur into her mother's ear.

Her mother never replied.

Aunty Agnes wouldn't ask Marjorie how Elise was after these visits. She knew better than that – even if she didn't know enough to realise that Marjorie might not even have been to the mental hospital at all.

Marjorie always telephoned the farm, though. Every month. Because how were they to know whether she had visited or not? Certainly Elise wasn't in any fit state to tell them. And all Marjorie had to do anyway was visit the confessional and say, 'Bless me, Father, for I have sinned. I have been telling lies,' and everything would be alright again.

Bill would ask about Elise, though. Or Pa would ask. Depending on who got to the telephone first. And Aunty Agnes would always listen. Aunty Agnes and the Sacred Heart of Jesus.

'How's your mother then?' Bill would ask.

'She's alright.'

'How are you then, Marjorie? You keeping your chin up? Aunty Agnes says you are doing a fine job at that library.'

'I'm alright.'

And Pa would say: 'Oh, it's you, then. How's that mother of yours? It's about time she started coming good. She's been bloody months in that place. She coming good yet?'

'She's alright.'

'What about you then, girl? Are you coming good?'

'I'm alright.' As she wondered at the spindly voice of Pa that crept now through the Bakelite. *Pa's voice is not steady on its feet anymore. These telephone lines are wearing him out*, she would think.

'Everybody roundabout's been asking after you. I let them know I reckon you're coming good,' her father would say.

Coming good? Or going bad? Marjorie would wonder. And Marjorie would listen to the dry whisper of her father's voice and ponder on what had gone wrong with the modern telephony system that it had lately turned her father's voice into the sound of a thousand wheat husks in the wind.

'Did your mother ask after me?' the wheat husk voice might ask.

Marjorie would shrug. 'No.'

'Your father's thinking of coming down. What do you think, Marjorie? I can't seem to make up my mind on things these days. He's just been down. What's he gunna do while Elise just stares at him with those eyes of hers and never a word to say?' Pa might ask.

'Is the ploughing finished?' asked Marjorie of the spindly voice.

'Why don't you come up and help with the ploughing? There's still a bit to be done,' the voice might reply. 'You could tidy up about the place for us. We rattle around in the house by ourselves these days, I don't mind telling you. This house has too much of a man's feel about it and it could do with a girl's touch now even if I do say so myself,' Pa's delicate, skinny voice might offer.

'I don't think so.' Marjorie would shake her head at the telephone on the wall.

'Put Aunty Agnes on, love,' Bill would say.

'Put Agnes on, girl,' Pa would say.

And Marjorie would hand the Bakelite receiver to Aunty Agnes. She would wander off down Aunty Agnes's hallway and into her bedroom. She would shut the door – softly. And lean against it – carefully. And watch the gentle city lights outside her bedroom window as the whispers went to and fro between the adults.

'It is funny how silent a screaming place can be,' Marjorie said one Friday night after she had truly been to visit her mother. She said it to the front door as she slammed it shut.

'What's that you're saying, Marjorie?' asked Aunty Agnes. She had rushed from her kitchen when she heard Marjorie at the door and now she stood and she wiped her hands over and over on her apron as her eyes went red. Because she had recently indulged in a timid hope that things were beginning to come good for Marjorie. 'That sounds like nonsense talk,' she said. 'You stop with that, you hear?'

'Lonely too,' Marjorie said. 'A messy heap of lunatics all cluttered together and tripping over themselves in their own little imprisonment creations. All shouting or crying or muttering or screaming. Which is ridiculous. Because no one hears. Because they are all deaf – by choice. They don't want to hear anyone or anything. Not even themselves.'

'Don't talk about the less fortunate like that, Marjorie.'

Marjorie had taken off her double-breasted, worsted wool coat and matching hat with velvet trim and had flung them at the hallstand while she was talking. She was peeling off her gloves now, carelessly, as you would a peel a banana. She tossed those just as carelessly in the same direction. She paused then, after all the tossing and flinging, to straighten Aunty Agnes's pearls that Marjorie now wore. 'Oh no, Aunty Agnes,' she said. 'They are not the less fortunate. We are. We are the ones who have to slog on in the realities of this world. We are the ones left behind to face things, to clean up the mess, while they flee and fuss and pamper themselves in their madnesses.'

'Marjorie! You are being cruel and unchristian. That comment is uncalled for!

Marjorie shrugged. 'Thank you for that, Agnes, you sound just like my mother. And that is certainly just what I need! Any chance of a cup of coffee?'

*

It ended up taking the best part of a year for any proper words to be spoken on those fitful visits to that mental hospital. Which gave Marjorie plenty of time to perfect her encrustations. No soft, delicate baby coral for Marjorie. Running helped with the process. Marjorie hadn't let the city stop her running. After all, she had run from the Mallee there to this city here, so she just kept on going all through that year. But she ran on her own these days. There was no Ruby. No Jesse.

She would run early in the mornings before work. Especially on Fridays. Especially on the Fridays she had appointed as mental hospital visiting days. Running around and about the streets and lanes, train lines and yards and factories. All around this lovely place. Running with all those dependable engines. She would run past the awakening trams – blinking and shuffling and screeching their morning calls. Their mouths yawning open and shut. She would run alongside the solid, dependable trains – shunting and shoving at each other in the goods yards. She would circle around lines of utes. Empty. Waiting quietly to lend a hand. Marjorie loved these engines. All that metal. They smelt like blood. Marjorie ran for a year before her mother spoke.

'There is no tablecloth.' Those were the first words Elise said to her daughter at that mental hospital.

Marjorie's arms jerked up and folded themselves across her chest. She lifted her chin and did her best to glare at this mother of hers who had killed Ruby and then abandoned Marjorie for nearly a year. 'You talk, Mother,' she said. 'I am here, and your words are for a tablecloth.' And Marjorie didn't go back there for a long time.

Chapter 16

IT SEEMS THAT those few words were enough to satisfy Elise, though. She didn't seem to mind that Marjorie didn't go back for months. Elise retreated back into her silence and didn't say anything more to anybody until well after a specialist book conservator had taken Marjorie under his wing at the library. 'You have a talent for fixing all things material in this library, I can see,' he had said.

'I don't know about that,' she said.

'Well I do. It is a delicate and precise art. And you could be really good at this. How would you like to become a book conservator?'

Marjorie flushed. A lifetime being paid to fix broken things. Who could conceive such a mighty thing? So that was that. Marjorie began training as a conservator. She became officially responsible for saving things. If those things needing saving had been made out of paper, that was. She was a dab hand at saving those papery things.

And Marjorie loved her work. It was a place of organisation and logic and trustworthiness. It was a place where precious things were held gently and treated kindly. And given a place to be. There was nothing at all shifty about her work.

Even when Ruby interrupted it. Like she did sometimes. There she would be. Ruby – drifting there in the corner of her bedroom while Marjorie straightened the piles of broken books stacked on her bed. One side of Ruby's face hidden by the room's soft shadows. One side – the still beautiful side, turned to Marjorie. *You know you are incorrectly using the word 'ephemera' to describe your work, don't you?* she would say. *Ephemera means 'something of no lasting significance'. That is not how you would describe your work, is it? Or is it me, maybe, that is of no lasting significance? Or is that you, perhaps? Is that how you are describing yourself now?*

Marjorie would stop. 'It's old newspapers today,' she said as her pillows began translating themselves into fragments of torn newsprint. But Ruby was never interested. She didn't look at Marjorie. So Marjorie ran her hands down the length of the starched linen tablecloth on her bed. 'Are you still there, Ruby?' Marjorie whispered. She didn't turn around to see.

No. I'm not here. How can I be? You know that better than anybody, don't you?

But Ruby had gone too far. 'You have gone too far, Ruby. That is much too far. That is too much,' Marjorie cried.

And Marjorie jerked and flailed herself awake. Waking to a city swaddled in morning mist. Holding its breath within the softest of breezes. That mist surrounding and dampening the distant trams as they clattered and called to her. The air secure with the remains of last night's rain and that morning's coffee. Marjorie waking to the taste of a Mallee dust storm in her mouth.

She flicked back the hair that had fallen across her face – glistening black like it was wet. Like the leaves were now on the tree outside her window. They were quiet, absent-minded leaves. Absorbed in their job of hoarding the rain hanging murky in the air. Not at all interested in a stark, brutal dream that has assaulted a girl just now on the other side of the window. Marjorie sagged there in her bed. Dawn was creeping into her bedroom. She watched it greet her stained-glass window. Dawn sun battling the mist – a weak skirmish as it tried for a foothold on the day. Fragments of it playing in the tree in Aunty Agnes's front yard, lighting up the rain-drops wobbling on the branches. Marjorie's head turned and she watched that. Watching it hard. Blinking so very hard. So that her eyes could do a proper job and stay dry and hard. Dawn never compromised. It was like engines – always there. But not everything in the world was safe like that. Marjorie knew now that most things were unpredictable, like bees. And Marjorie knew all about the danger of bees.

She blinked and did what she always did these days. She went to work. Her father and Pa were coming down for the weekend.

*

'Marjorie seems to be getting back on her feet, don't you think?' they whispered. Their hope cradled in their gentle talk, speaking softly when they thought she wasn't watching.

Marjorie pedalled away at the Singer sewing machine.

'Does she have any friends yet?'

Marjorie could glimpse Aunty Agnes shrugging. 'The sewing is good for her. She is always making something. And she helps me about the place,' she said.

'That young lad Jesse keeps on asking after her. At least she still has him,' said Pa. His words were constricted. He was choking the life out of them in a death-tight grip because he knew that words were weak and could turn on you anytime and betray you.

Aunty Agnes nodded. What could she say? She could say: *I know. I have seen each letter as it arrives. I have heard the postie blow his whistle, I have seen him put another one in the letterbox, I have collected it and put it on the hallstand for Marjorie when she comes home from work.* She couldn't say that, though. Not with Marjorie over there in the corner pretending she couldn't hear them.

'What about that job of hers? That still going alright?' asked Pa.

Yes, it is, thank you, Pa. It is going quite nicely, Marjorie whispered to herself.

'It's time we went. Do you want to come and visit your mother, Marjorie?' Bill asked as he stood up from the kitchen table.

Marjorie treadled hard on the Singer sewing machine.

'Marjorie?'

Marjorie laid her hand flat on the comfort of the raw silk trussed and trapped with its multiple stabbings from the machine needle. She looked up at the face of her father, then across at the face of Pa. She looked back at her father – at all that worry piled up and hiding behind the grip of hands on his hat and in the bend of his shoulders. She shook her head. 'I don't need to,' she replied. 'I visited my mother a couple of weeks ago. You go on without me.'

But Marjorie made a mistake. She shouldn't have listened to their drought-stricken, rickety voices. She shouldn't have glanced at Pa and seen the shameful, unmanly beseech of his eyes. She shouldn't have then turned away from that to look instead at the face of her father. Where she was waylaid. Where she didn't have any time to duck out of the road of the pain that charged at her – tearing past all that piled-up worry, all that strangulated love, to hit her in the face. Marjorie surprised herself then by deciding she had no choice but to offer a bit of ointment for the pain. What else could she do? 'She spoke to me last time I went,' she offered. 'She said, *There is no tablecloth*.' Marjorie said no more. She didn't move to explain when 'the last time I went' actually was; or if any words had been spoken since.

Aunty Agnes and Bill and Pa didn't notice those left-out things, however. The three of them were open-mouthed and struck silent at the thought of those four wonderful words so magically appearing from Elise. Marjorie wasn't, though. She bent her head to return to the solace of the sewing.

'She's on the mend for sure then,' said Pa when it was obvious the Singer sewing machine had stitched up the possibility of any further words from Marjorie. He stood up to go. 'A woman's on the mend if she's talking, that's a fact.' He nodded. 'And you're up and about too, working in that library of yours. Not lying around all day in your bed. You'll be right as rain soon enough, Marjorie. You keep on. You keep your chin up, girl.' He nodded and nodded.

So Marjorie put her chin up and watched the three of them walk out of the kitchen. Then she lowered her chin again and went back to her sewing.

And went back to her real Friday nights. Where she was spending her time since those four words ventured into the air, now bent on trying to understand, even just a tiny bit, about what purgatory would be like for someone like Elise. Or for someone like herself. Because though Aunty Agnes would say over and over, *It was an accident, Marjorie! Nobody is to blame. Just a terrible accident*, what would kind, wrinkly old Aunty Agnes know?

Here's how Marjorie went about that: she would walk past all the concert halls to see what was playing. She would stand in foyers or sneak up to doors – to listen to the familiar beauteous sounds on the other side – to graft the singing of the city onto the singing of the Mallee. But it was always such hard work. So Marjorie would stop when those sounds began to make her eyes water. She would spend hours in art galleries – wandering and staring. At drawings and paintings – her fickle, watery eyes searching for signs of balance. For evidence of blame. Or hints of love without madness.

Until Marjorie was discovered. 'This can't be where you do your charity work.' It was one of the boys from work, standing over her as she drank coffee at the cafe outside a theatre one Friday night.

'No, it isn't,' was all Marjorie could manage.

'I'm going to this show. Come with me. I have a spare ticket.'

How could Marjorie refuse? She badly wanted to, but a real lady wouldn't refuse – that would be bad manners. And bad manners on top of her never-ending lies was starting to add up to a very long purgatory. It was *My Fair Lady*, though, and she didn't really want to be stuck in any theatre with all those songs. Not being able to run off if it all got too much. But Marjorie went anyway. And she tried hard not to let those songs – and one particular song – wear her away.

She didn't get worn away, though. Marjorie seemed almost the same at the end of the show as she was at the beginning. So she started going to more shows. And more theatre. And more galleries. And the opera. And the ballet. And Marjorie really did believe she was getting away with it. Because they were very crafty those songs, those art galleries, those plays, those operas, all those beautiful costumes. Because they were not a downpour that rushes down the dry creek beds and rips and gouges at a person's insides and their outsides as it tears past. They were like the best of spring rains that make your face lift to the skies. That soaked you right through before you even knew it. Until your eyes were transparent and you could at last start to truly look at a young girl that would become your mother and whose very life had prevailed on such things as these in the city. You could actually start to see how this young girl who would become your mother might have been if the Mallee hadn't interfered.

Even so, it was spring before Marjorie went back to the mental hospital to set the table again. And it was Jesse who made her do it. Not that he knew anything about it.

'There's another letter for you, love,' Aunty Agnes had called as Marjorie closed the front door. 'It came in the mail today,' she said.

Marjorie stopped halfway through pulling off her gloves. There it was. *A much-travelled thing*, Marjorie thought. *It must be bushed. It is a long way from there to here. How many post offices? How many miles on a postie's bike? How many hours on Aunty Agnes's hallstand?* She gazed at it. It was lying delicate and mysterious – just like all its predecessors – on the polished wood, patiently waiting for her to get home from work. It looked fragile and beautiful – like the spring's first fallen rose petals. But the delicate beauty of roses can be a trap for the unwise. Because roses are thick and fast with thorns. They always come together. It is a package deal, and when you love the rose you have to face the probable consequences.

Marjorie was tender as she picked up the letter. Somehow, this time, she had run right out of being brutal and merciless at its innocent arrival. She didn't screw this one up, crushing the words within to smithereens. She didn't shove it in her handbag then march to her bedroom and take it out again to grind the screwed-up ball of a rejected letter into the surface of her dressing table. Marjorie walked slowly to her room this time and laid the letter carefully on top of the pile of all those other screwed-up, straightened-out, unopened, unacknowledged letters.

Because Marjorie was no lady. Because a person of good manners would have responded to mail by writing some sort of a letter in reply. But Marjorie had not done that for any of the other ones. And she wasn't going to do the right thing for this one either.

Marjorie did respond, though. She responded by visiting her mother.

*

'I keep getting these damn letters from Jesse,' Marjorie muttered at her mother. She had finished setting all the tables and was now standing beside Elise at the empty fireplace. So she said it to the chimney bricks, really.

'I've got a whole bloody suitcase full of them now. Bloody hundreds of the things!'

Elise might have nodded.

'Bloody hell, Mother! Why does he keep on writing them? What does he want? Do you even remember Jesse?'

Elise sighed a short, sharp sigh. She might have nodded.

Marjorie snapped open her handbag and pulled out her nice new gold-plated cigarette case and proceeded to light a filter-tip cigarette.

'Hey! You can't smoke in here,' said a white-coated one.

'This is a chimney right here. I can so,' said Marjorie. She didn't bother to offer her mother a cigarette. Marjorie knew that her mother's views on the value of a beautiful voice would not have disappeared along with that voice. Instead, she placed a cigarette centre stage between her perfectly red-lipsticked lips and beamed at the white-coated objector as she flicked the lid on her matching cigarette lighter.

'Yes,' whispered Elise to the chimney bricks when Marjorie left. 'I do.'

*

Marjorie might have spoken to her mother about Jesse's letters but that didn't stop Jesse. His letters kept on turning up – quietly, carefully, gentlemanly, stubbornly. And so did he. The letters made a good job of panicking Marjorie every time their delicate, papery selves arrived. But it was his face that terrified her the most. It was so ephemeral, so intransient, this face. A face that flickered at the edges of her mind. Flickering far longer than any decent flicker should. Every time.

It would happen outside her work. The work that Marjorie loved. This job that gave her organisation and logic and trustworthiness. A job that was about reparation, restoration: finding a right and proper place for broken and fragile things. Making them better for all the world. Marjorie rescued the discarded. There was nothing unsteady about this place.

Except for those times Jesse caught her out. She would be about to ascend those marvellous front steps and pass into the comfort of the building's purpose and design. But her elegant, confident walk would be tripped up when her eyes caught a glimpse of a face in the nearby hustle. A shock of recognition across a rolling sea of faces. A fleeting meeting of eyes across the crowd. Undecided eyes that could never make up their mind whether they were green or brown, thick dark lashes under warm brown hair curling recklessly down a forehead. Before the face was gone.

It was always a momentary thing. But a moment can be a very long time. And that moment was all it took – every time it was all it took – for the traitorous memories to burst out of their hiding places, dragging a whole lot of things with them. It would be Wheat Bag Boy. Staring right at her.

'It's Jesse. It's not just his letters. Now he's started turning up as well. I get just a glimpse of a face in the crowd, then he's gone. And weeks and months might go by.' Marjorie was sitting on a chair. Elise was sitting beside her. They were at a window. Elise had abandoned the fireplace some months ago and her real estate of choice these days was this particular window.

'It is a many splendid thing.' Elise nodded at the window. She didn't look at Marjorie. She might have been talking about the perfect lawn outside. And it was so perfect it didn't need any more words. So Elise didn't say any more words.

'He was there again. I keep seeing him.' Marjorie was staring out at the lawn now too. It was early summer and the grass was ripe, expectant. Marjorie studied it with her mother – those perfect lines of mowing. It could have been a proud English lawn out there, it was so perfect in its lines.

'It is good to see them,' said Elise.

Marjorie nodded. She agreed. The many lines of a decently mowed lawn were always good to see.

'It is very good to see you, Marjorie,' Elise then said. Also to the window.

Marjorie's mouth fell open. Her head turned. Marjorie thought then that she might as well have been a clock because it seemed like it took one whole hour and a thousand thoughts for her head to turn towards her mother.

Why is that? Marjorie would think in that long head-turning hour. *Why is it good to see me? I have burnt your beautiful first-born daughter. It seems like only yesterday I did that. She didn't deserve to be burnt. She is grotesque now. Shoved under that pile of dirt and stones. Out there in the blazing sun. Smothered by plants that dutifully lie down on top of her and die, each time, with her.* And Marjorie had to blink very, very hard. Maybe the blinks were the second hands.

'And don't sit there with your mouth open like that. Do you want to catch flies?' said her mother. Marjorie stopped blinking and just sat there and let the water in her eyes do its business. Elise reached out and took her daughter's hand and they stared out at the perfect lawn.

'Mum spoke to me tonight.' Marjorie was speaking softly into the telephone mouthpiece, forgetting that the words might need a boost as they had quite a long way to go. She heard her father heave in a chest full of breath.

'What did she say?' he asked, his words wobbly and flattened from the weight of the heaved in breath.

'She said, *It is very good to see you, Marjorie . . . And don't sit there with your mouth open like that. Do you want to catch flies?*' And Marjorie was still as she listened to that heaved-in breath sigh itself out in a long thin line, down all those miles from there to here. Marjorie didn't feel any need to convey other words that had been spoken that day. Because everybody knows a mother is doing alright if she could remind her daughter once more of the perils of swallowing flies.

And Marjorie almost forgot about Wheat Bag Boy for a while. Because after more than a year Elise was now starting to look around. She was starting to find her way out of the labyrinth. And so was Marjorie. But, as with any labyrinth, finding the way out on your own is not an easy undertaking. Because a labyrinth is an intricate and cryptic thing. So, without even discussing it, they joined up and walked the labyrinth together.

*

'Do you think Ruby is alright?' was Elise's next question to the window. The city was turning its thoughts to Christmas and the sprinklers were spraying the sunlight outside. 'We don't see very much of Ruby here anymore, do we?' Elise said. Then she turned from her habitual contemplation of the immaculate lawn and looked directly at Marjorie – before turning to look around the room for Ruby.

I don't suppose we do. There's not very much of her left to see anymore, was Marjorie's first thought. Which was followed quickly by: *And no. I don't think she is alright at all.* 'No. We don't see much of Ruby anymore, do we?' Marjorie said softly to her mother.

But Marjorie was lying to her mother. Because Marjorie did see Ruby. She saw more than a bit of Ruby – even if there wasn't much of her left to see anymore. She didn't see her every day. And she never knew where she would see her. But suddenly there Ruby would be. Sitting at a reading table, engrossed in a book at Marjorie's work, her lovely red hair falling all about her, one side of her face perfect and peeping through, shining and serene. Or leaning against a lamppost waiting for a tram. Or smiling at her from a passing car.

And of course there were those dreams, too. Marjorie saw a lot of her there.

'I am not running off and leaving you, Ruby,' Marjorie said. 'I can never leave you. Because there is nowhere I can run from you. I take you with me every single day,' her dream cried.

*

'How is your father, Marjorie?' Elise asked at the next visit. She started looking around for Bill. 'I want to go home with Bill. When is your father going to take me home?'

'Dad's not coming tonight. He has just been down, don't you remember? He won't be down this weekend, Mum,' Marjorie said.

'Could I go home with you then, Marjorie?' Elise asked, her soft grey eyes pleading.

'No,' Marjorie said.

Elise reached over and took both of Marjorie's hands. 'I'm sorry, Marjorie,' Elise said.

Marjorie was uncertain these days about the return of her mother and she jumped a bit at Elise's apology. She didn't take her hands away and she didn't take her eyes away. But Marjorie was wary. Because she was not yet sure what her mother might be sorry for. Or whether she should be more sorry than her mother. So Marjorie never said anything to that.

*

Despite the cloying grasp of the mental institution, Marjorie could see now that Elise was trying hard. And it was working. Marjorie watched as her mother slowly crept about the place, collecting as much of those shattered, scattered, scorched bits of herself as she could find. And Marjorie watched as her mother did her very best to mould all those bits back together into some sort of recognisable thing. And did the best she could to look out for her visiting daughter and to speak to her the lucid truths of the insane:

'Ruby is dead, isn't she? We will never see her again.' It was Elise, wading in a sea of Friday tears who said this to Marjorie on one of those visits, more than a year and a half after that cleansing fire that burnt Ruby away.

'Yes, Mum.' Marjorie nodded. 'That is correct. Ruby is dead.' She nodded and nodded at Ruby, who was there for Marjorie, at the back of this tidy room – one side of her caught by the shadows, the perfect, lovely, unscathed right side of her face looking at Marjorie. Her hair catching and glinting in the soft afternoon light as she smiled. But Marjorie knew what was on the other side. Marjorie kept right on nodding. She had seen that other side again just last night.

'I didn't mean it,' Elise whispered.

Who ever really means it? thought Marjorie. She stared at her weeping mother.

*

'Condemnation is of the devil, Marjorie. I have learnt that,' Elise whispered to Marjorie one Friday as autumn leaves drifted down. 'And self-condemnation is a haughty thing. It is not helpful. It does not participate in healing. It has done me no good, Lord knows, and it will do you no good, Marjorie. We will never be able to get out of this place with that self-condemnation you insist on carrying around all day.'

'I am not the one stuck here, Mother. I can leave anytime I like,' said Marjorie.

'You don't leave here, Marjorie,' said Elise.

Marjorie looked away from her mother and watched the ward orderly scratching the sunburn peel on his arms.

'But you could leave here if you were willing to climb down off your high horse, Marjorie,' Elise pleaded. 'You will not find solace from up there and it is far too high up for you to ever find your own forgiveness, let alone your mother's.' Elise started wringing her lovely hands. 'It is too cloudy at those heights for you to see the world as you should; you won't make sense of anything from up there. A person's restitution does not often abide in the heights. The air is too thin.'

Marjorie reached out and stilled her mother's hands. 'It doesn't hurt up here on my high horse, Mother,' she answered as dead burnt skin fell in a shower at the feet of the orderly.

'I beg to differ. You are not right,' said Elise. She pulled out one of her hands and patted Marjorie's hand as it detained hers.

*

'Why do you do it, Marjorie?' Elise asked as the windows stood firm against the early winter rain.

'Do what?'

'Work to revive all that beautiful broken paper. Resuscitate all those lovely damaged items from their certain death.'

Marjorie shrugged. 'Because it is inappropriate for them to die. They are considered by many to be as good as dead. Useless and worthless, not good for anything. But I am very good at putting them back together again. They are much more than good for something when I have finished with them.'

'What about books? Do you save them too?'

Marjorie smiled. 'Yes. I love fixing books. I don't care how damaged they are.'

'Are you good at your work?'

Marjorie shrugged. 'I keep being asked to do it, so I must be,' she said. 'I am being properly trained as a conservator,' Marjorie added.

'That is a good thing to do, Marjorie,' said her mother. 'Fixing broken things. Ruby would be proud of you, I think.'

*

'I don't have to worry here, Marjorie,' said Elise on another wintry Friday. 'I may never be good enough, but this place harbours humanity enough for me.'

'What do you mean?' asked Marjorie.

'The people in this place are all shocking in their private mental illnesses. They have enormous secrets and burdens to shoulder, day and night. It is a sad place. Lord knows they are suffering here.' Elise shook her head. 'There is clemency in this place for me because the people here are much too busy to care that I am not good enough.'

Marjorie could think of nothing to say. So once again, as she had done so many times now on these visits, she took her mother's hand. Because what words can ever be said that will wash away somebody's not being *good enough*?

'I am so sorry for what happened, Marjorie,' whispered Elise. 'I am so sorry.'

'I know,' said Marjorie.

'I am so sorry, Marjorie,' Elise said again.

Marjorie could see herself in the window. Her reflection was staring at her. 'I, too, am so sorry, Marjorie,' Marjorie whispered to herself.

*

'I would like to start drawing again,' said Elise as she watched the early blossom on the almond trees outside.

'Why?' asked Marjorie. 'It's a bit dangerous, isn't it? Aren't you worried your friends here might suddenly grab your things and stab each other up the nose with the hard end of the paint-brushes? Or drive the pencils through their own eyeballs?'

'Don't mock other people's pain, Marjorie,' said Elise. 'That is a cruel thing to do and you are not a cruel person. Besides, you would be better off trying to manage your own pain.' She nodded gravely at Marjorie, and Marjorie had the decency to feel shame. Which was not lost on her mother. She wanted to comfort Marjorie, so Elise looked for some other words that might do the job. 'You look like a lady now, Marjorie,' she said, and she smiled.

Marjorie jumped. 'What?'

'However, you don't talk like one. Even after all these years. It is *I beg your pardon*, not *what*.'

Marjorie smiled.

'Also,' Elise continued, 'I have found there is a piano here, so, I have started playing it.'

'When? When did you find this piano? How long have you been playing?'

'Oh, quite some time. I don't have to tell you everything about myself, Marjorie. Do I?'

'No,' said Marjorie.

'And I have formed a choir as well,' Elise said.

*

'Mum is playing the piano again,' Marjorie told the telephone lines. 'I've seen it. The piano.' She listened to the sudden jerk in her father's breathing.

'She really is on the mend then, isn't she?' His voice was wobbly, juddering.

'I think she is, Dad. She said she wants to start drawing again, too. And she has formed a choir.'

'A choir! Who with?'

'Her friends there. That's what she says.'

'Well. That'll be a sight. Won't it?' And they both laughed. They were timid and fragile and glad. All up and down those telephone lines.

*

It turned out the piano was a good one. It was a concert grand piano brought along and then left behind by a previous inmate – who had, years back, launched their own personal finale off the lichen and slate roof of the laundry block onto the lawn waiting below. This concert grand had been waiting for Elise for years. And Elise did have a concert – for nobody in particular – one day on that circumspect green lawn. 'We are going to have a musical recital,' Elise informed the orderlies. 'We will be performing on the front lawn. So, if you would kindly move the piano out there, I would be very grateful.'

Elise played the piano; Elise conducted her ragtag choir; Elise sang. And Elise created some magic for them all – and for anybody else who wanted to listen. With her singing and her playing and her rolled-up newspaper for a baton. She pushed back, for just a few wonderful minutes in the middle of that lawn with its distant border of wrought iron. She pushed against the murky confusion that swirled about and entangled them, the bewildering violence that haunted them, the chaos from the voices that wearied their hearts.

305

Elise's fellow inmates sang and sang. And Elise's voice joined in and carried them all over the beautiful wrought-iron gates to wherever they wanted to go.

The superintendent of the mental hospital wasn't partial to acknowledging magic. But he was quick to capitalise on the obvious value of the sort of thing he could see out of his office window, below him there on his pristine green lawns. He called the newspapers. He called the relatives of the inmates. And he required from Elise and her floridly mentally unstable colleagues a second, more proper concert. Which Marjorie and Aunty Agnes and Pa and Bill were invited to attend.

And which was better than the first one and got Elise in *The Argus*. And *The Age*. And *The Herald*.

But not out of the mental hospital.

*

Not all the newspaper reporters gathered on the lawn for the superintendent's concert were fooled, though. Some of them smelt the bakings of a good story wafting around that grand piano. 'Where are you from?' they asked Elise quietly and quickly, before the superintendent could prevent her from answering. 'You shouldn't be here in this mental hospital. Why are you in here?'

Elise didn't have time to tell them everything. But she told them enough. Enough for them to climb aboard a faded red rattler the next week and head out of the city. They headed straight for the Mallee, which had thrown out Elise and Marjorie, and had buried Ruby beneath its red sand.

'You would have seen her in all the papers,' they said, waving an armful of them around in front of all those tins of powdered milk and packets of self-raising flour.

'We only get the mail and papers twice a week here. Maybe they haven't arrived yet,' said Mrs Cameron as she tidied her own pile of the very same papers.

'There was a concert.'

'Was there indeed?'

'Yes there was. In a mental hospital. Why is she in a mental hospital? Isn't there another daughter? Where is she?'

'You'll have to go now,' said Mrs Cameron. 'I don't have time for tongue-wagging about other people's business. And perhaps you two could find something better to do with your own selves than meddling in the lives of a decent family just trying to get on with things.'

'We're just doing our job. Reporting the facts.'

'I have to shut the shop now,' said Mrs Cameron.

*

'You must know something about her,' they said, pencils in hand, standing outside the post office, baking in the heat of a Mallee drought.

'Yeah. We do,' said the circle of men in the dirt out the front – theirs legs planted, their arms folded, their eyes locked.

'What can you tell us?'

'You're the reporters. You find out.'

'Wasn't there some sort of an accident in the family? Something to do with a house fire?'

'Was there?' the men said.

'That would be none of your business,' someone said. And they all nodded.

'Got to round up that mob of sheep; finish off that fencing; check those dams; get back to the missus,' they said as they jumped in their utes and sprayed those blokes

307

from the newspapers with a shower of red dust and white limestones.

*

The reporters tried the local pub that night. But everybody roundabout had told Bill and Pa by now, so everybody was ready and waiting. And nobody was planning on making it easy for them. The locals lined up all along the bar. Scrupulously facing the publican, their collective backs ignoring the attempts of the reporters to find a spot there. The bar had turned into an impenetrable barrier, a water-tight line of country cold shoulders. The publican handed Pa and Bill their beers, and Pa and Bill, beers in hand, turned to the reporters. 'None of this is any of your damn business,' Bill said.

'By the crikies, you're right there, Bill,' grumbled Pa.

The two of them stood shoulder to shoulder. They took a long drink from their beers, watching the reporters over the top of the froth until their glasses were empty. Then they put their empties daintily on the bar, before turning back to stare at them again. Pa took his pipe out of his top pocket and clamped it between his teeth. Bill folded his arms tight across his chest.

'Gorn, bloody clear off now,' said Pa.

'It's going to be a hundred and ten in the shade tomorrow. You two should get on back to the city where you belong,' said Bill, his head nodding in the direction of the pub door while his eyes stayed on their faces. 'You've got no call to be snooping around here. Not in this heat.'

Everybody at the bar turned around. A solid line of those cold country shoulders turning, arms folding across chests, eyes joining Pa and Bill's to stare at the unwanted newspaper reporters blundering around in the heat and the flies. Those locals, those neighbours and family and friends, stood there in a mob and stared.

*

Elise concluded her mental hospital commitment some time after the visit from the newspapers. 'I am going home now, Marjorie,' Elise said.

Marjorie's delicate balance buckled – even after all these months of watching her mother find her way back down the path. 'Are you sure you are well enough?' she asked.

'I would hardly have been discharged and going home if they didn't think I was well enough, would I? Of course I am well enough. Because I never have an opportunity to miss those damnable tablets here, do I? There is always someone hovering around dishing them out. And they refuse to leave until you have swallowed everything.' Elise stopped. 'What is *well enough* for anyone in this world, anyway, Marjorie?' she lamented.

'But what about me?' said Marjorie.

'You don't have to stay here, dear.'

'I can't go back with you. I won't go back there,' said Marjorie.

'You can, you know. If I can do it, then so can you. You are as well able to go back and face the music as I am.' Elise lifted her chin and glared. While Marjorie blinked and blinked. It was only when that salt water won the battle and flooded triumphant down Marjorie's face that Elise relented. 'Marjorie, we need to pardon ourselves,' she said. 'You cannot carry this burden on your shoulders for the rest of your life. Even if you are protected on all sides here by the brawny shield of paper and that papery sea of tranquillity that you work within.' Elise stroked the face of her daughter. 'Nobody in their right mind would have meant for any of that to happen,' she said.

'Have you counted them, Mum? Do you know how many days? How many months of Fridays I have been visiting you?' Marjorie asked. Her voice was tiny and lonely. Her mother was leaving her again.

'Of course I have been counting them, you silly girl. I am not mad. I have witnessed two institutional Advent and Christmas celebrations, and fasted through three mental institution Lenten seasons.' Elise paused and thought. 'And Lord only knows how many wheat harvests and sheep shearings I have avoided,' she said, shaking her head. Elise put her finger under her daughter's chin and lifted it so Marjorie had to look at her. 'And you have been visiting me for months of Fridays enough for you to look more beautiful than before all of them began.' She smiled.

'What will I do here without you?' Marjorie cried.

'You could start by reading all those letters from Jesse,' said Elise as she stood to kiss her daughter.

Marjorie straightaway forgot anything that she might have been doing. She was suddenly, completely still – hands full and face staring. Her handbag with its lipstick, its cigarette case, its tiny punched cardboard tram ticket – all held up in the air and arrested.

*

'What will you do back there?' Marjorie asked. She was helping her mother pack her things: clothes, drawings, pencils, sheet music.

'The first thing I will do is visit the cemetery,' Elise said. 'I will stand with your father in front of that hump of red dirt and limestones you talk about, Marjorie,' she said, her grey eyes large. 'My mind has cleared and I can weep now for what I have done to my beautiful daughters. I can pray that the one left behind will learn. That she will try to behave like the brave young lady she really is. And that she will turn and look a kindly young man full in the face. As she should.'

Marjorie's fingers splayed open and the pencils she was holding ran for cover on the floor.

Because how did Marjorie's breakable mother know that Wheat Bag Boy had been there once again? Jesse. Inside this time. Not just hiding in all those passing faces outside. Marjorie had looked at him. The other times she never needed to look. She would only need to catch a glimpse, before their eyes would rush to drag away from each other in the crowd.

He was different these days, she could see. But, then, so was she. The last few years had crept in on both of them; and she supposed those years had brought their own particular baggage along for the ride with him. Just as they had done for her.

But this time there was some other thing clinging about him. Some new wheat bag lumped on his shoulders. She felt her own shoulders shiver even now. Because this particular wheat bag of Jesse's was a wheat bag she recognised. Try as his face might to pretend otherwise, he was a man full of sorrows now. A person with a resignation of grief. And even though she might also try to pretend otherwise, Marjorie knew all about that.

Marjorie straightened herself to her full, stiletto-heeled height. A graceful dark-haired beauty in her Singer sewing machine Audrey Hepburn dress, surrounded by shipwrecked pencils. 'Only one daughter is dead,' she said.

'Are you sure about that?' asked Elise, shaking her head. 'I say my prayers that one remaining daughter is like a tree. Tall and elegant and beautiful in its bare winter glory. But not dead. Not really dead on the inside. And I long for spring to prove to me that it is still there. But I was never much good at gardening. All I could ever manage was those ridiculous plastic flowers and they are not alive. So I do hope you are right.'

Chapter 17

IT WASN'T A small room but it was made small by every available space being crammed full of material to fix things. And Marjorie was right in the middle of it, even now. Summer was back again. Autumn, winter and spring had already had their go – turning up to stare at Marjorie and to wonder about the courage of a mother who had scraped together enough of herself to leave the solace of insanity. Who had walked out of those beautiful wrought-iron gates with Bill and gone back to the Mallee to face the music.

But Marjorie was still there – still doing what she loved – restoring rare and damaged books. She was tranquil in her work among this prevailing, fluttering fragility. But tranquillity is often a flimsy thing – easily broken. Marjorie knew that better than most. So she shouldn't have been surprised when one day a voice smashed it. 'Hello, Marjorie,' he said.

Marjorie spun like a willy-willy, scattering her precious bits of paper everywhere. She spun right into the two hazel eyes of Wheat Bag Boy.

'Remember me?' he asked.

'Yes,' she said. Marjorie tried to get her eyes to move. But they wouldn't budge. She couldn't stop staring at this person she had last spoken to in that cemetery where Ruby's bones would now be brittle and alone, lying cluttered together under the dirt. *Although I have exhausted myself over the years trying not to remember you,* was what Marjorie wanted to say. But that was a lot of talking and this was the rare collection section of a library. And silence was golden. 'What are you doing here?' she asked.

Jesse Mitchell gazed at Marjorie in that particular Mallee way Marjorie had not felt for so long, and which she had mistakenly begun to think belonged to someone else now. She knew he was taking silent note of myriad tiny details that could be noted and recorded but not necessarily described. *Jimmy Waghorn taught Jesse to do that,* Marjorie thought with a sudden pang. And that pang did it. It upended her. Marjorie realised a whole trainload of her dead and buried past was starting to derail right now. Wheat trucks full of it. Right in front of her. She watched the train wreck from the inside of her eyes as she was grabbed and thrown, like a bale of hay off the back of a ute. As her dead and buried stuff spilt out in every direction there in her paper castle. 'What do you want?' she asked.

'I need to talk to you; I want you to talk to me,' he said.

'How long have you been here?' asked Marjorie.

'At this particular rare collection reference desk?' asked Jesse as his thoughtful hands rubbed the mellow wooden surface. 'Or in the city?'

Marjorie shivered. She wasn't about to ask Jesse to answer the second question. She reckoned Aunty Agnes knew the answer, though. And probably her mother. And her father. And maybe even Pa. *I know what you have done, Jesse Mitchell,* she thought.

'I am bent on pestering you for a talk. Make no mistake, Marjorie. I will do this until the flamin' cows come home,'

Jesse said as he looked her up and down. He noted the pencil skirt hugging her, the silk blouse, the pearls, the red lipstick matching the shiny red high heels at the bottom of those glorious legs he remembered so well. His mouth gave a hint of a smile. His eyes did their best not to stare. He gave a slight nod as Marjorie watched her careful life clattering down the embankments. 'Right now,' he said. 'I want to talk right now.' Jesse leant back against the polished wood of her desk and gazed sideways at her.

He looked so relaxed, leaning there. So calm, Marjorie half expected him to take out a tin and papers and start rolling a smoke. Or pull out a .22 rifle and take a shot at a rabbit. 'You know I can't talk right now,' she said.

'When could you ever talk?' Jesse responded as he settled further into the desk.

Marjorie looked around now to see if any of her colleagues was noticing. But Jesse had been watching them all along. He could see them all from his casual and deliberate positioning. Marjorie shouldn't have forgotten that about Jesse. She sighed. It was so hard to forget what you needed to forget, and at the same time remember the things you should never forget.

'Can I help you, sir?' One of her colleagues had come over to assist.

'I'll take this one,' said Marjorie into the awkward silence that had arrived with the helpful librarian and which was now just hanging there. It wasn't hanging over Wheat Bag Boy though. He seemed fine. Marjorie had to step over her strewn fragilities and leave them flapping and floundering there on the floor. 'You can go to afternoon tea now,' she said to the gawking librarian. He wandered off, surprisingly reluctant, glancing back a couple of times. Presumably to confirm

Marjorie had not changed her mind. Not because he wanted to get another look at that person with the strange-coloured eyes. Who had not yet stopped staring at Marjorie.

'I wonder if they're curious about a bloke like me being here?' Jesse wondered to the vaulted ceiling. 'I know I would be if I were them,' he said as he watched the sneaking, curious glances of eyes roundabout. 'And do any of them know where you've come from?' he asked, his eyes moving from face to face. 'I bet they don't. But I also bet they would just love to know. What do you reckon?' He turned his head just a fraction and looked Marjorie up and down once more.

Marjorie tried to act like the specialist materials conservator she was. She tried to stab Jesse in the eye with a look of contempt. But libraries were never a good place for violence – and especially not the conservation section. Her look failed. It changed instead to a look that noticed the lovely long fingers resting on the polished wood. She loved those fingers. One of those damned derailed wheat trucks just reminded her of that. It also reminded her that right now she didn't have much option. And that options had never been much available to her where Jesse Mitchell was concerned. 'I finish work in a few minutes,' she said, hurrying through her words to cut him off. 'We'll talk then. If you leave right now.'

Jesse considered the proposal for a downright wasteful amount of time. 'Good-oh, Marjorie,' he replied at last. 'I'll see you in five minutes.'

'I'll meet you on the steps at the front of the library,' she said. 'Now go. Please.'

Jesse seemed to take his own sweet time pushing himself off the reference desk. He turned to gaze at all the ears trying so hard to look like they weren't listening. He was tempted to nod and give a couple of those peeping faces a wave. That would stir things along. And she deserved it.

But he didn't. 'See you on the steps,' was all he said.

As he left, he gave Marjorie a wink and a Mallee nod, though. Which was more than enough for all those eyes roundabout.

*

Marjorie stopped just inside the front doors and scanned the crowd on the lawns in front of the library. All she could think of was the pile of letters from Jesse lying unopened and unanswered in her cupboard; she hadn't received a new one in a long time. She wanted to cry.

Shoving a pair of tortoiseshell sunglasses on her face, she stepped out of the shadows of the library and into the late-afternoon sunlight slanting onto the steps. She tried to look poised and indifferent as she stood there for what seemed like ages, looking for Jesse. And Jesse leant quiet against the statue for as long as he could – looking at her.

'Gidday again, Marjorie,' Jesse finally said as he moved away from the shelter of a bronze soldier on a horse and into the sunlight. Marjorie swung towards the voice. It was a quiet voice in a crowd. But she heard it. Even after all this time of forgetting, Jesse's voice had been lurking there in the back of her memory, waiting for its part in the concerto to arrive. And now it was playing. It was the sweet low sound of the cello.

'There you are. I've booked a table,' she said. And in saying it, and in seeing him twice in one day, Marjorie was suddenly back at Jimmy Waghorn's with Jesse. She fought it. But she was never as strong as the Mallee. So she headed off at a fast pace. Taking charge so as to maintain her fragile advantage.

To leave the Mallee behind. Wheat Bag Boy would have to puff and get red in the face if he wanted to keep up. She would have run if she could.

But Jesse didn't have a problem keeping up. He was at her side from the moment he emerged from the shadows of the statue and he stuck there – weaving through the busy streets and effortlessly keeping pace. He was like a sheepdog, the way he instinctively negotiated the moving mass of people. He was like a ball of spitty grubs in a tree the way he shimmered and swayed beside her – fascinating and dangerous as he stepped through the crowd. Ready to spit at anyone. Ready to spit the whole poisonous lot at Marjorie.

'Here we are,' said Marjorie arriving at a cafe and abruptly sitting down. Outside – where escape routes were enhanced. 'The waiter will be here in a moment. He's from Italy. He knows me. They make great coffee here.' Marjorie glared at Jesse, daring him to disagree. Pulling her cigarette case out of her handbag, she lit a cigarette and inhaled so the smoke could to do its work on her tight strings. She took her time, inhaling and slowly exhaling before she allowed herself to look at Jesse. He was leaning back. His chair tilted just a bit. Brown arms lightly crossed. Long legs loosely crossed.

'I reckoned you would still be smoking,' he said.

'Of course I bloody am. Why wouldn't I be?'

'Because it is unladylike to smoke.' Jesse smiled and pulled out his tobacco.

Marjorie's stomach lurched as she saw the tin, the packet of delicate papers, the box of matches. She turned to her own cigarette to smoke out the memories now buzzing in her head.

'And I am glad to hear you're still swearing. Even though I believe it's impossible for you to swear. Again because,

318

if I recall correctly, ladies do not bloody well swear.' It was his turn to blow out a puff of smoke. He watched it wisp away. Then turned to look at Marjorie

'Hell and damnation,' said Marjorie. 'What are you doing here?'

'I just wanted to see you.'

'Then why didn't you just sneak a look at me through a window and keep going?'

'I wanted to see for myself that you were alright.'

'Of course I'm alright. I'm not bloody dead, am I?'

Jesse looked at her while he thought about other dead people. And other dead things – like love. 'I think we need to talk,' he said.

'Crikey, Wheat Bag Boy. It's nearly four years since I last saw you,' she lied. 'What could we possibly have to say to each other now? The past is dead.'

Jesse looked away. He could see himself, a young kid, pushed over on his backside in the red Mallee dirt. He watched as he picked himself up and brushed the dirt off. 'You look fine,' Jesse said. He tried to keep sadness out of his voice. But it got in. 'Fine like a lady.'

'What do you mean?'

'I mean you look fine. Like her.'

'Like whom?' Marjorie asked very carefully.

Jesse knew it was risky. But no one won a war without taking risks. 'Like Elise. You look like her. Except for the hair, you look a lot like your mother.'

He struck swift as a tiger snake and grabbed her arm as she surged up from her chair. Her chair toppled backwards. It tried but couldn't regain its balance and it was the chair's turn this time to fall on its backside. But Jesse had Marjorie's arm.

He held her arm hard so she couldn't get away. Not without making a public spectacle of herself.

Jesse picked up her chair, still holding her arm. So they stood chest to chest. Eye to eye. On the pavement. 'You are a fine lady. Even if you do still swear and smoke.' He smiled at her. Well, at least half of his mouth smiled at her. The other half tried hard but couldn't really manage it. While he held her so she couldn't move.

Marjorie could feel him; she could smell that Jesse smell. She hadn't smelt that smell for so many years. But it wasn't that many years really – it just seemed like forever ago. And Marjorie also knew by now that four years could actually be an eternity. Marjorie breathed in that smell again, but even while she was breathing it in she knew she was making a mistake. Because she couldn't afford that smell anymore. It was much too expensive for Marjorie.

'Do you reckon we should sit down and have something to eat now?' said Jesse. 'The waiters are looking a bit worried they might miss out on a tip.'

Marjorie sat back down in her chair. Jesse ordered coffees to tie her down to a commitment.

'Here. Let's see if you still have the knack. Something to pass the time while we wait for coffee.' He pushed the tin, papers and matches across the table.

Marjorie tried to stop it, but a small smile escaped her mouth. She grabbed the tin and papers and matches. And Jesse sat back and watched as Marjorie, for the tiniest time, forgot. She forgot pangs, and a mad slaying mother, and a sister who couldn't stay. She remembered instead for a fleeting moment a boy who loved her and magical campfire nights and peppercorn trees and an old blue bench. 'That was good,' said

Marjorie when all was done but the butting out at the end of the smoking. She could have meant the smoke. Or something else.

'Why don't you ever go back?' asked Jesse into the last drifts of their smokes.

'Back where?' asked Marjorie as carelessly as she could.

Jesse placed his arms on the table and leant towards Marjorie. 'You know where I mean,' he said. His eyes refusing to let Marjorie off the hook.

'I went back.' Marjorie looked away to stop his eyes boring into her.

'I don't mean that time at the cemetery. I mean after that. You never went back. Did you?'

'I don't need to. Dad and Mum and Pa come down to visit me. There's always the telephone.'

'I don't go back much either.'

Marjorie looked at him in surprise. She wondered why she had not known that. 'Don't you live there anymore?'

'Haven't lived there for the last couple of years.'

'Why not?'

'Don't know,' he lied.

'I will never set foot in that place again.' Marjorie's red fingernails mashed the remains of the smoke into a pulp in the ashtray. 'It's getting late. I have to get home. Thanks for the smoke.' She got up and turned to run. Or at least to walk as fast as she could without drawing attention to herself.

'But you haven't eaten your tea,' said Jesse. 'You haven't even ordered it yet.'

'I don't have time now,' snapped Marjorie. 'And it's not *tea*, it's *dinner*. We eat *dinner* in the evening.'

Jesse ignored the rudeness. He also ignored the confused

waiter approaching with two coffees and a menu, and joined her on a double-time march back down the street.

'I need to talk to you again.'

'Why?'

'I haven't finished.'

'I have.'

'No, you haven't, Marjorie. You haven't finished.'

Marjorie glared at Jesse but he ploughed on. He could handle that look. 'Will it ever be finished for you?' he asked as they walked back past her library, now resting in the evening quiet. 'I want answers, Marjorie.'

'Well, you can't have them.'

'Why not?'

'Because I said so.'

'What are you scared of?' Jesse asked the back of her beautiful sleek head of hair as she tried to flee.

And there it was. Marjorie's determined march back to a semblance of safety was thrown off course. But she recovered well. So well that anybody other than Jesse would not have noticed.

'I'm not scared, Wheat Bag Boy,' she said, spinning around to face him. 'That scared Marjorie you are referring to, who ran around being scared in the Mallee – she doesn't exist anymore.'

But Jesse wasn't looking at her. He seemed to have already forgotten his question.

'I can always find you in there, you know,' he said, gazing up at the magnificent structure. 'I can always think of a million things I need to research about the Mallee. And it's all in there. Probably take me months. And if you are not there to assist me, then I am sure another librarian will.' Jesse moved his gaze from the beautiful repository to Marjorie. 'Surely one of your colleagues would be willing to help out a bloke who's come from the Mallee. Where you come from.' Jesse locked his eyes on Marjorie.

Marjorie couldn't remember Wheat Bag Boy ever beating her before. But Jesse Mitchell had beaten her. Many times. She tried her best to look him up and down. But she couldn't because his eyes wouldn't let go of her. 'For Pete's sake. Alright. One more time and then that's the end of it.'

Jesse smiled and nodded. Two muddy green eyes watching her. 'After work tomorrow then, fine lady?'

'No!' she said. 'I can't.' Then, 'Yes,' she said, trying to drag her eyes away.

'I'll be right here same time tomorrow. And if you don't turn up, I'll just have to come in and find you.' He smiled at her, then left her floundering there, gasping for air, as he turned on his heel and walked into the evening crowd.

*

'Where to this time, fine lady?' Jesse asked the following evening.

Marjorie said, 'I don't know. We can take our time. I don't have to work tomorrow. You choose.'

'Right-oh,' Jesse said after a moment's hesitation. 'Let's just wander off and see what comes up.'

So that was what they did. They wandered through the sunset into dusk, and through dusk into evening. They wandered from evening into teatime. They wandered far into the night and right through it, all the way to the next morning.

They didn't run – not this time. They didn't stoke a campfire. They didn't sit on an old blue bench within arm's length of a protective and patient peppercorn tree. They couldn't sit still like they used to. So they wandered up and down streets wide and hustling and bustling with the energy of the night-time city. They roamed tiny laneways, cosy with small talk and small groups. They strayed into parks and sat on iron benches – carefully not touching each other – and looked at the possums and the stars.

But they did talk. And after a while, it was almost like it used to be. But it didn't start out that way.

'You don't ever want to go back home?' Jesse's question seemed to take both of them by surprise as it barged in suddenly.

'No, I don't. I like it here. Why should I go back? I can have a bath anytime I feel like it here. I don't even have to wonder if the windmill has been turned on or if the dam is full before I do.'

'It's not such an easy thing to go home, is it?' Jesse said, ignoring Marjorie's watery explanation.

But Marjorie wasn't listening to Jesse. 'You know that the Mallee root is not a root at all but a stunted, twisted under-ground trunk? Did you know that?' Marjorie scowled.

'Yeah,' said Jesse.

'And what about that layer of kerosene we used to put on top of the water in the tanks to suffocate the mossies? Remember that?'

Jesse nodded. 'Yeah, I do,' he said. 'But I don't see why you should concern yourself with that anymore. Not when you haven't set foot in the Mallee since that time you visited the grave.'

Marjorie's voice, heavy and bitter, had trailed off down the street, though, so she couldn't answer straight away. 'What about you?' she asked gaily when a bright voice finally came back, leaving its heaving bitterness around the corner some-where, back with all those other soggy, encrusted memories. 'What do you like about it?'

'The night-time in winter – frost on the fences, those bright stars everywhere, and foxes calling. The smell of a full bag of wheat in the summer sun. And the smell of a shearing shed.' Jesse stopped. He could have added a few other things to the list:

—Night-time campfires near an old peppercorn tree.

—An old blue bench.

—Jimmy Waghorn.

—A strange and consoling friendship with an

extraordinary and melancholy friend.

And he could have mentioned other things as well. Like the echoing mystery of looming Furphys, thirsty for water; wind-mills and their Southern Cross fins, creaking and cranking and labouring to catch that waft of wind; a few thousand head of brown lanolin and wool roaming contented in the stubble. Or the damn trouble with families. But he didn't. He busied himself instead staring into the trees above their heads.

Marjorie broke the silence. 'I miss the rain, Jesse,' she said. She was quiet as she said it. 'I miss hearing it pelting down on a tin roof.'

Jesse nodded.

'People here don't drink rainwater.'

Jesse turned and looked at her. 'I know. Strange, isn't it? Why do you reckon that is?' he asked.

Marjorie shrugged. 'Do you remember how we would stand in puddles after a good rain? When there was a bit of a breeze rippling across the puddle? And if you looked at the water long enough you felt like you were sailing away on the puddle?'

Jesse nodded and smiled.

'And that's the other thing I miss,' she said at Jesse's smile. 'City people don't head outside to sniff the coming rain. They don't stand in rain. Everyone has an umbrella here. It seems it is best not to let the rain touch you.'

'Yeah.'

'I really don't know why, though,' said Marjorie. 'The idea is not to get wet, isn't it? If you get caught in the rain without an umbrella you use newspaper. You run around with newspaper on your head. Do you remember your father running around in the rain with a wheat bag over his head?' she said. 'Much better than newspapers.'

'I try not to remember my father,' he said as he stubbed out his smoke.

Marjorie went stiff. She knew she was precarious these days – more than she imagined Jesse could know. She was sharp, like all the bleached fence posts and rusted fencing wire and blackened tree stumps standing surrounded and trapped in their perfect crystalline salty prison. Nowadays she was brittle and frayed and paper thin, like the beautiful books she fought to conserve. And she was a fool. She had forgotten about Jesse's father.

She looked up at the evening star high above the tree. She knew what Jesse meant about the stars littering the Mallee sky. The stars were demure here. They didn't jostle – pushing and shoving for their bit of space in a black velvet sky that spread from one side of the world to the other. They didn't cram here. They were shy. They hid their real selves behind a veil here. Marjorie looked at that one fearless star and said nothing for a long, long time. Until the star gave her enough courage to look Jesse full in the face. 'You know why I left. But I don't know why you are here,' she said so quietly the noise of the star almost blotted out her words.

'No,' said Jesse. 'I don't know why you left.'

'Why are you here, Jesse?' Marjorie asked.

*

They were in a tiny coffee shop when dawn started creeping in. It was Marjorie's choice of table. At the back. The coffee was good here, and the teapots were not naked. Marjorie was sitting against the wall and facing the door. They had somehow talked right through every hour of the night. Though neither of them had yet bothered to answer the other one's question.

They had separately and instinctively, in the still, ever-watching parts of their minds, noted the warnings from the trains. And the backup warnings from the trams. At one stage, at about the usual three-o'clock-in-the-morning time, a train whistled and they both stopped and looked at each other.

'Do you remember the trains?' asked Jesse.

'Yes.'

'Right about now we would pack up and you would run off. I used to watch you,' said Jesse. 'Every time. I would stand there and watch until you had disappeared in the dark.' He stopped and shrugged off the memories.

But Marjorie could not allow any old campfire, old blue bench, peppercorn tree, Jimmy Waghorn, night-time friendship back into her life. There was no space left in her life anymore for such things. She stared at her coffee: espresso with milk. Jesse was having tea: strong and black with sugar.

'Coffee always reminds me of you and your mother. She was the first person I ever knew who drank coffee. I always loved trying that coffee,' said Jesse.

Marjorie watched him over the rim of her cup. *Do you remember that old percolator of your mother's, popping its brown bubbles into its glass lid on that old wood stove?* her coffee whispered to her. *And do you still think of that time you gave Jesse a cup of Elise's coffee?* Marjorie could not free herself from the coffee percolator's sweet reminiscences. The thoughts had escaped before Marjorie could stop them. She tried to shove them back in but they were out for good now. She sighed – she couldn't help herself. Forgetting was such damn hard work. Her eyes gave a quick dart at Jesse's teapot. Just to make sure that it was properly clothed. She looked back at Jesse across the gulf. Separated as she was from him by this small cafe table with its prim little teapot, perching clothed and confident within its rightly placed tea cosy. Quarantined there by an all-consuming farmhouse kitchen fire that was as insistent and as eternal as Elise's jocund plastic flowers, even four years later.

Marjorie shook her head to dislodge the memories. 'I have no space left in my life anymore, Wheat Bag Boy,' she said.

'What?' said Jesse.

'That was years ago, Jesse,' she said. 'I have no space left.' And she dismissed him with her cup of coffee.

'Do you think you will ever go back, Marjorie?' Jesse asked. 'Do you ever think going back is something you should do?'

'Why would it be something I should do?'

'I dunno.' Jesse shrugged. 'Catch up with your folks? See how your mother is going? See what everybody is thinking . . .'

'No,' said Marjorie. 'I do not think I will ever go back. And I do not have to go back. I know what's going on. I told you. Elise writes to me all the time. They all come down to see me. Even Pa. And there is such a thing as a telephone, you know. I talk to them all on the phone.' Her eyes flashed as she watched him over the rim of her cup.

Marjorie's surveillance of the teapot hadn't escaped Jesse, but he didn't say anything. He looked out instead at those few valiant city stars now being pushed aside by the dawn and left Marjorie to the teapot for a long while. 'Stop calling me Wheat Bag Boy,' he said finally. 'I have a name.'

Marjorie jumped. As hundreds of memories surged and broke her barriers and flooded everywhere. Unwanted memories of a much younger Marjorie taunting a stricken and secret boy. A hundred Jimmy Waghorn images followed through the breached levee of her mind. Followed by pictures of a boy who later repaid that taunting with a strange and wonderful friendship, who dared to love an angry and frightened girl.

'I'm sorry, Jesse,' said Marjorie. 'About the leaving.' She glared at him before turning to glare at the fading stars.

'That's it?' said Jesse.

'That's it.'

'Why didn't you tell me?' Jesse asked.

Marjorie stared at the footpath. 'What was there to tell? There was nothing to tell. It was all very clear what had happened. My mother was a raving lunatic. Ruby fell on the stove and got burnt. Because of me.' Marjorie stopped talking. She moved her stare from the footpath back to the teapot. 'I screamed out to Ruby for help. And she came running. And she ran right into the fire. I killed her,' whispered Marjorie to the properly clothed teapot. A slight shudder rippled across her shoulders. Marjorie needed to stop this conversation. She had to help her eyes, which were blinking hard. 'Ruby's skin was falling off, like bark off a tree. Have I told you that already? Her hair was all on fire.'

329

'You should have told me.'

Marjorie looked at Jesse. She so wanted to be tough. She so wanted not to crumple and cry like a city girl would. 'There was no time,' she said. 'I had to get the train.'

'You left me there. I waited for you for nights and nights and nights at Jimmy Waghorn's place, Marjorie,' he said. 'Just me there, Marjorie. Waiting for you to come back.'

Marjorie didn't answer that. Her eyes moved back to watch the retreating stars. 'I told them they should put Ruby out of her misery,' she said. 'I didn't have any time to tell you that. I didn't have any time to tell you I suggested they get the gun and shoot her. I had more important things to attend to.'

Jesse sat for some time, watching her turned-away face. 'All the locals know about the tea cosy hat,' he said.

Marjorie winced.

'You know how it was,' he said. 'After the concert and everybody roundabout saying Elise was a local treasure, and them all pitching in to help Bill. Well – after Ruby died – when your mother came back from the mental hospital – the locals organised a working bee at your place.'

Another good reason to be scared of bees, she thought. 'Do they hate me?' she asked.

'No. Nobody hates you. Do you think the locals blame you for what happened?'

Yes! thought Marjorie.

'Sorry, Marjorie,' Jesse said, not quite knowing what he was apologising for. 'But no one blamed you. It turns out that they all had a fair idea about what might have been going on. And everybody knew it was an accident. Nobody blamed your mother, or you. Everybody knew it was just a terrible accident.'

Marjorie stared into her coffee cup.

'If you have so successfully forgotten the kindness of the locals, I wonder what else you might have forgotten over these last few years, Marjorie?' Jesse went on. 'Have you forgotten the campfire nights at Jimmy Waghorn's place?'

'Of course I haven't forgotten,' said Marjorie. But the effort of all this remembering was taking its toll. Her face slipped and tripped under the impact. She fought to keep the wobble away from her mouth and the water out of her eyes.

'Do you remember the plasticine statues she made?' he asked.

'How could I forget them?'

'I stole one of them.'

'I know you did. They all got ruined in the end, don't you remember? I was glad you took one. I sometimes dream that it might still exist – that you saved it from death by madness.'

It was Jesse's turn to be taken aback. He wasn't sure what to say, so he said nothing. But he wanted to say this: *What else have you dreamt of over these past years, Marjorie? Did you ever dream of you and me?*

Marjorie looked at him. She was inscrutable. Non-committal. She might just as well have been one of those Mallee stars in her inscrutable non-committance.

'What about paper?' asked Jesse. 'Can you make a paper dress?'

Marjorie swallowed to stop the sigh that had filled her throat and was trying to make a run for her mouth. Her eyes didn't move from Jesse's face. She could have said any number of things to that. Things that would have made Jesse nod and smile. She could have said things like:

Yes. I am a dab hand on the Singer sewing machine now, as a matter of fact. I could make a paper dress now if I wanted to.

331

Or: *What about that soggy tomato sandwich you gave to Ruby and me in the school library that day? Do you remember that?*

Or she could have said: *Paper is nothing to be afraid of. It is not plastic.* She for sure could have said that.

But she didn't say one word. Her face was a still-life portrait of obscurity. As Marjorie watched herself standing at the dangerous edge of a salt lake, she could see the sand underneath – smooth, perfect, glazed by the unmoving water and the sun. And she was afraid because she knew too well what was underneath. 'It's late. I had better be getting home,' was what she did say.

'What's the hurry? You don't have to work tomorrow?'

Marjorie ignored Jesse. 'You can walk me to my tram stop if you like.' And she surged up from her chair and walked away.

*

'Do you think about Ruby much?' Jesse asked. It seemed to the night that this man had waited all night to find the right place to ask this question. But no places had really offered him any help. They were at Marjorie's tram stop now, waiting for her tram. So the night could see that this looked like the last place Jesse had left.

Marjorie stilled. It was a question of only six words – not a very big question. But even so, it swamped her with memories: of a Ruby who had always been there for her, of a Ruby who constantly saved her, of a Ruby who eventually died for her. Of a lock of sweet red hair preserved between the pages of a stolen sketchbook. She shrugged and fixed her eyes on the tram tracks. 'I don't see much point in thinking about Ruby anymore,' Marjorie lied. 'What's done is done.'

The tram tracks didn't notice, and if they had they wouldn't have cared. They heard much worse than that pitiful lie every day. They just kept humming to themselves and ignored the sad and angry young lady on the platform. Beautiful and ossified at once. Jesse though, as a rule, didn't tend to lose things, so that imperceptible stiffening of the shoulders and the ever-so-slight hesitation before the reply was not lost on Jesse. He filed it away with the swallowed sigh he had spotted earlier. He could see a sigh, or a lie, on a person's shoulders – day or night.

I talk to her every day, Jesse, was what Marjorie would have said if she was able to. *I see her from time to time, Jesse. I see Ruby.* 'What's done is done, Jesse,' was what she said instead.

'You know there's a drought up home?' Jesse said.

'What? Of course I know that.'

'A lot of folks roundabout are worried they are going to lose their farms.'

Marjorie swung around to face Jesse. She hesitated. Then she shook her head. She was dismissive. 'How can you lose a farm, Jesse?' she said. 'It's a permanent bit of land. It's not a screwdriver or a spanner that you can just throw down somewhere and then forget where you put it. You don't see ex-farmers wandering around confused and vague, squinting and frowning, work hats pushed back on the backs of their heads as they scratch absent-mindedly, saying, *I used to have a farm somewhere hereabouts, but I must have put it down someplace. Can't for the life of me remember where I put it . . . By the cripes, now I seem to have lost it . . . Any of you kids seen that farm?*

Jesse ignored her. 'Blokes are talking about having to walk off,' he said.

'And how can you *walk off*?' said Marjorie, shaking her head at Jesse. 'No one really *walks off*, do they? They go under. That's a fact. But they don't walk off. Most Mallee farms, if I recollect, are a long way from anywhere, and where are they going to walk to? No. It would be plain stupid to walk and Mallee farmers are generally not stupid. They won't walk off. They'll drive off.' Marjorie folded her arms and turned back to watch the tram track. But she wasn't finished. 'The Mallee has lots of ways to make people lose,' she said softly to the tracks. 'There are lots of other things besides a farm that you can lose. You can always get another farm. But there are some things you can never get back. And some things the Mallee will never let you forget.'

'I know what you mean,' said Jesse. 'Without ever meaning to, and without ever forgetting you, somehow I lost you. But you seem to have done a fine job of forgetting me.'

Marjorie stopped looking at the tracks. She looked at Jesse now and shook her head. What did Jesse Mitchell know of anything? He only knew half of this. He was only half right. Because she had no trouble forgetting Wheat Bag Boy; but she knew full well she would never be able to forget Jesse. Despite her best effort.

'I've done fair enough without you, though, over the last couple of years,' Jesse said. 'I've lived. I've managed.' He nodded at her. 'Thank you for asking, Marjorie.'

Marjorie froze.

Jesse watched her: her eyes staring at him, her body – so familiar, and yet not – lit by the soft glow of the streetlamp. She turned back to watch the approaching tram. It was slowing as it came down the line – waving its antenna at them, hissing and screeching as it stopped. One elegant shoe was placed on the second step, one gloved hand on the railing before Marjorie turned to look at Jesse. 'Goodbye, Jesse. Thank you for the visit,' she said, holding out a hand.

'I heard your mother is singing again,' said Jesse.

'Yes, she is,' said Marjorie. 'She started singing again before she left the mental hospital. It's doing her good. She's been talking to me about her singing all the time lately. My mother's singing has generally been a good thing.'

'They're putting on a concert back home, I heard. It's for the drought relief.'

Marjorie's eyes narrowed. 'I know that. Mother talks to me about that all the time as well,' she said. 'But why would that be of any concern of yours, Jesse?' Her voice floated down from the tram step, soft and suspicious.

Jesse ignored it. 'Your mother is organising it, apparently. It's a big deal.'

Marjorie's eyes were guarding hard now. 'How would you know, Wheat Bag Boy? You don't even live there anymore.'

Jesse didn't seem to hear. 'I heard it's going to be just like the concert where she won the plastic flowers. You might have very successfully forgotten quite a few things about the Mallee, but I can bet you won't have forgotten those plastic bloody flowers, Marjorie. Have you?' said Jesse.

His words had been quiet until now. But, though he didn't mean them to, now these words of his were rushing and trampling at Marjorie. She swung around. She staggered on that tram step, her arms held out against those words with their mad talk of plastic. She wanted so much to say, *Is my mother alright, do you know? I worry!* She wanted so much for Jesse to comfort her like he used to do. But she was afraid. Not just for her mother, but because she could see that this odd sort of a Jesse standing in front of her was afraid too. But why should he be afraid? So all she could do was repeat herself. 'How do you know all that? You don't even live there anymore. Why don't you live there anymore, Jesse?' she asked.

It was Jesse's turn to shrug shoulders. He turned away from Marjorie.

'We haven't finished this, have we, Jesse?' Marjorie said. She watched as Jesse stepped back, tucked his hands underneath his folded arms and leant against the light pole. Marjorie looked down at him. And now she had to choose. But she didn't really have a choice. 'You can't just turn up after all these months of lurking around out there in the crowds and then think you can simply disappear off into the crowd again. We need to finish this, Jesse,' she said.

Jesse looked up at her. He nodded. 'We sure do. I'll come over to your place,' he said.

'You don't know where I live.'

'Of course I bloody do,' he said.

A look, washed over with all sorts of sadness and regret, fled from Marjorie's eyes at that. She tried to grab it. But it was too late. It was out. *Of course my Jesse Mitchell would know that*, she thought as she watched this particular, peculiar Jesse Mitchell lumping his strange and secret yoke across his shoulders. 'Why have you been sneaking around the city these past few years, Jesse? I've seen you. You know I have seen you. Why have you been spying on me all this time?' she asked.

Trams are not as forbearing as wheat trains and this tram was getting a bit impatient. It clanged at Marjorie to get a move on, so Marjorie decided not to wait for Jesse to answer. She turned instead to obey the tram. The tram took hold of Marjorie and the doors slapped shut.

Jesse watched Marjorie. He chose not to let the tram know the answer to Marjorie's question. 'I waited for her for nights and nights at Jimmy Waghorn's place,' said Jesse instead to the side of the tram. 'She left me. Just left me there at Jimmy

Waghorn's place.' Marjorie walked to the centre of the tram. Jesse gave her a small smile. His arms were still folded across his chest, and his hands were grabbing hard at his elbows. But they still managed to give Marjorie a finger wave. And his head gave her a nod.

But Marjorie was creating a nuisance of herself with the tram and the tram had had enough. So it took off, hissing and clacking and clicking. Marjorie watched that Jesse Mitchell through the tram window as the tram, gathering speed, dragged her away.

Jesse stood in the space created by the tram stop light, watching Marjorie and the tram disappearing into the dark. Jesse stood and watched. Until the safety of the still-dim street swallowed the tram with Marjorie and her cargo of questions. He stood. Just like he used to do at Jimmy Waghorn's place. Before he turned and walked in the other direction. Until the next time. Just like he used to do at Jimmy Waghorn's place.

Chapter 18

I<small>T WAS AN</small> indolent city summer day. A lazy and soft afternoon – not like summer in the Mallee. But there was
nothing lazy and soft about these two. They were like the
dust cloud running and churning and choking behind the
harvester – trying to keep up as the harvester raced to get
the wheat off before the chasing rain. They were, once more,
carefully not touching. Sitting opposite each other under the
apple tree in Aunty Agnes's backyard. But they *were* talking.
'I don't dwell in the past, Jesse,' Marjorie said.

'So you say, Marjorie,' said Jesse.

Marjorie's eyes flashed at Jesse. 'I have moved on, Jesse. I am
making a life for myself. A good one. You need to find out how
you can do the same.'

'Do I? So I can have a life just like yours? I don't think so.'
Jesse shook his head.

'You need to stop writing those letters.'

Jesse stopped shaking his head. He swapped to nodding
slowly instead and said nothing for a while. Then he leant
forward, put his elbows on his knees. 'And just what would
make you think I haven't already?' he said.

Marjorie's head jerked. She folded and tried hard not to
crumple. Because despite what she was saying to Jesse, and
despite what she told herself, and especially because of what

she had been doing for all of that morning until nearly lunchtime, what Jesse had now said was just about the last thing she needed to hear. His letters – even when they were unread – kept her away from the edge of the salt lake. They kept her on solid ground. But Marjorie had a job to do so she wasn't going to answer that. 'What do you reckon it is about mothers and everyone always having to run away, Jesse?' Marjorie asked instead. Even though she had known for years the reasons for mothers and everybody's running. Even though she already knew what Jesse might say. Because when she had arrived home after the night out with Jesse, she got out all Jesse's letters and she read them. She smoothed them out and stroked them gently then she started with the first one and didn't stop until she had read right through to the very last. She had spent hours looking at all Jesse Mitchell's words about mothers and running. 'What do you reckon it is?' Marjorie asked.

Jesse winced. 'You tell me, Marjorie,' he said.

'I have already told you what I think about that, Jesse. Many times.' Marjorie settled herself. She clasped her arms and fixed her eyes on Jesse so he could not turn away. 'I read every one of your letters last night,' she told him. 'So. Now it's your turn. You tell me.'

It was the middle of the afternoon, but the two of them could have been back in the Mallee in the middle of a night sitting around a campfire. Marjorie sat as she had once done before – she did not stir, she did not intrude, while Jesse talked to her as he had done one time before about a mother and a father. This time, though, Jesse talked until he had no words left, until he ran out of things to say.

Once, in those long-ago campfire times, Marjorie could have put an arm around Jesse, and that was all she would have needed to do. Words would not have been necessary. But the two sitting there in the shade of the apple tree were no longer Jimmy Waghorn campfire night-time friends. They were different people now. She couldn't do that anymore. So Marjorie spoke. 'I am so sorry, Jesse,' she said.

Jesse stared at Marjorie. 'Why?' he asked. 'What for?' Then he shook his head and turned away and neither of them spoke for a long time.

It was Jesse who talked first. 'I need to tell you something else, Marjorie,' he said to the back fence he was staring at. 'I didn't just take a glorious tiny plasticine horse. I have taken something else as well.'

'What?' she said. 'What else?'

'The old blue bench,' said Jesse, his eyes leaving the fence and turning now to stare across at Marjorie. 'I took the bench. I've got Jimmy's old blue bench.'

Marjorie's lungs sucked in a huge mouthful of air.

'Where is it?' she asked.

'At my place.'

'Where at your place?'

'Out the back.'

'Where out the back?'

'Under a tree.'

'Do you light a fire?'

'Yeah.'

'Is the tree a peppercorn tree?'

'You'll probably have to find that out for yourself.'

Marjorie's eyes were tired. She hadn't had much sleep. And now here she was with some sort of a Jesse Mitchell again. And he was talking to her again. And now Jimmy Waghorn's old blue bench was somewhere here as well. It was too much.

She sat there looking at Jesse as her eyes gave up the battle. As two pearls tipped over their edges. The pearls clung for a bit on her eyelashes before starting down her face. She sat there, as the late-afternoon light bickered with the early dusk. 'I would like to see that. I would like to sit on that bench again one day,' she said.

'Yeah,' said Jesse. 'I reckon you would.'

Neither spoke for another while. Marjorie was thinking about an old blue bench. Jesse wasn't, though. He was thinking about something else. He looked across at Marjorie. It could have been another one of those Jesse Mitchell sizing-up looks, but it had too much sadness soldered onto it to be just that. 'You're still running, aren't you?' he said.

And again, he'd caught her off guard. She took a long time to answer. 'Yes,' she said. 'Yes I am. Sometimes. It helps.' *There are no blazing, jostling stars now, though; no sentinel frosts,* she thought. And if she had thought some more while she was staring right at Jesse she would have thought that running is not always about leaving. It is not always about getting away. And she might have said, *Running can be about finding your way, you know.* But she didn't. She said, 'And I always make sure I am home before sun-up.'

'Me too,' was all Jesse said.

The sun was trying hard not to leave them in darkness because it knew Marjorie had something else to say this day about running: 'I'm going home for a while,' she said.

'Why? I thought you never wanted to go back.'

'I'm not going to up stumps and move back there, Jesse. I know I said I would never go back but now I need to. For Mum. I'm just going to go for a few days. My life is here now. And I happen to think my life these days is alright.'

Marjorie watched Jesse as she said this, her eyes skimming his face, looking for signs of quarrel, daring him to disagree. But all she could see were confused eyes: eyes that didn't know if they were supposed to be the colour of gum leaves or the colour of wheat bags; eyes that were uncertain. So Marjorie said something else: 'But I have been worried for a while that my mother might be not very well right now. Like that time with the bees. And those awful plastic bloody flowers.' Marjorie stopped. 'And now you turn up,' she went on. 'And you talk about the concert and you talk about the plastic.' Marjorie stopped again because she didn't want to talk about the other times – with the tablets, and the fires.

Jesse nodded. 'Is it the drought fundraiser, do you think?' he asked.

'Who knows?' Marjorie shrugged. 'Yes. Probably. But who ever really knows? Anyway, I can tell that Dad is worried, so I've told him I'll come home for a while and give him a hand. I thought that might have been why you finally stepped up and spoke to me instead of running off like a squib into the crowd. I thought maybe you knew something and were worried about my mother.' Marjorie smiled a raggedy smile in Jesse's direction.

Jesse's face reddened. 'I could come with you,' he said suddenly. 'I could give you a hand.'

'How exactly would you give me a hand, Jesse?'

'I might give your mother a hand. Sing in her concert.'

'You can't do that, Jesse.'

'Why can't I?'

'You can't even sing.'

'And how would you know that, Marjorie?'

And the sun, which had already stretched itself as far as

it could go across the yard, was at last overcome by the talk of those two under the tree – and by the night shadows. The shadows were hard pushing at it now, and the sun was stumbling and trembling towards the back fence. Marjorie and Jesse sat as the sun, red-faced and worn weary, was shoved, and fell over the fence into the shadows of the vacant block behind.

*

Jesse wasn't the only one who, over the years, had been tiptoeing around the perimeter of Marjorie, hiding behind sandhills and silos, lugging their own burdens of things that needed to be said, dredging patterns and ciphers in the sand as they passed, like stumpy-tailed lizards in the night. A gauntlet of womenfolk was piled up on the crushed-quartz platform that day, waiting for Marjorie. They pushed ahead of her father, who had come into town to collect her while Pa waited back at the house with Elise. Those women hunched together there, each with a hand as an awning against the glare, their hankies flapping at flies, as Marjorie stepped down from the carriage into a brutal Mallee summer day.

Marjorie looked at the small, boiling bunch of them in the heat. She was taken aback, but she nodded at them. Not to say *hello*, as they might have assumed, but because she didn't think she had any other choice. Because even though it had been a lifetime ago, she recognised this group straight away; she could see it as plain as day. It was sitting there on all their hot faces and suspended there in those waiting eyes: floating either plaintive or hopeful. Anybody else might think it a strange place for them to gather, these shuffling women, their shoes trundling in the sun. But it was not strange. It was the certain and right place. Because these women were a mending party, a sewing guild. They were all of them in the business of mutual darning and patching. They were there because they had for a long time accepted the collective benefits of everybody getting around everybody else, gathering quietly in their clusters with their Birch Quick Unpicks and their darning mushrooms – giving a person a hand when there was a great deal of individual unpicking and redoing that needed to be done in life.

'Marjorie, love,' said Aunty Thelma as she kissed her on the cheek. 'Thank goodness.'

'I've missed you, dear,' said Mrs Cameron. 'Let me look at you,' she said as her ample arms surrounded Marjorie.

'Shirlene Doherty is organising the supper for your mother's concert. She volunteered,' said Aunty Kathleen. 'She has also offered to drive you out to the cemetery. Daylight or dark.'

Marjorie looked across at Shirlene Doherty's face nodding away in an effort to dislodge its weight of apprehension. 'I'm making your mother's meringues. That's what I'll be bringing for the supper,' said Shirlene. Her nodding head was working hard.

Marjorie had used such a lot of words over the past couple of days with Jesse Mitchell. She looked around at the women bundling around her. She opened her mouth but no words would come out, so Marjorie realised she must have used all of them up and now she had no words left. But she thought something. Marjorie's eyes turned to Shirlene Doherty. *Thank you, Shirlene Doherty. Thank you*, thought Marjorie as her father stepped forward.

*

And now Marjorie was back in that house again. Bill had transported Marjorie and her fine city suitcase with its brass hinges and triangular corner guards and fleur-de-lis pattern down the dusty miles and through all the slumping wire gates to the farmhouse. So here she was. In the kitchen once more.

She was scanning her mother's face as the two of them sat there at the old kitchen table. The north wind was rattling and slapping on the other side of the closed back door. It was tormenting the place: thumping roundabout; skidding against the bedroom window where she had dumped her suitcase; clouting the tin on the roof.

A fan moved in the kitchen – dull and despondent in its failing efforts to battle the day. The cocky divided his time between spreading his wings before its spiritless efforts and eyeing Marjorie out of his side-on head. Elise was talking and talking as her hands fluttered through the air. 'I am putting on a concert recital,' she was saying.

And Marjorie sat stiff with fright as bits of her mother's glitter hovered and piled around the room. 'I know. You have told me all this before. Why are you telling me this?'

'These are unhappy times. Everyone here is struggling. We all need this concert, Marjorie.'

'Why do you need it? What is it going to give you, Mother, that you need?' Marjorie asked.

Elise's hands cut short their fluttering. They stopped in front of Elise's face and she peered through their spread fingers at her daughter. 'I don't know what you mean, Marjorie,' she said. 'What are you saying?'

'I am saying: *Are you alright?* I am saying: *What are you going to do if they give you more of those plastic bloody flowers?*'

Elise smiled then. She flicked her stilled fingers back into life. Flicking them in Marjorie's direction. 'You don't have to worry, Marjorie. You know I do not commune with those flowers anymore. They refused to provide any solace for all those months at the hospital and I don't expect them to start now. I am dead to them, Marjorie,' she said. 'And that language is uncalled for. You are not a filthy little guttersnipe. I am so glad you have come back, Marjorie. This concert will be much more marvellous than those recitals I performed in my wrought-iron-emblazoned mental institution. Those newspaper reporters will have another think coming after they have seen this.'

'Who is looking after you? Are you taking enough care of yourself?' asked Marjorie as she watched the glitter of her mother's mind swaggering in the weary waft of the fan.

'Oh. I don't have time for that sort of thing now. I have a drought relief opera in the Mallee to produce.' Elise smiled gaily and patted Marjorie on the arm. 'That boy Jesse Mitchell is going to come back. He is thinking about singing in my production. He might come up from the city on the train. Or drive a car. I don't know which.'

'He can't do that!' said Marjorie.

'Do what?' asked Elise, momentarily mystified. 'Drive a car? I think he can.'

'Sing in your concert.'

'Sing? Of course Jesse can sing if he wishes. And I really don't think it is any business of yours, Marjorie, who sings in my recital. And I don't appreciate that tone, young lady!'

'Why would he do that? Why would you let him? He can't even sing!' said Marjorie, ignoring her mother.

But it seems that answering Marjorie's questions was another thing that Elise didn't have any time for at the moment. 'His mother, who is very devoted to my work, told me he might be interested,' Elise continued, her words getting faster and faster.

Elise was in a hurry now because the words were jamming and piling and anxious to get out of her mouth. 'I am hoping Jesse will have a tenor voice. I need one of those. He will be untrained, of course, but so is everyone out here in the dusty middle of nowhere. And we don't ever let that stop us.'

Marjorie had another go. 'Jesse can't just turn up in town again out of nowhere and think he can butt in on your concert, just like that.'

Elise stopped. She was taken aback. But only for a moment. 'Well of course he can, you silly girl. Why could he not?' she said.

'Because I said so. Because you don't even know if he can sing. You have already admitted that.'

Elise wasn't heeding her, though. 'And his mother has quite a nice little voice too. You could take a leaf out of their book as far as devotion goes.' Elise was nodding enthusiastically at Marjorie. 'I will teach Jesse how to sing – if I need to,' Elise said, almost as an afterthought.

Marjorie turned away from the singing lessons and devotion. 'There will always be droughts, Mother,' she said. 'They are as eternal in this place as the salt and the sand. You don't have to do this if it's too much for you.'

But Elise had forgotten for a moment about the perpetually returning droughts. 'It is a terrible thing that happened to Jesse's father – that accident. It is a wonder his mother can sing a note at all after that.' The glitter jostled and crowded. 'Why are people not more careful, Marjorie? Farming is a perilous thing.'

'Jesse told me about it,' said Marjorie. She might have sounded dismissive, but she really wasn't. It was just that she was concentrating on her mother, wanting to grab Elise and swat at that simpering glitter floating all around her. 'You need to look after yourself. There will be no concert if you don't look after yourself.'

Elise pulled away from Marjorie. Her beautiful hands danced again in the air between them. 'I am looking after myself in an appropriate manner, Marjorie,' she said. 'Considering the circumstances. Any decent person could expect no more of me than I am so far managing in heat such as this. Could they?'

'No! You're not looking after yourself! And you damn well should be. And yes, I can. I expect so much more,' said Marjorie. Her chair toppled as she reached and grabbed to hem in the cavorting hands.

*

Marjorie was shivering in the heat by teatime. They ate: Pa at one end of the table, Bill at the other end. Elise was sitting in her seat with her back to the stove. And Marjorie, shivering, sat alone on the other side of the table.

'Where are your tablets?' Marjorie asked as she handed her mother a cup of coffee.

'They're on the mantelpiece,' said Pa, watching Elise over the top of his saucer of tea.

'They are not necessary,' said Elise.

'I am waiting to see you swallow one,' said Bill, clearing the dishes from the table, keeping an eye on Elise as Marjorie reached for the tablets.

It was a summer night. They might have finished their tea, but it would be a while before it got dark. The north wind had gone home for the night, though. Bill and Marjorie and Pa glanced away and noticed, and glanced away and held their breath, and slurped their tea and clattered the dishes in the slowing light of the kitchen as Elise put a tablet in her mouth and swallowed her coffee.

'I've got some traps to check down by the shearing shed,' said Pa to Marjorie as the last of the dishes were put away with the last of the daylight and they were as sure as they could be that the tablet was gone.

'I'll help your mother in the lounge room with the piano practice. You two go and check on me traps,' said Pa, nodding in the direction of the back door. Marjorie's eyes widened. She was about to say something about Pa and classical piano and operatic competence but he saw her look. 'Go on, you two, don't just stand there,' he said. 'You think I don't know about how a bloody piano works after all this bloody time?'

So it was Marjorie's turn now, all these years later, to stand there in the quieting heat of a Mallee summer twilight. To stand there with Bill at the shearing shed yards. To lean her elbows beside his on the rough chopped rails. To stare with him at the gruff loveliness of a Mallee farm preparing itself for a well-earned night's rest after defeating a day sent to oppress.

'We've done our level best,' said Bill to the retreating swelter in front of him.

'I know,' said Marjorie.

They stared at the Mallee trees on the fence line in the distant gathering gloom.

'I'm fretting. I have to admit it, Marjorie. Fretting from daylight to dark that your mother is forgetting to take those tablets,' said Bill.

'It won't be forgetting, Dad,' said Marjorie. And Marjorie couldn't help but tally up all the other forsaken tablets lying about in the past, and the fire that swallowed them instead. Such tiny things, such giant penalties. 'So much glitter. I get frightened when there is so much glitter around,' she said. Her voice was soft in the dusk.

Bill nodded.

'People roundabout have pulled together, ya know. The womenfolk have been doing what they can for your mother since she came back home this time. Since Ruby. Everybody hereabouts appreciates why you've been needing to stay in the city with Aunty Agnes. Kathleen . . . Thelma . . . Mrs Cameron . . . even that Shirlene. But it's a shame it had to take what happened here for them to see how it can be for someone like your mother.'

Bill stopped. You might have thought he had finished. But this was a hard conversation and he was hoping for some help from the darkening furrows – which all ignored him. So he had to push on alone. 'It's not the same without you here, Marjorie. I'll admit that,' he said. 'It's not the same without your sister.' Bill's eyes were on the paddock in front of him. They were blinking fast and hard like Bill wanted to really make sure that paddock understood all this before it disappeared into the dark of the night. His voice dropped then to a sound as quiet as the mopoke. 'I was thinking your mother had finally got the better of this place. But I can't help thinking the tablets just aren't doing their job lately,' he said.

Marjorie nodded.

'Your mother needs this concert, Marjorie.'

'I can see that. I wish she didn't, though,' said Marjorie.

'By crikey, everybody hereabouts needs it too,' said Bill. 'Your mother has given everybody a bit of optimism with this concert of hers. There's folks here that see this concert as a means of holding out for one more season. A lot of folks round here seem to be pinning their hopes on your mother, you know.'

Marjorie's head stared straight ahead.

'And all the locals are behind you too, Marjorie. There's no point dragging it all out again, but everybody knows what's what. Your sister wouldn't want you brooding over things like this. You have got to put it behind you, girl.' Bill's head went up and down, up and down, up and down.

Marjorie's head didn't move.

'I'm counting on you. You know that. It'll only be for a few weeks, but if you can keep getting those tablets into her and help her through this concert, she will be back on an even keel and then all this will be over. You can go back to the city then. When she's calmed down. Some of us are a bit worried this concert business is turning out to be too much of a weight for your mother. If you can just help her like you did last time at the mental hospital. You know what I mean. She's a thoroughbred, your mother. She's not like you. She's not built for heavy loads like this – all that hope pinned on her. Not in this heat.'

Marjorie's eyes moved themselves from considering the distant scrub. They turned to study her father. *How?* she wanted to ask her father. *I don't really know how I helped my mother last time. So how can I help her this time?* 'What is she doing with all that paper? What is she planning on doing with all those packets of crepe paper piled up everywhere in the kitchen?' she asked.

*

Bill hung about the kitchen the next morning. He came in after milking the cow and put the milk bucket on the bench. But instead of heading out the back door again, he sat down at the table. Next to Pa. And opposite Marjorie.

Elise was in her seat next to the kitchen stove. Near the old coffee percolator. Jauntily defying the heat of the stove and the prospect of a replication of yesterday's over one hundred and ten degrees in the shade.

'Cup of tea, Dad?' asked Marjorie.

Pa's fingers were moving up and down on the table. Marjorie looked at his spindly face with its patches of sorrow sewn in behind the stubble. Once his fingers would have been drumming.

'Cup of coffee, Mum?' she asked.

Pa's fingers reached for his pipe. He pushed tobacco into the bowl.

Nerves jangling and clanging all around the table were adding to the already heated day. But Elise didn't notice. She wasn't jangling.

'I've done my level best with your mother over these past weeks – got her cups of tea – even made sure there was plenty of milk and always one of those useless saucers of hers – too small for any bloody good – underneath,' muttered Pa between puffs of pipe lighting. 'But caring for the likes of your mother is no job for a man. A man's not built to be good at this sort of thing.' His teeth clamped down on the pipe. His eyes blinked hard.

Elise smiled at the stove.

Marjorie turned to her. 'Your concert is going well then, Mother?' asked Marjorie.

Elise smiled.

Pa jiggled.

Bill stood.

'Well, you had better start taking those tablets again, Mum, if you want it to stay that way,' Marjorie said.

It was the kind of bald, no-nonsense statement that sat well in a Mallee environment. Bill and Pa each sucked in a breath, though. Because pared-back, skun-rabbit talk was never what Elise appreciated and Marjorie should have remembered that. Marjorie's sentence hung there waiting for Elise, but Elise did not take offence. She seemed unperturbed by it. She knew the reasons for things being as they were. 'The tablets have gone stale from the heat. I am sure of it. They are rancid. They have weevils in them now. So I won't be taking them anymore. Besides, I feel so happy and full of beans lately. I don't need those tablets,' Elise said. Her smile brightened. She stood up.

But Marjorie was too quick for her mother this time. She lurched – just like she had done years ago – pitching herself towards that stove, and this time Marjorie got there first, and this time she didn't stumble. 'You don't want to have to go back to the mental hospital though, do you, Mum?' Marjorie said as her arms reached for the mantelpiece, as she snatched the hiding tablets.

Elise gaped at her daughter. Dismay replaced the smile. But not for long. It was quickly shoved aside by bright glittery confidence. 'I am well able to take care of myself and to know when, and if, I need to be taking any tablets!' said Elise. 'And you would do well to remember who you are, Marjorie. We do not interrogate people about their private medical matters. And we do not mention mental hospitals in polite company. For pity's sake!' she said. She folded her arms and her lovely grey eyes were no longer soft. Glitter swirled, cavalier.

Marjorie shoved the tablets in the crook of her arm. She turned from her mother and surveyed the room. 'What is all this paper doing in the kitchen?' she asked.

'It's a bloody mess is what it is,' said Pa. 'It got the better of me last week and I tried to clean it up. A kitchen's no place for all this,' he said, his arm sweeping. 'But I caused such a ruckus with your mother that I had to bring it all back again.'

'Unformed costumes,' said Elise. She ignored Pa as she grabbed Marjorie by the arm. 'That is what all this lying about paper is. Because they will not come forth and be made. I am struggling with them. They threaten me and will ruin the recital. All that indolent paper lounging around in the corners like it has nothing better to do. It is overwhelming.'

'You are making the costumes out of paper?'

'Yes. Crepe paper. Do you remember Ruby's dress?'

Do I remember Ruby's dress? How could I ever forget that dress? How could I forget one single thing about Ruby? thought Marjorie. She wanted to say, *No!* She nodded instead. She looked at all the piles of crinkly coloured paper waiting in the corners.

'It is not actually the paper's fault,' said Elise, waving distractedly at it. 'The real reason is that I just don't have the time for so many costumes. There are so many good people singing who actually don't know how to and I have to show them. And you know that an opera must be magnificent in every way. It must have grace and beauty in style as well as sound.'

Pa muttered quietly to himself. Elise peered at him. 'And Bill's father sitting over there is no help. *He* can't sew,' said Elise.

But paper had always been waiting in the wings, ready for the rescue of many, even if Elise's lack of time wouldn't permit. And it did its job once more in that farmhouse kitchen. It had already whispered to Marjorie, from its various dusty kitchen corners, of the possibilities of medication and magic to aid nerves in need, once again, of a tuning fork. And Marjorie had taken seriously the anxious whispery papery talk leaking steadily towards her out of the shadows like water escaping through the red dirt of a broken channel bank, and she had then talked about it to her father the night before. 'I can help you, I think, Mother,' said Marjorie carefully. 'If you will let me. I will sew all the costumes for you – if you will take all the tablets for me.'

Bill and Pa's air was stuck in their chests as they waited.

'It is a treadle sewing machine. You will sew backwards. You will not make costumes. You will unmake them with all your backwards treadling,' said Elise, shaking her head, dislodging fragments of glitter. 'I might make many wonderful papery costumes – sewing and sewing into the dark of the night. But time has deserted me. There is not enough of it left now. I could sew and sew, but I still wouldn't get them all done in time. I will be found wanting. I will not be good enough. I could take all the medications in the world prescribed by that insane asylum that you so rudely speak of, Marjorie, but it is not magic, you know.'

'I have learnt,' said Marjorie. 'I know how to treadle front-wards. And I also know how to treadle backwards, if needs be.'

'How do you know?' asked Elise.

'Aunty Agnes showed me.'

Elise stopped. She was astonished. She thought about her daughter's declaration. And the glitter paused – unsettled, uncertain. 'I could try taking the tablets then. If you do not inadvertently sew backwards,' Elise said, contemplating the prospect.

'That's the way, love,' urged Bill. 'Go on. Marjorie's good at it. Aunty Agnes told me. She makes all her own city clothes now.'

'Good,' said Marjorie. 'You and I have an understanding then.' She nodded once at her mother before raising her hand and pointing her finger. 'But if you ever stop taking the tablets, I promise you I will destroy all the costumes I have made.' Her pointed finger moved in warning. 'I will screw them up – the whole lot – and burn them, every single one of them.'

Elise's eyes were wide as they followed Marjorie's pointing finger. Elise considered this a more than fair bargain. Because she believed Marjorie. And she well understood about the circumstances and reasons for things being burnt. And she also understood lofty consequences where concerts were concerned.

Pa took his pipe out of his mouth. 'Then that settles it, doesn't it?' he said. 'Why are we all just sitting around flapping our gums? There's work to be done. Take a bloody tablet, Elise, and let's get on with this concert you're doing.'

Pa and Bill and Marjorie watched while Elise swallowed a tablet. 'Elise, love,' Bill then said, his voice gentle, 'you make sure you keep taking that medicine. Because if you don't, I reckon Marjorie intends doing something about it.'

Marjorie's arms had folded themselves again. 'I promise you I do so intend,' she said. 'I will get Aunty Agnes to call the mental hospital the moment you stop taking the tablets and I'll see about taking you back there myself if I have to.' No more words came out of her mouth. They didn't need to.

'Too right about that, Bill,' said Pa. 'And I'll give the girl a hand.' Pa's chin was stubbly and wobbly – keeping company with the words wobbling out of his mouth.

'And you, girl,' Bill said, turning to Marjorie, 'I hope you really can sew.' Bill's face tottered a bit under the unfamiliar, uneven weight of a grin – a grin only big enough to fit one side of his mouth, but it was there: the first grin for many a day. Then

Pa and Bill and more than a decent measure of hope stood up and walked together out the back door and into the sagging heat.

*

Elise marvelled at her daughter. Marjorie sat in that house, and Marjorie and her mother's Singer sewing machine treadled together into the late hours of the days and the early hours of the nights. And the prowling heat and the pervading glitter could do what they liked, but they were no match for that old Singer sewing machine with its confidently treadling Marjorie. And just like Elise had done all those years ago, Marjorie took in her arms those piles of rustling crepe paper packets and created magic. It was a garden that she created. But Marjorie's garden was not a plastic garden full of glee and gloat. It was a whimsy, a soft whispery papery garden. It was a chimera. Crepe paper costumes blossomed everywhere in that kitchen. They flourished there, clustered around the Singer Sewing Machine in their myriad colours, in their flounces and folds, their crimps and their pleats. They jostled and rustled – every colour under the sun that had been lucky enough to be put into crepe paper.

Elise was bolstered by all that paper magic steadily spreading through her kitchen. She swallowed her tablets – day by day, costume by costume, rehearsal by rehearsal. And her courage grew. So even though she would still, at odd times of the day or night, find herself in a struggle against her enduring secret lack of grace, she was able to swallow again and again and again. And she was able then to rise up and slap and kick and clout and sweep nearly all of those noiseless murmurings of her secret failings out the back door, where they withered and frizzled in the heat of the drought.

And Marjorie and her father and Pa watched as the glitter dwindled from the air around Elise. They watched as that glitter shifted and shuffled and settled instead on those lovely crepe paper costumes clustering and bunching in all corners of the kitchen. Until Elise was calm and sure from all those swallowed tablets, and the costumes were fine and magical with all that glitter. And it was time for all that paper splendour to be taken to the town hall for the concert.

Jesse saw them first. Jesse was standing in the middle of the stage. He was stewing. But not from the heat. His two-toned eyes were wary. They couldn't make up their mind whether to survey the pile of papery costumes now transported and clustered and whispering to themselves behind the stage curtains in the dusty little hall, or to glue themselves onto Marjorie. Because this was the first time his eyes had seen Marjorie since their time in the backyard at Aunty Agnes's place. 'What's all this then, Marjorie?' he asked.

'What's all this then, Jesse?' said Marjorie. And her face was as wary as Jesse's eyes.

'What?'

'You. Back here in this place. Sneaking around and taking singing lessons from my mother and planning on singing in an opera.'

'I told you I might lend a hand. I'm not bloody sneaking.'

'And I told you that you couldn't sing.'

'And I asked you, if I remember rightly, how would you know?'

Marjorie stared at those lovely undecided eyes and they stared right back. 'When can I see you, Marjorie?' Jesse asked.

'No time for that. You have to make sure you have that singing voice all properly tuned up.'

'I can spare some time; I don't have to be practising all day.'

'Well I can't. I have no time to spare. I am very busy making things. These are all the things I've been busy making,' she said, waving her arm at the costumes while her eyes stayed where they were. 'These are the costumes for the opera.'

Jesse looked at them. 'They're all women's dresses. Where are the men's costumes?'

Marjorie smiled a smile of sweet and subtle reprisal. 'Everybody in the opera will be wearing a dress. Women and men. The play requires it. There's one there for you. I made it myself.'

Jesse's eyes moved from one end of the papery cluster to the other. He looked worried. 'They're all made out of paper. Like that one Ruby had.'

'Yes, they are. Every one of them.'

'Do you think that's a good idea?'

'Ruby will be thinking it is a very good idea, Jesse.'

'What about Elise? Does she think it is a good idea?'

'It was her idea.'

'Alright then.' Jesse nodded slowly to himself. 'So. What we have here then is everybody wearing a dress. A dress made out of paper. The men too.' His slowly nodding head was dubious. His eyes couldn't make up their mind either.

Chapter 19

EVERYBODY IN THAT little Mallee town who was willing to give it a go had been practising for this concert for months by now. They were like a country league footy team in their fervent training with the sniff in the wind of a grand final opportunity. Except they were training for their voices to be singing an opera not their legs to be kicking a footy. They had been drawn together from farms in every direction and they were dogged now in their determination to have a collective go at this bizarre city-singing grand final. Even Jesse – that last-quarter, late-season ring-in – was training non-stop. It was *Turandot*. Nobody knew what inspired Elise to choose *Turandot*. Hardly any of the locals thereabouts had ever even heard of *Turandot*. They had shaken their heads. Not just at the grand and peculiar notion of an opera daring to be sung in their little old town hall, but at the much greater peculiarity that had led to them putting their hand up to actually do the concert. How had Elise managed to persuade that motley crowd of ordinary Mallee folk struggling to do their best in the middle of a drought to stand on a dusty stage and sing an entire opera in the middle of a summer that seemed like it was never going to end? A summer that had discourteously refused to provide any one of them with even a half-decent harvest.

'Heard you're gunna give Elise's fancy singin' a go,' they might have been heard to say.

'Yeah. Ya're prob'ly thinkin' I'm mad as a cut snake, but I'm givin' it a burl,' they perhaps could have been heard to reply.

'Can ya sing?'

'Dunno.'

'Better than sittin' home and watching the crop die before your eyes though, eh?'

'Yeah. There's that for sure.'

So what better choice was there than *Turandot*? It was a crazy choice and a crazy opera. An Italian opera based on a German adaptation of a Persian poem about an Asian princess and a Chinese warrior which is sung in Italian, and described by those who know of such things as a flawed masterpiece. And it was now going to be sung in the middle of a Mallee drought by people wearing dresses made out of paper. So *Turandot* was perfect.

There were, however, a number of operatic shortcomings that were a struggle for Elise from early on. The concert had no orchestra. Just Elise and a violin player. Just Elise and a piano player. But everybody knew that all along and they didn't mind. And no conductor. Just a baton carved by Bill from a bit of a Mallee stick, and Elise. And everybody hereabouts knew that as well and thought that a Mallee stick wielded by Elise was as good as any that the city might have to offer. And no principal singer – just Elise. And no knowledgeable, tuxedoed devotees of the opera to fill this small Mallee town hall – those who might have been acquainted with a bit of Italian. Just all those locals – loyal and stoic and courageous – there with their singular Queen's English and in their Sunday best. And everybody knew that too.

Try as everybody might, though, the singers could not help worrying about that one particular, sticky defect: that the opera was going to be sung in a foreign language and nobody was going to understand any of it. And no matter how they whispered quietly to themselves about it, they had no answer for such a lumpy problem. 'Elise, we'll be singing the whole thing in a foreign language,' Aunty Kathleen, the elected spokeswoman, had pointed out early on as gently as she could.

'That's right. The opera is sung in Italian.' Elise smiled.

'But we can't talk Eyetalian. You can't expect everybody to learn Eyetalian as well as learning to sing just for this. Can you?' asked Shirlene.

'Does anybody know an Eyetalian that maybe could put it all in English for everybody?' suggested Mrs Cameron.

But Elise would not be dissuaded. 'We are singing in Italian as Puccini intended. We will not desecrate it. But Elise was used to life flinging barriers at her, and used to facing any number of inadequacies that had been upended in her path, so the dearth of Italian understanding wasn't going to damage Elise. She had foreseen this difficulty and she knew what to do. 'Don't worry. I have always had a solution,' she said. 'Our *Turandot* will not fail because of our insufficiency in the Italian language. I will assist everybody here throughout the concert. All of you will learn the words – in Italian. You will sing in Italian. And I will be there to support any in the audience who lack understanding in anything but English.'

'I think that might be the entire audience,' suggested Shirlene.

'Quite so, Shirlene,' Elise agreed, nodding.

*

Elise's drought relief fundraiser was a sell-out success. The hall was jam-packed on the night of the concert. Locals turned up in drove after drove. They came from every direction, leaving plumes of Mallee dust to hang on the horizon in the warm night air. Cars cruised disbelievingly then resignedly past the front of the hall and down the road as their occupants realised they were not going to be able to park right out the front, or even in the now-full vacant block next door. Everybody for miles around marched themselves and their Sunday bests up the path to the front entrance of the hall, where they had to throw in a heap on the floor their Mallee sensibilities of tolerable personal space and stuff themselves precariously close together on the hard, wooden benches. Folks settled in, hauling their inadequate single-language competencies with them, and filled that hall past its brim.

Marjorie was near the stage. She had appropriated a place at the very front for herself, Bill and Pa. The three of them were sitting now in their front-row seats, with Marjorie in the middle. They were staring up at the dark dusty red curtains straddling the stage front. Shielding, until they were ordered to do otherwise, Marjorie's mother and her troupe of singers with their songs of love and betrayal in a language no one could understand. But all those opera-singing locals there behind the curtain had not worried about any of this for a long time. All of them, up there now, ready and waiting behind the stage, dressed in their paper costumes, were confident that Elise had fixed the Italian problem.

And Elise had. Elise didn't let down anybody in that packed-out little hall. The curtains moved aside and there was Elise facing the audience, standing in front of her lined-up, rustling, magical singers, her Mallee-stick baton in hand.

'This is a story about mistakes people make, and love and fear, and having to live, and having to die. It is about death. It is about trying your hardest even if it means dying. It is about trying even when you don't understand. It is about triumphing against the odds. It is about love.' Elise's smile was radiant. 'And it is also in Italian. Which I will translate for you all. From time to time.'

And so Elise did. From the moment those curtains drew aside, Elise would turn to her operatic audience whenever it occurred to her and she would call out the story, while those beautifully ordinary, courageous country folk rustling on the stage in their crepe paper sang their Chinese story in their dusty Italian Mallee accents. They sang the whole night through, as best they could, to their utmost, in their magical crepe paper costumes. They sang and held their chins up against failed crops and dying sheep and bone-dry dams. They sang for the beauty of human frailty in the face of almost anything. They sang.

'This one is for you, Ruby,' Elise called as Jesse's mother sang her aria. 'The gentle, faithful Liù who was willing to kill herself for love because someone she adored took the time to smile at her.'

And just about everybody from hereabouts knew what that meant. 'Ah . . .' sighed nearly all of the hall as Jesse's mother sang:

'That was won by such flame
I will love even you
Before this dawn
I will close my weary eyes.'

Bill and Marjorie and Pa weren't among the sighers, though. They sat silent. They stared up at Elise and Jesse's mother.

Then Bill reached for his daughter's hand and patted it as Marjorie blinked and blinked and Pa cleared his throat.

'This one is for you, Marjorie,' Elise called again as Elise sang Turandot's aria. 'A beautiful ice princess who thinks her only option is to kill anyone who tries to love her.' Elise waved her baton for the chorus to join in.

'And now Jesse, with his beautiful tenor voice, will sing "Nessun Dorma",' Elise called over her shoulder to the audience.

'Think about this one, Marjorie,' cried Jesse, joining Elise in the calling-out. He stepped forward in his crepe paper. 'He's saying: *None shall sleep, even you, oh Princess, in your cold room. But I will succeed. Vincerò!* That's what this song is about.' And he walked to the front of the stage, his crepe paper Chinese warrior creation shoving and rustling and glinting on all sides.

But what Jesse and Marjorie weren't to know was that they were not the only passengers able to catch a train out of the city and into this town. That stage fright had crept on board one day as well and found its way back, even after all these years. It had snuck once more into this small dusty place and had been hiding out backstage in the town hall for days. And now it grabbed Jesse and strangled him hard. After all his days and days of practice – hours spent rehearsing with Elise in the middle of this stage with the daddy-long-legs quivering and trembling in the corners; hours spent practising by himself in the dark of the night under the reproving glare of the sandhill, or all alone in the middle of the day on an idle and wasted farm – now he couldn't sing out what was there in front of him. And it was such a little song. It was only three minutes long. Not even half enough time necessary for an adult to drown in a dam. But Jesse stood voiceless.

Elise saw it. 'Stage fright has no part in our production, Jesse,' she murmured, stepping up to his side. 'It is a thing devoid of all mercy. Don't worry. I have encountered it many a time and now I will help you defeat it. We will not stumble,' she whispered into his face.

But Elise couldn't do everything. She couldn't help everyone at the same time. She had to turn her back on the chorus to help Jesse, and the chorus faltered straight away without Elise and her Mallee-stick baton. It lurched and stumbled as Calaf blundered against his supposed triumphant assurance that he would win the princess when the new day dawned.

Bill stood up then. He inspected the teetering debacle in front of him like he was inspecting a line of dead rabbits hanging off the back of the ute. He squinted at the piano player and the violinist. He peered at the chorus. He looked at Elise and he looked at Jesse. Bill straightened his tie, buttoned his suit coat, picked up his hat, lifted his head high. He turned then, as if to walk out on the shame of the shambling chorus, the disgrace swarming in Jesse's eyes at his suddenly faithless voice. But Bill wasn't going to do that. He was turning to his daughter. 'Look after this,' he said as he gave Marjorie his hat. Then: 'I'll do the conducting, Elise,' he called. 'You help the lad with the song.' And Bill leapt onto the stage, grabbed the stick of Mallee from his wife and started conducting. Because he had heard this song enough times in his life by now to know what to do.

And out of the blue Marjorie was standing now and she was yelling. 'Sing it, Jesse. Sing it!' she yelled.

Then Pa was standing beside her, charging in like he was the nineteenth man just given a chance to run on the field in this grand final: 'Gorn, you lot, don't just stand there gawping like a flamin' stupid chook cooking itself in the midday sun – get singing, ya fools,' he ordered the chorus. 'Give that stick what for, Bill,' he bellowed to his son.

And Elise stood with Jesse and led him into 'Nessun Dorma'.

'That's the way, lad! Give it what for!' roared Pa.

'Keep going, Jesse! Keep going!' called Marjorie.

They were the coaches, those two. There on the sidelines and shouting their encouragements. But not everyone was pleased:

'Quiet down the front there,' called someone.

'Shut up, you two, will ya!' called someone else.

'Leave 'em alone. You're the ones who should shut up! You shut up!' called someone else.

'Yeah,' called Pa. 'If ya're not gunna lend a hand, then just shut ya bloody trap so we can all hear the lad sing his song.' Then he and Marjorie sat back down to hear the singing.

And that Mallee, with its bald and scabby paddocks, its stinking poverty-stricken dams, its echoing empty rainwater tanks and its silent useless windmills, stopped. Because what else could it do? It stopped as Jesse sang out his song. It stopped as Elise turned and led her little troupe again. It stopped as they sang past Calaf and his successful riddles, as they sang through Puccini's unfinished end, as Calaf gave Turandot another chance.

Marjorie stood up again when all the singing was done. It wasn't to call out anything this time. She stood because her mother deserved it, and Jesse deserved it. And she knew about standing ovations now, on account of having lived in the city for a few years, even if no one else in that hall did. And wasn't that what any decent person should do in the face of such humble magnificence?

She stood there, alone, against the salt water and the salt crystals and the encrustations of her own private concoctions. And clapped and clapped and clapped. Standing by herself there in the middle of that roiling sea of applause as everybody from roundabout – all those faithful aunties and uncles, all those locals doggedly looking after their own – acknowledged this little Mallee masterpiece.

'We can do an encore if you wish,' called Elise to the hall. 'You can all join in.'

'Yeah! Go on. You and Jesse do that song again,' the hall cried.

So they did. Bill conducted and Elise and Jesse sang 'Nessun Dorma' one more time. Her little opera troupe chorus sang, her miniscule orchestra played, as Elise called the words to the audience.

Marjorie stood, and Pa stood up beside her, and Marjorie and Pa sang with them. And so did everyone else there in that little hall. While that dusty stage, jammed full with its brilliant crepe paper rustling and glittering and crinkling, sang with them. And it turned out that Elise was right about the tablets not being magic. Because all the magic that Elise said wasn't in her tablets was in that town hall in *Turandot*. It was jam-packed with it.

The superintendent of the mental hospital had tipped off the newspaper reporters, of course. 'An operatic recital in the middle of nowhere,' he had said. 'It will be marvellous. A testament to the recovery of patients from my institution.' The newspaper reporters weren't so sure. They had been to this town before and they knew what to expect. But they could sense a good story either way. So, armed with pen and paper, they returned, and squashed themselves against the back wall of that packed-out little hall to watch this Mallee *Turandot* unfold. It was boiling in there with that crush. Sweat smothered their shirts, and their mouths hung open. But not because of the heat, as you might think. It was because of *Turandot*. They forgot themselves and their duty at the back of that little town hall. They clapped and clapped along with all those locals. They rushed to write it up as the most marvellous of crepe paper operas in a nondescript dusty town fighting hard not to die of thirst in the middle of the Mallee.

But nobody from hereabouts really cared two hoots about what was written up in the city newspapers. They weren't too concerned at all about what might have been said. They wouldn't have bothered to pay two bob for any of that. '*Vincerò*,' called Elise. '*Vin-cer-ò*,' sang Marjorie and Jesse. '*Vin-cer-ò*,' Pa and Bill, the aunties and uncles and the whole lot of them sang. '*Vin-cer-ò!*'

Jesse stood in imposing spangled splendour in the fanciful paper dress that Marjorie had sewn for him. He stood straight and tall now, right there in front of Marjorie and her encore. He didn't move. The whole hall clapped and shouted and whistled at Elise's crepe-papered musical masterpiece while a crinkling and rustling Jesse looked down at Marjorie from his dusty stage. Then Jesse moved. He moved his head just a bit, just enough. It was that slightly angled, slight downwards tilt. He gave Marjorie a Mallee nod. Right there. And Marjorie couldn't help herself when she saw that. One side of her face scrunched up just a bit so that half her mouth tilted up in an almost smile, and one eyebrow raised itself just a little, and one eye just about winked at him. And when Jesse saw that, he gave her one of his Jesse smiles. He gave it sweetly and softly as he stood there beside her triumphing mother so it floated out over Elise, out over Bill and Pa and the aunties and uncles, out in full view of all those locals, and it settled ever so quietly on Marjorie.

Marjorie's face couldn't help itself then. Before Marjorie even had time to weigh up the very real consequences of her face behaving like that, her face took that smile and gave that smile right back – straight away.

*

When can anyone ever really know about a thing? When do you get to nod and say, as you stare off down the track, *Yep, we could all see that coming – saw that a mile off*?

And how does a thing ever find its ending? Can you chase after it and grab it and throw it to the ground? Or is it best just to stand back and watch it? Leave well enough alone. Watch that willy-willy feeding on itself – lurching and swaying in the dust and the heat – crazy and wild and ruinous and beautiful. Watch it until it wears itself out tearing across the stubble.

And what if you could have seen that thing coming a mile off? Would you have tried to run and grab it and throw it to the ground? Would that have made it any easier for Marjorie? Would that have meant, in the long run, that things might have had a chance to turn out as something else altogether? Because no matter where Marjorie might end up there would still be all that Mallee somewhere with its relentless eternal implacable semi-desertness to contend with. Even if she might end up as far away as the city.

But maybe Marjorie knows now that things can always have a chance to turn out as something else altogether from what a running girl might have first thought. Especially when you can know you have done a good thing – and you know

now that you can walk off down that track. And the dust on that track will sigh under your feet as you pass. It will remind you for sure that there will always be this Mallee. But it will tell you also that this city is a solid thing. With its autumn leaves and its laneways, its Aunty Agnes and its asphalt, its trams and its coffee. And that just for you, in or out of the Mallee, with or without Ruby or Jesse, there is – watching and waiting for you – all that paper. All that piled-up, inexorable, indomitable, uncompromising fortune of broken and damaged books.

That's when you can know for sure.

Glossary of Terms

I HAVE DEVELOPED a short list of terms used in my book in response to a few questions and sometimes puzzlement about their use.

Some of the words I have used seem to be specific to the area of the Mallee I know: words such as *swaggie* and *spitty grubs*. Others seem to be particular to country living. Or perhaps unique to the time frame in which the story is set. The list is not an expert-reviewed, authoritative work, but is my parochial explanation.

Swaggie:
Most Australians and New Zealanders would know the term 'swaggie' as an itinerant or transitory worker. These swaggies were common during the Great Depression. These (mostly men) would arrive at farms and request work in return for food and a place to stay for a while. There were a few of these old men in the Mallee area where I grew up. They were not itinerant but were living in sparse accommodation (sheds or old settler huts) on various farms. Even though they were no longer travelling around, we referred to them as 'swaggies'.

Furphy water cart:

The Furphy Water Cart was an essential piece of survival in the early Mallee. These cast iron water carts were the invention of the Furphy family in Shepparton, Victoria. There is no permanent water supply in the Mallee area where I grew up. And in the early years of settlement there was no channel system either. So Furphies found their way onto most of the Mallee farms as an essential and practical means of carting and storing drinking water. In my childhood the Furphies had lived out their days as water carts and were just used as cast iron water tanks that filled when it rained. Furphies were used by the AIF in the lead-up to the First World War. There is a body of thought that ascribes the origins of the saying 'telling a furphy' to soldiers gathering around the Furphies and swapping stories of the war.

Water bag:

Hessian water bags were another essential Mallee item. These bags were made from hessian with a wire handle and usually a ceramic spout. Before filling, a new water bag would be soaked in water to expand the hessian fibres. Once soaked, the bag would be filled with rainwater and then hung in an appropriate spot – usually on the front of a ute or tractor; or under a verandah. The damp hessian kept the water cool; and if properly soaked before use, the water bags did not leak.

Spitty grubs:

The term 'spitty grubs' was used in the Mallee for the larvae of the Spitfire Sawfly. The larvae cluster together in large balls of squirming grubs on the branches of eucalypt trees. When provoked they will ooze a mustard-coloured liquid as a deterrent. They don't spit. Mallee children would poke the grub balls with sticks to get them to 'spit'. We believed they were poisonous but they are not.

Sheep in a line:
Sometimes Mallee paddocks were cleared of too much vegetation leaving sheep without adequate shade on a hot day. If sheep were in a paddock without shade on such a day they would congregate and form a line against the sun so that one side of the sheep was shaded. They would then create their own (albeit paltry) shade for the whole mob. Each sheep would tuck its head into the available shade of the sheep in front of it. You could see an entire mob of sheep standing in such a line of manufactured shade. I don't know why people think sheep are stupid.

Flies on backs:
A heat wave in the Mallee is debilitating and shade is essential. Mallee people who were out in the sun would attract flies looking for shade. Flies could congregate on the backs of any human willing to stand still long enough for them to land. You could sometimes see hundreds of flies silently camped on someone's back.

Acknowledgements

'THANK YOU' SEEMS such a modest expression to be loaded with all the weight of my immense gratitude.

Thank you to the wonderful Bruce Pascoe. 'You keep writing, girl,' he nodded at me a couple of years ago. I am sure Bruce Pascoe has no idea how much those few words from such a wonderful man meant to me. He encouraged me. So I did.

My heartfelt appreciation and respect goes to my wonderful agent Catherine Drayton and her assistant Claire Friedman: for seeing something in this book. Then offering to lightly lead me on the sometimes tangled walk through the scrub until we could all see what the proper shape of this story should be. I would be still wandering somewhere out in that bush without you.

I have lived so many moments of grateful appreciation for all that brilliance stacked there at Pan Macmillan. To Mathilda Imlah for agreeing with Catherine Drayton, and deciding to give me a go, (and also for your humour). To my amazing editors Bri Collins and Ali Lavau for your perfect, painstaking dedication. To Georgia Webb for chasing up the articles. And to Clare Keighery and all those wonderful Pan Macmillan people for your various, astonishing artistry in making this book look so lovely.

There are many people – friends and family – who have read and critiqued and argued and encouraged. Thank you to my sisters Jennifer Lawson and Sharon Baragwanath for your early and late reads and encouragements. And to my friend Marty Moser for reading an early draft and encouraging me mightily by leaving me a phone message to say it was good. I have loved sharing the road with you all.

Thank you also to my sisters-in-law Judy de Bono and Lois Krake for your reads and your comments and encouragement. (Lois, I have included a glossary to explain the very specific usage of the term 'swaggies' in this book.)

A special thank you to my friend Heather Crawley for your generosity in taking the time to read this during a hectic time in your own world; and for your then wise words. I hope you like the 'Nessun Dorma'.

Particular thanks have to go to Graham Brinsden and Carolyn Emonson. Two special friends, both of whom have spent nights and nights listening to me read the early form of this book. Thank you Graham for your solid truth that never wavers despite the look on my face. And Carolyn, thank you always for your encouragement – always wrapped around intelligent, informed advice; and for our shared love of a good book that now spans a half century.

My uncounted thanks must go to lovers of books everywhere. Because without all that collective partiality and belief in a good book to solve most of the world's woes this planet would not be as bright as it is. So thank you to publishers, booksellers, readers, writers, educators and librarians everywhere who never tire of showing people – big and small – the matchless wonder of reading.

And lastly, to the younger Brinsdens: Daniel and Karli, Victoria and Emmeline. All of whom have supported me weirdly and faithfully and lovingly throughout this journey by never having read any of this book. Now you can.